KT-118-189

# WITCH-BEAST

*Bernard King*

**SPHERE BOOKS**

First published in Great Britain by Sphere Books Ltd 1989
This edition first published by Sphere Books 1996

Copyright © 1989 by Bernard King

This is a work of fiction, and while locations are based on fact all characters are
entirely imaginary. Any apparent resemblance to actual persons, living or dead, is
purely coincidental.

Printed in England by Clays Ltd, St Ives plc

Except in the United States of America,
this book is sold subject to the condition
that it shall not, by way of trade or otherwise
be lent, re-sold, hired out, or otherwise circulated
without the publisher's prior consent in any form of
binding or cover other than that in which it is
published and without a similar condition
including this condition being imposed
on the subsequent purchaser

Sphere Books
A Division of
Macdonald & Co (Publishers)
Brettenham House
Lancaster Place
London WC2E 7EN

## 'YOU HAVE SERVED ME WELL. NOW IT IS TIME FOR YOU TO REST!'

She clutched at her chest, feebly at first, then with a stronger, more convulsive movement. Panic mounted with her increased heart-rate, panic which surged beyond her servitude, screaming admonitions in her failing ears. For a moment a raw foetor swept into her nostrils, then faded. She tried to speak, to call out, but her throat was dry and the words wouldn't come.

The creature reared up on its hind legs, resting its cruelly-taloned forepaws on the back of the chair opposite. Those eyes, big as saucers, burned unremittingly into her own, dimming the rest of her shrinking world with their brilliance.

And if our life were less confused by the sounding tides of action, in its clamour unpropitious to the fine attention of the soul, we might more often hear to our peril such words as those which made the hero Odysseus fear. For we stand upon a greater height of years than those who have lived before us; were there more lulls and pauses in the rumour of the world, we might catch echoes out of a vaster distance, and know a wider trouble than they.

W. Compton Leith, *Sirenica*

To the
four-foots
I have known
– greater souls
in lesser bodies

. . . And For Simon

Ellie took the stick from the big white Newfoundland's teeth after the ritual brief tussle. She threw it again, watching it turn end over end as it described a long curve in the air. Leader was already chasing after it, ears and coat streaming behind him in the April morning, before the stick hit the grass close by the bench.

She watched him run, large and handsome, a flash of white fur against the burgeoning greenery of St Katherine's Gardens. She watched him in a way she'd never done before, both proud of the large animal which had replaced children in her life, and sad that this was to be their last run together.

'Will you understand?' she asked softly, her breath steaming slightly in the early chillness. 'Will you understand and . . . forgive me?'

Suddenly Ellie Pasciewicz felt cold. She huddled in her anorak and began to follow Leader towards the stick. On the bench beside the path an old lady was sitting with a carrier bag. Not a tramp, Ellie thought. Plain, serviceable dress. Once fashionable, perhaps, as fashions for the elderly shapeless went. Strange that she was out this early, sitting around in the cold like that. Still, the elderly had to fill their time with something, and she knew from seeing her grandmother that they didn't sleep very much, or very long. Sleep must be the elixir of life, Ellie thought. Sleep and you live. Live and you have to . . . leave Joe.

And Leader.

Oh, he was a good enough man, her Joe. He provided. He worked hard. And he didn't knock her about. Not yet. But that bloody drinking was getting worse and worse. It had always been bad, but she'd put that down to him being a foreigner in a strange land, probably even continuing the customs he'd been brought up with. But not to the extent he was doing it now. Not to the point where their marriage wasn't a marriage any more.

Ellie had tried talking to him, but it didn't work. How could it? He was rarely sober enough to take any notice of her. Or Leader. Really she didn't like leaving Leader behind with Joe, but there wasn't any choice. She had to get away, and the only bolt-hole open was back to that same mother who'd always said her marriage to a Pole would turn out badly, and who'd made it clear that she'd put up with Ellie, but not with Leader.

'Not with a dog that size, my girl. It's only a maisonette, not Buckingham Palace.'

The Newfoundland bounded past the stick and then turned and went back for it, picking it up in his powerful jaws. He had a full pedigree and had cost Ellie quite a lot of money, though she'd told Joe she'd got him from a home. He'd have calculated the cost in beer and vodka otherwise, and had even less time for the dog than he'd bothered to give it already.

Her bags were packed and Joe was still snoring. His partner would call for him and run him to the car repair shop they ran together in Uptown. He'd wake up at the last minute, throw on a sweatshirt and jeans under his overall, and hardly notice she'd gone. He'd be too busy trying to put his head back together for that.

And if he did? He'd shout. She'd shout back. Then she'd make a run for it when the taxi came to take her to Monkhampton Station.

Leader's tail wagged. His teeth were clamped about the last stick Ellie would ever throw for him. He turned to face her as she advanced across the grass, then set down the stick and went over to the bench. His wet nose nuzzled Gertie Tomkins' stockinged knee. Gertie looked down at him.

Their eyes met.

We know what we have to do. We know what's coming, that we have to face up to it, to prepare. We each have our tasks to perform, animal and human.

'Leader,' Ellie called. Then, more firmly, 'Leader!'

Dog and woman surveyed one another in unspoken communion. In that place, at that moment, *something neither human nor animal spoke to both of them*.

Ellie rushed up, her breathless arrival breaking the spell. Leader barked once, then turned away from Gertie to rub his head against Ellie Pasciewicz's thigh.

'Sorry,' she smiled at Gertie. 'I hope he hasn't been annoying you. He usually ignores strangers.'

Gertie Tomkins smiled back ''S all right, dear,' she replied. 'He's a nice dog, he is. Well, be seeing you.'

She rose stiffly to her feet and began to walk away. Ellie bent down and snapped the lead onto the Newfoundland's collar. Their last walk together was almost over.

The stick lay on the grass, its purpose fulfilled. Ellie began to walk the animal towards the exit to the park, not sparing Gertie a backward glance. If she had done she would have seen the old lady walking along as if never a twinge of arthritis had ever crept into her joints, breaking twigs from the budding trees and putting them into her carrier as she went.


There could no longer be any doubt. It was beginning.

Harker had been through the cuttings index time after time, seeking references he might have missed, cross-checking, always suspecting the possibility of error. Somewhere there would be a flaw in the reasoning, a question as to the validity of some of the evidence. After all, it was speculative, to say the least.

Yes, somewhere he'd find a discrepancy. Somewhere it would be wrong.

But it wasn't.

It hadn't even been his own investigation, not in the beginning. It was the previous Antaeus Professor of Folklore and Related Studies who'd begun to collect and examine apparently unrelated data and formulate the hypothesis. Old Willington-Cartier had been popularly regarded as eccentric by

3

his fellows and students, a fair achievement for a Folklorist. Normally the rest of the academic world had a distressing tendency to dismiss them as irretrievably nutty. Maybe if they'd seen the index they might have changed their minds.

Harker shook his head sadly. No, the old gent wasn't mad. His nickname came from his courteousness and the shock of white hair which seemed to stand straight up from his scalp, rather like Einstein's, but it was no indication of his capabilities. He'd reasoned it out, step by step, pieced it together, fragment by fragment, and Henry Willington-Cartier had got it horribly right.

'There is never an end, young Andreas,' he'd told Harker when the latter had been one of his students, nearly thirty years before. 'There are only beginnings. And don't you think of them as new beginnings, either. No beginning is anything more than a logical progression from what has gone before, even if we're not always able to determine the species of logic employed to progress it. Really there are no beginnings and no ends, but for our purposes such accuracy would create impossible obstacles. So, having postulated a continuum, we now virtually ignore it.'

No beginnings, no ends. Just a progressing continuum of actualities. But that didn't stop *it* beginning.

The old man's notes had been as thorough as the index, making terrifying sense. So had his *modus operandi*:

Examine current trends in Western Society. Note the progressive pollution and destruction of the environment which civilization grew up in. Note the increasing acts of violence and terrorism, the acceptance of violence, and worse, as a daily fact of life. Note the decline in Christian values and in the open practice of Christianity itself. Empty churches like, for instance, St Katherine's in Monkhampton. Appreciate the concomitant deterioration of the species *homo sapiens* (!) as they wanted the goodies now, not in the afterlife. Note the increasing tendency for overt governmental assistance in distress areas (not just *distressed areas*) to be declining. Note the increase of sexual liberty in the sixties and the decline of the

4

same, through fear of AIDS and HIV, in the eighties. It's still there, but now it can kill you.

Postulate a link between these factors. Not so unlikely. Crimes of violence and sex crimes were intimately linked, as was the decline in Christian values. As was the lack of concern for the environment and human life as gross materialism increased. Postulate this connection and what did it yield, the old boy asked?

The beginning.

Harker shrugged in deference to Willington-Cartier's memory. Okay, Henry, progression towards change in the existing continuum. Is that better?

It wasn't. For all its more complex language it meant the same thing. Andreas Michael Sebastian Harker, Antaeus Professor of Folklore at Cambridge University, stood before the window with its stone mullions, looking out and down at the evening creeping insidiously across the court. The old gent had chosen his successor well. There had always been an ideological sympathy between the two men, even if they were separated by more than twenty-five years. Now this sympathy, this legacy of posthumous postulations and hypotheses, was creeping out of the grave and into Harker's soul.

'What we fear most, my boy, is what we are obliged to face,' his predecessor had once said. 'Men have faced up to the phantom hound, Black Shuck. Men have faced up to the horrors of Nazi Germany. Between myth and reality there is no division when it comes to fear. Roosevelt was less wrong than limited by his context when he said that we only have fear itself to face. Certainly fear is something to be afraid of, but there is more reason to believe that what we have to fear is what we believe to be reality. And belief is what creates reality, you know. Perhaps the thing we have to fear most is belief.'

Harker shuddered. It was down there, amongst the students fleeing their studies for pleasures of the opposite sex or real ale. It was out there in the countryside, from the fens to the broads to the Cotswolds and beyond. It was in the air and sweeping across the seas. It was not believed in yet because it

5

had yet to gain credence in the mind of the populace, but that didn't stop it being there, this nameless thing.

And it was nameless. Not even old Henry had given it a name. It had been too dreadful and too alien in its implication for mankind for any kind of appellation to be successfully descriptive. He might have called it reality, for his finding proved that it was real enough, but reality was too abstract a concept, paradoxically, to label it with. It didn't suggest the horrible potential of the . . .

What was it? Real, yes. A belief, yes. But *what* was it?

When old gods die new ones are brought to birth. Man would never know them as gods, though. Not in the way he had known Christ and Zeus and Allah. The signs were there for any with the wit to perceive them to see, though they weren't the traditional portents of translated prophets or stars hovering over stable-blocks. They were more subtle, less recognizable than that. And more dangerous in their very subtlety.

And more real.

In the abstracted remoteness of Harker's snug, book-lined study they were real enough. How much more sinister they must be out there, in the real world, in the universe of Porsche and Dunhill and YSL and Our Price Records. They could turn off the TV and still the VCR. They were Space Invaders, not from above but from below.

No, it wasn't beginning, Harker conceded. He'd been wrong to think that. He'd been limited in his thinking, something he must never be again if he or anyone was to survive. His assessment of the evidence had misled him. It wasn't beginning at all. It was much worse than that.

It had already begun.

# LEADER

'Hey, you see that? Looka that bastard turn over. Wheee.'

Joe Pasciewicz laughed gruffly and waved his beer can towards the TV. Beside him, at the other end of the sofa, Johnny Crashaw nodded and forced a smile. Once the car had stopped sliding Stuart Whitman pushed open the door and crawled out, gun ready.

It was a little ritual for Johnny. Neither he nor Joe was the right side of forty any longer and both would have felt ridiculous in the youth scene of discos and theme pubs. In their separate ways they were both single, Johnny through his wife's death from cancer two years earlier, Joe through Ellie finally getting fed up with his drinking a couple of months before.

Her parting words still smarted. 'Bloody Poles,' she'd yelled at him, just before she slammed the door hard enough to rattle the glass and went off to her mother's. 'All the same. All of you. Bloody manic depressives or alcoholics the whole bloody lot!'

S. Whitman hauled the bad guy out of the upside-down sedan and stuck his magnum up the creep's nostril. Joe drained his can and tossed it vaguely towards the waste basket in the corner. It hit the rim and fell, rolling a little way across the stained carpet. Joe reached for another can.

The two men worked together, partners in an Uptown repair shop. They worked hard and played hard, mostly apart. Johnny played a lot of poker and had two or three steady girl-friends, though he always thought the expression a misnomer for women over thirty, which they were. Joe's play consisted mostly of drinking and watching the occasional porn video. With Ellie gone and no kids he'd turned in upon himself, feeding on his subconscious lusts and hatreds. It wasn't healthy, but it worked.

9

And yet one legacy of Ellie remained. It was starting to make its presence felt again, howling hungry and imprisoned in the garden shed. Ellie's mother had never liked dogs, so her daughter had left Leader behind, reluctantly, never thinking Joe capable, for all his faults, of venting his spite on a dumb animal.

Leader wasn't dumb, though. He was proving that right now, towards midnight on a Thursday, as Joe and Johnny went through their weekly ritual of drinking themselves stupid in front of the box. Part of Johnny wondered why he stuck with the date. It left him hung over and trying to light his welding gun with a trembling hand next morning. He'd crash on Joe's sofa to save driving home and hate himself when he woke up. But the hating wasn't always in proportion to the booze. Often it was because of his own cowardice, he secretly admitted.

Cowardice about Leader.

'Fuckin' dog,' Joe growled.

The Newfoundland in the shed, underweight, badly wormed, sleeping in its own excrement, howled again.

'Fuckin' neighbours complain to me,' Joe repeated. 'Keep your dog quiet, they say. I keep him quiet if he don't shut up.'

Johnny finished his beer and opened another. 'Let him be, Joe,' he said quietly. 'You know what they say. It's a dog's life. Why don't you feed him something or clean him out?'

The ring-pull hit the carpet. There was no point in being tidy, the way Joe kept house these days.

'I feed him. He get food. He shit too much. He too fuckin' noisy. I'm fixin' that. Slowly, I'm fixin' that.'

*Blazing Magnum* was moving towards its climax. Stuart Whitman had set up the blind girl in the hospital and his sister's murderer had taken the bait. Soon there'd be that amazing flashback, Joe remembered from the first screening. Soon that naked girl, tits wobbling wildly, would smash the other woman's skull to pulp as she groped her boyfriend.

Leader howled again.

Johnny knew what was coming. He swigged hard at the beer and shut his eyes at the thought. Maybe Joe'd hold off, this once. Maybe Leader'd keep quiet. Maybe horse-skin coats'll be the rage this summer. Or flying rats.

The killer began his confession. The flashback started. Three naked or half-naked people, a man, a woman and a girl, started sporting through the mansion. Juicy flesh.

Joe never showed his friend any of his porn tapes. He was old-fashioned enough to be ashamed of his open secret. But he'd openly drool at milder stuff like this on television. The candlestick began to rise and fall. So did the girl's breasts, nipples stiff with promise. So did Leader's ululations.

He gritted his teeth and watched on, loosening his belt. As the boyfriend stared appalled at his young lover, the belt slipped through the loops on Joe's faded jeans. His generation had grown up in jeans. They were still in jeans now. One day, if they lived that long, there'd be pensioners queueing in post offices for their payments in jeans.

The flashback finished. It got boring after this. Chase through hospital and Stuart Whitman shoots down helicopter with handgun. And it looked like, and had to be, a model. They never crashed the real thing, for two reasons. One, too hard to get the pilot out. Two, too expensive for the budget. That's why they always crashed aircraft just behind a hill, where you didn't see them hit. Just a fireball the other side of the horizon where the oil-drums went up.

'I come back,' Joe grinned, his belt free of his jeans and clutched firmly in his right hand. 'Have another beer, Johnny.'

Johnny watched him go and had another beer. Tomorrow he'd do it, finally. Tomorrow he'd take his courage in both hands and do what any one of Joe's neighbours should have done. He'd phone the RSPCA and report, anonymously, that Joe Pasciewicz was ill-treating a dumb animal. Dumb animal.

Leader howled again. Obviously Joe hadn't reached the shed yet.

Stuart Whitman shot down the chopper.

Joe unbolted the shed, trying to close his nostrils against the noxious exhalation of faeces and ammoniac urine which would greet him when he opened the door. The Newfoundland was a big dog. It voided a lot of waste, mostly liquid in one form or another since Joe had got haphazard with its diet. It stank.

Not its fault, perhaps, but that didn't make the smell any better. Especially to someone like Joe who'd never liked dogs and only put up with the beast for Ellie's sake. They'd not had any children, without ever really knowing why, and Leader had been Ellie's substitute. But he wasn't Joe's.

'Just keep your trap shut,' Joe snapped.

Leader tried to push past him, to escape into the night, but he was too weak, despite his size. It's hard to tell when a long-haired animal is under-nourished, but the Newfoundland obviously was. The tight arch between ribs and lumbar vertebrae showed that, as did the ears, tight on the skull, and the way that Leader stood on his pads instead of digitigrade – on his toes – like they normally do.

He barked weakly, forced back into his own filth, his white coat soiled and matted to a brownish fawn. The belt flashed and pain stung into him.

He yelped.

The belt swung again. And again.

No imprisonment for mistreating a dog, Johnny decided. Fine, probably. Yes, there's bound to be a fine. And a ban on keeping the animals. Joe's never wanted to, so that won't hurt him. And he's not short of cash, so the fine won't hurt him either. You never know, they might even save the dog.

Oh Joe won't like it, but he doesn't have to know it's me. The RSPCA'll see to that for me.

Tomorrow.

I'll do it tomorrow.

Leader's yelps became submissive. Weakened by misuse, virtually helpless against its well-fed and well-boozed master, the animal sank into a painful and submissive silence.

Was this all that remained by way of attention? Scant rations and a beating? Wasn't there sunlight out there in the daytime? Wasn't there grass to roll upon, a place that wasn't made of wood that retained the reek of bodily waste? There had to be a way to reach it. There had to be.

That was the first objective. Once that was achieved there'd be time to conceive the second. And there was a second. There had been a second ever since the first blow had fallen, since the water-bowl had first become drained. Since the food hadn't come on time.

The second objective was what a human might have called revenge. To Leader, however, it was simply punishment, and obedience to a new and greater master.

The belt flagged as the arm which wielded it grew tired. The dog was already silent, but its silence hadn't saved it from that further beating, the beating which said you've-dragged-me-down-here-you-fuckin'-cur.

And I will again, Joe Pasciewicz. You punish me, yes. But I punish you first, in the only way I have left. In the only way I can.

Johnny didn't hear the silence when it came. *Blazing Magnum* had finished and the next programme, which he'd turned up, was a heavy metal band in noisy concert. It wasn't his kind of music, but it was loud and legitimate, and that was all that mattered. Except for that phone call in the morning.

He made himself the same promise every week. Every week Leader began to howl. Every week Joe went down to shut the dog up.

Johnny sniggered through the beer. Shut it up? Wasn't it shut up to start with? Wasn't that why the poor bugger was howling? Well, he'd make that call. Tomorrow.

Leader cowered, eyes frightened, brain determined. Look right, be right, it finishes. For now. Hold on. Stay alive. Preserve what strength you can. Whatever is to come, be it death or liberty, it has to be better. It will never be like it was with Mistress again. Too much has changed for that. But it has to be better.

Just hold on. Fight again tomorrow, if there's still a little strength. But hold on.

Humans have a god. Do we? If you're out there, somewhere, will you hear me if I pray?

I don't have the human way of making sounds, so will you hear me? If you're not a human god you will. You have to, if you're there.

Joe's belt was back in place when he returned, securing his jeans. He sat down heavily and opened another of the endless supply of cans. He needed another drink after that.

'What this, Johnny?' he asked, his tongue and brain confused.

'Whitesnake in concert,' came the detached reply.

'Fuckin' crap. Anything on Channel 4?'

'You don't like Whitesnake?'

Joe shrugged and raised the can to his lips. 'Not my music. Anything on Channel 4?' he repeated.

'Some documentary about the shipyard at Gdansk,' Johnny conceded, knowing the reaction he was likely to get.

Joe beamed and flicked the remote control. Johnny Crashaw groaned inwardly and retreated towards the morning. He'd ring them in the morning. It might fuck Joe up a bit, but it would do wonders for Johnny's state of mind. If he lasted that long in his resolve.

And if Leader was still alive.

Out in the shed Leader lay upon the stained boards. He'd pushed what filth he could away with his paws to clear that precious area. He looked at the bolted door, the bolt on the outside, and remembered the way he'd been able to turn door handles in times long vanished. Now, if the catch had only been *inside* his prison he'd have been out of here long ago. That old cliché about dumb animals wasn't true. Oh, it might take a while to learn how the humans made things work, and it might take acquired skills to master them, especially as only the humans had that remarkable toe on their up-paws that could hold things by folding over the others. The opposable thumb, they called it. It was like having two paws on each forelimb. No wonder they had the advantage, especially as they didn't have to try to run on them.

Leader was still smarting, but he accepted that. It was the price of his punishing Joe Pasciewicz. Possibly there would be an occasion in the future when he'd be able to do more, but he had to conserve what he still had. Even licking his wounds was an extravagance, and he'd learned not to do it because of the way it weakened him.

For now, stay alive, he told himself. The rest will follow.

Solidarity was being smashed, slowly and politically. Joe groaned, Johnny closed his eyes and began to doze. It will be over soon, was his last conscious thought. One way or another, it has to finish soon.

In the shed, alone, weak and smarting, Leader thought exactly the same thing as he settled his muzzle down onto his forepaws.

The waste bin was full. No point in trying to get the can into it. He'd pick it up tomorrow, perhaps. Joe dropped it onto the cushions beside him and opened up his last beer for that evening . . . morning. Friday now.

Another fuckin' Friday.

Why wasn't that dog dead yet?

Tomorrow he'd stop feeding it permanent. That'd teach the bastard animal. Have to die then.

After all, Ellie wasn't coming back, and that was all that mattered in Joe's world.

He thought.


Johnny Crashaw lit the welding gun with the now traditional shaking hand and fitted the new sills to the decaying Ford Cortina. Across the workshop Joe Pasciewicz was rubbing down, ready for a paint job, and the lads were figuring out how to mask a wheel-well.

Johnny turned off the acetylene gas at the cylinder and set down his gun. He pulled off his mask and checked about him. No-one was watching, all too involved with what they were doing, or trying to do. He slid towards the office.

The phone sat there, waiting. He'd already looked the number up. Now he dialled it.

'Your call is being diverted at no extra charge . . .' said the recorded voice.

Johnny cursed silently. They didn't make it easy, did they.

The new number rang. The same caring voice Sally was to hear some hours later answered him.

'I . . . I want to report a mistreated animal,' Johnny began.

'May I have your name, sir?'

'Let's keep my bloody name out of it, can we? This isn't a hoax. It's taken me quite a while to get round to making this call.'

'As you wish. Where is the animal now? Can you tell me what it is?'

'Yeah. It's a Newfoundland dog. Name of Leader.'

'And the name and address of its keeper?'

He told the caring voice, in a rush. Then he put the phone down and slid back to his welding. Somehow the dog didn't matter any more. All that mattered was that sick feeling in his gut, a feeling that was part sympathy for the starving Leader, part betrayal of his friend and partner.

After all, what did the dog really matter? It wasn't as if it was a man, or a little girl that was being abused. Just some dumb animal. That's all.

Still, he'd done it now, and he'd done it without giving his name. Joe'd never know, unless he told him.

And Johnny certainly wasn't going to tell him.


He heard the footsteps approaching the shed. Outside it was day, and a bright day at that, despite the grime which crusted the windows. Somewhere there was a world of grass and sun and trees. Not here, though. All there was here were stained boards and that reek of filth he'd grown used to, and the nagging, half-forgotten pain that had long since gone beyond hunger.

Sores had begun to open, causing suppurating patches in the matted fur, where the belt had drawn blood. Leader's left eye had closed from bruising along the bony ridge of the orbit. Whereas before he'd managed to stand with difficulty, now he was wondering why he needed to stand at all. You could die in any position.

He struggled onto his feet, pressing down on the straightened forelegs to take the effort out of his hind-quarters. Death wasn't coming yet. Not before a little more defiance. Staying alive and on your feet was defiance, of a sort. So was howling.

They'd do. They'd have to do. They were all he'd got left.

The two uniforms picked their way down the overgrown garden path towards the shed. The RSPCA Inspector, Terry Morris, glanced at the beat copper beside him. 'Jesus.' he muttered grimly. 'You can smell it from here.'

'Dead?' the policeman asked.

Terry shook his head. 'Hard to tell. I've smelled it this bad and still found something alive before, but it's usually had to be destroyed. There comes a point where no amount of care will save an animal.'

'So you reckon we're too late anyway?'

'I didn't say that. God, what a stench. There's no fresh faeces anywhere around, so it's been doing its business in there for . . . weeks, probably.'

He was a short man, stockily built, with prematurely grey hair and a fresh, fair complexion that never looked as weathered as it should. His pale blue eyes could express an amazing range of emotions within a very short space of time, but right now they were glazed with sympathy and dread at what he expected to find. That didn't mean he was going to take chances, though, and he was wearing stout leather gloves, just in case.

'Do I have to come in with you?' the copper asked, his nose wrinkled and his eyes looking somewhere else. 'I mean . . .'

'I know what you mean. No, this is my job, not yours. You're just here to make sure we observe the niceties, whatever they may be in a situation like this.'

17

He reached out and unbolted the shed, positioning himself to block the opening as the door swung outwards. A wave of filth and decay rushed towards him as the foul air inside struggled to replace itself and failed. He gagged momentarily and turned his head, eyes swivelling to make out the interior without him having to breathe it.

Leader was panting with exertion. Two sets of footsteps meant that it wasn't Joe on his own. And despite the reeks of waste and neglect he'd scented strangers. That could mean anything. It could even mean an end to his torment. Yet whatever it meant he'd face it on his feet.

He could only wait. There was no strength any more for escape. A few yards, maybe, then his legs would give way and he'd collapse, ready for the kicks and blows which would force him to find the energy to be driven back into his prison. That's how it worked with Joe.

But this isn't Joe, he told himself again. This could be better, or worse than Joe. It could be a new beginning, or the end. Or a hopeless neither.

'Bloody hell!' whispered the man in the navy sweater and the peaked cap. Then: 'Okay, easy boy. We're not here to hurt you. Easy now.'

Leader struggled to remember. These sounds were gentle, soothing. A thousand years ago his mistress had made sounds like those. Good sounds. *Safe* sounds.

'That's a Newfoundland?' the copper asked, keeping well outside the shed as Terry moved carefully inside. 'I thought they were big buggers?'

'They should be,' Terry told him.

He extended a glove for Leader to inspect. The nose wrinkled and an appallingly grey tongue made a limp attempt at a lick.

Always games with humans. Do what you're supposed to and you stand a chance of staying alive. This time you have to get it right, because if you don't there isn't going to be another chance.

'So what's the damage?' asked the policeman, edging a fraction closer.

'That's hard to say. Badly undernourished,' Terry observed, running a gloved hand over Leader's back and flanks and feeling the bones beneath the filthy tangle of discoloured fur. 'Some nasty sores and bruising as well. He's been beaten and starved. He must be one hell of a creature to have stood it this long. Good dog. Good boy. We'll soon have you out of here.'

He didn't try to stroke or pet Leader too hard. It was almost impossible to know what wounds he might be disturbing if he tried. Instead he slung his arms beneath the Newfoundland and lifted it up. Easily.

'C'mon, boy. Let's go.'

As he carried Leader from the shed a neighbour peered over the low fence, nodding sagely. 'So you're taking the poor bastard away, are you?' the man asked. 'About time you boys did something useful.'

Terry stopped for a moment. 'Are you the person who called us?' he inquired.

'Me? No, not me. None of my business.'

'Cruelty is everybody's business,' Terry said firmly, then continued towards the van parked on the road. The beat copper had opened the rear door for him and Leader was laid gently inside on disposable litter. 'That's a good boy,' Terry smiled, closing the door.

'Right, I'll leave you to it, then. Out of interest,' the policeman added, 'what happens now? To the dog, I mean? I know the bastard who got him like that won't cop more than a fine.'

'He would if I had my way. If it had been a child he'd go to prison. Sometimes I think there's no end to human cruelty and conceit. But that's not what you asked me, is it? I've checked with Salvation. Tom Greaves says he can take him for a while.'

'You reckon he'll make it, then?'

Terry shrugged. 'At least Greaves is a vet, so once the poor creature gets to Salvation it'll have every chance. It could be too far gone, but it was on its feet when we arrived, and that's a good sign. They're a strong breed, Newfoundlands. Working dogs. Like Labradors they were bred for hauling full fishing nets ashore, and they've been used for sea rescues. I'd say that one's as tough as any.'

He was on his way to the workshop when he noticed the new arrival in one of the pens. It was a large dog, long-haired, with a coat that was probably white all over. Despite Salvation's best efforts Leader still wasn't completely clean. It would probably be some time before he recovered sufficiently to shed the permanently stained hair and replace it with his natural colour.

Usually Pieter Hangel ignored the animals. They were a distraction with their crying and scrabbling. And they smelled. With the best will in the world it was impossible for them not to. Even *clean* had a smell to it. Yet this particular beast caught his eye for several reasons.

He squatted on his aged haunches and peered through the wire mesh. Leader, sitting before, rose weakly to his feet and padded across to the human with obvious effort. Man and dog studied one another carefully, neither getting too close to the barrier between them. Hangel's dark eyes stared straight and unblinking into the animal's light amber ones. Somehow Hangel had expected the dog's eyes to be dark, and was slightly surprised that they weren't.

From its gaunt appearance, even through its long coat, this creature had suffered. It had been imprisoned and starved. It had been beaten and deprived. Granpa Hangel nodded to himself. He knew all about things like that. He would never forget about things like that. Not whilst he had life and a number tattooed on his forearm to remind him.

'Listen to me, my friend,' he began, softly, his voice gentle and caressing, persuasive and calming. 'They are all beasts. There is no such thing as humanity. Only shades of bestiality. There is only the thickness of a strand of wire between kindness and torture. Nothing more.'

Leader's ears pricked up at the sound of the old man's words. Then they gradually lay back, away from the skull. His amber eyes half-closed and the corners of his mouth drew back without exposing the teeth.

Pieter Hangel understood. He'd seen enough of his son-in-law's charges to recognize certain facial expressions. This one was quite rare. Only a few breeds, Dalmatians and Labradors among them, and only a few individual other animals, achieved this particular look.

Leader was smiling back at him.

'So you know? You understand me? Yes, perhaps you do. We have this bond between us, you and I. We have the bond of our suffering and the knowledge of man's capacity for evil. And perhaps we have something more.'

Leader lay down, still smiling at the old man through the wire mesh. In his brain something was stirring, something he'd almost forgotten through the pressing needs of staying alive. His tongue flicked out around his mouth and he barked once.

It was enough, for then.

'You'd better call me Ben,' Detective Chief Inspector Wilson smiled, somewhat uneasily.

'That's fine by me,' came the reply, accompanied by a smile which the policeman found rather too polished and professional to be entirely natural.

Jake Lewis released his hand and waved him to a chair in the spacious reception area, his smile fading only slightly whilst Wilson sat down. 'Now,' Lewis continued, 'what can I do for you, Ben?'

'Simple enough. I want to see the town.'

Lewis nodded, his expression persisting. He lowered his head for a moment, affording the detective a perfect view of the spreading bald area sheltered amongst his tight black curls. When he looked up his face showed slight bewilderment.

'As you know,' he began, 'Monkhampton Development Corporation maintains a Visits Officer to show people moving to the town around the expansion areas. Can I start by saying

I'm slightly puzzled by your request to see me? Also, I've no doubt that your own people have given you a tour of your patch already. Now, if I put those two things together, and I think they belong together, I'm left with an obvious question, Ben. What exactly do you want from me?'

Wilson shrugged, uncomfortable in the suit he'd put on for the first few days in his new posting. Promotion to his present rank had accompanied the move from C Division, but a new area and fresh faces under his command conspired to add to the unsettlement he was experiencing.

He rubbed at his fair beard with thick, short-nailed fingers. Two or three loose blond hairs came away, dropping on to his dark tie and standing out like crescent moons. 'I want someone who can give me more than just the standard spiel,' he replied. 'You're a native. You can tell me more than someone who's simply doing a job here. If I'm going to do any good I need to get inside this town in a way your Visits Officer couldn't take me. I want to know what makes it tick. I want to know what the special problems are, ethnic minorities, that sort of thing. Are you with me?'

Lewis nodded slowly. He was puzzled to know exactly how Wilson knew he'd been born in Monkhampton. Then he remembered that one of the men now probably under the DCI's command was a neighbour of his, and had at one time been a newcomer himself. Chances were that Sergeant Pierce had been talking to his new chief, filling him in about Lewis's job as an Information Officer with the development corporation, someone whose job was defined within broad parameters as having the facts and figures of expansion at his fingertips, knowing what was going on and being able to explain it to strangers such as Wilson.

'You've had an Information Pack?' Lewis asked.

The detective nodded. 'Nearly 19,000 new homes, rented and private, in eleven years. Over ten million square feet of commercial and industrial premises. Nearly forty miles of new dual carriageway roads. And so on. It's impressive. Especially if you add on a population rise from 130,000 to nearly 180,000.

That's an awful lot of new people, Jake. And new villains, I expect.'

Lewis grinned in return. 'Some,' he replied. 'Don't forget that, under the Labour Government in the seventies, we were supposed to take what was described as a "proper social mix". Disabled, disadvantaged, that sort of thing. I know, I know,' he added, seeing the policeman's expression. 'I don't like that sort of sociological jargon either. And I put it forward as an explanation, not as an excuse.

'Still,' he continued, 'things have changed now. The Tories want us to sell as many of our rented homes as possible. They've cut back on funding and made the whole concept of new towns as a means of relieving inner city overcrowding unfashionable. That's why we started to see inner city development corporations, like Merseyside and London Docklands, moving into the area of urban renewal.'

Wilson felt his smile begin to return, this time a little more easily. 'That's the sort of thing I'm after,' he said. 'I really want to know what makes this town tick. I don't want the propaganda. I can get that out of your bumf. I need the background from someone who knows it, the who's-done-what-where-why. You've got a closing date, I believe?'

Lewis snorted. 'We have. First of December this year.'

'So you've only another six months to go. What happens then? To you, I mean.'

'Ever heard of UB40? The unemployment benefit form? That's what happens to me, unless something turns up.'

'Doesn't that make you rather bitter?'

'I went into it with my eyes open. I knew when I joined the development corporation that it had a finite life. I'm the only one I can really blame if I end up on the dole.'

'Well, at least I think you're a realist.'

Lewis gave him a long, searching look. 'I'll be frank with you,' he began. 'There's a certain line, a spirit of optimism and pride, which is supposed to run through everything I say. Now, I understand what you want from me, how you want me to help you. In order to do that I've got to give you the kind of

23

frank opinions that could get me booted the hell out of here. You keep them to yourself, I'll give them to you. Do I make myself plain, Ben?'

There was a stress on the name which made things perfectly clear to Wilson. He felt himself beginning to grin as he replied: 'Three hundred per cent. I can see I came to the right man.'

Lewis forced a laugh. 'Flattery doesn't get anybody as far as it used to,' he replied, 'but it still helps. Okay, copper. When do you want to start?'

'What have you got in mind?'

'You want to see the town? I'll show you the town. I'll drive you up every bloody street in the place if you want. Strictly, I'm supposed to stick to the expansion areas and tell you about our achievements, though that would have been a lot easier if we'd gone in for linear development. As we didn't, I'm going to have to take you through the old parts to get to the new . . .'

Wilson held up a hand. 'Whoa,' he muttered. 'I'm just a simple cop. What's linear development, when it's at home?'

The Information Officer nodded. 'Okay. There are two principal forms of new town development. Linear and satellite. Places like Northampton, which closed a few years back, were linear developments. That means that expansion took place in one part and followed a natural line of growth. If you like, they developed a block which lengthened to become a line. Satellite development means you do a bit here, then a bit over there, then a bit somewhere else, then a bit up north, then south-west. You establish a collection of development areas linked by an infrastructure, the road and services network, then gradually join them all together to make a whole. With linear development you're simply tacking a line-shaped development on.

'Now, Northampton's development in linear form was the reason it was the first of the third generation new towns to be closed down. It was easy to stop expansion there. There was no expensive infrastructure to be wasted by early closure. Now, although Monkhampton's gone in for satellite development, in partnership with the borough council, it was an existing town and most of the infrastructure was already there. That's why we're being closed down. Those satellites which aren't complete can fend for themselves and, probably, be taken over by private developers. If we'd been somewhere like Milton Keynes, starting from a green-fields site by laying down the infrastructure, we might have had a bit longer, but even M K's heard its death-knell now.'

'You sound a little cynical about it, Jake.'

'It's the only way to be in a development corporation that's closing down. We don't work for the coal industry. Our union's short on muscle, locally at any rate. There's no golden hand-shake at the end. Just the basic government redundancy terms, a week's pay for every year of service. It ain't going to go very far.'

It was the policeman's turn to agree. For a moment there was an uneasy silence. Then Wilson asked: 'When can you start showing me around?'

Lewis checked his watch. It was a little after half-two. 'Now, if you like. We can get the background detail out of the way on a general tour this afternoon and then handle any areas you have a specific interest in tomorrow. There's nothing on my desk that can't wait for a day or so. And we'll take my car, if you don't mind. One, I know where we're going, so I won't have to break off what I'm saying to give you directions. Two, I reckon I need the mileage more than you do. They might expect me to be on call twenty-four hours a day, but they don't pay me as if they do.'

For the afternoon and most of the following day they toured the expansion areas in the northern half of the town, seeing the prize-winning rented housing developments at Southlands and Woodville, touring the interminable, identical, beautifully-landscaped and soulless employment areas with their unit factories and individual site developments.

Wilson's introduction to Monkhampton wasn't exactly that of a stranger in an unknown land. He'd been born in London and had joined the force straight from school, training at the police college at Hendon. His early years, the ones which determined his C I D suitability, had been spent in Oxfordshire, an adjoining Midlands county, and several years at nearby Waventree as a detective sergeant had prepared him for a succession of postings which had brought him progressively nearer to Monkhampton. Now, with his new rank, came a new posting to the town he had never quite had the time to get to know before.

In many ways it was a disappointment. The town centre, gutted of most of its history in the name of redevelopment, losing seventeenth century coaching inns to banks and shopping arcades, took some coming to terms with. Most of it was still shabby and under-developed, consisting of areas which looked like bomb-sites and doubled as expensive, under-prepared car-parks. Lewis made no apology for these, merely remarking that the uncertain planning policies of the borough council, always hungry for cash, and the cutback in funds from central government which had doomed the development corporation, were likely to leave them an urban wilderness for many years to come.

Wilson's patch, Monkhampton A Division, covered the northern half of the expanding town and all of the town centre. B Division had the southern half and a good stretch of the county beyond, including a nightmare stretch of the M1, the first, oldest and most frequently repaired motorway in the country. It was a nightmare of traffic violations, accidents and sheer bad driving, and Wilson was intensely glad that for once the shit end of the stick had gone to someone else.

Lewis referred to their travels, somewhat cynically, as progress tours, cynically because the development corporation, suddenly out of fashion in government circles, no longer had either an industrial or domestic building programme. 'We had over thirty architects on the staff at one time,' he muttered. 'Know how many we've got now? Two. I ask you!'

The short, grim-faced, balding Information Officer soon showed his passenger how expansion had brought a new prosperity to the town, broadening its industrial base and reducing unemployment, even through the recession years of the early eighties. Without that influx of new industries brought by the expansion programme, he explained, the town of Monkhampton, dependent previously upon the leather trade, would have become as deathly and despondent a place as Corby after the collapse of the steel industry, requiring as much time, energy, money and development area status being pumped into its revitalization as Corby was taking.

Though Lewis declared himself a native, his voice bore little of the broad vowel sounds which characterized the local accent. Occasionally, for effect, he would parody his background with an expression like: 'Oi'm jus' orf dayn the ol' tayn,' but Wilson refused to be taken in by either his posturing or his occasionally vicious sense of humour.

Towards evening on the second day, after the schools had spilled out their shouting, liberated contents, and several of the street-lights, timers badly set, had decided to blink into an unnecessary and premature watchfulness, they were driving back towards the police station on Salmond Square. Their route took them past the central church of All Saints, described by Lewis as 'about the only consecrated traffic island in the country', over the complex of traffic lights on George Square and past the sprawling, slightly raised huddle of Victorian houses which bordered the dual carriageway on their right. Wilson knew what it was called by now. He'd been into its mazes with his own men and passed it several times with Lewis. Yet the usually garrulous Information Officer somehow never alluded to the area, which formed an island of earlier time in the midst of the developing wasteland just off the town centre.

'How about taking me into Uptown?' the policeman asked.

Lewis took his eyes from the road long enough to flash his passenger a questioning glance. Then he said: 'Nothing to see there. Just a part of the old town that hasn't gone yet.'

'Maybe it will give me some of the flavour of what Monkhampton was like before expansion. That could be useful to me.'

Something in the movement of Lewis's shoulders as he flicked on the indicator and moved to the outer lane of the dual carriageway suggested a shrug. All he said was: 'Okay.'

They turned off the broad ribbon of new road and passed beneath the streetlamp-lit shadows of the older quarter. The houses were set close together in narrow streets, some with cobbled alleys and cul-de-sacs leading off them. It seemed damp, and the wheels of the car threw up more water from puddles than they had done previously. Without any apparent alteration in the light the air about them began to feel thicker, more solid. The dark areas seemed blacker, and those beneath the lights were more yellow. Here and there a pile of freshly-swept rubbish glistened in the gutter, and a roadsweeper in corporation navy overalls pushed his green handcart along the deserted streets.

Here and there a head showed through the gap in ill-fitting, heavy curtains, giving a glimpse of life, or whatever passed for life, inside the crumbling houses. Occasionally a labourer, his clothing soiled and grubby with work-stains, trudged homewards through the damp. A short queue of tired, thin adults and children waited in the seedy, drab interior of an old fashioned fish and chip shop, taking their turn to approach the dingy chrome counter and depart with the precious bundle wrapped in curious pink newspaper.

Not the *Financial Times*, surely? Wilson wondered. Then he remembered the Saturday evening local sports paper, the Pink'Un.

'You wanted to see Uptown,' Jake Lewis grinned evilly. 'Here it is. Like it, Ben? Is it soulless, or has it got too much soul for you?'

Wilson suppressed a shudder. There was a depressing, deathly quality hanging over the streets and houses, as if some brooding presence in the towering bulk of St Gargoyle's had spread its bat-like wings across the lives of all within its reach.

'Tell me about it,' the policeman said. His voice was quiet and the words almost caught in his throat on the way out.

This time Lewis actually did shrug as he swung the wheel

28

and rounded an almost completely blind corner. 'What's there to tell?' he asked. 'Your own men must have filled you in about Uptown by now.'

Wilson nodded, more to himself than to the driver. 'Yes,' he agreed, 'they have. But I want to hear what you have to say about it. Will you tell me?'

'Okay.' The response was devoid of enthusiasm. 'We'll start at St Katherine's, if you like.'

He threaded the vehicle along the narrow streets and into an unusually large square which Wilson somehow felt to be the heart of the area. Even at a quick glance the policeman could see that it was something of an architectural junkyard, the properties varying widely in both style and purpose. One side of the square, the side from which they'd entered, was two solid blocks of dingy houses, ranging in height between two and four storeys, in the uniform red brick which characterized almost every building in Uptown. Between the blocks ran the road they had travelled. Wilson was a little alarmed at the way Lewis drove straight into the square, ignoring what was, theoretically, a T-junction, but the absence of traffic in Uptown was only equalled by the apparent absence of garages amongst its shabby houses.

Opposite them stood a row of tall, mouldering, detached houses. Many of them were empty, their windows boarded up on the ground floor behind the untidy hedges, and most of the glass broken away from the upper frames. Here and there a thin, unhealthy cypress struggled to keep its dignity, and the sad, broken remains of a vandalized monkey-puzzle tree sprawled defeatedly in front of one of the older houses. At a quick count only three or four of the properties appeared to be inhabited. Outside one of them a sign supported by two posts proclaimed: Salvation Animal Sanctuary.

The third side of the square boasted the bold, rotting frontage of an ancient shopping arcade, its interior, green and dirty-cream and poorly lit like the square itself, sloping tunnel-like away into whatever depths it possessed. Both of the shops flanking the entrance were empty, the doors shuttered and padlocked and the windows whitewashed. The whole idea of a shopping arcade in a development such as this struck Wilson as an anachronism, and he said so.

Lewis simply smiled. 'Temple to God,' he remarked, gesturing towards the old church on the north side, 'temple to Mammon.'

Lewis abandoned, rather than parked, the car in the deserted square. From a nearby house a head was thrust around the door, glinting eyes focusing doubtfully upon the two strangers. If there was any attempted secrecy in the observation it was entirely banished by the Boris Karloff creaking as the glass-panelled, sticking door was wrenched open from within. As Lewis and Wilson stepped out of the car and on to the cobbles the head was rapidly withdrawn and the creaking sounded again as the door was pushed quickly shut.

'The natives don't seem particularly friendly,' Wilson quipped.

Lewis peered at him from beneath scowling eyebrows. 'Uptown people keep themselves to themselves,' he said quietly and, the policeman thought, a little too firmly.

They began walking across the uneven cobbles towards the north side of the square. Above them, silent and broody, reared the spired bulk of St Katherine's. The church, grotesquely ornate, waited above the steps which led to a litch-gate in the high wall for them to approach. As Lewis held the gate open for Wilson to follow, the policeman noticed that there was only a neglected lawn with a few flower-beds around the church. As far as he could make out in the uncertain light there was no burial-ground attached to the church-garden.

'Where do they bury the dead?' he asked.

The Information Officer smiled grimly, his features darkened by the shadow of the rotting litch-gate above him. 'There's some plots to the east and north,' he answered. 'Most of the Uptowners seem to prefer cremation out at Milton, though. There's not been a burial here at St Gargoyle's for years.'

They crunched up the unweeded gravel path, past the

...ab...
...lows...

...side of the
...tone arch, to the
...hat's why it's called

...the porch roof, its wings
...or imminent flight across the
...ptown, sat a bloated, cat-headed,
...Strictly speaking it wasn't a gar–
...jecting spout to carry rain-water
...as it positioned in such a way as to
...served such a purpose. It sat too high,
...o ever have been a proper gargoyle. It
...oration, some whim of the Victorian-
...d created the monstrosity of St Kath–
...ved for a house of God.
...orch, stepping unhesitatingly beneath
...ter, and tried the inner door. It opened
...on the midnight-black interior of the

...more as a suggestion than an order. 'I'll

...e in the porch, struggling to read the
...ces pinned with rusty tacks to the
...ard. It was impossible to miss the odour
...hey gave off, despite the theoretically
...ir in the open porch. It was as if they
...time, lost to all but the ghosts of those

31

bro
56. 3.00
'This has b
it. I simply don't bel
'If it's in Uptown yo
walking back towards th
likely anything. Now, come o
the vicar didn't,' Wilson grumbl
'I'd have thought the kids wo
church.

He hadn't travelled three steps in
up his coat collar against the sudden
thrust his hands into the pockets. H
steam out in winter clouds, despite
June air outside. Concentrating as he
in temperature he found himself standi
staring up towards the sanctuary, befor
how he came to be there.

If the carving above the porch had
terior of St Gargoyle's was a positive r
the vaulted roof towered off into distan
manner of flying, creeping things might l
ed the arches, their spans supported as
corbels carved from a lighter stone. B
carpet of dust waited for his presence
serried ranks of collapsing pews, each
Victorian church furniture which res
monize with its neighbours, were co

32

tangled remnants of the lawn on either side. Wilson was
starting to feel the need to talk, if only to dispel and banish the
almost tangible silence that hung in the darkened air around
them. Besides, he sensed more eyes than he was prepared to
count peering between mildewed curtains behind dirt-crusted
window-glass. He wanted to turn, to startle the watchers by
looking back at them, but even if he did so he knew that m
of them were invisible, watching in darkened rooms, un
be seen with no light behind them to throw their sha
silhouettes out into the street.

As they approached the porch on the sout
church Lewis pointed up above its green-st
sculpture perched upon the gable end. 'T
St Gargoyle's,' he grinned.

Perched at the nearest end of
slightly furled, as if preparing f
attics and slated rooftops of U
dragon-tailed stone-carving.
goyle at all, having no pro
away from the roof. Nor
suggest that it had ever
too proud off the roof t
was simply a carved de
Gothic architect who ha
erine's on the site rese

Lewis entered the
the leering stone mons
beneath his hand up
church.

'Stay here,' he said,
go and find the lights.'

He left Wilson alor
worn, weathered noti
wormed-oak notice-bo
of mildew and decay t
cleansing effect of the
had become trapped in

who had worshipped in St Gargoyle's in the depths of its vanished past.

Without any warning the lights inside the church began to flicker on. In the sudden glare spilling out through the open door Wilson read the notices easily. Or, rather, he saw them easily. Reading them was more difficult because of the ~~owned~~, yellowed paper upon which they were written in ~~fa~~ded ink of a long-broken, forgotten fountain-pen.

~~BAPT~~ISM OF SARAH CROFTS, said one. APRIL 30TH ~~2~~ P.M.

~~b~~een pinned up over thirty years,' the policeman ~~r~~inging with incredulity. 'I just don't believe ~~bel~~ieve it.'

~~yo~~u can believe anything,' Lewis called, ~~th~~e entrance from the vestry. 'Very ~~come~~ in and have a look around.'

~~wou~~ld have torn it down, even if ~~add~~ed as he stepped inside the

~~int~~o the nave before he drew ~~the~~ chill of the interior and ~~h~~is breath threatened to ~~th~~e comparatively warm ~~w~~as on the sudden drop ~~stand~~ing in the central aisle, ~~befor~~e he really understood

~~been alarming the in-~~ ~~n~~ightmare. Above him ~~g~~ darkness in which all ~~l~~urk. Cobwebs festoon-~~t~~hey were by grotesque ~~b~~eneath his feet a thick ~~it~~ to disturb it, and the ~~was~~ a small masterpiece of ~~abso~~lutely refused to har-~~associ~~ated with the fungoid growths of damp-rot, white and leprous against the heavily-stained darkness of the wood. Before him as he approached, his feet leaving tracks upon the dusty tiles of the floor, the sanctuary stood empty and violated, the stone massiveness of the altar-table, bare of frontal and ornaments. Around him, about him, almost within him, fumed the distinctive, distressing odour of abandonment and decay, disuse and dissolution. St Gargoyle's was nothing more than an empty, godless shell.

'It hasn't been used for years,' Wilson snorted.

Lewis, close beside the ruined altar, turned his head and nodded to the policeman. 'As you say,' he affirmed. 'Yet this church is the heart of Uptown,' he continued. 'Haven't you wondered how I was able to turn the lights on? The electricity supply is still connected. And that's because the church is still in use, after a fashion. Oh, they have to clean it out every time, and that takes quite a bit of doing, and they don't, as you've pointed out, have services here any more. But it's still Uptown's heart. And in so far as a place can have a soul it's the soul of Uptown as well.

'Let me tell you about this place you insisted I should take you into, Ben. As I think I've said, Uptown is one of the few parts of this town to survive the expansion programme to date. But it's done more than just survive. If it had been up to the borough council and the development corporation Uptown would have vanished years ago. There's a London consortium all ready and waiting to buy up the land for redevelopment just as soon as the borough council's ready to sell. And the borough was ready to sell three or four years ago. Uptown's an anachronism, a proud, unyielding anachronism. It's half-empty and rotting on its foundations, but it's holding out against everything it regards as unthinking, unfeeling change.'

He paused, his eyes following Wilson's gaze about the decrepit interior. In a dark and distant corner something low and furry scuttled away.

'So what do they use it for?' the policeman asked.

Lewis shrugged. 'Meetings, discussion groups, that sort of thing. And residents' council meetings of course.'

'A residents' council? In a run-down rotting sewer like this? Why, half the buildings are empty. It's less than half a mile from the town centre, but it can't even sustain a proper range of suburban shops. Does *anybody* from the rest of Monkhampton ever come here?'

'Sometimes. Mostly newcomers, out of curiosity. Expatriate Londoners looking for something to remind them of Whitechapel in the sixties. And the Uptown Residents' Association is one of the strongest in the town.'

'That's as may be, but how do they keep the council from slapping on a load of compulsory purchase orders and tearing the lot down?'

Lewis shook his head and began to walk down to the vestry in the base of the tower. 'Their councillors are always independents, never politically aligned. Oh, the parties have tried campaigning here, putting their own people in to stand for the seats in local elections, but they never do very well. Uptowners have a very insular outlook. They keep themselves to themselves and they don't like strangers. They always return their own candidates.

'Now, you recall I said that the Uptown councillors were independents? Well, Monkhampton Borough Council is politically very finely balanced. The two councillors from Uptown exercise a quite remarkable degree of power in comparison to the people they represent.'

'So what you're saying is that their vote goes to whoever keeps Uptown standing? Is that how they do it?'

Lewis nodded. 'According to the discussion documents produced at the start of the expansion and redevelopment programme, which eventually became the Master Plan I gave you a copy of, Uptown should have been torn down nearly four years ago.'

'So why wasn't it? You can't tell me it's a healthy area for people to live in. Not now I've seen it for myself.'

The Information Officer snorted derisively. The sound echoed in the empty church slightly more than their dust-muffled, low-toned conversation was doing.

'As I've said before,' he explained, 'this is a partnership new town. That means that the borough council provides certain agency services, such as engineering works and housing administration, to the development corporation in order to prevent expensive duplication. Oh, we pay for the services all right, but it still works out marginally cheaper than setting up our own. Now, although Uptown is one of the areas designated for redevelopment it falls within the old borough boundary. That means we can only be invited to participate in its re-development by a direct request from the borough council, under the existing partnership agreement. And, in this case, we haven't been invited.'

'And the Uptown councillors are behind that, no doubt?'

'Yes, but there's another consideration as well. The council wants to retain control of the site and sell it to a developer of their own choice. That way they get the site value *and* rate income from whatever goes up in place of Uptown. In other words, development corporation keep your hands off our asset.'

'Meanwhile the people continue living, if that's the word, in this absurd collection of rotting slums.'

Lewis sighed loudly and turned back to face the policeman. 'I don't think you've understood anything I've said, Ben. They *want* to carry on living in Uptown. At least, until the development corporation's dead and buried. The Uptowners have fought expansion and redevelopment all the way along the line. They actually seem to *like* it here.'

He pulled back the heavy, mouldering curtain which closed the vestry off from the nave of the church. Myriad dust-motes flew like summer pollen into the dirty glare of the electric lights.

'So why don't they do something to improve the place?' Wilson demanded.

'Because they know they can't fight the council for ever. Sooner or later Uptown will vanish from the townscape of Monkhampton. It has to. Even its councillors recognize that it's an anachronism in the new, modern town.'

They stood in the vestry, its walls lined with empty pegs where surplices and cassocks had once hung, empty book-shelves which now held only the odd notebook, a damp, limp, children's Bible story-book from the fifties, and two or three dirty-green English Hymnals. In its centre stood a grimy table with four high chairs around it, the velvet upholstery of their seats faded, torn and chewed into holes by vicious rodent teeth. In one corner a plain wooden ladder led up to a trapdoor in the ceiling, giving access to the clock and bells in the spired tower above. The bell-ropes, their striped sallys grimed by forgotten hands, were tied to the ladder to prevent them dangling onto the table.

On the south wall of the tower a large patch of damp bore traces of a faintly-phosphorescent mould. In both the vestry and the church the sickly-sweet, nauseous odour of decay permeated both the fabric and the air itself.

'I've seen enough in here,' Wilson muttered. 'What time is it?'

Lewis checked his watch. 'Nearly six,' he replied. 'The local pubs will be open in a minute, if you fancy a drink.'

'Are there any pubs here in Uptown?'

'There were several at one time. I expect two or three will still be in business. The Shakespeare on Cattlemarket Road, or the Red Lion, but that's down on Station Hill. I know, how about the Battle of Inkerman in Inkerman Terrace? That's the nearest.'

Wilson smiled and began to move towards the south door. 'I've time for a quick half,' he answered.

'Good. We'll walk there. At the risk of putting you off whatever you'd intended eating tonight, it'll give you a more direct sample of Uptown's flavour.'

They left the car parked in St Katherine's Square and walked down through the deserted shopping arcade, passing its tiny shops with their windows boarded up or painted over. A wooden balcony ran along either side above their heads, painted in the same green and cream as the lower storey. The glass and timber roof above this was broken in several places, and Wilson felt himself tensing at the thought that the whole thing might come crashing down on them in a lethal rain of jagged splinters at almost any moment.

In the centre of the arcade a circular area topped by a glass and timber dome radiated smaller corridors off the main one. These had shops only on one side, their windows facing on to the dadoed walls which blanked off the stairways to the upper floor, consisting of tongue-and-groove wooden-walled offices and workshops. Here and there a handbill had been stuck to the painted surfaces, but there was very little graffiti, what there was being scraped into the surface rather than written with felt-tip pens or spray-cans.

Wilson felt increasingly ill at ease. The silence, broken only by their echoing footsteps, the lack of people, the closed shops, even the lack of rubbish in the corners and the usual evidence of night-time lovers seemed to be conspiring against him.

As they started down one of the smaller corridors the policeman stopped to study the graffiti.

KILROY WOSNT HERE. ELVIS. SUK THIS, followed by a crudely-drawn penis and testicles.

No rock-star names. Not even a twenty-year-old eulogy of the Beatles. No NF swastika or Nazi-parody JUDEN RAUS or NIGGER GO HOME. Nothing he couldn't have found cut into the timber walls of an army nissen hut thirty years earlier in the vanished days of National Service.

'Don't they have any modern vandals in this part of town?' he asked.

'A policeman complaining about a lack of vandals?' Lewis snorted. 'I don't believe it.'

'Neither do I,' Wilson replied, forcing a smile to mask his unease. 'In an area like this it's positively unnatural.'

He already knew that Uptown was probably the only part of Monkhampton where the crime-rate was actually showing a marked decline. This was the base reason for his curiosity about the area. It wasn't right. The poorer parts of any town or city, and Uptown was indisputably within that category, usually showed the greater incidence of criminal activity.

37

Mostly it was muggings and burglary, old ladies on pension day and homes showing the flashing timer of a video recorder in their windows. Uptown should have been a peak on the graph, not a valley. For football matches, demonstrations, parades, it was always Uptown that the extra men were drawn from first. The area was patrolled to a lesser extent than any other part of the town. Yet its sprawling urban decay, its environment of narrow alleys and lost ambitions, the obvious deprivation which stared from the eyes of its hungry children and the suspicion manifested by their elders, as if whoever it was had changed his mind about going out whilst there were strangers outside the house, made it an ideal breeding-ground for every kind of crime on the statute-books. It didn't make any sense at all. And the more Wilson saw the more he found his bewilderment increasing.

They turned left out of the arcade and continued down one of the wider streets. Other shops, scattered between private houses, lined their route, all of them securely closed. Turning into a side-street they found themselves in front of a dark opening off the pavement beside a large, high window, its surface frosted in Art Nouveau swirls. Above their heads a peeling painted sign hung from a rusting iron bracket. It showed, in the rays of a nearby street-lamp which wouldn't have looked out of place in an industrial museum, a British cavalryman with drawn sabre in the uniform of the 1850s. Behind him in orange and scarlet a cannon-shell was erupting as it hit the ground, making his horse rear up. Beneath its feet, on a black panel in plain white lettering, was the legend BATTLE OF INKERMAN.

Through the narrow double doors above four lethal-looking steps the sound of a juke-box spilled fitfully out.

'You made me love you, I dinna wanna do it, I dinna wanna do it . . .'

Lewis led the way up the steps. Inside the doors a corridor led down to an inner door marked Lounge. Beside them, as they entered, another door painted the same dull crimson bore the legend Saloon. Between them, in the centre of the blank,

38

yellowed wall, was an archaic-looking wooden cigarette machine.

'. . . yessa do, yessa do, you know I do . . .'

They walked down the corridor and into the lounge. The carpet beneath their feet was a dull, threadbare grey, ornamented with yellow and red scrolls. Wilson, approaching forty-four, remembered a similar carpet in his parents' lounge, thirty years before. The walls were gloss-painted, once probably white before decades of nicotine had done their work, and hung with garish prints of Crimean scenes which time had mercifully faded. The bench seats along the walls and the free-standing chairs about the table had red plastic seats which had faded to a different shade from that of the formica-topped tables.

The wooden bar, deep mahogany, looked as if it was original Victoriana contemporary with the building. Behind it the bottles attached to the optics looked as ancient as the walls, and the pump-handles glimmered sadly with the fitful dullness of unpolished, sweat-wiped brass. A barman, short like Lewis but contrasting scruffily with the Information Officer's careful dress, watched their approach through narrowed eyes. His expression beneath the poorly-concealed overhead lighting, was a long way from being welcoming.

'Somethin' I c'n do for you gents?' he asked, his voice oddly high-pitched against the deeper tones of the singer on the juke-box.

'You made me happy, darlin', you made mee sad . . .'

Lewis looked at his companion. 'Pint of bitter all right?' he asked.

Wilson was surveying the empty lounge, trying to shake the impression that he had stepped back into his adolescence. 'Mm,' he agreed, absently.

'Two pints of best, then,' Lewis smiled. The barman nodded, reached beneath the mahogany bar for glasses and began pumping the clear, red-brown beer into them.

'That's two-sixteen,' he said his voice devoid of expression, as he lifted them onto the bar counter.

Lewis paid, tried another wasted smile, then carried the beer over to a corner table. Wilson was already sitting down there, turning a blue glass ash-tray with a red motif at its centre over in his fingers.

STRAND, it said. FILTER-TIPPED.

'I used to smoke those when I was at Hendon,' he remarked. 'Remember Strand?'

' "You're never alone with a Strand"? Oh, I remember them. Blue and white packet. You know, someone once told me that it was the advertising that killed the brand off. People began to think that smoking them made you lonely. Silly, wasn't it?'

'How long have they been off the market? Eighteen, twenty years? What's the average life of a glass pub ash-tray, Jake? Six months, maybe, before some pissed-up idiot knocks it onto the floor? They make them out of plastic now. Or the good old tin ones, like that one over there.'

He pointed towards a SENIOR SERVICE ash-tray on the next table.

'How's the beer?' Lewis asked, changing the subject. He was beginning to share Wilson's unease about their surroundings.

The policeman took a long pull from the straight glass. He lowered it back to the table and wiped traces of the head from his lips. 'That's not bad at all,' he remarked. 'Whose is it?'

'Harrington's. It's a local brew. They've one of the last independent breweries operating in this part of the Midlands. Right here in Uptown, as a matter of fact. It's one of the few industries still surviving here.'

Wilson nodded. 'That's more like beer ought to taste like . . .'

He fell silent, suddenly aware that even the appreciation was taking him back several years. 'You know,' he resumed, 'I don't believe this place.'

'You mean the pub?'

'I mean the whole thing. Uptown. It's still living in the fifties. Just look around you. The juke-box is modern, but that's the only thing in here that is. The furnishings are ancient. That slot-machine over there's an original one-armed bandit, right down to the indian's head. It's a collector's item. Even this ash-tray. And the music. And the beer. And the street-light outside. It doesn't belong to the eighties and I don't suppose it ever will.

'I looked at the signs in that arcade as we walked through it. Bronco, Izal, hard loo paper. Vim. Brillo. Farley's Rusks. All old brands. Fairy Soap. Pears Soap. Carbolic. It's a nostalgia freak's paradise. I'd have thought some bugger would have been along with a screwdriver and had 'em away to sell before now. It just doesn't make any sense to me. No bloody sense at all. It's as if the people of Uptown distrust the present so much that they've shut it out.'

He drained his glass in several large gulps. 'Come on,' he said. 'I'll buy you one back and then I want to get back to the station. And after that I think I'll have an hour or so in the Central Library, if it's still open.'

Wilson carried their empty glasses back to the bar for re-filling. As he was returning to the corner table the lounge door opened and a younger man and woman entered. Lewis noted the welcoming smile they received from the barman and contrasted it to his less enthusiastic greeting when they had come in. As the policeman handed him his pint and sat down again with his own they made no attempt to resume their conversation. They simply watched and noted, each in his own way, the contrast presented by the young couple's arrival.

The girl had bobbed hair and a long skirt beneath her coat. The man wore a dated lounge suit and had an army-style short-back-and-sides haircut.

Fifties revival, Wilson thought to himself. Or was it fifties-original?

Double-breasted jacket with wide lapels. Wide trousers with turn-up cuffs. Plain black Oxford shoes.

'And when I tell them, an' I'm certainly gonna tell them, that I'm the guy whose wife one day you'll beee . . .'

'Evenin' Mike, Carol. What's it to be, then?'

'Pint o' best an' a port an' lemon,' Mike replied.

41

Carol giggled. She was quite pretty, really, though a trifle over made-up, Lewis thought.

'D'you think I should, Mike?'

'. . . they'll never believe meee, they'll neverr believe meeeeeee . . .'

Wilson carried their empty glasses back to the bar. 'Thank you,' he said as he put them down. As he collected Lewis and they made their way across to the door he felt three pairs of eyes stabbing into his back. When he pulled the door open he turned back and looked towards the bar.

Mike, Carol and the barman were all smiling at him.

At that moment Ben Wilson began to feel slightly sick. In Uptown it was Mike and Carol. Everywhere else it was Wayne and Tracy, and Tequila Sunrise not port and lemon. Either Uptown had deliberately and, within its confines, universally regressed, or it had deliberately stopped.

He frowned at the thought. Stopped? What the hell for? Why did people or places usually stop? Because they're dead? These people weren't dead. The place might be dying, but the people were alive enough, in their suspicious way. So, not dead. Then what?

Waiting? People stopped to wait. But what for? In a place like Uptown what could they be waiting for? The bulldozer?

He walked along beside Lewis as they went back to the car parked in St Katherine's Square, quietly wishing that he'd left well alone and stayed out of Uptown. It was going to worry him, he suspected.

But he didn't know how much. Or how soon.


Gertie Tomkins peered from behind her lace curtains, frowning. She'd been all set up and ready to go when that wretched car had driven into the square and stopped. And those two who'd got out and gone over to St Gargoyle's weren't Uptowners, that was certain.

There had been a lot of strangers in Uptown recently. Mostly they were business types with fancy cars. Probably what the man on TV called *yuppies*. Fancy name for smart-Alecs, Gertie thought to herself. And they'd all done what these last two had done. Gone over to the church, once with a priest who wasn't local. Gone into the old Emporium Arcade, after they'd stood about outside it, pointing and waving their clip-boards, talking gibberish in posh voices.

Well, sod 'em. Sod 'em all. She'd do what the *other* told her, not what those fancy-pants decided.

It wasn't fair, making her wait like this. Why couldn't they just have got in their car and driven off, instead of disappearing? Now she was having to hang about until they did.

Yes, sod them an' all. Maybe they weren't quite like the others, but they still weren't Uptowners. They'd have understood. They'd have smiled and stopped for a chat, looked right. Not strode about like they owned the place.

Which the rotten sods probably did already, or would soon enough.

She felt her lower lip tremble with suppressed emotions, a mingling of rage and excitement, with more than a little anticipation as well. Gertie didn't go out a great deal these days. She didn't need to, on the whole. The post office was only a few minutes' walk when she went out for her pension on Thursdays, and the grocer's in the same block supplied most of her food needs. There wasn't a great deal left over once the regular had been put aside for the bills. No looking round for fancy shoes in posh shops like Caroman's or posh foreign food in fancy restaurants. Mousetrap cheddar had always been good enough cheese, even if its flavour had begun to vanish as the texture grew more rubbery, year by year, without going off to fancy places that called themselves delicatessens.

She'd go out another once or twice a week, down to Mrs Blunson's in Inkerman Street for a gossip. Sometimes Mrs Blunson came to her. Sometimes that awful Mrs Crouch came as well.

Sod her.

But now, when Gertie *had* to go out, she couldn't. Maybe she'd made a mistake by sticking her head out earlier. Certainly they'd have heard the door creak, even if they hadn't actually seen her. Still, that couldn't be helped now.

She had to wait until they came back to their car and went away for good. The *other* wouldn't like it if outsiders got involved in what she had to do. Not that she was actually afraid of the *other*. Not at all. She just wanted to do the right thing and make everyone happy.

Oh, the waiting!

Perhaps if she sat down and turned the TV on time would pass a bit more quickly. Perhaps if she did that, though, she'd fall asleep and never go out. That wouldn't do. She'd be letting everybody down if she did that, even if she didn't understand exactly how. No, it was her duty to stand there at the window and wait for the strangers to go. They couldn't be too much longer. Not at that time of day. They'd want to be getting back to their fancy offices and fancy homes. That's what they'd want.

So, they wouldn't be too much longer. Not them.

Her legs and feet were beginning to hurt with all this standing. Since she'd had those pills off Dr Fowkes the swelling in her ankles had gone down a bit, but it was still an ordeal for a lady in her seventies to have to be doing sentry duty like this. If they'd been Uptowners she wouldn't have had to do all this waiting, she thought again.

Suddenly Gertie's eyes brightened again, renewing and re-affirming their focus after the dull introspection of a moment before. She stared obliquely through the window as Wilson and Lewis came back into view, walking towards the parked Sierra. One of the strangers unlocked the doors and they both got in. Then Gertie's waiting and muttering ended as they drove off out of St Katherine's Square.

Now, she thought. It has to be now.

She stepped out of her front room into the narrow hall and opened the front door, mentally cursing the noise it made. It'd be all right to leave it on the latch. She wasn't going to be gone long. Besides, the *other* would make sure everything was all right for when she got back.

44

Gertie set the lock, then bent down to pick up the plastic carrier bag. The bottles inside it clunked dully together, protesting the disturbance. They hadn't been easy to find at this time of year. The hardware shops usually didn't bother to stock their contents until the weather started to get colder. And she'd had to go outside Uptown for them. Not everybody knew about the *other*, and there was always the chance that questions might have been asked by somebody who wouldn't understand.

Carrying them back had been heavy for the old lady. She'd had to stop and rest several times, being careful to make sure nobody she knew saw her, just in case. Still, she'd soon be free of them now. They were making their last journey together, and it wasn't very far. Not very far at all.

She pulled the creaking door shut behind her and started slowly off across the square. It was a little before half six and she wanted to be done before the shift came off at Harrison's Brewery. The carrier bag grew heavier with each step, but she also drew closer to her destination, and Gertie gritted her National Health teeth, white and regular in their orangey plastic gums, and pressed gamely and determinedly on.

Soon be there, she told herself. Soon be there. Soon be done now.

Her original intention had been to walk around the edge of the square in case somebody noticed her, but the *other* had told her it didn't matter, not now. All that mattered was what she had to do, and really that was going to be easy enough.

Back on the kitchen table was the check-list she'd written herself, crossing off everything she was going to need as she'd bought it and put it in the carrier. When the last item was to hand and crossed off she'd emptied out the contents and rechecked them against her deletions before replacing them. Nothing had been omitted or forgotten. It was all there. All on its way to church.

At the litch-gate she stopped and set down the bag for a few moments' rest. There was plenty of time. Certainly enough for a small breather. From the porch at the other end of the

45

weed-strewn path the gargoyle grimaced impatiently, urging her not to be such a sluggard. Gertie scowled at the carving, then resumed both her burden and her progress beneath its now approving gaze.

Those strangers had come in here. So had the other ones, some of 'em. Those yuppie types. Sod 'em all, polluting the old place with their fancy notions. The *other* was right. It was time for a purgation, a cleansing.

And a new beginning.

The carving, half mammal and half reptile, disappeared above her as she entered the porch. Gertie was strongly tempted to set the bag down again and take another rest, but instead she pushed open the door with her free hand and stepped inside. The chilliness of the interior reached out for her, caressing rather than clutching with its touch. Old people get used to the cold too easily. It becomes a friend, a companion, instead of the masquerading enemy it truly is. She shuffled through the dust towards the rack of hymn-books at the back of the south aisle, then set down the carrier. Removing its contents one by one in the light spilling through the open doorway she mentally reviewed them once more against her memory of the shredded check-list.

A bundle of twigs broken from the rowans in St Katherine's Gardens and dried thoroughly. A weekly free newspaper, also kept dry. A firelighter. A candle. A box of matches. A plastic washing-up bowl. This had been large enough to fit into the carrier with everything else packed inside it, including the final items.

Two litre bottles of paraffin.

She'd probably have been able to find a candle in the church, if she'd looked, but the *other* didn't want anything left to chance. That was why she'd brought the newspaper, instead of ripping up some of the old hymn-books, which were probably damp anyway.

Her instructions were quite clear and Gertie carried them out precisely. She shredded the paper finely by hand and placed it in the plastic bowl before pouring the paraffin over it. She set the candle in the middle, making sure it balanced upright, then set the rowan twigs around it. The candle projected three or four inches above the paper and paraffin.

The next part was the hardest, physically. Going into the vestry at the base of the tower, its curtain still drawn back where Lewis had left it, she half-carried, half-dragged the four heavy chairs to where her bowl had been set up and stacked them above it. For good measure she tore up most of the hymn-books and placed them around the outside the bowl, sprinkling them with a little left-over paraffin. Holding the matches, she walked back to the doorway and felt beneath a wooden alms-box screwed to the wall. Her nails tore the tired, brittle sellotape and the key came away in her hand.

Nearly there.

Gertie didn't bother to look around her. She might have sent her mind back to remember a time, possibly forty years before, when St Gargoyle's had been filled with worshippers. They all prayed during the war, all of Uptown. They all prayed for some years after the war, before the *other* came. She'd been married here. In Coronation Year her hubby had been buried from here. Good times, sad times. But none of them mattered any longer.

She lit the candle and shuffled out, locking the door of the church behind her and throwing the key into the tangled grasses beside the gravel path. As she walked back towards the litch-gate she looked up at the grinning monster above the porch.

*There is life*, it told her, *in everything. Not just in man. Other things want to worship here as well, Gertie. You have helped them. Well done.*

Gertie smiled at the monstrosity. It was right, of course. How arrogant it was to think that only man might want to worship his creator. It made sense to think of other creatures needing to make obeisance. Hadn't the *other* told her something similar?

*Not all my worshippers have hands, daughter. Not all of them can open doors. You must help them for me. It shall be your task to take the doors away.*

47

And that was what she'd done. How long it was going to take Gertie didn't know. Probably the paraffin vapour would ignite long before the candle burned down to the twigs and the newspaper.

If they didn't have hands to open doors, then they probably wouldn't want pews to sit in. Or the roof which pampered man required to shelter his hairless body from the elements. Or bells in the tower to summon them to worship.

No, they would be summoned by something . . . *other*.

Ben Wilson was back at his desk when he heard about the alarm call. Christ, he thought, I was in that place just a couple of hours ago. It was too bloody damp and decayed to catch light. Even if it wasn't, it's a hell of a bloody coincidence.

He picked up the phone and punched out an internal number on the push-button dialling, trying to get hold of a recently-promoted DS he'd brought over from Waventree. A woman's voice answered.

'Kate, is Harry Chester there?' Wilson asked.

'He's gone off to get a witness statement on that burglary in The Avenue, sir,' came the reply.

'Okay. Look, get hold of him for me, can you? Get him to meet me at that fire in Uptown. And have a stab at arranging for our forensic people to liaise with the duty Fire Officer. There's a stink coming out of that place that's something more than just burning church.'

He spoke to the duty Fire Officer himself, later that night. By then St Gargoyle's was a gutted shell. It was the following day before Wilson was told that the alarm call which had alerted the Fire Service had come from outside Uptown.

Somehow that seemed to make sense to the policeman. Yet it also presented him with a riddle. Of all the houses facing the square not one occupant had either noticed that the church was on fire or bothered to report it.

But that was in the future. Now he was standing beside a fire tender, one of four, in St Katherine's Square watching the battle to save the church. The light June evening appeared to be going on indefinitely as the soaring, scorching flames lit up

48

the sky and the surrounding area. Hissing patches of steam jetted back through the shattering windows as firemen played steady streams from their hoses into the burning interior. Uniformed coppers patrolled, pushing back any Uptowner who might, in their opinion, be getting either too close or in the way.

The smoke from the fire went up into the night, rising in a flame-masking column in the still air. A police Sierra drove into the square and parked untidily. Harry Chester got out and hurried across to Wilson.

'You wanted me, guv?' he began.

Wilson nodded. 'Get round to the local paper offices,' he told him. 'I don't care who you annoy, but I want everything they've got in their library on Uptown on my desk first thing in the morning. Take Kate Jones along to help you carry it. Okay, Harry?'

Chester slapped a hand across his chest in a mock salute. 'By your command,' he grinned. Then, more seriously: 'You reckon this is arson?'

'It bloody well isn't spontaneous combustion,' Wilson answered him.


Gertie was feeling well-satisfied with her work as she opened the front door and went in. Yes, she'd done a good job. She had a right to be pleased with it. More importantly, the *other* would be pleased with it as well.

She walked through to the kitchen and put the kettle on for a cup of tea. A nice cup of tea after her work. And why not celebrate with a little drop of carefully-hoarded whisky in it? Maybe even a slice of fruit-cake as well.

The kettle boiled and she warmed the pot. Once it had grown almost too hot to hold she took the caddy down from the shelf and spooned some loose Ty-Phoo in before adding the rest of the water. There was a cup sitting on her draining-board beside the sink but it was old and chipped. The everyday cup. Not the right thing for a celebration. Not at all.

Gertie was about to reach inside a cupboard for one of her

49

bits of best china, one of the few surviving items from that tea service they'd been given as a wedding present, when her eye fell on the check-list on the kitchen table. That came first, she decided. The task wasn't properly complete with that lying around. She tore it up. There. Now, with that out of the way she could take things easy.

She'd take her tea and cake through to the front room once it was made. She could sit there and watch the fire start in comfort. It ought to be better than anything on the TV for once. There we are. Drop of milk. Strainer over cup. Pour. Now for that drop of whisky . . .

Gertie suddenly turned and looked behind her. It was completely irrational to suppose that there was anybody there, but it felt as if there was. Nothing to see, of course. Well, there wouldn't be, would there, gal? Not here there wouldn't. Nobody'd get in once she'd locked up proper.

She poured more of the whisky into her cup than she'd intended. The feeling that there was somebody there persisted, prickling at the short hairs at the back of her neck. It was still full daylight, and when the sun declined at the end of the day it came slanting in through the kitchen window anyway. Even so, the air in the kitchen seemed murky, as if there were shadows there that had no right to be. She felt cold and shivered to herself, her bones chilled even in June.

Not natural, that wasn't.

Gertie Tomkins suddenly felt uneasy about going through to the front. The kitchen was an extension to the rest of the two-up, two-down house that her late husband had built on, with a bathroom above it to replace that outside washhouse and water-closet. Beyond it was the stairwell and the old kitchen, now rather grandly called the dining-room. Then a short passage leading to the front door with a door off it to her front-room. In the unnaturally chill gloom of the kitchen that short passage seemed positively sinister.

She sat down at the kitchen table with her tea, the cake forgotten. Well, if she was honest with herself, it wasn't so much forgotten as ignored. The gloom seemed to be at its worst around the walk-in pantry door and Gertie didn't want to go through it unless she could help it.

This was all very puzzling, she reflected. The house had always been a friendly place, even comforting her by its friendliness and familiarity when her hubby died. For it now to have become sinister and threatening, isolating her in her own kitchen on a bright summer's evening, didn't seem either right or likely. But that, Gertie decided, was what had happened.

No, this wasn't right. Here she was, supposed to be having a quiet celebration, and she felt like a cornered criminal, in dread of the coppers moving in and taking her. She peered determinedly at the darkness, so thick now that it had almost congealed, and suddenly sat bolt upright on her wooden chair. There were lights in the dark. Lights that looked like slitted eyes staring back into her own.

Her ancient heart began to flutter. She felt its beat increase. She felt a cold, trickling sweat break out around her hairline.

Eyes out of darkness. Bright eyes. Eyes that were opening, growing larger. And larger.

She felt her mouth gape open in shocked surprise. Her hand, holding the cup, froze where it was, in mid-air. Her stomach felt suddenly sick and her temples throbbed with an increasingly irregular pulse.

A mouth formed beneath the eyes. With teeth.

Such teeth.

With an effort she set down the cup and tried to stand. Only then did she realize that her old legs didn't want to work any more. She wasn't only a prisoner in her own kitchen, she was a prisoner in her chair.

The eyes grew even larger. As a ghastly panic enfolded her in its clasp, as the hammering of her heart began to sound her death-knell, Gertie Tomkins realized what she was seeing. And why.

*You have served me well, Gertie,* said the *other*. *Now it's time for you to rest.*

She clutched at her chest, feebly at first then with a stronger, more convulsive movement. Panic mounted with her increased

heart-rate, panic which surged beyond her servitude, screaming admonitions in her failing ears. For a moment a raw foetor
swept into her nostrils, then faded. She tried to speak, to call
out, but her throat was dry and the words wouldn't come.

The creature reared up on its hind legs, resting its cruelly-
taloned forepaws on the back of the chair opposite, the one
that Marge Blunson sometimes sat in when she came without
that other woman. Those eyes, big as saucers, Gertie thought
briefly through her terror, burned unremittingly into her own,
dimming the rest of her shrinking world with their brilliance.

Her eyes went out.

She sat there, helpless, deaf, dumb and blind. Adrenalin
surged bitterly into her mouth before taste went for ever as
well. Now only feeling remained, the feeling of sheer horror
and the feeling of physical pain. Pain which shot through her
chest and paralysingly, agonizingly, down her left arm. Pain
which doubled her over, drawing her insides together like the
string tie of an old-fashioned pouch.

Then Gertie felt the hammering stop, and the darkness of
oblivion took over.


Jake Lewis spent the next day in the office, catching up on
some overdue paperwork and fending off the latest panic about
site completions from the General Manager. He'd always en-
joyed his job, but the approach of MDC's end-date was
making him lethargic and dispirited. It wasn't easy, sitting
there and watching the offices empty one by one, shunting the
furniture and the surviving staff into smaller and smaller
spaces as the waves of redundancy bit home. They'd even
given up on leaving parties after the final wave of outgoing
architectural staff had held what they called the Last Supper.

He heard about the fire in Uptown on the local radio on the
way into work. Jake tried to find some grim humour or irony
in the fact that he and Ben Wilson had been two of the last
people in St Gargoyle's. If either of them smoked then they
might even have started it, dropping a fag-end.

Well, he reflected. This was Friday, Arse-end of another bloody depressing week. No, maybe he was being unfair. Two days out of the office was hardly bloody depressing. It broke things up quite nicely, in its way. That Wilson was an OK copper. Still, he could afford to be. He had the rank. Chasing up the arrest record by persecuting the public wasn't so important once you made inspector.

After an alcoholic lunch in the staff bar he thought about ringing Sally and seeing what she was doing that evening. It was her half-day, though, and she'd be out shopping probably. To be sure he tried her home number and let it ring fifteen times before replacing the handset on his desk phone. He'd catch her later.

Later dragged slowly nearer. Just before he gave up on the week and went home he tried again. This time she picked up the phone at her end and he struggled to voice a cheery hello. It nearly killed him, but he made the effort. She could be cool enough without him pissing her off unintentionally.

She was cool enough anyway, and he wondered why he'd bothered to make the effort. After a few brief exchanges she slammed the phone down. She sounded upset about something, but that was hardly the world's greatest consolation.

He'd cheer her up. He'd wander round later with a couple of bottles of half-way decent plonk and a Petruccio's pizza or three. She liked Italian, he remembered.

Jake Lewis shook his head. Fuck it, he thought. I'll go down the cricket club instead. You can make the mistake of being too available, too bloody understanding. I'll let her stew in her own juice overnight and ring her again tomorrow. Besides, last time he'd gone down the club Mark Bentham's wife had been making eyes at him.

You never knew your luck until it happened . . .


Yeah, Tommy Junior decided. Amazing.

He always felt the same thing on those rare occasions when he was admitted to Granpa Hangel's workshop. It was a mingling of awe and pride, yet tainted with the contempt of one who has grown up in the age of micro-processors and quartz chronographs. The awe was for the old man's obvious skill and dedication to his chosen work. The pride was in knowing that the man who could do such things was his mother's father. And the contempt, less for the old man himself than for what he did, was a paradox which Tommy never bothered to reason out. Fourteen-year-olds can be like that sometimes.

The workshop, though, was definitely amazing. Not like his father's, which was a cluttered jumble of old cages, power tools, welding kit and garage equipment, collected second hand over the years to keep the Landrover running. Not like that at all. Despite being an old brick-built forge tacked onto the end of the outbuildings as an afterthought it was clean and impeccably ordered inside. Benches ran round three of the walls with drawers and cupboards underneath, drawers and cupboards which remained mysterious to Tommy, who had never seen any of them open and could only manage the odd haphazard guess as to their contents. Above the benches, shelves were bracketed to the whitewashed walls, some standing empty, some holding cases and half-assembled movements, others adapted to take larger tools, mostly different kinds of metal saws. There was old lino on the floor, worn and patched in places, and the ceiling was whitewashed like the walls, with a couple of strip lights hanging on chains. Beside the door stood several small sheets of brass, stacked against a variety of exotic woods. The door was wide, taking up most of the fourth wall, and unlike the drawers and cupboards it creaked alarmingly whenever anyone opened it. Except Granpa Hangel. He knew the knack of opening and closing it in total silence.

The old man was regular to the point of being punctilious in his habits, so it was only very occasionally that Tommy had to be sent to call him for a meal. Not that he minded, particularly being sent to the workshop. His grandfather never spoke a great deal, spending most of his time within himself, drawn back into the memories and secrets of his past, memories and secrets which probably had something to do with the C-212257 tattooed on his left forearm. There again, Tommy decided, he could just be thinking about his work, about what those clever, wrinkled fingers, the nails brown and horny and frequently discoloured with jeweller's rouge, were to achieve next.

The door creaked shut behind the youth. Granpa didn't like the weather getting inside the workshop, whatever kind of weather it was. It could upset the balance of a delicate mechanism, he'd once explained. That's why he kept it shut, supplementing the little light from the high window at the further end with the strip lights.

Pieter Hangel swung around on the old typist's chair to face his grandson as Tommy entered. He looked from the boy, dark complexioned like his mother, to the old station clock hanging above the door, its pendulum swinging in a steady rhythm. His seamed, haggard features, long-jawed and thin-lipped, the eyes dark, hooded pits below the bushy white eyebrows, the nose strong and his hair still a thick white thatch above the deeply-lined brow, settled on Tommy. The mouth slowly smiled.

'Your mother has sent you to tell me I am late for lunch,' he observed.

His voice rasped a little, rather like a Godfather in a mafia movie. Despite his foreign background his English was near-perfect. Tommy had never bothered to be surprised at this. After all, the old man had been in this country for over a quarter of a century before Tommy was even born, and if the boy could learn how to speak the language in the first few years of his life it was only reasonable that even an old man like his grandfather could pick it up over a twenty-five year period.

'You got it, Granpa,' Tommy answered him.

Hangel sighed. Ah, the idiomatic syntax of the young. It was yet another of life's absurdities that the tongue he'd struggled to master was so readily debauched by those who knew no other. If *he'd* said that, someone would have corrected the bloody foreigner.

'I forgot the time,' he explained superfluously. 'One does such things when the work is interesting. Only the bored are eternally watchful of the passing of time.'

Tommy stepped a bit closer. 'So watcha doin'?' he asked.

Somewhere in the hooded pits Hangel's eyes twinkled. The interest of others in his work was one of the few things which could stir a response in his distant soul. 'Come here,' he beckoned.

On the bench where he'd been working stood a peculiar contraption of brass mounted on wood. Inside a framework which reminded Tommy of the parallel bars over at the school gym were two round objects mounted horizontally on axles. Sorry, he corrected mentally, they're called arbors, not axles. One of the shapes was a fat cylinder, whilst the other, a spiral groove cut around the exterior throughout its length, was cone-shaped. A plaited brass wire, rather like the snares he'd seen his father cut off injured animals, was wrapped tightly around the fat cylinder and attached to the base of the cone. Outside the frame, at the front, a toothed wheel was mounted on the cone's arbor, held by a ratchet which permitted the two to move in opposite directions. And on the front of the cylinder's arbor an ornately-filed brass key was attached.

Hangel grinned. 'You know what this is, Tommy?' he asked.

Tommy shook his head. It looked like something out of the Science Museum. It had to be part of a clock, because clocks were his grandfather's hobby now as they had been his livelihood throughout his years in England. But where was the rest of the clock, the dial and hands and stuff like that?

'This is a demonstration model I've made for Estbury Technical College,' Hangel explained. 'It shows the workings of the fusee. Do you know what a fusee is?'

The boy shrugged. 'Sound like part of a gun, Granpa.'

The old man nodded. 'Things are not always what they sound like. You remember, when you were younger, you had a clockwork train? You'd wind it up and let it go and it ran. But as the power ran out it went more and more slowly, yes?'

'Yeah, I suppose so.' Tommy was beginning to wish he hadn't got himself into this.

'It went fast to begin with, then slowed down, then stopped. Now that was because the so-called clockwork didn't have a fusee, my boy. If it had, it would have run at the same speed all the time, until there was no power left. In here,' he pointed to the cylinder, 'is a mainspring, fixed at one end to the arbor and at the other to the outer drum-case. Without the fusee that spring would discharge its power at an unequal rate. You set the clock going at midnight, by two o'clock it says half past three. By half past three it says half past four. By five o'clock it says half past five. Perhaps at six it will catch up with itself, and then it will begin to slow. By eight o'clock it tells you half past seven, unless you have a fusee, to control the rate at which the power of the spring is released. You see?'

Of course he didn't see. How could he? No keyboard. No space invader sounds. No plastic or electricity.

'Sure. Looks pretty good.'

'But lunch is ready, yes? And you've come to remind me of the time, not to listen whilst your own food grows cold.'

Hangel stood up and put a thin arm around Tommy's shoulders. 'You open the door for me and close it behind,' he instructed. His grandson looked vaguely disappointed. He'd been hoping to see how the old man managed to open and close the door without it creaking. Not that the knowledge would have been any practical use. There was nothing in the workshop that would be likely to benefit Tommy. His mates wanted power tools, not the old hand-saws and horologists' gizmos that Granpa used. They wanted up-market chronometers, not bracket clocks that weighed a ton and filled a suitcase. Even that mysterious shape under the tarpaulin cover in the corner would probably take two kids just to lift it, whatever it was. And just assuming he swiped all the brass, he'd only get a couple of quid scrap value for it, and a hell of a bollocking if the family found out it'd been him.

Tommy did as he was told and creaked the door shut. Then he walked with Granpa Hangel under the plastic extension roof which sheltered the entrances to the other outbuildings on one side and stretched across part of the cage area on the other. The workshop smelled of oil and metal, like a garage in miniature, that warm but unappetizing odour of engineering. Out here the smell was very different, and stronger. A permanent reek of animal waste, disinfectant and, when it rained, the rankness of wet dog. Neither Tommy nor Pieter Hangel noticed it, though. They were both thoroughly used to the smell of Salvation.

As they passed its pen the large white Newfoundland, now well on the way to a complete recovery, bounded against the mesh and barked welcomingly at Granpa. He stopped in his stride and turned to smile at it. He nodded.

'Soon,' he whispered.

'Granpa?' Tommy asked.

'Hmm?' The old man turned to his grandson. The boy knew nothing of the bonds forged by suffering, the alterations to the mind it could cause, the differences in attitudes to life and purpose. But he might, one day.

'Soon, I said,' he told Tommy. 'Soon be time.'

'Time to eat, Granpa,' Tommy countered, his stomach crying out for burger and chips.


It was simply a doorway between two shops. Every high street has them, tucked away, almost invisible. This one was recessed about three feet, with a white door at the end of it and an electronic lock. The sign in varnished Letraset read OFFICE CLEANING AND MAINTENANCE LTD and, in smaller letters, UPSTAIRS. Nothing sinister about it. In fact the litter about the floor suggested that it might well be a favoured trysting place for young lovers with nowhere else to go after a movie or Big Mac.

For Sally, though, it would always hold a shudder. That's where it all began for her on a Friday afternoon.

At twenty-five Sally French was something of a career girl. Not executive material, perhaps, but a good enough legal secretary to have been head-hunted by her present firm. She was also extremely decorative, her hair worn long and with a studied wildness in its styling, her clothes as good as the exigencies of a single city life permitted, usually from Next, and her figure distinctly modelish.

Friday was Sally's half-day. The afternoon was usually taken up with a partners' meeting, with one of the articled clerks taking the minutes. A receptionist took incoming calls, which left Sally free to do the week-end shopping, working her way along the local shopping precinct and the older shops around it. Basic stuff, Fridays. Groceries. Saturday, if there was time, probably a hunt round the clothes shops and a sniff through Boots perfume counter.

The doorway was in part of a thirties redevelopment. At street level the shops were fitted with smart, modern fronts, plate glass and trendy logos. Only the cracked paving tiles, not replaced in some of the entrances, gave their age away. Above them, however, their age was rather more blatant, painted on for anyone who bothered to look up by thin-framed metal windows and plain, drab brick, not to mention the concrete sills stained with green, lichenous discolouration and pigeon droppings. You had to look up, though, and nobody really bothered. Not with the bright, gaudy wares displayed underneath. And, for the same reason, nobody ever looked at the doorway.

So far the afternoon had been pretty good. Sally had used up her week's supply of L Vs on her usual binge lunch (hang the calories – I can take it one day in seven, can't I?) at Trattoria Napolitana, veal washed down with a Fruili Cabernet Sauvignon by the glass. After coffee she'd started to work her way slowly towards the delicatessen where she bought most of the week-end food and the fruit shop which supplied the basics for working lunches Monday to Thursday. Now, at getting on for three-thirty, the carriers were growing heavy, but she'd promised herself a squint in Caroman's window for a new pair of summer sandals. Caroman's was outside the main precinct, though, beside the doorway, and she might not have a chance to do it tomorrow.

She didn't see him coming. She didn't really see him at all, which hardly endeared her to the police afterwards. No good description, no arrest. No arrest, no conviction. And not much nearer promotion, either. The first she knew was when he took her by the elbow and spun her, unresisting in her surprise, into the entrance to OC&M. The bags went with her, then dropped around her feet, spilling their contents and adding to the litter in the doorway.

He pushed hard at her, forcing her against the door. The pushing hand took a rough hold around her right breast, squeezing it painfully. The other hand flashed a wickedly-sharp blade in front of her eyes.

'Scream and I'll cut you,' he hissed. 'Purse!'

'I . . . I'm spent out,' she stammered, trying to think, trying to fight down the panic bile spilling into her mouth. 'Take the bags . . .'

'Don't shit me, you cow! Good clothes, smell good, you got money. Or cards. C'mon. Cash and plastic. Now!'

Sally felt the false edge of the clip-point blade slide into her left nostril. If it, or she, moved an inch it would slice half her nose away. For ever.

With fumbling fingers she unlatched her handbag and groped for the purse-wallet inside. The blade moved a fraction deeper, the point beginning to tickle up a face-destroying sneeze. Abandoning any thought of bluff or resistance she pulled out the purse and felt the hand move off her breast to snatch it.

The point lowered but remained substantially in place. 'Stay here,' the mugger hissed. 'Count twenty. I see you come out before then I'll come back and cut your fucking eyes out.'

He was gone before she could answer. Her chest heaving with relief she began to slide down the door, legs suddenly weak. It was over. She was safe again. However long it had taken, and it felt like hours and hours, it could only have been a few seconds.

For Sally, slumped there amongst her spilled groceries, the world going busily on with life only three feet away, it had been the first time. No-one had ever done that to her before. Okay, it might have been worse. He could have just stabbed her and taken the purse off her body. He could have forced her to do anything he wanted. Anything. That he hadn't would only come as a consolation later, after she'd seen the police and told them the little she could, after she'd reported the loss of her credit cards and that concerned looking copper had driven her home.

She still had her keys, and the policeman saw her safely into her flat and offered to make her a pot of coffee. Sally smiled weakly and shook her head, so the man said 'Okay' and left her to put her life back together. They'd wanted to take her to a hospital for a check-up but she'd turned that down. All she wanted was to be by herself for a while and sort through the range of emotions which the afternoon had confused her with.

The first thing Sally did was to run a bath. A shower was no use at a time like this. You couldn't soak under a shower. You couldn't lie back and massage that assaulted breast, washing away that grip which had only penetrated the protective layers of bra and sweater and jacket psychologically. Get the body right and the mind will follow, she thought. With luck.

She poured half a bottle of bubbles under the running water and stood there, frothing them up even more with her hand from time to time. Her clothes peeled off, layer by layer, tossed into the laundry basket to be sterilized and purified of the invading touch later. Naked at last, the afternoon still not dipping into summer evening, she wandered haphazardly into the kitchen and poured herself a stiff vodka and tonic from the small stock under the sink. Wash off the body, wash off the mind. Try not to dwell on it too much or too long. That way lies madness, she thought, wondering if she was quoting and, if she was, who from.

Sally took the vodka back to the bath and sank into the foam, feeling the water and bubbles soothe and purify her despoiled existence. If this was what being mugged felt like, she conjectured, then how much worse must the even more personal desecration of rape feel?

She wasn't religious, but she heard herself say softly aloud: 'Pray God I never find out.'

Outside the sky darkened. The day, which with a grim laugh she realized had been best described as muggy, was threatening to climax with a thunder-storm.

She soothed away what remained of her physical discomfort, stroking and washing the breast she was surprised to find unbruised. Chances were Jake would ring and propose something for the evening. It had been a couple of days so it was time for him to call. Well, this time he was going to be out of luck. He wasn't that good company, in bed or out of it, anyway, and Sally was in no mood to put up with anyone or anything she didn't have to.

She lay back in the bath, feeling the bubbles cover her chin, blowing a path through their close-packed mass as they approached the level of her mouth. It was all over bar the shouting, now, and the police would do whatever shouting they could on her behalf. Nothing left but to forget, though she knew she never would. It would be dangerous to forget. It would be dangerous because what had happened today could happen again. And again. And next time, or the one after, if she allowed there to be another time, could be so much worse. Next time she could well be cut, or beaten, or even raped.

She shuddered, hearing the water lap over the edge of the bath with the violence of her movement beneath the comforting blanket of foam.

What had that copper said? Not the young constable who took her statement but the older one, mid-thirties or so, in plain clothes? He'd wandered through the office and stopped, somehow attracted by the good looks which still shone past her fearful expression and mascara-run cheeks. The uniformed officer had deferred to him, called him sir. Ranking detective, probably.

He'd read her name off the statement form the constable was writing out in a spidery, scarcely-literate hand, and called her by it though he'd not bothered to introduce himself.

'If I were you, Miss French, I'd get myself a dog. A big one with a mouthful of teeth. German Shepherd or something similar. That puts these creeps off trying things like this.'

Good advice, Sally reflected. Then she sprang upright in the bath, bubbles flying, as she realized that her hair was getting wet.

She reached up to the towel-rail and found herself a bath-blanket, standing up and wrapping it around her body. She'd have to wash her hair now, and that definitely precluded doing anything with Jake for that evening. Except that the fridge was empty and she didn't have any cash until she got to her bank in the morning. Christ, was she glad they'd finally got round to introducing Saturday morning opening a few years back.

Okay, if he rang up he could feed her.

She drained the vodka and, wrapped in the huge towel, dripped into the kitchen to pour herself another. As she started it she reflected on the lunch she'd treated herself to at Trattoria Napolitana. It wouldn't hurt her to go hungry for a night, maybe sleep off the horrors of the day, by staying in. Jake could go play with himself after all.

The alcohol was beginning to take the edge off her anguish. Even so, the advice that copper had given her was still there, still working actively away. She'd never had a dog, but she didn't have anything against them. They'd just never somehow been a part of her life. Now that was about to change. Now she was going to take that plain-clothesman's advice and get one. A big one.

In the lounge she set down her drink and looked at the clock. Not yet six. She took Yellow Pages from the shelf beneath the phone-seat and flipped to the index at the front. *Animal Boarding, Animal By-products, Animal Feed-stuff* . . .

The phone rang. It was Jake.

'How's the light of my life?' she heard him grinning confidently.

'Not tonight Jake,' she told him firmly.

*Animal Services, see Pet Services 417* . . .

He felt crushed by the weight of her tone. 'Hey, what's the matter, Sally?' he asked her.

'Look, just leave it for now, will you?'

*Animal Sundry Mfrs . . .*

'C'mon, girl, this is Jake you're talking to. Is it something I've done?' His tone was beginning to grate towards the pathetic.

*Animal Welfare Societies . . .*

'Sod off, will you?'

She slammed the receiver down and picked it straight back up again before he could try to renew the abortive conversation. Then she dialled the local RSPCA number.

'A big one with a mouthful of teeth.'

The number rang, then stopped. A recorded voice cut in: 'Your call is being diverted at no extra charge. Please be patient.'

It rang again. A woman's voice, warm and somehow comforting and friendly, oozing care, said: 'RSPCA. How can I help you?'

Suddenly feeling committed Sally took a deep breath. A dog would alter her life, probably for ever. But hadn't that thug in the high street already done that this afternoon?

'I'm looking for a dog,' she said. 'I can give a good home to one. How do I go about it?'

'Where are you phoning from, caller?'

'Estbury Green, that's 0557 39771.'

'Your nearest animal sanctuary is . . . let me see . . . Well, there's no official RSPCA sanctuary in the area, but there's a private one we sometimes refer to. Call Mr Greaves on 0557 51412 at Salvation, St Katherine's Square, Uptown. Salvation is open Monday to Friday, nine to three.'

Sally nodded, feeling her towel slip, then realized her nod couldn't be seen down the phone. 'Fine,' she said. 'Thank you.'

Monday to Friday, nine to three. Salvation. Damn good name, that.

She put down the phone and wandered towards her bedroom. Time to dry off and put something on. Then she'd wash her hair.

Really, it wasn't so bad, she decided, finishing her drink and wondering about having another. You got this sort of thing everywhere these days, and by the law of averages it was a sad fact of life that she'd probably have had to face it sooner or later.

It could have been much worse. At least, despite the privacy of the doorway, it had been in the town centre, where rape would have been next to impossible. Now somewhere like Uptown, or one of the other, seedier parts of Monkhampton, that creature could have laid her down and taken *everything*. Not just her purse.

The thought of Uptown brought her back to Mr Greaves and his animal sanctuary. It wasn't really surprising that she hadn't known it was there. After all, she'd never had any reason to enter the depressing jumble of Victorian slums that bordered the dual carriageway beside the town centre. It wasn't noted for shopping or leisure centres or anything that could conceivably interest Sally. Why it hadn't been torn down years ago, especially in an expanding town like Monkhampton, was a source of wonder if you bothered to think about it.

Which Sally realized she was.

She made up her mind and fixed another drink. Dog, she told herself, nodding as much to find out if the booze was working as to agree with her own decision.

Big dog. Yes, Mr Policeman. Mouthful of teeth.

It snarled, baring savage, drooling fangs at faceless muggers. They ran away, shrieking.

Sally grinned. 'Good boy,' she whispered aloud.

Then the chill crept back and her hair began to prickle. Dress and wash it, she told herself firmly. You're trying to put yourself back together, not fall apart. And that's what you'll do if you carry on like this. Besides, there's absolutely nothing that can be done about getting any size of woofer, let alone one with big teeth and an outgoing personality, until Monday. And she needn't bother to phone. She had the address now, and she knew where it was. Easy enough to call in after work and see what they had. With big teeth.

Bright guy, that copper. Wonder if he's married?

Wonder what his name is, come to that?

And I wonder what he's got that I could take to?

She smiled and shook her head, letting the towel fall away
s she burrowed into a drawer for clean underclothes. What
1e copper had was what all men had. Nothing more and,
)oking at him, probably nothing less. Her mind was still a
ttle confused, for it hadn't been the policeman at all she'd
10ught of when she asked herself the question. It was this
1an Greaves who ran Salvation.

And what, she wondered, if what she could take to had
een a creature with four legs, not three.

Sally giggled. The vodka was doing its job and she was
eginning to feel much better.


he beat officers patrolled Uptown much more after the fire
hich gutted St Gargoyle's. Wilson realized that it was a
)licy of shutting the door after the horse was long gone, but
ith a greater presence and carefully picked constables he
)ped to build up a much clearer idea of what exactly was
ippening there.

Something was happening. There was absolutely no doubt
)out that. The only problem was to find out what that some-
ing was.

The Uptowners were more coldly polite than friendly, but
en Wilson told his men, and women, to keep at it. 'You'll
member from way back,' he informed them, 'that the book
resses *initiative and discretion* as a constable's chief weapons.
/ell, I want you hot on initiative. But I want you even hotter
1 discretion. Remember this is a traditionally low crime area.
on't stir things up. The folks there will have noticed our
creased presence for themselves without you stressing it by
)ur actions. I know it's a challenge, but I want you to achieve
)th high profile and low visibility. That may sound con-
adictory, but we have to know more about the area than we
), especially now the compulsory purchases are being served,

and to do that we need more help from the inside. We all want whoever torched that church, preferably before he torches something else, like a block of flats, for instance.'

And so the uniforms returned to Uptown, singly and in twos, always on foot. They walked and watched. They bade friendly good-mornings. They offered helping hands with trivia.

And learned nothing.

Gertie Tomkins was discovered dead at her kitchen table by Mrs Blunson and Mrs Crouch, who got no response to their knocking at the front and, figuring Gertie had to be in, went around the back to investigate. They saw her through the window and called one of the ever-present, ever-helpful coppers to break in. Wilson's fire-raiser was cremated without irony and her ashes scattered at the crematorium, as seemed to be the custom for Uptown funerals. About a dozen locals attended, together with the copper who'd found her, the copper who hadn't noticed the shredded check-list as he felt for her missing pulse. Marge Blunson had, though. Marge tidied the pieces of paper into her bag and burned them later. The *other* would have wanted her to keep things tidy.

A week had passed since the fire. Uptown remained quiet and, for the police, indefinably hostile. 'It's as if we weren't wanted there,' one officer said, 'as if we're somehow interfering with something they want to do.' How right he was.


The hammering began early, whilst Pieter Hangel was still dressing. His bedroom faced on to the square and he drew back the curtains to see what was causing the noise.

A truck had pulled up outside the old Emporium Arcade. Two workmen with stepladders were taking lengths of battening and stretching them across the ground floor fascia and the arched entrance, holding them in place with heavy nails.

The old man sighed and nodded, then turned away. It had to come sooner or later. The last shop had closed and the arcade was empty, its tenants forced out one by one by the consortium which had purchased it for redevelopment. All said and done it was a shopping arcade, not a right of way, and hardly anybody went through it any more. Even so, it was yet another signal of the coming end. With the church burned down and the first compulsory purchase orders being served on the residents Uptown was entering its death throes.

He finished dressing and stood watching for a while longer as the workmen continued their task. With the battening secure, sheets of heavy plywood were attached, sealing the glass in from vandals and closing the entrance. One of the panels was constructed with a frame and hinged door at its centre. This the men set in place last. One of them walked into the arcade whilst his fellow stayed with the truck, then he re-emerged and fitted a padlock to the door as he closed it.

There were still lengths of battening and sheets of ply on the vehicle. Granpa Hangel watched as the men got in and it started up, turning and heading out of St Katherine's Square towards the Inkerman Street entrance. Before the morning was done the Emporium Arcade would be closed for ever.

A knock came at his bedroom door and his daughter Mischa, Tom Greaves' wife, was asking why he was late for breakfast. He excused himself on the grounds of oversleeping.

'With all that noise outside?' she asked him. 'And you sleeping less than you did, as you're always telling me? Are you ill, Daddy?'

'No,' he answered gently. 'Not ill. A little restless, perhaps. I am always restless if I oversleep. My body is not used to the luxury.'

He placed a hand on her shoulder. 'Leave my breakfast,' he told her. 'This day I do not want it. I will take a walk instead, I think.'

Mischa wasn't entirely happy, but she knew her father well enough not to try and argue with him. He would be quietly immovable, like a cliff-face her words broke upon in waves, perhaps worn down the merest fraction, but not enough for her to see any effect, much less change his mind. She left him there and went back to the kitchen.

One side of his bedroom was lined with bookshelves, the wood groaning beneath the stacked weight of an untidy jumble of volumes. He walked across to the shelves and ran his eyes along the titles, reaching out as he found a spine labelled *Der Weg Zum Wahren Adepten*. He flipped through the well-thumbed pages until he found and re-read the section he wanted. The instructions were not exact, of course. Not for what he had in mind. But they could be adapted. The *other* would show him how to adapt them.

Mischa was out of the kitchen when he finally went downstairs. He passed through to the area behind the house where the animal pens were on one side and the workshops and storage areas on the other. Tommy Junior was at school and his father would be holding surgery at this time, so there was no danger of being overlooked.

Entering one of the workshops he emerged with his trouser pockets bulging. In one was a padlock and key. In the other, held in place with his hand and concealed partly in the pocket and partly up the sleeve of his jacket, was a twelve inch cold chisel. Rather than go back through the house he walked around it before heading down the front path and out into St Katherine's Square.

Pieter Hangel stood in front of the boarded-up arcade, surveying the bleak plywood exterior below, contrasting it with the ornate Victorian fascia still visible on the upper storeys. For some minutes he simply looked, his eyes ranging across the outside of the building. Then he walked off, following the route the workmen had taken, towards the side entrance in Inkerman Street. The men had finished their work there as well and had carried on to the other entrance in Inkerman Terrace, close to the public house. Here they were still putting up the battens.

The men exchanged friendly greetings with the old gentleman strolling by, hands deep in pockets. He carried on past them, now three-quarters of the way around the block, and turned left into Sebastopol Street. The Emporium Arcade had been built on a cross-pattern, rather like a church, with entrances at each end of the arms of the cross. For some reason the fourth entrance had been set at the end of a printer's yard which dipped away from Sebastopol Street between the houses. It consisted of a heavy but ordinary-sized wooden door, secured on the outside by a padlock and hasp. Hangel turned down into the yard and stood before it.

He took the padlock from his pocket and laid it on the ground at his feet. The cold chisel followed it as he examined the existing lock with his probing fingers. It was a good lock, probably about twenty years old, and it was going to take more than the cold chisel he'd brought to cut through it. Besides, he didn't want to make too much noise and risk attracting attention. There were too many policemen walking about Uptown these days to do that.

Was there a pair of bolt-croppers at Salvation? He tried to think his way through the tools lying around in the storeroom, to visualize them one by one and call up a mental image of what he wanted. The process consumed him to the point where he failed to hear the approaching footsteps behind until a voice said: 'Use these.'

The man wore a tweed cap and cord trousers. He had a dirty waistcoat on over his shirt-sleeves and looked as if he could have come out of a sepia photograph. His face was lined, stubbled and nondescript, with thin eyebrows and a curious blankness about the eyes. Pieter Hangel noticed this in passing, his attention chiefly focused on the bolt-croppers the man was holding out to him.

'The *other* told me to give you 'em,' the man added.

He took the tool and set the jaws about the staple passing through the hasp. As he pressed, the long handles closed, the jaws bit through and the old lock fell away with a dull clatter. He returned the bolt-croppers to the one who'd brought them, who turned and walked away without another word.

He replaced the lock with his own and pocketed the key. It didn't seem at all strange that the *other* should have sent him help. The *other* directed what he did, had even suggested the construction of the apparatus beneath the tarpaulin in his workshop, so it was not unlikely for others to be instructed in the same way. When he needed help that help was given, be it in the form of the printed word or direct human assistance.

Yet this was the first time that another servant had approached him. Soon they would all know one another, work with one another for the accomplishment of the *other's* purpose, he reflected as he walked out of the yard and back towards the Inkerman Terrace entrance. Could that mean he was about something of much greater importance than the mechanism in the workshop? Or was it simply that there was no purpose to the one without the other?

The Inkerman Street entrance to the Emporium Arcade was now completely sealed like the other two. The workmen and their truck were gone. Probably they'd already checked the Sebastopol Street entrance and thought it secure enough, assuming they even knew it was there.

Pieter Hangel went quickly back to the door at the end of the yard and unlocked it. He tried the handle and felt the door pull towards him at the top whilst resisting lower down. There must be a bolt on the inside, he decided, reaching for the cold chisel and using it as a lever. He was still remarkably strong for his age, his years in the camp having toughened him in his youth instead of taking the toll on his health they had done with so many others. He drove the chisel firmly home and leaned against it, feeling the door give slightly. Then he relaxed momentarily before setting his full weight on the projecting section with a sudden jerk. There was a muffled wrenching sound from within as the door sprang suddenly outwards. Pausing long enough to rub dirt onto the exposed wood to disguise the evidence of his work he stepped inside the arcade and closed the heavy door behind him.

In contrast with the dark shadows of the yard outside, and the dim length of the corridor leading from the door to the eastern arm of the cruciform arcade, the interior was bright with sunlight streaming down through the glass and timber roof above the walkways. The green and cream paintwork, peeling and blistering, reflected it back from the remains of its

71

glossy surface, sending it, refracted, into otherwise dark corners, exposing the grime and litter, some of it from the previous autumn's crop of fallen leaves, which had accumulated throughout the months of its decline and desolation. Here and there a stretch of the original Victorian tiles remained on the floor, cracked and broken, but mostly the surface underfoot was concrete, dirtied by countless feet to a grim slate grey.

Granpa Hangel walked out into the sunshine and looked up at the roof. The edges of the frames were grimed where the rain had washed sediment onto them. Some areas were cracked or broken, dark, dry stains on the concrete showing where the weather had penetrated. The whole arcade was still, except for the echoing of the intruder's footsteps, an echoing which grew greater as he approached the circular area at the centre, beneath the glazed dome receding overhead.

He stopped at the centre of the cross and turned slowly, looking down each of the passages in turn. The main arcade ran north and south, with shops on both sides. The transepts, as he regarded the cross-arms, were narrower, with shops only on the south sides.

Facing north he looked towards the St Katherine's Square entrance. Above the expanse of plywood and battens an area of glass still showed like the high window above a church altar. This was bigger than St Gargoyle's. This structure, deserted but not forgotten, as it was destined not to be forgotten for many years to come, was a cathedral by comparison. Now it was empty, dead. But it would come to life one last time, and the life it would know for that brief period would be more powerful than anything it, or Uptown, had ever seen before. The power it could store was immense, like an enormous mainspring. The very shape of the building, if the power was generated in the right way, would form a fusee to prevent its dissipation.

A giant clockwork structure made of bricks and mortar, of plaster and wood and glass. A power-house and a cathedral.

For the *other*.

*

Logic itself demanded the meeting, and eventual mutual acceptance, of Leader and Sally French. Sally had convinced herself of the need for a large animal, her decision boosted by Ben Wilson's casual remark about a mouthful of teeth. Leader had the teeth and, once recovered through Tom Greaves' care, a paradoxical leaning towards the female of the human species. It didn't matter that Tom had nursed him back to health personally. A man had put him in that terrible condition. A man could do so again. Even Tom. A woman, Ellie Pasciewicz, had loved him. *Ergo* Sally would love him. Animal Q.E.D.

All in all, she reflected, Sally's interview with Tom Greaves hadn't been the easiest few moments of her life. The grizzled vet, old beyond his years, his close-cropped hair and beard greying rapidly, had asked uncomfortable questions and seemed to distrust her brunette good looks from the start. Probably, she decided charitably in retrospect, his knowledge of Leader's past had played its part. The animal obviously deserved better in the future, and Tom was determined to see that Sally would be caring for him properly.

At first sight she had to admit her circumstances for caring for something the size of a full-grown Newfoundland didn't look that good. Single girl, out at work five days a week, living in a flat didn't particularly sound to her the ideal recipe for canine happiness. But she'd toured the pens between the house and Granpa Hangel's workshop and the large white dog had immediately caught her eye. To say it was love at first sight would be over the top a fraction, but between Leader's attraction to her as a woman, and therefore safe, and her appreciation of the creature's full beauty, now that it had put on weight again and its coat had renewed itself, even the fastidious Tom Greaves found little room for argument.

'The flat's just across the road from a park,' Sally persisted. 'And it's quite large, really. Honestly it is.' She was sounding like a schoolgirl and she knew it. It worked on Jake Lewis, so why shouldn't it work on this dour man with the yea or nay?

Tom's broad shoulders eventually shrugged, albeit somewhat resignedly. Anybody who was prepared to try this hard

73

wasn't doing it on a spur of the moment whim. 'It's my usual policy to see the new home and approve it before I let the animal go,' he cautioned, knowing it was useless. This woman was prepared to knock a few walls down to convince him her home was large enough, if she had to.

Sally nodded, fervently. Tom asked her to complete the usual Salvation forms. She did so in record time. 'I'll have everything ready when you come to inspect, Mr Greaves,' she beamed at him. 'Absolutely everything.'

She'd not been able to read everything behind the shrug. It concealed a multitude of thoughts and rationalities. Leader was a big dog and took a lot of food. And space. Both were commodities Salvation didn't have too much of. That, however, was always less of a consideration than the quality of life the creature had a right to expect. That was always the most important of many considerations.

Tom insisted that she go back out to the pens. 'To say goodbye,' he smiled, though that was far from his main reason. He wanted to see if that first, immediate interaction between woman and dog would be repeated, to point out to her one last time the disadvantages of a large dog in terms of housing, feeding and, certainly not least, veterinary bills. He might just as well have saved both his breath and the effort. Sally was convinced. So, from his facial expression, hind quarters bent and body low to the ground, one paw raised as if asking her to play games with him, ears down and mouth open, panting slightly, was Leader.

One last stab at making things difficult was called for. 'I'll be round on Wednesday afternoon, sometime just after lunch, if that's all right,' he told the working girl, knowing full well she'd normally be at the office then.

'I'll take the afternoon off and be waiting for you,' Sally responded, archly. 'They owe me some time, and I can't think of a better way of using it.'

She wasn't going to budge an inch, Tom reflected.

She said her goodbyes to Leader through the mesh and walked away. His amber eyes followed her as she made her way back between the pens. He barked once, then again. At the last moment, as she was almost out of sight, Sally turned and waved to the animal.

He bounded against the unyielding mesh, seeking a way through it. It wasn't fair that this comfortable woman was going away and leaving him there. Her scent, despite the masking odours of perfume, was friendly, not unlike Ellie's had been. She looked right and seemed right.

Just like the one that the *other* had told him to look out for.

He'd heard the conversation at table that evening, between his daughter and Tom Greaves. It had been sporadic, interrupted as it was by Tommy's pleas about that new computer program if he did well in the end of term exams, but there'd been sufficient of it for Granpa Hangel to realize that there was someone interested in the big white in pen five.

His son-in-law seemed reserved, uncertain, not going into the economics or extolling the suitability of the potential new owner, so a resolution wasn't automatically in the offing. Even so, the old man realized that it was only going to be a matter of time before he needed to act, to fulfil the instructions he'd been given.

A great deal of the preparation had been done already, out there in his workshop. What there was lay beneath the tarpaulin in the corner, unexplained and inexplicable. That it was clockwork went without saying. What it was actually designed to do, however, most certainly did not.

He'd delayed long enough, he decided. The commands were clear enough when they came. The difficulty wasn't with understanding them, but with the nature of their origin. How could he possibly begin to explain that they simply sounded inside his head? Another mad old foreigner, his brain unhinged by those wicked Nazis. That's what they'd say. And that's why Pieter Hangel said nothing.

But why obey them in the first place? they'd ask him. Why not ignore them altogether? Do you always do everything you're told? If you were told to go and lie down in the middle of the motorway, would you be daft enough to do it? Why don't you discriminate? You're old enough and not quite senile yet.

They wouldn't understand. Not the way he understood. Not the way that white Newfoundland in the pen understood. That's why he worked alone, in secret, on the instructions he'd been given.

By the *other*.

If they'd been spoken to by the *other* they'd understand. They'd leave him alone then, to get on with his work. The *other's* work. But it was impossible to tell who the *other* spoke to and who he didn't, and there could be few enough around here to share Pieter Hangel's understanding of pain and bestiality. Leader had come closest. It still showed here and there on the large animal's exterior, and in its eyes.

He'd known those eyes the moment he'd first looked into them. They mirrored his own. This was the one the *other* had chosen, beyond any small shadow of doubt.

The evening dragged on. Tom was in his office, catching up on the inevitable paperwork. Tommy was in his bedroom, studying for those exams and the reward he hoped they'd bring. Granpa sat with his daughter Mischa, a slender, dark woman in her late thirties, who'd married the young vet Tom Greaves fifteen years before. They watched television, Mischa dozing off from time to time. Being Tom's nurse as well as his wife was hard work, especially when she had to be Tommy Junior's mother too.

Anglia Reports finished. It had covered the expected summer death toll on the A11 and had been about as relevant to Monkhampton as a Christmas drink-drive campaign in March. Pieter Hangel hauled himself out of his chair, nudged the sleeping Mischa gently, then went off to the kitchen to make a hot drink for them both. The weather was too warm for it, really, but domestic rituals gave some much-needed stability to the old man's uncertain world. Once the mugs were ready he carried them through.

He wasn't tired. As he grew older he found himself sleeping less and less. Besides, he couldn't sleep tonight until he'd done what he'd been told to. His daughter, however, had to winkle Tom out of the office and prise her son away from the computer keyboard before she could go to bed herself.

The box was still on. A late film was running, the 1939 version of *The Hound of the Baskervilles*, with Basil Rathbone playing Holmes for the first time. It struck Granpa Hangel as particularly appropriate, so he settled down to watch whilst Mischa finished her drink and got the rest of the household ready for bed. He was often the last one up, so nobody would be suspicious or realize that he was simply waiting for them all to go to sleep.

The others came and made their good-nights to him where he sat. Howls echoed across the Devon moors. Richard Greene, not realizing the significance of his missing shoe, demanded: 'You surely don't believe in that ridiculous hound legend?'

Granpa Hangel smiled knowingly.

The household settled for the night around him. The occasional bark sounded from outside. He turned off the light and drew back the curtains, looking out across St Katherine's Square. Terraced houses opposite, an alley leading through to St Katherine's Gardens. The ruin of St Gargoyle's grotesque and menacing to one side. More terraces and the façade of the old Emporium Arcade on the other. Here and there the odd light still showed through the thin curtains of an upstairs window, but otherwise the square was deserted except for the occasional parked car, rusted and battered beneath the harsh yellow glare of the street-lights.

For a moment he thought he glimpsed a shape out there, large, dark and four-legged. He blinked and looked again, seeing nothing, and returned to his seat in front of the film.

*Hound* finished. One of the continuity announcers was interviewing himself to fill a break in the all-night programme. Sport next.

He switched off the set and listened to the house around him. Except for the occasional, familiar creaking of the property settling itself, it was as silent as the world outside. Granpa Hangel stood up and made his way quietly through the dark towards Tom's office. Once there he opened the key-cupboard, its contents lit by the light from the street-lamp outside. His fingers closed over the padlock key for pen five.

He didn't bother to close the cupboard again. He could do that when he brought the key back. Instead he went back through the house and out to his workshop at the rear. Most of the animals were asleep as he passed them, but Leader, a white shape in the night, was standing alert, watching and knowing.

Noiselessly, as usual, the old man opened the workshop door and stepped inside, closing it after him. The technique was really very simple. The door dragged on its hinges, but with the thickness of the sole of the old man's welted shoe under the leading edge it rose enough to prevent the sound. With the door closed again he switched on the light and bent to remove the tarpaulin from his construction. He set the mechanism out in the clear floor area at the centre, then turned off the light and opened the door once more.

Leader stood beside the pen gate, waiting silently. Granpa unlocked it and withdrew the padlock hasp from the metal keepers, pushing the gate open just enough to permit Leader to squeeze through. Once outside he sat quietly at Pieter Hangel's feet until his liberator pointed towards the workshop. Without a sound he padded towards it and went in.

Once they were both in the workshop Granpa closed the door and turned on the light again. The floor area was now mostly taken up with a large five-pointed star, built in sections of cut brass and standing on tiny feet which raised it slightly clear of the floor. The central area created by the lines formed a regular pentagon and was completely empty. Leader stepped over the exterior construction and into the pentagon without a command being uttered. There he sat, waiting patiently.

In the valley between the two northernmost points stood a carefully made clockwork motor, complete with fusee to control the discharge of its stored energy. This connected to a chain, rather like an elongated bicycle chain, which ran beneath the brass lines of the star, connecting the constructions at the points. Each of these latter items was different, yet they all shared a certain bizarre similarity, being mostly constructed from the same sheet brass as the star itself.

Leader faced the clockwork motor from inside the star. Granpa Hangel knelt outside the assembly, a series of small manual switches, rather like model railway points, beneath his outstretched fingers.

'The five senses,' he began, gesturing around the star. 'The five doing points of man or any other animal. In man they are the two hands, the two feet and the mouth. In you they are the four feet and the mouth. Those are what things are done with, places are gone to, food is caught and devoured with, fights are won or lost with. Five doing points, five senses. And from the five comes a sixth, which is the sum of the parts and something more. The essence of the being.'

The Newfoundland stared at this old man, his head slightly to one side. He'd heard humans speak before, but never quite like this. Usually he could tell what they wanted of him by the sound of the voice alone, by its tone of patience, or pleasure, or anger. But this went beyond simple tone identification. For the first time he heard individual sounds and realized that each had a meaning of its own, just as the structure of a bark or howl had meaning.

'The five points of doing you know. The five senses you know, Leader. Yet you may still learn more about them. See. Hear. Taste. Smell. Feel,' he gestured to the points of the star randomly. 'Three of these are grouped together upon the lower points of the pentagram. They are Taste, Smell and Feeling.'

Pieter Hangel flicked three of the switches. The clockwork whirred, driving the chain beneath the star. Leader turned, his amber eyes fascinated as the constructions at the points leaped into mechanical life. A brass paw, suspended by rods, closed upon a piece of fur to represent feeling. A dog's head, the jaws hinged, bit into a lamb's kidney until the blood oozed from the fresh offal. Another head, the nose tilting from side to side, descended into a small posy.

'These are ways of *knowing*, as indeed are the others, my friend. But they are limited by distance. So are sight and hearing, but they permit a greater range.'

Leader panted, his tongue lolling. He heard the old man's speech and recognized the individual words within the overall pattern. More than that, slowly but surely he began to realize that he had not only heard them, he was beginning to understand them as well. He licked his lips. He sniffed for the old man's scent along the brass lines of the pentagram. He raised a paw and touched the shiny, smooth, night-cold surface. He looked up at Granpa Hangel.

'Yes, my friend,' Granpa nodded. 'The time has come for you to know. The *other* wants you to. Now, be still a moment longer and watch.'

He flicked another switch. The clockwork whirred again. On the fourth point a tiny pair of bellows, attached to a dog-whistle, compressed, sounding a shrill ultrasonic note.

Leader growled.

'Your species has better hearing than man, better hearing than most creatures upon the face of this planet. Possibly only the *chiroptera*, the bats, have greater auditory powers. Or perhaps I should say they display greater auditory powers. You see? I have read much, studied much, to be ready for this time, Leader. I have to be ready so that I may make you ready. The *other* has required that of me. Now, one last point.'

At his command the clockwork struck a match to a candle by an ingenious arrangement of wires and pulleys. The candle lit and the match burned out, clogging the mechanism with charcoal. It didn't matter. It only had to work this once.

'The light which permits one to see. Oh, I know you have better night-vision than we humans. But you also have better smell and hearing and a less jaded sense of taste. You may have been denied the opposable thumb by evolution, Leader, but you are superior for all that. You and your kind are the coming man, not the theoretical superman of the Nazis or the evolutionary postulation of bio-chemists. *You* are the future.

That is what the *other* wants, you see? This is what we have to work for.'

He stood up, easing his cramped legs out of their squatting position beside the switches, now all depressed. He smiled down into the amber eyes which looked up from the central pentagon.

'Five senses,' he reiterated. 'Yet they are five in one, making a sixth. Combine their powers. Add the range of the greater to that of the lesser. Think of smelling as far as you can see, of seeing everything that you can hear, of touching all, tasting all, within that extended orbit. You have what man calls the spirit, embraced within those powers. You may see its reality and, more than that, encounter it with the other extended senses. Your power is already greater than man's. Now, with the senses combined and amplified by one another, your power is infinite. Truly god-like.

'You have been chosen,' he continued, whispering now. 'You were not named Leader for nothing. I know that you understand me. Now, make your answer. Let me understand you.'

The Newfoundland growled and grunted, struggling to articulate sounds that it was physically unequipped to cope with. After several moments, dejected and frustrated, it whimpered and lay down, its muzzle resting on its folded forepaws.

'You can do it,' Pieter Hangel hissed. 'You can do it. Do it. Do it!'

He heard. He understood. His canine brain screamed: How?

Granpa Hangel beamed. 'Like that,' he urged. 'Like that, Leader. I heard you. I *understood* you.'

You . . . understood me?

'I did. I did!'

You understand me now?

'I do, Leader. I do. Yes, I hear you. I may not answer you the same way, but I hear and understand. Have *you* understood what I've told you?'

I . . . think so, Pieter Hangel.

81

'Then show me. Show me, Leader. Let sight be gone.'

He watched the candle. Leader's eyes were focused upon its flame, drinking in the mere trickle it gave compared to the electric light which bathed the interior of the workshop. The seconds passed, pregnant, anxious. The candle remained alight.

The strip-lights above them pinged and went out, leaving them in the uncertain illumination of the flickering candlelight.

Pieter Hangel grinned and clapped his hands silently together, checking the sound of their meeting at the last moment. 'Now,' he urged. 'Hearing. Let me hear you. In silence.'

Leader concentrated upon the dog-whistle. The miniature bellows slowly filled themselves. Then emptied.

Granpa Hangel heard the shriek inside his own brain. He clapped his hands to his ears, eyes rolling, nodding so that the entire upper half of his body shook with the effort.

The note died away. In the candlelight Leader was watching him.

'Good. Very good. And now the other three. Smell. Taste. Feel. Be them. Do not despise them. Simply *be* them. Now!'

Leader turned inside the inner pentagon to face the three lower points. His eyes blazed in the darkness, big as saucers. Take them within, he thought. If they exist within, then they no longer need to exist without.

The brass shapes buckled. The paw flew apart, shredding the fur beneath it. The nose shattered, shredding the flowers. The jaws buckled and exploded, shredding the kidney and compressing it until fragments flew outwards to spatter the whitewashed walls of the workshop.

Will that suffice? Leader enquired, shades of expression already manifesting in his unspoken words.

'More than I dared to hope,' Pieter Hangel answered. 'The *other* chose you well, Leader.'

The animal nodded. So often the suffering of my kind is vain and pointless, he began. This time I have been fortunate. There is a woman who smells right who will come for me.

You and the *other* have shown me things I would not have dreamed of before. I know, now. I *am*, now. I am Leader.

'You are Leader. It is more than just a name. It is a state of being.'

A transitory state of being, Pieter Hangel. This is only my beginning. It is not my end. Now, you must take me back to my pen, where I shall simply be a dog again. Then you must clear the evidence of this night's work away and go to your bed.

The old man nodded. The Newfoundland stepped out of the pentagram and stood waiting for the workshop door to be opened. Once it was he padded silently to his pen and slipped inside. Granpa Hangel replaced the padlock and refastened it. Then he returned to his workshop, dismantled the star and stacked it back under the tarpaulin. His work, for the time being at least, was done.


The power of the *other* extended out across the darkness. It sought. It probed, seeking for the minds of its servants.

It roamed the night, touching worshippers and unbelievers alike, giving nightmares to some and visions of pleasures as yet untasted to others. It felt for weaknesses and grasped for strengths, counting, waiting, planning.

Some heard and understood. Others experienced without knowing, without their conscious minds remembering. Yet they had felt the touch of the *other* for all that, and they could never be the same again.

Most of those it touched were for the future, for work yet to be done. Two, however, were for now, and it found them where it expected to, in Uptown. One was a prisoner in Salvation. The other was a prisoner also, trapped by her memories and her loneliness, in her terraced house in Inkerman Street. Singly both entities were nothing. Together they would serve, and serve well.

The mongrel bitch was getting on in years, feeling her age,

noticing the greyness about her muzzle whenever she caught sight of her reflection in a puddle or a pane of glass. Her joints were stiffening and her periods of sleep were shorter and less regular.

The old lady in Inkerman Street was much the same. Stiff joints, grey hair, tired limbs. The mongrel had lost her owner during a cold spell the year before. Marge Blunson had lost her husband several years ago. Now even her female friends were starting to die off around her. They were both lonely, both ready.

The *other* was aware of this. There was little it didn't know. Yes, these two were right for what they had to do. They would work well together.

It reached. It penetrated. It spoke.

The mongrel, Mary, raised her head from her folded fore-paws and looked about in the darkness. Through the wire mesh she caught sight of the large white Newfoundland, head alert, amber eyes glittering in the night. In Mary's brain a species of understanding began to grow. In Mary's heart an expectation, almost forgotten through the lonely months, took hold again and strengthened.

*You see?* the *other* told her. *I can be kind.*

Marge Blunson stirred in her sleep, then awoke. For a moment she sat blinking in the darkness of her bedroom, her tired old eyes struggling to adjust to the thin light filtering through the curtains. Then she began to smile.

What a wonderful dream it had been. Such a simple idea, yet so charged with the power to end her loneliness, to re-vitalize her inner desolation. Why hadn't she thought of it her-self?

She began to nod. Yes, she'd do it. She'd do it tomorrow. She'd sort through her wardrobe and find something really nice to wear, then she'd go up to Salvation and find herself a dog. That'd fill the lonely hours and bring her back to life. Bring both of them back to life.

And something more.

*

84

'Just a little mongrel,' Marge told Tom Greaves. 'I don't want nothing special, you know. Just a companion. Not too big, mind. I can't afford to keep a big dog. And it wouldn't be fair. Not in a little house like mine. And he needn't be young. I'm not so young meself,' she giggled.

Though she didn't realize it herself, Marge Blunson's request was epoch-making. In the twelve years since Tom Greaves, always too soft with animals, his partner said, had withdrawn from regular veterinary practice and set Salvation up, Marge was the first Uptowner to offer a home to one of his animals. The kids came around, of course. They looked and decided, and Tom sent them away to come back with their parents. They never did, though.

It wasn't that the locals didn't have pets. Occasionally, very occasionally, Tom would be brought an elderly animal whose owner had died. Cats and the occasional stray dog prowled the streets at night. Old Murphy made the trek to the shops with his brown and black mongrel, fat, tired and lame like himself, tied on a hairy string lead. They had pets, but they found them for themselves. They never asked for them from Salvation.

He took her through to the pens and she picked out a mongrel. Somewhere in its white and brown splotched ancestry there was some Fox Terrier. The head was brown, darkening to black around the muzzle, though the black was beginning to grey with age. The short tail still managed to stand up and wag on occasions, and the contracted legs, suggesting a touch of Basset Hound, gave the bitch a squat, compact appearance suggestive of an odd-coloured Dachshund.

'Her name's Mary,' Tom said gently. 'She's probably about ten, which is getting on a bit for this size of animal.'

Marge's old eyes twinkled. 'She's perfect,' she said. 'A little love. Ain't you, eh? A little love.'

Marge looked up at Tom Greaves. 'I'm loosin' all me friends, you see? Ol' Gertie went two days ago, leastways that's when we found her, Effie Crouch an' me. I need a bit o' company, Mr Greaves. Your Mary'll do that for me a treat.'

Tom nodded. 'Let's go back to the office then, Mrs Blunson. We'll take a few details, then you can go home and get ready to share it with Mary. I'll come and take a look at you in a few days and then, if I think Mary'll be happy in her new home, she's yours. I have to do that, you understand? It's only fair to the animal.'

Marge understood. She dipped into her savings for a wicker dog basket and laid in a supply of Pedigree Chum Mixers and tinned food. She found an old basin for a water-bowl and a heavy baking tin she'd never use again, not for Yorkshire Pudding for one, for Mary to eat out of. She bought a posh lead that lengthened and grew shorter on its own and had a disc cut with 'Mary' and her address on it. All told the old dear had a very busy and expensive couple of days, rushing off to strange shops and digging out an old blanket to fold up for the basket.

Tom Greaves duly came and inspected, and was happy with things on Mary's behalf. Later that day he walked around from Salvation with the ageing mongrel in a wicker carrying basket that had seen better days. As soon as she was out Mary leaped onto Marge's lap and started licking her face like a puppy.

It was going to work out well, Tom grinned to himself. The two old ladies obviously adored each other right from the start. And why shouldn't they? Marge seemed nice enough, and Mary's friendly disposition had been enough to save her from a lethal injection, despite her age, for several months. It looked as if it was going to be a happy ending, and Tom liked happy endings.

The very next morning Mary and Marge took their first walk together in St Katherine's Gardens. To start with Marge kept the mongrel on its expanding lead. In a few days, when they were more used to one another, she'd take the risk and let Mary run free.

Marge took the lead in one hand and a plastic, leather-look shopping bag in the other. In this was a carrier-bag and an old fire-shovel from a broken companion set. Mary sniffed trees

86

and frisked on her lead. Then she found a patch which suited her and deposited a brown mound on the grass. Carefully, like a good citizen, Marge took out the plastic bag and the shovel and scooped the mess up. Then she went over to a similar deposit nearby and did the same.

Then she looked around for a third.

Two mornings later the carrier was full. Marge and Mary didn't go straight home from the park that day. Instead they walked on past the house in Inkerman Street into St Katherine's Square. Since the fire the square was looking even more desolate than usual, with the gutted church on one side and the deserted Emporium Arcade, its front now boarded up but with a small, padlocked workman's door in the bleak plywood fascia, on the other.

Uptown was finally beginning to die. Somehow the councillors had slipped up and the first of many compulsory purchase orders were about to be served. In a few months, by Christmas rumour had it, the whole area would be levelled, including the house in Inkerman Street and Salvation itself.

The animal sanctuary would survive. Tom Greaves had seen this coming and registered as a charity. The local authorities were aware of his work and sympathetic. Salvation would make out, somehow.

Marge tied Mary to the litch-gate and started up the path, the mongrel's questioning eyes following her. The porch was roofless now, the stone monster broken and blackened where it retained a tenuous perch above the entrance. Beyond it sections of beam projected above the shell like decayed fangs biting at a hostile sky. A scaffolding barrier barred Marge's way, a sign bolted to it proclaiming: UNSAFE. DO NOT ENTER. She ignored both the sign and the barrier, squeezing around them, staining her coat with soot from the stones she touched.

The House of God, once proud and bright with praise for the deity, was charred and defeated inside. The damage was much too great for the locals to be able to raise the cost of repair, even if they'd wanted to. And the diocese was under pressure from other sources now. It had been some time. There'd be no help for St Katherine's from there. Some day soon, just before the demolition teams moved in, some nameless bishop's deputy would come along with his mummery and perform the service of deconsecration, taking away the small, inscribed stone slab from the middle of the altar table.

For now, though, the slab was still there, the core and essence of the holy place. Here was the thing Marge was seeking, the thing Marge picked her way through the fire-stained rubble to examine.

Still there. Still sacred. Still properly a church. Just as the *other* had told her it would be.

She believed in the *other*, and she wasn't alone in her belief. There were plenty in Uptown that had been spoken to, convinced, prepared through the years. They'd do what was expected of them, what they'd been told to do. They'd lead the bright-eyes in the true path, show them the way so that they in turn could show their own kind, and their own kind could show other kinds in their turn.

Soon now, quite soon, a new paean would rise in this very place. It would be a hymn of praise, an act of worship and magic unlike anything which man had seen go before. It would be her doing, and the doing of those like her. But her own voice, she knew, would never be a part of that demented jubilation. It couldn't be. Its cadences weren't right.

But the *other* would remember her, remember what she'd done to help it happen.

Marge raised her eyes to the ruined sanctuary window above the altar. 'Tell me the way, master,' she whispered imploringly. 'Show me the way, monster.'

Master and monster, and nothing in between. How could there be? Marge asked herself. How could you divide the indivisible?

She set down her shopping bag and removed the straining carrier from inside it. As she stood there by the altar, the ruins about her brilliant light and strong shadow in the morning sunlight, she took hold of the carrier carefully and inverted it, depositing its foul, carefully gathered contents on the holy slab. The empty bag, brown-stained and nauseating, she discarded.

Liberated from its confines it began to sink together into a reeking pyramid of animal faeces. It wasn't Marge's place to shape the mess. The true worshippers would do that, those for whom the shape they created would have a greater meaning. For now it was sufficient that the raw materials were there, waiting for pads and claws to pat and rake out the shape which no man had ever knowingly seen before. How could she begin to shape it? She was as ignorant of the final form it would assume as anyone else might have been. All that mattered was that it was there, that the worshippers would come and create their own image, though possibly not in their own images as man had conceitedly done, and make worship and sacrifice before it in the same way that those other priests, those two-legged priests, had worshipped and sacrificed before the cross of Christ throughout the years.

She surveyed the disgusting mound. 'You are here already,' she whispered to it. 'You are here, feeling and seeing and listening, even as those before me claimed that Jesus heard and saw. But you're different. You're . . . other. You don't hear the prayers of men, his whining pleas for the help he's forgotten how to give himself. And you shouldn't. Why should you?'

A stone moved behind her. Then another. Marge turned and peered through her age-rheumed eyes to make out the dark shape which was approaching through the ruin. She stood quite still, trying to tune her ancient senses, trying to see the newcomer as he moved from shadow to brightness and back again.

A few feet away from her the dark shape stopped, its eyes stabbing into her. 'This ain't a safe place any more, love,' it began. 'You shouldn't ought to be in here. Didn't you see the sign?'

A constable, bless his little pointed helmet. And worried about her.

'I just came in for a last look round, you see,' Marge told him, smiling like everyone's granny. 'Just a last look round, that's all. Walking me dog and I thought I'd have a last look round.'

The policeman nodded and cast his eyes up towards the ruined roof. ''Spect this was a good church once,' he offered. 'They'll pull it down soon.' Then: 'You live round here, love?'

They'll pull it down? *They* will?

'Just down Inkerman Street.'

'Do you, eh? Thought I recognized you. Mrs Blunson, ain't it? You remember me. PC Forrest. When you found Mrs Tomkins . . .'

Marge shuddered. She picked up her shopping bag and gestured towards the altar. 'There's vandals been in here already,' she said.

'Vandals?'

She shrugged. ''Spect so. Can't see as anyone normal'd want to do a thing like that. All that mess and foulness. Nothing sacred these days, is there?'

PC Forrest looked at the mound of faeces and screwed up his face. It hurt his sensibilities, seeing that pile of stinking ordure settling itself into the holy table. He took out his notebook and jotted something down, checking his watch as he did so. Not his place to move it off, no matter how nasty it was, and he certainly wasn't going to volunteer.

After all, it was just a ruined church. Nothing more.

He shook his head. 'Nah,' he sighed. 'Nothing sacred.' Then: 'Had your look, Mrs B? Come on, then. Let's get you out of here in one piece. Then I'll walk you home. It's just another ruin now.'

She smiled and began to shuffle out ahead of him. 'As you say, young man, just a ruin. Even our god has given up on it.'

But not the other god, PC Forrest. Not the god we'll never know or understand. He's not given up.

In fact he's only just beginning.

Marge stopped to untie Mary when they reached the litch-gate. As she did so she looked up at the policeman beside her, frowning slightly. 'Don't I know you?' she asked. ''Part from the other day, that is?'

'Be a few years back if you did,' he answered.

Her face brightened with recognition. ''At's right,' she smiled. ''Ain't you Tom Forrest's kid? That's it. You're little Billy Forrest, used to live down Alma Terrace. Knew you was familiar, see?'

PC Forrest nodded. 'That's it, Mrs B. You got it.'

'You were a right little sod. Broke one of me winders once. I had to get yer old man to come round an' fix it. Still,' she sighed, 'that were the better part of thirty year ago. Say, didn't yer old man want you to get a good job an' get out of Uptown? So you join the bobbies an' end up back here again. Bit of a joke, ain't it?'

'Depends which way you look at it,' he told her, smiling.


Resigned he might be, but Tom Greaves hadn't run out of ploys yet. His visit to Sally's flat, 'Wednesday afternoon, sometime just after lunch,' actually took place shortly after 4.30, just as Sally would have been finishing work anyway. So I'm being petty, he told himself. Yet there's something about this pairing that worries me. I don't know exactly what, but the feeling's there none the less, and I can't ignore it.

He found the address in Estbury Green easily enough. The flat was on the ground floor of a converted Victorian semi and was, as Sally had insisted, quite a substantial residence in its own right. Altogether there were four flats in the house, one on each of the three floors above ground and the fourth in the basement. This last was quite small, having been converted from the original cellars, but Sally's, and the two on the floors above, had the traditional high-ceilinged, spacious rooms which the exterior would lead a visitor to expect. In addition the garden was quite large, stretching back a good thirty yards to the backs of the narrow terrace on the other side of the block.

Despite his late arrival she greeted him with a smile and no sign of anger or impatience. He entered brusquely, determined to simply check the preparations for Leader's well-being and go, but ended up sitting down with a cup of coffee despite himself. Eventually, when he got up to go, he was forced to admit to himself that whatever was worrying him was unlikely to surface as a result of his visit.

She's even right about the park, he thought. Estbury Green itself was just across the road, with a pedestrian crossing less than fifty yards from the front door. Leader wouldn't be confined either in the flat or out of it.

Everything seemed perfect.

'So I can pick Leader up on Friday afternoon?' she cooed.

Tom nodded reluctantly. 'I'll have him ready about two. Come for him then.'

He wasn't prepared for her throwing her arms around him and kissing his beard. As she did so the last traces of misgivings melted away. There was no reason to doubt the suitability of Sally French and Leader any longer. The two most important considerations were patently fulfilled. Dog and woman liked one another. Dog and woman would be living in an environment suitable for both.

Tom left the flat smiling, waving goodbye to Sally, who watched him go from the main entrance. Leader's time of suffering was now well and truly behind him. Sally's, however, was now about to begin.


Sally skipped her usual lunch at Trattoria Napolitana. She was too nervous for anything more than a cheese roll, bought at the Scotch Bakeries and eaten in small bites whilst she watched her watch in St Katherine's Gardens. Schoolkids, released for lunch, kicked footballs about, despite it being the cricket season. Here and there a courting couple, out of the office for half an hour or so, lay down and did ambiguous things in the dry summer grass.

She checked her watch again. Time moved so slowly when

you were waiting. The minute hand had crawled through a whole three segments of the dial since she'd looked last.

Fourteen minutes to two.

Salvation was less than five minutes' walk from here. No point getting up before five to. Tom Greaves might be convinced, but she wasn't about to do anything to jeopardize his conviction. She wanted Leader with a fervour that was at least equal to a lover's, and that meant she turned up at Salvation absolutely on the dot of two.

The thought of lovers reminded her of Jake Lewis. He hadn't bothered to contact her since she'd brushed him off on the day of the mugging. Chances were he was having it off on the quiet with that creep Bentham's wife. Christ only knew they'd been ogling one another hard enough when he'd taken her to the cricket club. Well, if he wanted that kind of trash, she was well rid of him.

Sally thought back to a few films she'd seen. Heroines met all manner of heroes when they were walking their dogs. So Estbury Green wasn't exactly Central Park. So what? The same chance turned up, no matter where you lived. And Leader was distinctive enough to generate all manner of chances.

C'mon, Sal. Citizen Quartz time again. Eight minutes to.

Another three minutes. Then she could get what Jake called her pretty, tight little bum off this hard wooden seat and go and collect Leader from Salvation. New dog, new life, she told herself, thinking again of that handsome, white-coated animal with the bright, pained eyes and the facial expression she could only describe as a smile. So man had far more facial muscles than any other species. So what?

One minute.

Sally French started counting. Fifty-eight, fifty-seven, fifty six . . .

Planning. Organization. Accuracy. Everything a legal secretary ought to be. She thought back to that rhyme she'd memorized when she'd been working in press relations:

> I have six honest serving men.
> They taught me all I knew.
> Their names are What and How and When
> And Why and Where and Who.

Get it right. Twenty-one, twenty, nineteen, eighteen, seventeen . . .

Stand up. Smooth your sweater. There isn't a man born who doesn't appreciate the outline of a good pair of breasts. Use 'em.

Smooth your skirt. Don't worry about looking too perfect. There's the walk between here and there to wrinkle you up naturally. Look right. Be right. This is important to you.

She started out of St Katherine's Gardens, smiling archly at a passing male stranger who caught her eye. Younger than Jake. Good looking. Then she sighed. Chances were she was in the wrong place at the wrong time. She didn't like Uptown, so she was unlikely to be there to see him again. Besides, she liked the older men she'd met better than the younger ones. They had two distinct advantages. One, they knew more and had taught her quite a bit. Two, they seemed to appreciate what she was prepared to do for them much more than men her own age. They took her for granted.

So, Jake had taken her for granted in his way. Bugger Jake. If he couldn't be bothered to make contact she didn't want to know. And she bloody well wasn't going to. So there!

She reached St Katherine's Square and checked her watch again. Two minutes to. Sally was timing it well. She wasn't to know that Granpa Hangel wouldn't have approved of her battery-powered timepiece. Nor did it matter. All that mattered now, or for the foreseeable future, was Leader.

The high house towered over her. So did the sign outside it. She started up the path and rang the bell.

Somewhere within earshot, albeit across Monkhampton town centre, a clock struck a faithful and quartz-electronic accurate two.

Granpa Hangel opened the door to her. She'd never seen

him before and his dark, sunken, haunted eyes worried her initially.

'I . . . I'm Sally French,' she muttered, her voice suddenly so low that she doubted if this obviously elderly man could hear it.

'You are expected, Miss French,' Pieter Hangel replied. 'Come through. Come through.'

She followed him through the ground floor of the house, familiar to her as Salvation's office, and out towards the pens at the back. Her heart leaped as she saw Tom Greaves standing there. Beside him, out of his pen, Leader was sitting obediently.

Until he saw Sally again.

Leader barked once, then stood up and bounded towards her. For the first time Sally felt the power of the animal as he reached her and, springing up, set his forepaws on her shoulders to lick her face. She staggered briefly back beneath his weight, then checked herself and stood firm. Impressions still counted, and this could well be another of Tom Greaves' tests for pet and owner. She threw her arms around him, not appearing to mind the dog-breath on her cheek, scruffling her fingers in his fur.

'Leader,' she said. Then, again, louder: 'Leader!'

Greaves watched in silence. So did Granpa Hangel.

'Down, boy,' Sally ordered. Leader lay down at her feet, obediently.

Tom Greaves nodded. Granpa Hangel's mouth moved, almost silently.

'Remember,' he whispered.

Leader remembered.

Sally smiled, reaching down and patting her new pet. 'Good Leader,' she said. 'Good dog.'

Leader panted appreciatively.

'He's all yours, Miss French,' Tom Greaves said, smiling. 'I hope you've brought your lead with you.'

'How could I forget it?' Sally smiled disarmingly back. Leader barked. Happily.

It was, as a human might have said, all coming together.

Ben Wilson, had he been asked, would have described Harry Chester to polite company as a long streak of nothing spectacular. He was aware that the description wasn't exactly accurate, but it served. Chester was well over six feet tall, dark haired and lantern-jawed. He looked more like an undertaker than a copper, had an unruly sense of humour at times, and despite being married with two young kids and a bloody gorgeous wife had an eye for the ladies. Oddly enough the ladies seemed to have an eye for Harry Chester as well.

Wilson had first noticed him at Waventree. On reflection he decided that wasn't exactly the truth either. Chester had been pointed out to him as being a mate of that mad bugger Ferrow, who'd later been posted to Corby and then promptly vanished off the face of the universe. But Chester had good qualities, and when Ben Wilson had been picking his team for Monkhampton Harry Chester had been a willing choice, especially with a promotion to sweeten the move.

They sat together at a corner table in the dated, plastic and formica interior of the Battle of Inkerman, drinking their pints of Harrington's. Chester's long frame had folded untidily behind the fixed table, and the smoke from his unthinking and interminable cigarettes was getting up his superior's nose. Their conversation, to begin with, was desultory, for Chester at least was aware that they were still on duty, even if they were perched in this god-forsaken pub at the time. After a few brief opening remarks, confined on the whole to generalities, Chester took the bull by the horns.

'Look guv,' he began, 'supposing you tell me why I'm here. Come to that, supposing you tell me why *we're* here.'

Ben Wilson grinned. 'We two police officers are sitting here as a public relations exercise,' he replied loudly.

The short, scruffy barman peered across at them from behind the bar counter, his eyes alert and unfriendly. It was getting on for nine and the Battle of Inkerman had filled up more than on the previous occasion Wilson had been in there with Jake Lewis.

Harry Chester snorted into his beer and set the glass down quickly, wiping his nose as he did so. *'Public relations?'* he stage-whispered.

'That's it, Detective Sergeant,' came the equally loud reply.

'It's not my place, guv, but if you asked me I'd say you were outta your fuckin' tree.'

Ben Wilson frowned for a moment, then winked. 'Play it my way, Harry,' he answered. 'Okay?'

Chester shrugged. 'You're the guv'nor. So, do I shout as well?'

Wilson extended his left hand, palm down, and wagged his fingers. 'Not shout, exactly, more don't worry about being over-heard.'

'That's fine by me, guv'nor,' came the noisy reply.

Conversation in the bar about them had suddenly become muted. Both men sensed the change and moderated their voices accordingly: DCI Wilson said: 'It's interesting what we've been finding out since the fire here in Uptown.'

Chester blinked. 'Sure is,' he affirmed. 'Bloody fasci-nating.'

'Yeah. Especially the way it's starting to tie together.'

'You mean the way the church burns down, then someone dumps a pile of shit on the altar?'

'That's exactly what I mean. It's all starting to fit the pat-tern.'

Harry Chester got as far as 'What . . .' before his shin was kicked under the table. 'What . . . about another pint, guv?' he asked, hiding his grimace behind finishing his glass.

Wilson drank up fast. 'Good idea,' he said. 'After all, we've got all night if we need it.'

All night? In here? Bloody hell!

He picked up his chief's glass and made his way to the bar, the opposition seeming to melt away before him and leave easy access to the frowning landlord. ''Nother coupla pints,' he grinned. Then, mischievously: 'Is it always this quiet in here?'

97

The conversations around him resumed. It was their turn to be a little too loud.

He paid for the pints and carried them back through the melting drinkers to where Wilson was sitting. He took a swig from his own glass before sitting down again.

'Cheers, Harry,' the guv'nor volunteered.

'Yeah. Down the little pink hosepipe, all the way. You were saying about the pattern, guv.'

'Well, I put some clever little bastards at Cambridge on to the available facts we've gathered. I told 'em everything, no matter how trivial it sounded to me.'

Chester grinned. Okay, Wilson, let's play the game back at you. 'And what did they come up with?'

'An anti-religion, Harry.'

The DS took another pull from his glass to mask his features. What the hell kind of bullshit was the guv'nor coming up with now? 'Anti-religion? You mean like Satanism?'

Wilson shook his head and smiled condescendingly. 'No, not Satanism. That's simply anti–Christian, they tell me. This is something much more subtle.'

Chester couldn't hide his scowl this time. Jesus H. Christ, he thought. These blokes must think we're a couple of loonies. Then he looked around him.

Nobody in the entire bar was laughing.

He decided to push things a stage further. 'Then what is it like?' he asked. This was all starting to sound like one of Bob Ferrow's fantasies, and Harry Chester had no intention of doing a wobbly into nowhere. Not if he could help it.

'I can't answer that, yet,' Wilson responded. 'But I will be able to, quite soon. Something tells me though that quite a few of the people here in Uptown know the answer already. Ever ask yourself why that church hadn't been used for so long, Harry?'

He hadn't, but this wasn't the time to say. Instead he answered: 'Yeah. That struck me as odd, guv. Not like the clergy to leave fertile soil unploughed.' He grinned at his use of the metaphor. He normally employed it in quite a different context.

'Oh, they tried, hard enough. I tracked down the last incumbent yesterday and asked him why the diocese had given up on this area. Know what he told me, old Father Granville?'

'Can't say's I do. I'd like to hear it, though. There's a few others might as well.'

He looked around him. Conversation resumed again, but muted, as if straining ears were afraid of missing something.

'The old boy said they just stopped coming, even the regulars. He dug a few out and asked them why. Never did get a straight answer. Just sort of formed an impression that there was something else in their lives, something that hadn't been there before.

'Something replacing their religion.'

'He tried to find out what it was, Harry, but they wouldn't tell him. He half-wondered if they knew what it was themselves. They had a sort of name for it, though. They called it the *other*.'

A door opened. Somebody came in, somebody went out. The door closed.

'Like another god?' Harry asked, interested despite the charade he felt he was playing.

'Like no god Father Granville had ever heard of. Finished your drink, Harry?'

'Just about, guv. Good pint, that. Think I might make this place my local.'

Wilson smiled wryly. They stood up and began moving towards the door. Nobody was standing even slightly in their way. In the doorway Wilson turned and looked back, aware of the watching eyes even before he saw them.

'Night all,' he grinned.

The door swung shut behind them. At the top of the steps Wilson paused, a finger to his lips, but their own silence wasn't necessary. The Battle of Inkerman had exploded back into raucous life. A figure, dark against the light from inside, tore open the door, saw them standing there and darted rapidly back inside.

They walked up towards the car which they'd left in St

99

Katherine's Square. The night had been still and warm, with only the muted rumble of traffic on the dual carriageway in the distance. Now, as Wilson and Chester progressed up Inkerman Street in the evidential northerly direction, skirting the block which housed the sealed-off Emporium Arcade, they became slowly aware of a totally different sound. Harry Chester heard it first and stopped in his tracks to prevent his footfalls on the uneven paving slabs masking it from his ears. Two paces ahead Ben Wilson also stopped, turning back towards his sergeant.

'You hear it, guv?' Harry asked.

Wilson nodded. 'I hear it.'

In the darkened neighbourhood, quite close, a dog was howling.

Then another. And a third.


Marge Blunson had been sitting knitting, the TV, sound down, flickering in the background. She looked up as Mary left her basket and began whining and scratching at the door.

'You don't go out at this time, my little love,' she told the mongrel. 'You've done your doings for tonight. Nearly time for bed, now, you see.'

Mary's scratching increased. She barked once, then again, then moved back away from the door, ears pricked.

Marge eyed the bitch curiously. 'Something the matter, Mary?' she inquired.

Mary went to point, body forward, short left foreleg slightly bent and raised. Then all four feet were on the threadbare carpet again and her body was straining back against them, as if threatening a crouching posture. The ears began to flatten back against the skull. The eyes narrowed. Her mouth opened, as if to bark again, but Mary remained silent.

Her mistress set the knitting aside and turned off the television, as if the silent picture was preventing her from hearing something. She stood up, her features serious. Then she began to smile.

Mary's attitude remained strained and increasingly aggressive. The lips drew back around the bared teeth, her long, terrier muzzle frightening and fearsome in its display. She growled deeply, as if from the very bowels of her being.

Marge moved over to the door, showing no fear for her stockinged ankles, one of them clad in the extra layer of a crepe support bandage, 'It's all right, little love,' she told Mary, her voice more understanding than soothing, 'Make sure you come back to me, though. No sodding off, now.'

The mongrel didn't seem to hear. Foam was flecking its lips now, and saliva hung like cobwebs between her exposed teeth. The growling strengthened and began to rise in pitch.

The old lady opened the door and Mary bounded out into the hall, towards the front door. Marge followed her and opened it. Mary bounded out into the night.

An unearthly screaming mingled with the howls. Harry Chester looked at his superior.

'Sounds like a she-cat with the hots,' he grunted.

'Sounds like half a dozen she-cats with the hots,' Wilson came back. 'This is a bit bloody odd, strikes me. Cats and dogs together, Harry?'

'Only when it's raining,' Chester quipped.

Ben Wilson shook his head. 'Forget the humour,' he ordered. 'Let's get to the car and get back to the nick.'

Chester shrugged and began walking again. 'Was all that gospel back there?' he asked.

'In the pub? Yeah, I suppose it was. I did talk to Granville and he did tell me about something the people here call the *other*. He didn't know what it was, though.'

'And the Cambridge bit, guv?'

'Yeah, that too. That was Granville's idea. He'd been trying to make head or tail of this place, but he gave up eventually. By that time he'd put quite a file together, though, so he referred it to some bloke the bishop's secretary knew. Some egghead called Harker. I spoke to him earlier today.'

'So what'd he say?'

Wilson shrugged. 'Not a great deal. But he's interested. I promised him a squint at that stuff you and Kate got from the newspaper files. He might be some use.'

'You mean there could be something in that god shit you were giving the natives?'

'You saw their faces, Harry. You tell me. Oh, some of them thought we were a coupla' nutters, but there were others hanging on every word. That's why we went there tonight. I wanted to check out whether old Granville was off his head or not.'

'And?'

'From the reaction we got I'd say he's as sane as you or I. And that's not saying much. I've always believed that normal people don't become coppers anyway.'

They were nearly at the corner of Inkerman Street and St Katherine's Square. Without either of them noticing, their voices had risen in volume throughout their conversation, as had the growing cacophony of animal sounds about them.


Tom Greaves made his last round of the pens and enclosures earlier than normal that evening. He hadn't so much chosen to do so as had the choice thrust upon him by the behaviour of his charges.

In all the years he'd been running Salvation he'd never heard a racket like it. Without exception every animal in the place was giving some kind of voice and struggling to get out. Dogs howled, cats screamed, even the family of gerbils he'd taken in were emitting their almost sub-sonic squeaks and leaping for the roof of their cage.

It was unearthly.

For a man who had dedicated his life to animals the word didn't come easily. Animals were creatures of earth. Even the squawking cockateel had to touch base from time to time. He stood in front of its cage and watched it beating its foot-long wings, yellow crest up and beak open in the general cacophony.

Usually he'd put his finger to the bars, nail upwards, and play 'chicken' with it, daring its wicked mouth to take the tip off. Tonight, though, Tom decided to leave well alone.

He searched Salvation for a reason for their behaviour, but didn't find one. If it existed at all, he decided, it was cerebral, not physical.

What the hell am I thinking? he asked himself. Cerebral? Forget it. Non-tangible is closer. Let's not carry anthropomorphism too far. They're only animals, after all.


Ben Wilson and Harry Chester reached the T-junction of Inkerman Street and St Katherine's Square and began to walk towards the DCI's parked car. Only when they were some ten paces from the vehicle did they notice the eyes which were watching from the edges of the square.

Harry's mouth fell open. His guv'nor grabbed his sleeve. 'Keep walking,' he hissed.

The eyes moved closer, ringing them around.

'What the fuck . . .' Chester left the oath unfinished as his mind focused upon the grim unreality of their situation. Every way he looked, every step he took, it seemed that the entire four-footed population of Uptown was drawing closer, furred and toothed and voicing its displeasure.

'Do you see . . .'

'I see it, Harry. Let's just get to the car and fuck off out of here.'

Dogs and cats advanced together through the evening, eyes blazing, teeth bared. The howling had given way to low growls as the quarry had been sighted. Now even they were ceasing as the ring of fangs and claws closed around the policemen.

Drawing closer. Ever closer.

Wilson shuddered. *If* they attacked, and they bloody looked as if they were at least thinking about it, there'd be no escape if they hadn't reached the car. And what a death it would be, snapped at and worried by a hundred small, foam-flecked mouths, torn and shredded by claws that, at first, could only sink deep enough to cause pain or discomfort, not real damage. Jesus! Even crucifixion had to be more merciful than that!

A thousand tiny bites and slashes would redden their flesh. They'd bleed out their strength, there on the cobbles, watching it puddle about them in their fear of the inevitable, engulfing end.

It would take time, and pain, and terror. It would last for the rest of their lives. It would literally worry them into their graves, as a fox is torn and bloodied and worried by the hounds that close upon it. It would destroy them, agonizingly, for ever.

If they didn't reach the car. If the animals attacked. And from the look of them they were going to.

Wilson felt in his pocket for the keys. Get one door unlocked and they could both pile in. Problem was getting that door unlocked. Oh shit.

His fingers closed on the keys and felt through them for the one which would unlock the door. The creatures, slinking low but moving with remarkable speed, were gaining on Chester and himself second by second.

The last few feet wouldn't matter. They'd be a series of leaps and springs. Instinctively they'd forget about the car and try to ward off the attack. That's what'd kill them. The instinct to survive.

Something told Ben Wilson that's what the animals were counting on.

If ever I've shat on anybody it's coming home to roost, Harry Chester thought. If I get out of this I'll be the nicest guy in the world.

Six paces. Five . . .

Another couple and we can beat the rush, Wilson decided. One more step and we're safe.

Four . . .

The eyes grew brighter and larger. And terrifyingly and suddenly closer. Claws scraped on the cobblestones. Wilson slowly withdrew the car keys from his pocket. The old Tarzan movies said to do it slowly and easy. No sudden moves.

He gripped them hard. His hands were sweating badly and his mouth had dried.

Three . . .

The creatures were almost at their heels, crowding closer around the two men and their car. Chester flashed a look at his guv'nor. They're holding off, it said. We're going to get out of here in one piece. Ben Wilson said nothing. He simply reached the car and forced his trembling fingers to fit the key into the lock.

Why doesn't somebody see? he asked himself. Why the fuck doesn't someone notice what's happening? They must have heard that hellish racket earlier. Half of Monkhampton must have heard it.

The door opened. Central locking released and Harry Chester reached for the handle on his side. The animals tensed.

And sprang.

Wilson and Chester leaped inside. Chester booting a spaniel in the teeth as it snapped at his leg. A cat launched itself at Wilson who slammed his door shut on its head, crushing it to pulp and trapping the dangling, bleeding body outside the car. Animals scrambled over the boot and hood, finding purchase on the painted metal wherever they could. They flung themselves against the glass of the windows leaving smears of saliva staining them. They slashed and chewed at the tyres. Chester hauled his leg inside and pulled his door on to the skull of a young alsatian. As he opened it slightly to thump the half-blinded dog's head out of the way a massive black tom, eyes ablaze, leaped through the gap at Wilson's head.

The key was in the ignition. The wipers were on, batting the lighter beasts away from the windshield. Mary grabbed a blade in her terrier teeth and rode with it, trying to fight it to a standstill. As it snapped away the effort hurled her clear of the car. She landed in a mêlée of crowding cats, the wiper-blade still projecting from her clenched muzzle.

Its claws dug into his scalp as the black tom-cat, screaming angrily, tried to crawl around Wilson's head to his face. His features screwed up with pain he yelled: 'Get the fucker off,

Harry!' as the motor turned over and he slammed the car into gear. Chester, his knuckles bleeding from punching the alsatian in the mouth, reached for a heavy torch under the dash and swung it against the cat's ribs. They crunched inwards with the impact and it tore free, wailing in agony, taking raked clawfuls of Wilson's hair with it. Streaking both his scalp and its own black fur with a dull, glistening red, it tumbled into the back of the car and lay still, staining the upholstery in its dying.

They lurched forward, the remaining wiper clearing the smears from Wilson's side of the screen, the battle-scarred tyres crunching as they lurched over their attackers. Blood sprayed up and obliterated Chester's door-mirror. Bestial shrieks and howls of pain and outrage surrounded them, briefly drowning the roar of the accelerator. Then, as they began to gather speed and slip free of the chaos around them, circling the Square to head back down Inkerman Street, a single howling ululation echoed out of the night. Clear of the pack, hurt but secure within the vehicle's body-shell, Wilson involuntarily slowed to listen.

A single note echoed through the sudden stillness of the evening. Even their attackers seemed to ignore their own pain and anger as it rose sharply, then began to break into a series of harmonics. Wiping the blood from his scalp away from his eyes, Wilson struggled to keep a mental count.

. . . Terrathree . . . Kartefour . . . Pantafive . . .

Slowly, very slowly, the unearthly sound began to die away, still breaking in harmonics.

. . . Oktoeight . . . Novenine . . .

Gone.

Wilson gunned the motor. 'C'mon, Harry,' he grunted. 'Casualty for patching up and rabies shots. Thank Christ it's not that porridge in the gut stuff anymore. While we're getting there call this in, will you. I want every loose animal in Uptown rounded up and impounded. Whilst that's going on it's house to house. Every pet owner gets asked where little fuckin' Fido was tonight. Dogs, cats, rabbits, even the bloody budgie. The works. Liaison with the RSPCA if they have to, but not one single syllable to the press. We're not going to look more like a pair of pricks then we already are. Jesus!'

He lurched the car into Inkerman Street, half-blinded by the rivulets still trickling from his matted hairline into his eyes. Harry Chester let out a low whistle and looked briefly back through the stained rear window at the animal carnage the vehicle had left behind in the square. Then, flexing his injured knuckles, he reached for the radio handset. 'Question, guv?' he ventured, white-faced and still shaking slightly.

'Yeah?'

'What the fuck was that noise back there? Where'd it come from?'

'That's two, you bugger,' Wilson grinned. 'Okay, let's start with the second one first. It seemed loudest to me as we drove past the old church, so chances are that's the source. As to what it was, your guess is as good as mine. What d'you reckon, Harry?'

'Christ knows. If it wasn't bloody impossible I'd have said it was a wolf.'

Ben Wilson nodded grimly and wiped at his eyes again. 'If it wasn't bloody impossible that'd be my guess as well. Now make that fucking call, will you, sergeant?'


Marge was reluctant to open the door again, not now Mary was back inside. The knocking persisted, though, and she reasoned that whoever it was could probably see a chink of light through the gap in the heavy curtains and know that there was someone inside.

She'd grown up in an age when you saved everything. Brown paper. String. Old cocoa tins. And especially electricity. Her reasoning didn't run to leaving a light on when you went out to convince would-be intruders the house was occupied. That was sinful then, and now, on a pension, downright impossible.

'You stay here, little love,' she told Mary, closing the front room door behind her as she went out into the unlighted hall. Her son had insisted she fit a chain and spy-hole to the front door before he was killed in that accident, and Marge looked through the spy-hole first.

Blue uniform, from what the street-lights in the late dusk showed her. Policeman. Again. There seemed to be policemen everywhere these days, none of them like the local bobby she'd known as a girl. All so young and so suspicious of everything.

She unlatched the front door but kept the chain on, peering through the narrow opening.

'Sorry to trouble you, love,' (they *all* called you love these days) he began. 'Do you have a pet animal of any kind?'

She smiled through the crack. 'Why yes, young man. I've a little dog I got from that nice Mr Greaves at Salvation. Why are you asking?'

She ought to have known better, she told herself. They never answered a straight question these days. They just came back at you with another. This one was no different from all the others.

'Has it been out at all tonight?'

'Only to do what it had to, you know, spend a penny. Why?' she persisted.

'Were you with it?'

'I never go out without my Mary, constable, and she never goes anywhere without me. We've been together all night. Never out of my sight, you see?'

# HARKER

Andreas Harker presented himself to the desk sergeant shortly after nine a.m. The policeman eyed him with obvious distrust and perhaps a tinge of amusement. Certainly his appearance was hardly standard for Monkhampton, though it would have aroused little comment in the broader confines of a university city.

The professor wore his brown hair, now more grey than brown, parted in the middle and long at the sides, giving his strong-featured face the appearance of a lion's head with mane. His eyes were deep-set and nearly black, giving an impression of tropic heat which was belied by his pinkish skin. Despite the summer warmth he wore a heavy tweed suit with gold watch-chain splashing the matching waistcoat. His fingers were heavily ringed and he carried a gold-headed cane like something out of *Pride and Prejudice* or Dickens. In place of a tie he displayed a carefully-tied cravat with a cameo stick-pin at the centre.

'And who might you want to see?' the sergeant asked, not entirely believing the vision before him.

'I am expected by Chief Detective Inspector Wilson,' Harker replied. 'Kindly inform him of my arrival.'

His voice was soft and, on the surface, polite, though there was an undertone of authority which put the sergeant's back up.

'Detective Chief Inspector Wilson is a very busy man, *sir*. Is there anything I can do for you?'

Harker flicked his gaze briefly heavenward, then turned its full, dark power on the recalcitrant copper. 'You misheard me, sergeant,' he began firmly and with no attempt to hide the authoritarian note this time. 'I said I was expected. My name is Harker. Professor Harker. I have driven over from

Cambridge at Wilson's request to be of service to the police. Not to be messed about like a naughty schoolboy in front of a bullying prefect.'

The sergeant reeled visibly. This man undoubtedly had an unusually strong character, despite his garb. The policeman opened his mouth for a riposte, then thought better of it and rang through to Ben Wilson's office. 'There's a *Mr* Harker to see you, sir,' he grinned, watching the professor fume out of the corner of his eye.

'Ye gods and little fishes,' Harker groaned. 'I thought the police were at least supposed to convey the impression of being efficient.'

'Have him shown through, sergeant,' Ben Wilson instructed. 'And it's Professor Harker, not Mister.'

The sergeant replaced the phone and detailed a constable to look after the desk for him. Then he came through and led Harker into the bowels of the police station, eventually pausing before and knocking on a door panelled with frosted glass. Without awaiting a response from inside he opened it and peered round.

'Professor Harker,' he stated flatly.

The small office comprised a desk with swivel chair behind it, two institutional easy chairs in front, windows, also frosted, in the wall opposite the door and a bank of filing cabinets behind the desk. It was sparse, almost spartan, and the only impediments to an impression of ruthless efficiency were the ring-binders stacked on the floor beside the desk and the mountain of folders, most of them open, which cluttered its surface.

If Harker's appearance came as a shock to Ben Wilson, then the reverse was equally true. The professor hadn't quite expected Wilson to have fair hair, and the beard was positively out of keeping. In his experience a neat moustache was about all that any copper managed to get away with in terms of facial adornment. Nor, he had to admit, had he expected Wilson to be quite so young, comparatively speaking, in view of his rank.

Harry Chester had folded his length inelegantly into one of the two chairs facing the desk. Both he and Wilson rose as Andreas Harker politely and ironically thanked the desk sergeant and stepped into the office.

The professor shook hands with Ben Wilson, noticing the stitches projecting from the DCI's blond hair as he rose. Harry Chester extended his hand as he was introduced, then waved it with an apologetic grin, showing off his bandaged knuckles to best advantage.

Formalities over, Harker settled into the unoccupied chair, crossing his legs and steepling his fingers. 'You gentlemen appear to have suffered a small misfortune,' he observed.

Wilson scowled, more out of concentration than anything else, as he attempted to form an impression of their visitor that went beyond his exterior. Chester's eyes flashed to his guv'nor and back to Harker as he said: 'That's one way of putting it. It rained cats and dogs last night. On us.'

'I take it you are speaking literally, not figuratively, Mr Chester?' the professor enquired.

Harry's grin faded. 'Too bloody true,' he answered. Then, looking across the desk: 'Shall you tell him or do I, guv?'

'I think the first thing is to find out if Professor Harker intends to help us, Harry. He probably doesn't love us too much right now. Not the way my call hauled him out of bed last night and asked him to drop everything and get over here first thing this morning. He's probably wondering what the hell it's all about. Right, Professor?'

Harker shrugged. 'Most of the policemen I've known have been, or claimed to be, overworked, Mr Wilson. Thus I deem your reasons to be other than merely causing me some minor inconvenience. In your own good time you'll tell me.'

Wilson thought back over this. It seemed to be politely saying hurry up and take your time. Let's hope Harker isn't always this obscure, he thought.

'Coffee, Professor?' Harry Chester asked.

'I assume it's from a machine?'

'Yeah. 'Fraid so.'

'Then I'd rather have chocolate, if that's possible. I admit it's a trifle early by today's standards, but cocoa, or even mocha, was a favoured morning beverage amongst the gentry in the eighteenth century, albeit their morning usually began around two in the afternoon.'

Chester flashed Wilson a *Christ! We've got a fruit-cake here* glance, then left the office to feed the machine in the corridor outside. Wilson grinned.

'My sergeant's finding all this a little hard to cope with,' he began. 'Which isn't to say I'm not either. You had all the relevant information up to last night, Professor. Disused church burns down isn't much, on the surface. But that church shouldn't have been disused. It's in the sort of area that still houses regular church-goers. And it shouldn't have burned down. I've a copy of all the relevant reports here. They all suggest arson. And why, with the church burned down and the site about to be sold to a development consortium, would anybody bother to desecrate the altar with a pile of dog-shit? Oh, did I tell you it was dog-shit? Not our job to clean it up, of course, but it struck me it could be useful to have a sample analysed. And that's what it was, all right. Traces of grass and soil mixed in with it. But it gets weirder, Professor.'

Harker nodded. 'I wouldn't doubt that for a moment,' he replied. 'Before you continue, though, I'd like to know what was used to start the fire, if I might?'

Wilson opened a folder and flipped through the tag-bound pages. 'Paraffin, candle, newspaper,' he listed aloud. 'Some sort of plastic container and dried vegetable matter . . .'

'Which was?'

'Hm?'

'The vegetable matter. I take it traces were analysed? What was it found to be?'

Wilson flipped more pages. 'Here. Twigs of wood. Mountain ash, if that means anything to you.'

Professor Harker's expression didn't change, but his voice lowered slightly as he replied: 'It means a great deal to me, Mr Wilson. The ash tree in general has a wealth of superstitions associated with it all over Europe and the northern hemisphere. The world-ash of Norse mythology, Yggdrasil, held the whole of creation, for instance. The mountain ash, however, *sorbus aucuparia*, is supposed to be particularly useful in the aversion of evil. It's also known as the rowan, quickbeam and witch-wood, to give you three of its many other names. A cross of rowan tied with red thread is sovereign against witchcraft. I myself have seen one, thrown over the railings to land amongst the group of standing stones known as the Whispering Knights, which forms part of the Rollrights in North Oxfordshire. And before you think such practices have died out by now, that was only about ten years ago.'

The thought crossed Wilson's mind that Harry Chester had been right. Harker *was* a fruit-cake. Still, he was there, and something just might come out of all this, so keep listening.

'So they burned the church down, using this . . . rowan . . . to avert evil? They thought the church was evil, is that it?'

'Probably. That would also explain why they didn't worship there. Hence my suggestion of an anti-religion earlier.'

'So the church was haunted, or bewitched?'

'Not in the way one normally thinks of such things, Mr Wilson. The answer is yes. But it was haunted and bewitched by the Christian religion, not by any traditional form of ghoul or ghost or what-have-you. The evil spirit was Christ himself.'

'So it *is* satanism . . .'

Harker shook his head. 'If that were the case they wouldn't have used rowan, which the Devil is traditionally allergic to. As I've explained before, on the telephone, anti-religion and satanism are quite different. But I interrupted you. You had more to tell me, I believe. About the dog-dirt?'

'Now that's one of the oddest things about this,' Wilson replied. 'It came from more than one animal.'

'All dogs? No cats?'

Wilson shrugged. 'We only took a small sample, just to determine whether it was human or not. I can't really answer that.'

115

Harry Chester returned with a plastic tray and three steaming cups. 'Here's your chocolate, Professor,' he said, handing one to Harker. 'Your coffee, guv, and one for me. Have I missed anything?'

'Bit early to say, Harry. We're still talking round it. I haven't told the professor about last night yet.'

'When it rained cats and dogs on you?' Harker sipped at his chocolate, his dark eyes peering piercingly through the steam.

'That's about the strength of it,' Wilson answered. 'We'd been having a drink at a pub in Uptown, trying your idea out on the natives. They surprised me, Professor. They seemed to take it seriously, as if we were on to something. Well, we started walking back to the car and this bloody awful howling and caterwauling started up. We'd left the car parked near the church, and as we approached it we were surrounded by a solid ring of cats and dogs closing in on us. We reached the car all right, but we had to fight them off. They attacked us. And the vehicle. The whole bloody lot of them. As we drove away there was a howl from the church and they pulled back. It sounded to me like a wolf. I know that's impossible, 'specially as I had the zoos checked to make sure, and the local authority registers for wild animals kept privately, but that's what the sound was like.'

'You've had injections against rabies, I take it?'

'Yeah,' Chester sighed. 'Casualty did that when they stitched the guv'nor's head back together and wrapped up me knuckles.'

'I had a house to house done after that, as well as rounding up every stray in the area. Nobody admitted having a pet out on its own and we only picked up five moggies and a couple of mongrels. Yet there had to have been about a hundred and fifty of the four-footed bastards after us. We even checked Salvation, the local animal shelter, but we didn't have any joy there, either. Tom Greaves said that his lot had been making a hell of a racket, but not one had got out.'

Harker thought for a moment. 'When you say dogs and cats together, were there terriers there with the other dogs?'

'Terriers, collies, even the odd guard-dog. The works.'

'Dog and cat in harmony isn't as uncommon as people generally believe. What is unusual is that the combination worked on such a scale, and that it worked from dog to dog as well. There are, as you must know, both aggressive and submissive breeds. The reason I inquired about terriers is that they can normally be counted upon to 'have a go' at almost any other type of dog. Now that *is* unusual. To my untutored brain it suggests some type of over-riding directive. Or common purpose, if you prefer.'

Harry Chester sniffed. 'Only common purpose I saw was them trying to turn us into Kattomeat.'

'You say they only actually attacked when you reached your car?'

Wilson nodded. 'They left it too late. They could have had us sooner.'

'Then dare I predicate their behaviour as a warning? Perhaps a retaliatory warning?'

Wilson and Chester looked at one another. 'Just what are you getting at, Professor?' Wilson inquired.

'Simply this. You make noises to the locals in the public house. They make noises back to you as you return to your vehicle. Except that it's the animal, not the human, locals, that return the . . . shall we say, favour?'

'We roust the locals and they set their livestock on us?' Harry Chester demanded incredulously. 'That's wild, Professor!'

'So is what happened to you last night, Sergeant Chester. But it's happened before. Animal attacks on humans, sometimes different kinds of animals acting together, have increased in recent years. Oh, they've been isolated incidents, and none of them involving as many creatures as you suggest, but they've happened none the less. I believe that you came too close to something last night, and were "warned off" in some way. I have postulated an anti-religion to you. Supposing I now say that this anti-religion is also non-human in origin?'

'I thought they all started with a god?' Wilson queried.

117

Andreas Harker permitted himself his first smile since entering the office. 'That depends upon your point of view, Mr Wilson. I would say that they usually begin with the human development of a myth or legend, from which a deity is eventually brought to birth. Such is not the case on this occasion. There is development of a myth, yes. But it has not been developed by humans. It has been developed by the animals themselves.'

'An animal religion? With respect, Professor, you outta your tree?'

'Not at all, Sergeant. There are precedents, at least ideologically, if you know where to look for them. And before you expostulate that the ideologies are human-originated I would add that they are mostly based on observation. Some animals appear to sense the presence of ghosts or unseen entities, suggesting they recognize life-forms invisible to our perceptions. Most primitive societies, past and present, though there are declining numbers in the present, draw no distinction between beasts and man. They share the same world and, in so far as anatomical differences permit, the same aspirations and abilities, albeit to differing ends. If man makes worship, there is no reason why animals shouldn't. The fact that we don't know anything about their deities is neither here nor there. By the doctrine of animism everything that exists has a spirit as well as a body. Oh, Christianity denies the idea of an animal soul, or at least its exponents do, but they also claim to turn bread into meat, and the meat of godhead at that. Now which of the two would you say is the more rational? No, don't try to answer that.

'Most primitive gods,' Harker continued, 'are both human and animal. The idea of totemism derives from man and his totem beast sharing a common ancestor who was both. Ever read any Tarzan books, Mr Wilson?'

'Years ago, when I was a lad.'

'Burroughs knew Africa very well, both the continent and its inhabitants, animal and human. He speaks in *Tarzan of the Apes* of travellers who had seen the earth drums that the great apes used during the Dum-Dum ritual. He says, and I quote, that this rite was the predecessor of "all the forms and ceremonials of modern church and state". Whilst he does not expostulate as to the deity invoked by the Dum-Dum he leaves little doubt that it was religious in origin. And before you tell me it was a fictitious invention, it wasn't. I've checked other sources against him.

'Moving forward, into Western society, we encounter *Das Tierdrama* in the works of the modern American satanist Anton LaVey. Whether the Illuminati origin he claims for the ritual or not is accurate doesn't matter. What does is that it admits of man's quadruped origins and their legacy. The participants hold dual animal and human identity, travelling back along the evolutionary scale to a time when they were neither or both. Perhaps the new anti-god that your Uptowners call the *other* is exactly that. Neither or both. Don't let your eyes glaze over, Sergeant Chester. This is what you brought me here for. I may not be making sense to the police mind, but I could very well be making truth.'

'Animals worshipping a god of their own?'

'That, despite its irrationality, is the obvious explanation, Mr Wilson.'

'Animals didn't burn the church down,' Harry Chester countered.

'Neither did a good Christian,' Harker snapped back. 'Do you have another explanation? Am I wasting your time and mine?'

'I wouldn't go that far,' Ben Wilson told him. 'You have to admit, though. It all sounds pretty far-fetched.'

'So was the Titanic encountering an iceberg where it did. But that didn't stop it happening. Did your men check the church when they were searching Uptown last night?'

The sudden switch caught Wilson unprepared. He was tired and his scalp was still smarting, both from the cat's claws and the glancing impact of the torch which Harry Chester had killed the animal with. To do him credit he only hesitated in thought for a moment. Then he said: 'They had a look inside. Didn't find any animals hiding there.'

'They were only looking for animals, I suspect. Not for anything else. Would you like to show me that church, Mr Wilson?'

Chester looked at his guv'nor. This was getting positively bloody looney. If there weren't any animals in the church what the fuck else could there be?

'Bearing in mind you've brought me here from Cambridge to help you, that is,' Harker added.

'You think there's something to find in the ruins?' Wilson asked.

'I do.'

'Would you like to tell me what it is?'

'When we get there. I'll tell you before you see it for yourself. I'm aware that you think me at the very least a little mad, Mr Wilson. Perhaps I am. I've spent most of my life interpreting data that most people would immediately dismiss as superstitious rubbish. This projects in what I say and even in the way I appear to you. It will benefit us both if I offer a token demonstration that will leave you convinced I am either hopelessly wrong or absolutely spot on. What do you say?'

Wilson shrugged. 'Why not?' he ventured.

Andreas Harker stood up. 'Then shall we be about it?' he enquired.

Harry Chester hauled his long body to its weary feet, grinning broadly. This nutter was digging a pit for himself. If he even hesitated on the edge Harry was going to be there to push him into it.

'I'll get the car round, guv,' he beamed. 'Next stop St Gargoyle's.'

Wilson nodded. Chester left the office, still grinning.

'Do you think I'm mad, Detective Chief Inspector?' Harker asked.

'I think you're unusual, Professor Harker,' came the response. 'And the unusual is always a little worrying to the police. We like things nice and orderly and predictable. That keeps a clear difference between the good guys and the bad guys. Would you mind if I had a look at your cane?'

'By all means. I left my sword-stick back in the rack at Cambridge, if that's what you're looking for. I may be . . . unusual . . . but I'm not mad enough to walk into a police station carrying a concealed offensive weapon.'

He tossed the stick across the desk, catching Wilson by surprise. Even so he caught it and threw it straight back, unexamined. To his amazement Andreas Harker had his hand extended, waiting for it, before he had begun the return throw. Plump running to fat he might be, Wilson thought. Slow he isn't.

'Wouldn't you like to search me for firearms?' came the question. 'Perhaps I carry a pistol loaded with silver bullets in case I encounter a werewolf.'

Ben Wilson relaxed and chuckled softly. He was beginning to like this oddball egghead. 'If you do,' he began, 'hang on to it, Professor. It just might come in handy before we're done.'

'That's most kind of you.'

Was there something there, in those disturbing dark eyes? Something that told the copper everything he could say or do would seem ineffectual to Andreas Harker? Or was it simply a recognition and tacit appreciation that Wilson, at least, was prepared to listen, no matter how unlikely the theories and ideas put forward by the professor? Only time would tell.

If there was time, Wilson reflected. St Gargoyle's had been out of use for a long time. Now, in the space of a few days, it had burned down, had animal faeces stacked up on the altar and . . . howled at him. At him, or at the animals which had been attacking him?

The phone rang. He picked it up and listened. 'Okay, Harry,' he responded. 'We're on our way.' Then, to Harker. 'Car's out front, Professor. Let's go see what you want to show me.'

At that time of morning, with the worst of the rush-hour traffic out of the way, the drive to Uptown only took a few minutes. As they entered the area Wilson told Chester to drive slowly as he took Harker verbally through their experience of the night before. As usual they parked in the deserted St Katherine's Square.

Professor Harker eyed the burned-out shell of the church. Its Victorian-Gothic style was more grotesque and menacing in ruins than it had been before the fire. It seemed to leer at them where it waited for the inevitable attention of the demolition crew, its blackened, crumbling tower stabbing at the late June sunshine. Its very bulk appeared to conceal an undisclosed threat, a menace which, despite their stolid police background, even left Wilson and Chester a little uneasy as they approached it.

At the litch-gate Harker held back. 'I'm sure you are aware that I could have come here before I met you this morning,' he began. 'I give you my word, however, that I did not, that I have never entered this church before in my life, either before or after the fire. And my word still means something to me, Mr Wilson, as anyone who knows me will tell you.'

He continued to tell them that he would only follow them into the ruins once they had sought out and proven, or disproven, the presence of what he had then told them to look for. It struck the policemen as rather a theatrical way to go about things, but then, they reasoned, Harker seemed pretty theatrical and unreal altogether.

They left him at the litch-gate and made their way up the weed-grown gravel path to the broken porch. As they squeezed around the barrier Chester said: 'He's gotta be wrong, guv.'

'About this?'

'About the whole fucking thing. It's too far out. *Too* far.'

Ben Wilson nodded grimly. 'I hope to Christ you're right, Harry,' he said. 'If you're not, if Harker's only half-way there, we've got more on our plate than any copper's had to handle before. Bust the bad guys and the public loves you. Bust their pets and the world's gonna fall on our heads.'

They moved carefully, eyes sweeping above and around for any sign of falling masonry or fire-charred timbers. Their feet crunched the layer of dried-out charcoal and cinders which covered the tiled floor. They twisted their way between the haphazard remains of the sooty furniture, blackened, blistered pews and the fallen pulpit, moving slowly closer towards the sanctuary and the altar table.

Both men could tell at a glance that the pile of faeces was still there. Nobody was going to remove it as a gesture of good-will, not with the church sealed off and patently dangerous. And the authorities would be a long time sorting out whose responsibility it was. From a conversation with the diocesan office Wilson had gathered that a minor cleric was likely to get the shit-end of this particular stick before the complicated ritual to reconsecrate and then deconsecrate St Katherine's began. The church would have to be reconsecrated before it could be closed. Protocol demanded that reverence for even a decaying House of God should be observed and seen to be observed.

It was still there. The rank smell had subsided to some extent and it appeared to be drying out and solidifying. They drew closer. The sun was above and behind it, partially concealing its shape in shadow. Even so, as they approached, both Wilson and Chester knew that Andreas Harker was at least partially right. It wasn't the rough mound it should have been, the rough mound that PC Forrest had reported on. It was taller, more irregular, as if it were reaching up towards the ruined sanctuary roof above.

They reached the desecrated altar and walked around it, viewing its contents as closely as their noses permitted. Harry Chester realized that he was breathing faster as his eyes took in the details Harker had described to them. Ben Wilson knew with a depressing certainty that the sick feeling in his stomach had nothing to do with the beer they'd drunk in the Battle of Inkerman the night before. It might, though, have something to do with that howling.

'Examine the pile of faeces,' Professor Harker had said. 'I believe that its shape will not be natural, that it will have the appearance of having been, or begun to be, modelled. You may not recognize the form . . .'

He was right enough there. It didn't look like anything they'd ever seen before. Possibly it would eventually take on a shape that was part-beast, part-human, but it was too early to tell.

'. . . either now, in its incomplete state, or even later, when and if it is completed. You may be able to tell from the impressions left in its surface what kind of being is performing the modelling, however . . .'

The marks on the striated surface of the shape, Chester convinced himself, were ambiguous. Whatever joker was into shit-shaping wasn't going to get his hands dirty, that was for certain. He was using short sticks or pointed twigs to sort the form out.

'That's how he's doing it, guv,' he told Ben Wilson. 'The sick bloody creep's doing it with sticks. It has to be that. It can't be what that bugger Harker says it is. No way.'

Wilson turned away, fighting the contents of his stomach. He'd done his stint of motorway patrol many years ago. He'd seen the broken, bleeding bodies cut out of the wrecks. He'd heard the screams and shrieks of whole families trapped in 'burners'. They still haunted his sleep. In his early days with the CID he'd come to terms with the cruel, ghastly damage that humans can inflict on one another in terms of murder and mutilation. That had made him sick as well.

'Get Harker in here,' he told his sergeant through gritted teeth.

As Chester retreated back along the ruined church Ben Wilson tried some deep breathing. Slowly his guts calmed to a state closer than they had been to normal. It wasn't what he'd seen that had upset him, but the implications behind what he'd seen. Chester was wrong, very wrong. It wasn't some nutter shaping a pile of dog-shit with a pointed stick that had made those marks. Not at all.

Harry Chester put his head back around the barrier. 'He's coming, guv,' he called.

'Okay. Now get forensic over here. I want a cast making. And get me a photographer as well, Harry.'

Professor Andreas Harker entered the ruins, poking obstructions aside with his cane. He approached the altar with his dark eyes twinkling triumph.

'Am I "back in my tree" as your subordinate would say, Mr Wilson?' he enquired.

Wilson looked at the academic. Harker shouldn't be smiling like that, he thought. He shouldn't want to be right.

He kept his opinion to himself. Instead he asked: 'Will you take a look at this, Professor?'

Harker moved around the altar and followed the line of the policeman's pointing finger. He studied the impression in the faeces for some moments, then said: 'It appears to be the print of a large, clawed animal. Doubtless the creature which has been modelling this idol.'

'Idol? This pile of shit?'

'Certainly an idol, Mr Wilson. For all their protestations that it is there simply to represent the power of Christ and not to receive veneration in its own right, the crucifix which stood here formerly was an idol.'

Wilson sighed. 'Okay, I'll leave that aside for now. Any ideas what exactly made this print?'

Professor Harker shrugged. 'It's too big for a cat, unless we start thinking in terms of the Surrey puma. Probably a big dog, I'd say.'

'Like a wolf?'

'Wolves aren't the only creatures which howl, Mr Wilson. Dogs howl, you know.'

Councillor Geoff Reardon (Independent-Uptown North Ward) was, to put it mildly, still bloody furious. He was cross with himself, yes. He was also cross with fate. Mostly, though, he was damn bloody cross with that white shape which had appeared in his headlights the night before, whatever it might have been.

After the sub-committee they'd adjourned as per usual, to the Red Lion, where Geoff had sunk his customary skinful. Still, he was a large man, fat by his detractors' standards, and reckoned he could cope with eight or nine pints, no trouble. What he'd forgotten was the hip-flask he'd been attacking as decision after decision went against his area. Somehow the balance of local power seemed to have shifted, excluding his best efforts in some unspoken but definitely real conspiracy.

As per usual the Red Lion. As per usual the drive home afterwards, except that it hadn't gone as per usual, sod it! He'd known he was a bit over the top, but there was nothing new in that, nothing at all. All you had to do was tell yourself you were a bit far gone, keep an eye on the white line and think everything through deliberately. And it was only a couple of miles, all said and done. No problem.

Except for that bloody white thing.

There he was, holding a steady thirty-seven up the urban dual carriageway (and they weren't going to bust him for that!). It was virtually deserted at that time of night and the jam sandwiches were easy to tell by the rig on the roof. Getting near the lights by the multi-storey car-park. Slow down, select nearside lane. Indicate. Check lights. Green. Accelerate on to left filter.

Told you there was no problem. Nearly home.

Courting couple on the path want to cross. They'll wait. Yeah, that's Mike James and Carol . . . what's-'er-name.

White flash.

It was there, in the headlights, all white fur and teeth. Too bloody close.

Geoff swung the wheel hard to the right. The white thing disappeared as his Allegro stormed towards the curb of the filter reservation. Maybe I ought to take my foot off the accelerator he thought as Mike and Carol loomed closer.

Who pushed who clear he couldn't tell as the Allegro mounted the kerb and trapped flesh against the metal barrier. For a slow-motion moment the windscreen splattered with red rain. Geoff reached for the wipers, then realised the seat-belt was biting into his chest and someone was screaming outside. The screaming grew louder as Mike's face shot up the bonnet and hit the windscreen, lips crumpling and teeth shattering on the glass. By now Carol was screaming as well.

The blue light came predictably flashing out of nowhere. The patrol car screeched to a halt, the sound of its tyres masking Carol's hysteria and Mike's whimpering, shattered pain for a few protracted seconds. The Allegro chugged with an irregular note which implied something was slightly buggered. Uniforms flashed outside the car, then one leaped away to radio for an ambulance.

Bloody awful meeting and now this. He began to sober up fast. I'm not going to talk my way past this one, Geoff thought.

He reversed back fast, his offside lights shattering against the police car, compounding his problems. Mike was howling as he slid off the bonnet and broken bones, released, stabbed through the flesh of his legs seeking to escape his body.

Geoff opened the door and tumbled out towards the road, staggering to keep his balance. Carol was swaying, moaning, crying. The sounds were muted because she'd wrapped her arms tightly across her face to block out the terrifying sights around her. Mike, at her feet, was pumping out his blood in a fountain, the spurts from his ruptured femoral artery soaking her dress.

Geoff staggered around in a circle, looking for the white thing, not finding it. He lurched over to Carol and put his arms around her, trying to soothe her into a less distressing silence. The uniform was bending over Mike, improvising a tourniquet from its blue tie. Its companion finished on the radio and strode grim-faced towards the hapless councillor, a small black plastic box in one hand.

The ambulance came and removed the bits of Mike that were still working, pausing only to wrap Carol in a blanket and shoot her full of sedative before bundling her into the back as well. The councillor, one of the patrolmen said, could be checked over by the police doctor when he took a blood test to confirm the breathalyser findings. Maybe in an hour or so, he grinned vengefully. The ambulance crew knew it would be faster than that. The police weren't going to let their evidence filter out of Geoff's bloodstream by delaying.

They bundled him into the back of the patrol car and one drove him to the station while the other waited for the breakdown truck. The damage to the car was mostly superficial, so they towed it to the police station for a quick forensic check-over. Every little helps in the current tangle of drunk-driving laws, they reasoned. There was always dangerous driving, even if the blood-test showed up negative.

Geoff phoned his solicitor, who phoned his wife. When they'd done with him she drove him home in the still-bloody Allegro, shuddering as she did so. They'd had the compulsory purchase order two days before, and now this. Her world, never ideal, was crumbling around Mrs Reardon.

She dumped him in a chair for the night and went off to bed. In the morning he was still sitting there, mumbling angrily to himself about a white shape. Grim-faced she washed the traces of dried blood off the motor and drove it round to Joe Pasciewicz' body-shop. Joe checked it over, not asking how it came to be that shape, and promised to work long hours until it was fixed. He rang for the parts (new bumper, bonnet, offside wing) while she was there. Mrs Reardon didn't bother to ask the cost. Geoff's insurance could take care of that. With his licence as good as gone they might as well do something for all those premiums.

Whilst Messrs Wilson and Chester, and the peculiar Professor Harker, were probing the mysteries of a pile of animal droppings on the fire-stained altar of St Gargoyle's, Joe sat down and stared at the front of the Allegro. The nearside wing would knock out and fill. He'd promised it fast so he might as well start on that whilst he was waiting for the replacement panels. It wouldn't take long, but there were other jobs promised for that day, so he decided to get them out of the way first. After all, Councillor Reardon hadn't managed to stop them serving his business with a compulsory purchase order, so he probably wouldn't be that much use in finding alternative cheap premises. Favour given, favour owed, after all.

It was late afternoon when he finally got the job under way.

Once forensic and the photographer had finished in the ruins of St Gargoyle's, Ben Wilson broke a length of wood from a charred pew and moved towards the disgusting shape on the altar, intending to shovel it off and pound it flat. He was about to do so when Harker stopped him, sharply.

'No!' the professor commanded. 'Leave it there.'

Wilson looked at him sternly, unused to having his decisions questioned by mere members of the public. 'It should have been cleared off long before this,' he snapped. 'There's no way I'm letting this farce continue, Harker.'

'Listen to me, Detective Chief Inspector. You brought me here. You doubted what I had to tell you, until you saw this. Now you at least suspect that I could be right. If you want my help, don't touch that idol. Leave it there. Have your men check and photograph it daily. It's not finished yet.'

The policeman lowered the length of scorched wood. 'What good's letting it get finished going to do us?' he demanded.

'How do you think we can put a stop to what's happening here if we don't understand it? We have to learn as much as we can, Mr Wilson, and this is one of the few things that can help us to learn. And before you challenge me again, I'm not speaking simply as a disinterested academic. I'm trying to think from your point of view.

'Tell me, what's your next move? Paw-print every large dog in Monkhampton until you get a match? So you find out which dog is shaping the idol. What do you do then? Get a canine psychologist to analyse its reasons? Sit it under a bright light and give it the rubber truncheon third degree until it answers you in a series of coded barks? I hope that sounds as downright silly to you as it does to me.

'Supposing you *did* find the animal responsible. You can't charge it in law. The days of burning pet toads and goats as witches' familiars are long gone. You can't even say it's a danger to the public in any way and have it put down. If it's an unclaimed stray you could have it destroyed, but I doubt if it will be. Dogs that size get noticed and rounded up quite quickly. Besides, whatever it is, it didn't arrange to collect and carry that pile of faeces on its own. Somebody put it there in the first place. Somebody human. Find them and you start to get some answers, perhaps. Answers in plain English, not woofs and yips.'

Wilson grunted and threw the piece of wood away into the fire-stained body of the church. Harker was making sense. The sight of that paw-print in the pile of faeces was so outside a rational explanation that for a little while it had distorted his own rationality.

'Come on, Professor,' he said wearily. 'I'll buy you lunch in the Battle of Inkerman.'

'Now you're making sense,' Harker grinned. 'We can extend your exercise of last night with Sergeant Chester a little further. If, as you say, the local populace appeared to be taking notice of what was said then, I think I can find something to rattle their ears a little more with.'

They left the ruins and walked back down the gravel path. As they passed beneath the litch-gate Wilson's eyes swept the buildings around the deserted square. Here and there a net curtain twitched in a window as a watcher hurriedly withdrew. There might not be anyone in evidence, but they were being watched for all that.

As Harker and Wilson left the square and began to walk down Inkerman Street, Marge emerged with Mary for their pre-dinnertime walk. It gave both of them an appetite, Marge believed. She saw the two foreigners and passed them without speaking, the mongrel, off her lead, at her heels. As they drew level, Wilson was staring at Mary, briefly remembering an impression of a dog about that shape and size wrestling with one of the wipers on his car the night before. The policeman shook his head. How could that docile, elderly creature have been a part of the yelping, howling, slashing horde which had menaced Harry Chester and himself the night before? Why, the creature didn't even look at him, even seem to notice he was there now. It couldn't be the same animal.

Could it?

And if it was, how did he prove it? POLICEMAN SNATCHES PENSIONER'S PET, the imaginary headline screamed at him. SAYS TINY MONGREL TRIED TO KILL

HIM. God knows Anderton had done enough damage to police credibility without him trying to charge an ageing dog with attempted murder, he thought.

Harker felt the changes in the man walking beside him. When they passed by he turned and looked back at the old woman and her companion. What could possibly be sinister about a pair like that? he asked himself. A line from an old song hummed through his head.

*Little old lady passing by . . .*

He thought briefly back to the files relating to Willington-Cartier's index, sitting on his desk in Cambridge. Right now he could be sitting in the Gardenia Restaurant in Rose Court, tucking into *pastourman* and drinking Demestica from a plain glass tumbler. Instead he was walking along with a policeman he'd only just met, a medium-typical specimen of breed, suspecting little old ladies of harbouring guilty and anti-human secrets.

Yes, it had begun. Whatever *it* was. And something told Andreas Harker that it wasn't going to be over for a long, long time.

They reached the Battle of Inkerman and ascended the narrow steps. Once inside the hush emanating from the three or four regulars there ahead of them was even more noticeable than it would have been had the pub been crowded. Wilson bought pints of the local brew and ordered sandwiches from the gruff landlord. Then he led Harker across to the table he'd occupied the night before, aware of the eyes watching over their glasses in silence.

The policeman didn't bother to raise his voice this time. There were few enough people in the bar for them to be able to hear him easily. 'You said there was something that could shed a bit of light on what's happening here in Uptown, Professor,' he prompted.

Harker smiled and tasted his beer. It wasn't exactly what he'd have chosen to drink, but it wasn't bad either. He listened as he tasted, waiting through the silence for some conversation or other around them to resume. It didn't.

He set down his glasses. 'Tell me,' he began, 'have you ever heard of Black Shuck?'

'Only this morning. You mentioned him . . . it . . . earlier, back at the nick. Sounds like a pirate to me.'

'A fair assumption, Mr Wilson, albeit an inaccurate one. Black Shuck is the phantom black dog of East Anglia. And not just East Anglia, I might add. It has different names in different areas. Barguest, Shug Monster, Hairy Jack and so on. Reported sightings range across the Western world from Europe to North America and back. In this country alone it's been seen from Cornwall to the Outer Hebrides . . .'

'Okay, so maybe I should have heard of it before. But what's this Black Shuck got to do with our own particular witch-beast, or whatever it is?'

'Patience, Detective Chief Inspector. I'm coming to that in my own good time.' He looked up and noticed the watching eyes suddenly and sullenly avert. Then he drank some more of his beer, relishing his unofficial audience.

'Most of the sightings are historical,' he continued, 'but many are well-documented for all that. In East Anglia in particular, though also in other places, there seems to be an affinity between our phantom dog and churches. The earliest mention we have is in the *Anglo-Saxon Chronicle* for 1127. A whole pack of the beasties were seen in the sky over Peterborough and Stamford, both religious centres. In Elizabethan times Black Shuck entered the church at Bungay in Suffolk, killing two and mysteriously dessicating a third. Later he progressed to Blythburgh nearby, where there are said to be marks on the church door, made as he entered. There he killed another three, as well as burning and, in the words of the man who recorded the incident, himself a clergyman, 'blasting' many more.

'Now, these are just a few out of many incidents, but if we compare them to the data we so far have available on the incidents here in Uptown we shall notice some remarkable similarities.

'Number one. Black Shuck is capable of producing fire. St Katherine's was destroyed by fire.

'Number two. Black Shuck is a very large dog. The paw-print we found in the church belongs to a very large dog.

'Number three. Black Shuck is responsible for people dying. You and Sergeant Chester almost died last night.

'Number four. Black Shuck is credited with at least human intelligence to go with his demonic origin. Your creature has to be super-intelligent for its species, though I suspect its origin to be slightly less spectacular than Shuck's.'

'Now, I admit that the connections I have postulated are rather tenuous ... Oh ...' He broke off as the sandwiches arrived, viewing them with disdain. I really should be in the Gardenia, he thought, 'Thank you,' he said flatly. 'As I was remarking, the connections are tenuous, but they exist, never-theless. And there's one more thing.'

'Which is?'

'Which is quite apposite, I believe. In the Burnley area Black Shuck is known as Striker, and one of his major character-istics is the ability to voice deep and protracted howls. Does that sound familiar to you, at all?'

Wilson's answer was to take a large swallow of beer and tear a ham sandwich in half with his teeth. He pushed the protruding end into his mouth and chewed sullenly. As he finished he said: 'Let me get this straight, Professor. There's a phantom black dog that howls, starts fires and kills people in church, right?'

Harker shrugged. 'Reasonably close,' he conceded.

'And you're saying the creature's come west to Monkhamp-ton?'

'Well, there have never been any recorded sightings from this precise area, though they have been noted in Lincolnshire to the north and Cambridge to the east. And let's not forget that this country is traditionally incorporated into East Anglia. Both your so-called local television stations transmit from Norwich, even if it is 130 miles away. But it could just as easily have come south from Burnley, or west from Worcester. Or even north from Devon or Somerset or Wiltshire. Geo-graphically speaking, Monkhampton would be a logical focus for its countrywide activities.'

'So we're on the look-out for a huge black dog that's more likely to kill us than let us kill it. Is that what you're saying?'

'Traditionally a large black dog, about the size of a calf, with a shaggy coat and blazing eyes the size of saucers. And yes, it usually burns to death those who molest it in any way.'

Ben Wilson shook his head. 'Now it's my turn to think you're out of your tree, as Harry put it.'

He'd forgotten about the audience propped against the bar. He'd even forgotten about Harry Chester, until he mentioned the sergeant's name. Yet the moment he'd spoken he regretted his words. Something inside warned him that Harker might be nearer the truth than any of them yet suspected.

Andreas Harker stood up, leaving his beer half-drunk and the unappetizing sandwich untasted. 'Then I'm sorry we've both been wasting our time,' he said curtly. 'I'll bid you good day, Mr Wilson.'

He was almost at the door, leaving Wilson half on his feet to stop him, when Harry Chester entered.

'Sorry I took so long,' the sergeant grinned. 'You'll want to hear this, Professor. And you, guv.'

Harker turned and looked back at Wilson. The policeman shrugged. 'Okay,' he scowled. 'I spoke out of turn. Let's hear it, Harry. All of us,' he added, glaring pointedly at Harker.

Harry sat down and the professor resumed his seat. 'They've identified the cast as definitely dog,' Chester began. 'Probably somewhere in size between an Alsatian and a Great Dane, though they're still working on the breed.'

'Not the size of a calf?' Wilson sneered.

'Could be, eventually,' Chester answered, obviously puzzled by the remark. 'Depends on whether it's stopped growing yet. But there was something else as well.'

'Scorch marks?'

'Not on the dog-shit guv. Only on the altar itself, but we knew about them already. No, the guy who was taking the cast noticed a hair in the print and bagged it for the lab. Like the print, it's solid dog.'

Harker and Wilson exchanged glances. 'Do I ask him or do you?' the professor demanded.

'I do,' Wilson replied. 'What colour was it, Harry?'

'Allowing for discolouration, due to the matter it was found in, they tell me it's white, guv'nor. Pure snowy white.'

Their lunch continued uneasily once Harry Chester had joined them in the Battle of Inkerman. Ben Wilson, conscious of his lapse from grace, not to mention having refuted data which could well support his own theories in front of the locals, struggled to make amends with the now rather prickly Harker. In his turn the professor was puzzled by the white hair, yet also somewhat relieved. Black Shuck had always been thought of as a spectre, a ghostly visitant from beyond the realms of man. To find it alive and well and modelling faeces in a burned-out church would have been slightly too much to cope with. He'd probably have wondered himself whether he was treed or not.

Wilson repaired the damage as best as he could and the three men eventually parted, if not the best of friends exactly, at least on speaking terms. Wilson and Chester were to repair to the police station to check on any further findings from the lab. Andreas Harker was to return to Cambridge and his work on the Willington-Cartier index. Each of them felt that the situation, whatever it might actually be, was still unresolved, though only Harker carried a true sense of dark foreboding locked inside himself.

The afternoon wore on towards evening. In the repair shop off Sebastopol Street Joe Pasciewicz worked alone on Councillor Reardon's bent Allegro. Johnny Crashaw had taken the afternoon off, as he seemed increasingly to be doing, to see one or other of his women. The apprentices knocked off at their usual time, Youth Opportunity Programme rates not exactly encouraging them to do overtime.

Joe slipped a trolley-jack under the engine mountings and lifted the front end clear of the garage floor. He crawled underneath with a lamp to check the extent of the damage from below and to work out the feasibility of beating out the wing that wasn't bad enough to be replaced. Afterwards, when he'd climbed to his feet, he opened his locker, and took out a bottle of vodka. Twisting off the metal cap he swigged a slug of the clear spirit neat from the bottle before replacing it.

There was no way he could get up inside the wing to knock the damage out without taking it off, and if he had to cut it off he might as well replace it. The alternative was a filler job from the outside, and Joe mixed up a wodge of the grey, resin-based compound before cleaning off the area around and inside the dent. He was slapping it roughly into place when the sound of feet outside told him the shift had changed at Harrington's brewery, just half a block away. That meant it was gone seven.

He roughed the filler into shape, leaving it proud, and swigged some more of the vodka whilst he waited for it to go off. The body shop was virtually windowless and they worked most of the time by artificial light, so Joe didn't notice when dusk began to gather outside. He sanded the filler and primed it, setting the blow-heater up to cook the paint dry. Once it was, a couple of coats of matched top-coat would finish that part of the job and he could go home. He'd been down to the shop at lunchtime and traded in the pregnant gang-bang video for one with what was euphemistically called water-sports. Maybe about nine he'd finish up and go home with a four-pack and watch it. Yeah.

For some reason the top-coat didn't want to dry when he sprayed the first layer on. Joe moved the heater as close as he dared and finished the vodka ahead of his schedule. It didn't seem to touch him any more. Maybe he should have bought another bottle whilst he was in the supermarket. Vodka came cheap from the big boys, and it all tasted the same to him anyway.

It was almost nine when he decided the paint was dry enough for him to spray the last layer on. The porn video was calling to him by now, inviting him to view those lacey women

136

with their bursting bladders. 'Go on, Joe,' they invited. 'Go on home and watch us piss.'

He shook his head free of the vodka, or as free as he was going to get it, and wagged a finger at the brown-paper package, reproving it for tempting him. Not fair, he thought. Not fair you tempt your Joe with these thoughts. I got work to finish. I promise quick job. I keep promise.

He could always leave the fan-heater going all night and chance the result. The only problem with that was that it wasn't as young as it used to be and it might just spark off if it ran too long. With the amount of paint and thinners in the body-shop there'd be a hell of a bang if it did. Still, he could risk a quick walk round to the Pakki shop for another bottle to keep him company while he was waiting.

He opened the door and stepped outside, surprised to find how dark it was now. The longest day had only just come and gone, so it had to be quite late. He checked his watch and found it was getting on for ten. Better hurry, Joe thought. Shop shut at ten. Pakki prices bad enough. Pub prices fuckin' criminal, yeah?

He reached the corner off-licence, just as the woman with the caste-mark was about to turn the sign to CLOSED. He persuaded her to let him in, oozing Eastern Europe charm through the vodka. He always charmed this one. She looked so Western with her wavy hair and high cheekbones. He could give her one or three, he grinned to himself.

She handed over the vodka with her usual smile, dark and exotic and promising something she was never going to deliver. Joe paid up and left, standing alone on the pavement as she closed the door and locked it behind him. Another chance gone. Fuck it. She'd probably be a disappointment anyway.

Joe made his way back into Sebastopol Street and returned to the body-shop. The heater was still blowing, still drying off that last coat of paint. He looked at his watch again, wondering how much longer it was going to take.

He was still wondering, the cap now off the new bottle of vodka, when he heard the noise outside.

*

Straight after lunch, with Andreas Harker on his way back to Cambridge, Ben Wilson looked in on roll-call for the new shift. He was painfully aware that he'd been spending a great deal of time on puzzling over a situation that, whilst it might be menacing, was unlikely to yield before ordinary police methods. Police time, especially his own, had to be justified, and he was reaching the point where it was in danger of being wasted pursuing some of the wildest theories he'd ever heard.

He resolved to concentrate on the facts, such as they were. At least Harker had led him to two new ones, the paw-print and the hair. Large white dogs needed exercise. That meant walking the bloody things. Public visibility.

There were two ways of finding the beast. One was noisy and would attract unwelcome attention, demanding answers he didn't have. That was an appeal through the press. He already had the civilian PR fending off inquiries about the previous night's house-to-house. Was there a rabies scare? Why were the police wasting time playing dog-catcher instead of leaving it to the local authority? Couldn't the LA cope? Why Uptown?

No, not the press, he decided. That left the second way. Brief the beat bobbies and wait for them to call in if they spotted the creature. It shouldn't take them long, he decided.

It didn't.


Sally hardly had her key in the door before she heard the enthusiasm on the other side. It started with a muted movement, then progressed to a bark, low at first, then another, louder bark as Leader's nose picked up her scent. As she turned the key there was a faint scrabbling. She'd have to find a way to cure him of that. Sooner or later he'd damage the inside of the door and she'd either have to find a boy-friend who knew how to fix it or stump up to the landlord for a new one.

As the door swung inwards the opposition retreated to the centre of the room, mouth open, tongue lolling, panting expectantly. It was nearly six and Sally was later than usual. Because of this her welcome, when it came, was more powerful and delighted than usual. Leader bounded the short distance across to her and leaped up, licking her face. As she staggered backwards he leaped down again, executed a small jump, sniffed her skirt and barked again.

All fun-loving, contented dog, she decided.

She knelt down and scruffled in his fur, patting his head and neck and tickling him under his lower jaw. An uncle of hers had bred Dachshunds, and he'd once told her that if you stroke an animal under its chin it can't take your hand off. Not that a Dachshund could, but a rogue Newfoundland might have a good try, and the two of them were still comparatively new to one another.

'Good boy,' she told him. 'Good Leader. You're pleased to see me, eh?'

He barked, hoping the sound conveyed appreciation. Humans seemed to have a talent for stating the obvious, he decided. In retrospect, though he hadn't realized at the time, hadn't been *able* to realize at the time, Ellie had mostly stated the obvious. 'Good Leader. Want to go for a walk? Hungry? Want to play?'

'Was nasty ol' Joe unkind to you, then?'

Sally stood up and walked through to her bedroom. 'I'll just change, then we'll go for a walk,' she called.

By now it was familiar enough to have become ritualized. Even if Leader hadn't understood the meaning of Sally's words he'd have figured the sound out by now. She said the same thing every night.

He tried the door whilst she was out of sight. He'd always been good with doors, but since he'd managed to get out the night before, Sally had taken to dropping the snub-catch on the yale inside, and double-locking it from the outside when she went out. He could turn handles. He was even tall and skilful enough to twist the oval yale-knob from the inside. But he couldn't manage that little snub-catch. Not yet.

Sally re-emerged in slacks and a tee-shirt, the formality of her office dress discarded. She was carrying his lead and eyeing him with feigned ill-humour. 'Where *did* you go last night?' she asked him again, the memory of those brown-stained paws she'd had to wash still fresh in her mind.

He made no response. It wouldn't help Sally to know that he understood the question, that since that night in Pieter Hangel's brass pentagram he'd understood almost everything that humans said. He didn't have the means to explain to them. Not without betraying the special abilities which the *other* had seen fit to grant him, and he wasn't going to do that.

Not yet.

Instead he waited whilst she clipped the lead to his collar and found her keys again. She'd let him off the lead, once they were in the park. She only kept him on it until they were across the main road outside. He didn't resent the constraint, knowing as he did that it was for his own protection as much as it was for Sally's peace of mind.

They left the flat and walked along the pavement to the crossing. Leader sat at the kerb, automatically, knowing that it kept his human happy. He watched the lights change and knew to go, but was canny enough to play dumb, seeming to require a short, sharp tug on the lead to get him to his feet again.

'There's my Leader,' she said, once across, praising the inevitable in the same way that she'd stated the obvious earlier.

They entered the park. Estbury Green was Monkhampton's largest park. It had once formed part of the grounds of a local family's home and been given to the borough in Victorian times. It was typical of its period, complete with cast-iron bandstand, aviary and monkey-puzzle trees. The lawns were well-tended and the grass always appeared cut to optimum length. The cast-iron gates, painted a slightly jarring shade of green, stood open from dawn to sunset every day, no matter what the time of year, not so much through the borough's good will as because it had been a stipulation of the bequest which had granted them the park. Somewhere there was still an Estbury who might notice and claim it back if they defaulted, not only depriving the public of a prime facility but also turning a fat profit on the urban open space by judicious sale.

Sunrise was early and sunset late at that time of year. If they wanted they could have the better part of three hours in the park together. Sally would tire before then, though, and take Leader home for them both to eat. She slipped his lead and let him run free, knowing that such a large animal required more exercise than she was prepared to cope with, especially after a day in the office. Leader leaped off across the grass, then stopped, turned and barked at her.

Stick, he ordered.

She stared at him, not realizing the origin of the thought which had flashed into her mind. She looked around the grass at her feet, unwilling to break anything from the trees, clad as they were in their summer foliage. A few feet away an old, well-chewed length, abandoned after other dog and owner games, lay waiting.

Sally picked it up. Leader took a step forward and barked excitedly. This was how he'd acted before, he remembered, in those days when games still had some meaning in his life.

'Is this what you want, Leader?' Sally said, asking the obvious once more.

He began to lope towards her. She drew back her arm and pitched the stick into the air. It turned end over towards the bandstand, a streak of fast white fur bounding after it.

Leader brought the stick back. Sally threw it again. And again. They wandered past the bandstand towards the aviary, oblivious of the other people around them, not even seeming to notice the uniformed constable discreetly speaking into the radio clipped to his tunic.

Just after a quarter of an hour later, as they were both beginning to tire of the game and think about going home for something to eat, an unmarked police car parked on double yellow lines outside Estbury Green. Ben Wilson stepped out, locking the driver's door after him, and started into the park.

Despite its size it only took him a few minutes to find the person and animal he was looking for.

Okay, so there were bound to be other people with large white dogs in Monkhampton, and as Harker had pointed out he could hardly arrest the beast for modelling dog-dirt when and if he did find it. But somehow the creature, whoever it belonged to, was at the centre of what was happening in Uptown, and the policeman felt that any answers he might be lucky enough to find would probably be connected with it. For that reason alone it had to be found and, he reasoned, found fast.

Other beat constables would doubtless sight other dogs. They'd radio in and leave their messages. Harry Chester could take another, Kate Jones a third. Sooner or later they'd get them all. Just a matter of time. Always time.

He strolled casually towards where Sally and Leader were both thinking about abandoning the stick. The Newfoundland saw him first and turned towards him, barking sharply. Sally followed Leader's amber glare.

'I know you,' she began. 'You were at the police station when . . ' her voice tailed off. The memory was still fresh and painful. She'd washed the clothes she'd been wearing during the attack, then thrown them away. They'd never feel the same on her again.

Wilson nodded, squatting on his haunches and trustingly offering Leader a hand to lick. 'Miss French, isn't it?' he asked, looking up at her. 'I see you took my advice about the dog. He's a beauty.'

Sally beamed. Only a few days maybe, but it was already turning into love-me-love-my-dog. She'd half-fancied this copper even before she'd washed the mugger's touch off her body.

'You didn't tell me your name, officer,' she admonished.

'Sorry.' He stood up, extending the hand Leader had been licking. 'Ben Wilson,' he told her.

They shook hands. 'And what are you, Ben Wilson?' she asked, holding the grip a fraction too long. 'C I D? One of the big boys?'

For a moment he wondered exactly what that last remark was referring to. 'Detective Chief Inspector,' he said at length. 'Yeah, you could say I'm one of the big boys. So, do you live round here?'

The address was on record. He could find out for himself easily enough. Leader's head nudged his thigh playfully soliciting the hand again. All dog. He squatted again and took the animal's forepaws in his hands, checking them over for telltale brown stains. There were none.

'Just over there,' Sally gestured. 'I've got a ground floor flat. Look, Leader and I were just going home, Mr Wilson . . .'

'Ben.'

'Ben. If you're not on park patrol, it's about the time I usually have a drink. You're welcome to join me. If you'd like to,' she added quickly.

'You know, I could do with a drink,' he answered. 'Look, give me the house number. I've just got to call in, let 'em know where I am, and then I'd like that very much. Okay?'

'Okay.' See you soon, Ben Wilson, her eyes said. 'C'mon, Leader. Home and food.'

He watched them make their way to the park entrance, then started back towards his car. As soon as he'd radioed in his location he locked the vehicle again, then decided to move it to a more acceptable parking space nearer Sally's flat. The short drive gave him some extra time to think.

The coincidence of having seen Sally before made things so much easier. She couldn't have had the dog that long, but they'd obviously taken to one other quite quickly. Yeah, Leader fitted the general description, but Uptown and Estbury Green were the better part of five miles away from each other. There didn't seem to be a link. Besides, he was all dog.

And then the little nagging doubt crept in.

Those little nagging doubts were what had pushed Ben Wilson to his present rank. He didn't call them hunches. After all, he was an ordinary, workaday British copper, not Sam Spade or Perry Mason. But whatever he called them they seemed to work nine times out of ten.

All dog.

Suspicious of strangers. Friendly once owner had shown acceptance. Soliciting play once they'd shaken hands.

Licking his hand before they had.

That dog had accepted him too quickly. Too easily. It seemed intelligent enough, so there had to be a reason, Wilson thought, leaving the car at the kerb and walking towards the flats.

An answer flashed through his mind. He rejected it immediately, then began to wonder and brought it back for review.

That dog knows you're a copper. You've seen suspects behave like that. Get in. Ingratiate. Throw suspicion somewhere else. That's what they do.

He shook his head. C'mon, Wilson. That way lies paranoia. Or the truth?

Now who's outta his tree? Look, take it bit by bit. If you're right, you'll soon know. If you're wrong, what the hell's wrong with a drink with a good-looking girl for once? You never know, you just might think a bit better if you wind down some.

He reached the door and rang the bell. Behind the door, couchant, Leader simply waited whilst Sally French answered it. He looked at his forepaws again, the paws Sally had washed clean. The paws Ben Wilson had just examined.

He saw the first black hair.

Though he had been careful to conceal his feelings from the policemen, Andreas Harker was something more than simply cross as he drove back to Cambridge. For Harry Chester to dismiss his theories, the professor felt, would be par for the course. The man displayed the pedestrian, almost loutish mentality which Harker's previous dealings with the police had led him to expect. Wilson, though, ought to know better. There was a man with both the rank and the intelligence to understand what was happening, if he chose to. That he didn't choose to, Harker reflected, could be positively tragic.

He turned off the A604 before it joined the M11 and drove into the city centre, turning into Trinity Street, then into the college grounds and parking in his reserved space. Crossing the court towards his rooms he attempted to assess exactly what his feelings really were. He was angry, yes. But he was more than just angry. He was, he admitted to himself, also badly frightened.

The act he'd put on for the benefit of his companions at the burned-out church had surprised even him. His assumption of what they'd find on the altar was as much guesswork based on theory as anything else. To have been proven right was more than satisfying. To have seen the actuality, however, had scared the hell out of the academic.

All right, the hair they'd found had been the wrong colour for Black Shuck. That didn't really matter. Almost anything could be shaping the idol, perhaps even a succession of almost anythings. The base theory still stood, even if Wilson and Chester were too bound up in their pedestrian logic to admit it. The evidence, every scrap of it, tied in to the Willington-Cartier index and its prognostications.

He climbed the carved oak staircase to the upper floor where his rooms were. Unlocking the main door he walked straight through to the study. Taking a worn tissue from his pocket he checked his sword-stick, wiping the surplus oil away and making sure the blade came free of its scabbard easily. Despite what he'd told Wilson that morning it was his constant companion, and he hadn't needed to return to Cambridge to fetch it. The world, for anyone who had read the index, was a more terrible place than it could ever have appeared to those who hadn't.

Wilson's joke about the pistol with the silver bullets for killing werewolves hadn't been that far from the truth, either. Unlocking a drawer of his pedestal desk he removed a battered wooden box and raised the lid. Resting inside, in a series of compartments lined with faded red velvet, were a bullet-mould, nipple-wrench, screwdriver, a silver flask, a small metal box and last, but by no means least, a humble but efficient

1865 Colt pocket revolver. He'd bought the weapon some years before as an antique. A friend in a local ballistics lab had (quite illegally) reproofed it for him and parted with a small supply of percussion caps and black powder, the contents of the metal box and the flask. The moulded lead balls which it fired reposed in an integral box, the hinges broken and the small brass handle tarnished almost black, wrapped in tissue paper.

Harker sat down and removed the revolver, probing each of its five chambers from the breech end with a pencil. Having made certain they were all empty he loaded each in turn with a measured amount of powder from the flask and one of the lead balls, each of which was fractionally oversize to ensure it held both itself and the powder in the chamber. Finally he removed five percussion caps from the tin and placed one over each of the nipples on the hammer end of the cylinder.

He laid the fully-loaded pistol on the desk in front of him and stared at it, sitting back, arms bent and fingers steepled under his chin. Andreas Harker had always sought to be a model citizen. The possession of this weapon, loaded as it was, constituted a serious and anti-social offence. To carry it, as he now intened to, was even worse. By way of authorization he shifted his gaze to the Willington–Cartier index, then nodded slowly to himself.

Yes, he was justified. Whatever he might encounter that night would be hostile, most likely. If it wasn't then he was taking the risk for nothing. That, however, would mean that he was wrong about everything.

One thing still puzzled him. The longest day, the Summer Solstice, when the powers of nature rather than the powers of man were at their strongest, had come and gone without incident in Uptown. Whatever the force they called the *other* was planning should have taken place then, he reasoned from his knowledge of witchcraft and demonology. If it hadn't, as was patently the case, there was a reason for it.

Harker had to know that reason. He had to know it because without it he had no idea of the time-scale involved before the *other*'s intentions came to fruition. And without that knowledge he had no idea how much time was left for him to stop it.

If he could.

Almost without thinking he slipped the revolver into his pocket and stood up. He'd ignored those dreadful sandwiches in the Battle of Inkerman and he was feeling quite hungry. He checked his watch and found it was a little after four. Fine. He could make Monkhampton by half five and get something to eat before the night's work commenced.

The drive back to Monkhampton was uneventful, now that it was possible to bypass Godmanchester and Huntingdon proper. He parked his car in a side-street on the other side of the dual carriageway to Uptown and found a rather unhygienic Greek restaurant. Two pittas, two *shevtallia* and a couple of skewers later he felt much better. Leaving the car where it was he went in search of a pedestrian crossing and started on foot towards his ultimate destination.

Outwardly, at any rate, Wilson was beginning to relax. He sat flopped in Sally's comfortable sofa, a generous gin and tonic in one hand and Leader's head nuzzled under the other. Sally was sitting opposite in an armchair, legs drawn up under her, nursing her vodka and digesting the scene.

'Beautiful dog,' the policeman ventured. 'He is a dog, isn't he? I mean, not a bitch?'

'Yes, he's a dog,' Sally smiled archly. 'I hope you're better at telling the difference with humans, Ben Wilson.'

He eyed her carefully, just long enough to bring the suggestion of a blush to her cheeks. 'No trouble,' he grinned. ' 'Cept with the odd leftover hippie. And some of them are very odd.'

'So what were you doing in the park? Litter deterrent squad? Or you just felt like some exercise. Do you live nearby?'

Wilson shook his head. 'Not so's you'd notice. Tell the truth I just felt like getting out of the office for a while, and this is a part of Monkhampton I've not seen much of. Yet.'

He took a swig of his drink and looked down at the white Newfoundland curled up beside him, eyes closed, breathing its way into a post-prandial doggy-nap. The bowl Sally had set out in the kitchen had vanished before Wilson had reparked the car and reached the front door. Leader was still slightly uncertain of his good fortune and tended to be greedy with food when it was available. The dog snored softly and slightly altered its position.

'Bet you feel more comfortable with him around,' Wilson continued. 'Leader, isn't it? Do you let him out on his own yet?'

Innocuous question. Stay friendly and interested. Let's do this quietly and there might be a chance of something more later.

Sally shook her head. 'Not yet. I have to watch him, though. He's good with doors, even bolts. He's very bright. And yes, he's a great comfort. I come straight home and pick him up before I go shopping.'

It wasn't worth mentioning that he'd got out by himself the night before. This was a social visit, at her invitation, after all. She followed her words across the room with her eyes. This guy Wilson seemed all right. Better looking than Jake. Okay, if they got into any kind of relationship it was bound to be erratic. The job called for odd hours, unlike her own. But he was easy to be with, so far.

So, keep him interested. No heavy pauses.

'What's your taste in music, Ben?' she asked, setting her drink down on an occasional table and getting up.

He shrugged. 'Pretty easy,' he answered. 'Most things, really. Not punk, though. I was too old to stand even a chance of coming to terms with punk.'

'That's funny,' she pouted, lying, 'I was too young, granpa.'

She crossed to the CD player. 'More your time than mine,' she remarked, loading the deck and programming the tracks. Then she came back and sat down.

He felt the air about him tingle as the clear sound began to fill the room. Muted thunder was followed by a rain-tinkle intro. Jim Morrison crooned: '. . . Riders of the storm . . . Into this house we're born . .'

'Yeah,' Wilson agreed. 'Right on.'

He sat back and let the music of the Doors wash over his mind. He'd been at school when this came out, when Morrison died in Paris in 1971.

Wilson looked down at the sleeping Leader through half-closed eyes, still looking more relaxed than he actually felt. He couldn't press the question of the dog too hard, too quickly, he told himself. There were other considerations here. A growing friendship to name but three. Yet through his lashes he began to notice something he'd not spotted before.

There were the beginnings, faint but still present, of dark striations in Leader's white fur.

He opened his eyes and bent over the dog, his fingers gently parting the hairs, singling out the strands of darkness. Sally watched him in silence for a moment, then asked: 'What's the matter, Ben? Found a flea?'

'Found a few dark hairs,' he announced. 'If you bought Leader as pure white you were done. Looks like he's shot with black.'

Sally had sat down again to listen to the music. Now she stood up and went across to the sofa, kneeling at Wilson's feet, moving his hand gently out of the way so that she could examine her animal for herself. She looked up at the policeman.

'You're right. I never noticed those before. Still, Mr Greaves didn't mention anything about his background to me. It seemed to be some kind of rule that they didn't at Salvation.'

For a moment Wilson thought his heart had stopped. He still couldn't be sure, but he had a link with Uptown now. As the first erratic thump sounded in his ears he tried to sound casual as he asked: 'So you got him from Salvation, Sally?'

'It seemed the logical choice,' she answered, still probing Leader for dark hairs. 'There're enough unwanted dogs in this world without me going out and buying one from a breeder.

And Mr Greaves is a very careful man. I had a struggle to get him to part with Leader. It was love at first sight, if you know what I mean.'

'I've got a pretty fair idea,' Wilson told her softly.

He suddenly realized that their faces were less than a foot apart, and that neither of them could think of anything to say. Jim Morrison went into *Moonlight Drive*. Their personal silence grew longer and deeper.

He'd kissed her almost before he realized. She drew back in mock alarm, peering at him, then offered her lips again. This time there was no hesitation on either side.

'What's an old-fashioned girl like you doing with a rat like me?' he asked her.

She wrapped her arms about his knees and looked up at him. 'Who's old-fashioned?' she queried.

Leader slept on beside them, lost in a strange new world of different colours and values, his mind reaching out through his dreams to other creatures in other places, awakening them, instructing them.

'Got any favourite take-away?' Wilson asked. 'Assuming you're not going to kick me out, that is.'


Harker approached the ruins from the north side, avoiding the open expanse of St Katherine's Square. About him the Victorian huddle of Uptown was well into the summer evening. Here and there children played ancient games of tag or bounced balls off the brickwork. Mostly they fell silent and watched him as he passed, making him feel more conspicuous than if he had crossed the empty square alone. Only the bolder spirits continued their play with a species of bravado which appeared wholly out of place to the academic.

Yes, Uptown was dying. More and more houses were being boarded up as the landlords sold out under the compulsory purchase orders. An air of desolation now mingled with the decaying squalor of the centuried brickwork, ageing both the district and its inhabitants from the comfortable familiarity of the past into a council-block future. It was all over bar the shouting for the bricks and mortar, and the few faces Harker saw showed it all too clearly.

Some of them, however, showed more. A sort of resolution, even optimism, which belied both their circumstances and their expectations. He reflected as he walked that it was almost as if they expected a new Messiah to arise and order their lives into new and different patterns of contented service.

'When the music's over,' sang a CD player somewhere else in the town, 'turn out the lights . . .'

The ruined church rose before him. After a false start up one cul-de-sac and a careful look up another he finally found the way through the maze of houses to the north side of the churchyard and the burned-out Devil's Door beyond. His feet echoed on the cobbles unnervingly, despite his crêpe-soled shoes. There was to be no secret kept from Uptown, he thought morosely. That individual dwellings might harbour a degree of non-human awareness he was prepared to accept from what he knew of the workings of the PRS. But that an entire area could feel as if it knew what he was going to do, before he even knew himself, was both an outsize puzzle and the promise of an overwhelming defeat to come.

Even so, Andreas Harker continued towards the station he had selected for himself that morning. The north gate was locked and he had to climb over the rough wall, making his way along it to a point where the massed summer nettles were not too bushy on the inner side. Here and there a star-shaped flower peered grimly through the tangled vegetation, dark and solemn and poisonous. Tiny somethings started and scuttered in the grass as he dropped down into the churchyard and looked around to see if he'd been observed. No curtains twitched. No silver-mounted dark blue helmet bobbed up with the traditional 'ello 'ello 'ello.'

He used the sword-stick to beat his way through the tall grasses towards the depression which had once been the path on this side. Here the weeds had taken a firmer hold, choking one another in their struggle to bury the gravel from sight completely. Close beside it, near the church, an antique yew brooded upon its ruined dignity, almost half of its gloomy bulk scorched away by the fire.

No-one had bothered to bar the north entrance to the blackened ruins, the wall and the gate, locked for as long as most people could remember, together with the stings and thorns of the rampant flora, forming an effective enough barrier for normal situations. The precaution on the other side had been nothing more than a token acknowledgement of an obligation. After all, why bother? The whole thing's coming down soon. No point in throwing good money after bad.

Harker cast a wary eye over the débris about the base of the wall, then surveyed the situation above him, wary of loose blocks badly set in heat-ruined mortar, drying timbers contracting and loosening their last tenuous perch in the warmth of the evening. He listened for sounds of movement or life. There was only the faintest breeze to stir the grasses. Nothing scuttered, all movement stilled as tiny eyes watched the intruder from their secret sanctuaries. A solitary bird sang above him, taking wing and fluttering away as he stepped through the gaping archway of the Devil's Door into the silent desolation of the church.

Despite its rooflessness the interior was darker than the churchyard outside. Roseate sunlight slanted low across the rubble, staining the sanctuary and the inside of the north wall with orange-red patches and splashes, contrasting starkly with the soot-blackened surfaces they stained. Harker checked his watch, standing in shadow, and realized by the faint luminosity of the face just how dark some areas of St Gargoyle's really were.

Nearly 9.30. Sunset.

The night starts here.

He picked his way carefully, watching his feet, towards the charcoaled mass of the pulpit, negotiating the fallen length of the brass lectern, its varnish scorched away unevenly, giving the heavy eagle the appearance of suffering some strange metallic leprosy. Above him a burned-off beam, sticking out like a broken snake-fang, creaked to itself but held its position. He stared at it for several moments, trying to decide which way to jump if it should fall.

When he reached the pulpit he kicked an area around it clear with his shoe, then took a couple of folded rubbish bags from his pocket and slit the plastic open with a small penknife. He laid them on the cleared area and weighted the corners down with bits of rubble. Now at least there was somewhere reasonably clean he could sit or lie down when he felt like resting. With that prepared he stepped away and peered up through the gathering gloom into the sanctuary. A slant of sunlight fell to one side of the shaped heap of faeces, the dust-motes trapped within it swirling like an iridescent ground-mist about its base.

Slowly, very slowly, straining to keep all his senses alert in the danger of the ruin, Harker started towards the altar. His crêpe soles crunched on broken glass and charred wood littering the tiles underfoot. His eyes swept the walls and the brighter, though still darkening, sky beyond the vanished roof. The shaft of sunlight winked out suddenly, leaving the disgusting, half-formed idol squatting darkly before him. In the deepening shadows it seemed larger, more powerful, more *formed* than he remembered.

He walked around the altar, studying what he could see of the shape and wishing he'd remembered to bring a torch. No, it hadn't changed. It was exactly as he had first seen it that morning, except for the marks left by the attentions of Wilson's forensic team. Nothing sinister in itself. But in its implications . . .

Harker shuddered to himself, the taste of half-digested kebab repeating from his stomach into his mouth. The world was very sick if things like this could happen. Oh, the animal that had shaped the mass this far was a marvel, a prodigy all right, but it was also a freak, a wonder and a horror.

Come on, Harker, he told himself. Forget what you told that policeman. Shuck's only a legend, not a reality. *This* is a reality, and that means that there's some logical explanation for it.

Like there's a logical explanation for me driving sixty miles to spend an uncomfortable night in a ruined church like some chump of a ghost-hunter?

He felt the comfortable bulk of the revolver in his jacket pocket, then moved his hand to the rear of his trousers and touched the hip-flask through their fabric. At least there'd be a modicum of comfort in the darkness. Then, in seven or eight hours, he could find a transport café for breakfast and return to Cambridge none the worse for making a fool of himself in private.

The last of the sun-splashes faded away, leaving St Gargoyle's and its single human occupant to the strengthening grasp of the night. Harker finished his circuit of the burned-out shell and returned to his prepared patch of polythene, taking out the hip-flask and swigging a mouthful of the brandy it contained. To settle my stomach, he told himself. Or my nerves.

He considered his last mental statement. Yes, he was beginning to feel apprehensive, but not for any particular reason. Probably it was just the unfamiliarity of his surroundings that was starting to get to him. The blackened walls soaked up what little light there was from the waning moon, what little reflected sunlight still tainted the open sky above him. Outside the walls the few scattered dead slept dreamlessly in their graves. Inside all was silence and shadow, save for the settling sounds of the dying church and the rustling of Harker's clothing.

A dark splotch flitted overhead. Then another. The academic felt his heart leap, then realized that bats had resumed their habitation of the ruined tower. Just bats. Not vampires. Not nameless harbingers of terror. Just bats. Probably *pipistrellus pipistrellus*, Europe's commonest bat. This being June there'd be little batlets for the so-called flying mouse to feed. In the summer maternity was everywhere you looked. Even overhead in the crepuscular darkness of the dying day.

He'd never had an irrational fear of bats, or toads, or snakes, and the dark flying tatters were in their way a comfort in his lonely vigil. They were something else, both alive and thoroughly natural, inhabiting the ruins.

And yet, he felt, quite irrationally, there was also something more.

Leader dreamed on, his bulk occupying a half of the sofa that Ben Wilson could have put to better use. The policeman pulled himself away from Sally long enough to go out for pizza and a bottle of chianti classico.

Tom Greaves, taking a night off from paperwork, tore himself away from the TV and made his last round of Salvation for the night. The animals were quiet, even sullen, but he put this down to the weather. It looked as if it was going to be a long, hot, dry summer from the lack of rain.

Tommy Junior had abandoned his computer in favour of the first television screening of the (chopped) film of Whitley Strieber's *Wolfen*, and was sitting with his mother and Granpa Hangel. He couldn't understand why the old man didn't appear to be interested in the tale of secret dog-like creatures dwelling in society's underground.

'Ah, fiction,' Granpa told him. 'Fact is much better.' Then he went to sleep.

Joe Pasciewicz ignored the rattle of the door. Just some drunk with a skinful too early on his way home, he thought. That never happen to me, he grinned at the Allegro, tasting his new bottle.

The rattle persisted. 'Fuckin' drunk,' Joe grunted.

Something scuttered on the tiled roof of the body-shop. Something flitted, a passing shadow, outside the window at the further end. Joe faced the door and threw out his arms like a crucified Polish Christ, the bottle still clutched in his right hand.

'Go home, piss-head,' he called.

The rattle stopped. The silence echoed back around him, even blotting out the humming whirr of the fan-heater. 'Fuckin' goo' job,' he muttered.

Then the scraping started.

It began softly at first, a scratching that had no apparent origin, unless the piss-head outside was trying to find a way in with his fingernails. Yet it had to be more than that. If it wasn't, how come it was on the roof as well, and outside the window, scraping, scratching, clawing?

Softly, then louder, gathering strength and volume. Growing in intensity.

Joe looked from roof to window to door in patent disbelief. He searched his vocabulary. He found.

'Creeps,' he yelled. 'Fuckin' creeps. Why you do this? I get you I tear your balls off! Go home, fuckin' creeps. Go 'way!'

He swigged hard at the bottle. It solved most of his problems, usually. Maybe it'd solve this one as well.

The silence resumed.

'Bastards,' he smirked at Councillor Reardon's car. 'They know I mean what I tell them. They piss off.'

The fan-heater hummed the only answer he was going to get. He nodded to it and gingerly fingered a test area of paint inside the wheel-well. It felt dry. He studied the partly-consumed bottle of vodka as if it was an old friend instead of just a transitory companion. 'We go home,' he announced to it. 'Go home, watch our tape.'

Inside the brown paper bag the lacey women smirked and postured invitingly. The thunder came.

At first he thought it really was thunder. It wouldn't have surprised him, after the long dry spell they'd had so far. Certainly the sound on the tiled roof reminded him of falling rain. Scrit-scrat. Pitter-pat. And the sound at the window. And at the door. If the body-shop hadn't been built into a terrace he'd probably have heard it on the outer walls as well.

He switched off the fan-heater and listened, his heart beginning to flutter despite the alcoholic anaesthetic he'd consumed. This wasn't a drunk, or drunks. There was more to it than that. While he was by the switches he cut the electric light for a moment as well so that he could try to make out whatever was outside the window.

A huddle of shapes. Shadows. Noisy shadows.

Shadows not afraid of being noisy. Shadows with a purpose.
A purpose.

He focused on the thought and lurched towards the door.
His foot tangled into a cable and he pitched over, catching his
forehead on the Allegro's offside door-handle. Cursing roundly
he turned the light back on once he'd clambered to his feet
again.

The noise had solidified, strengthened, built itself into a
constant and unending peal of thunder. It had life and vigour,
and an unholy power which was somehow directing it.

Joe touched his forehead and looked at the moist redness on
his fingers. Some bastard was going to pay for that, he scowled.
Some bastard was going to pay for spilling his blood. And for
making him afraid.

Yes, he admitted to himself, he was afraid. That noise was
too much for the origin he'd first ascribed to it. Drunks
wouldn't be on the roof and at the window as well as at the
door. It was something else. Something frightening.

He picked up a tyre-iron. 'I kill you, you fuckers,' he muttered grimly. He moved towards the door.

A thought struggled past the vodka. Whoever was out there
wasn't on his own. There had to be three of them, at least,
from the sounds he'd heard. There was no way that less than
three could make noises on the door, the roof, and at the
window at the back. Joe hefted the tyre-iron in his grasp and
decided it didn't matter. The one at the back would take time
getting to the front of the body-shop. The one on the roof
would have to climb down, or risk breaking a leg or his neck if
he jumped onto the cobbles outside. He'd have had plenty of
time to send the first one packing by then with a smashed
wrist.

He turned the latch on the inside and heaved the door open
with a rapid effort, leaping back as it folded inwards.

Joe stood there, growling to himself, staring out. His eyes
swept across the road, looking for the troublemakers. Only
when he dropped them to pavement level did he see the

humped, squatting silhouettes with their glittering, eager, night-bright eyes.

They stood up and moved into the light spilling out of the body-shop. He saw them, wondered at them. He saw the silent snarls and the teeth, wicked teeth, sharp and vicious teeth, exposed behind them. He tried to count but the vodka wouldn't let him. As he dropped the tyre-iron from shock-weakened fingers and began to take the first of several faltering steps backward his eyes stayed with them, no longer challenging.

The animals matched his speed, pace for pace. The distance between them wouldn't begin to close until Joe was backed up against the further wall of the workshop. And once he was there, trapped against the bench, ringed round with teeth and claws that could shred him in brief and bloody seconds, he'd have nowhere else to go.

Except where those teeth and claws might take him.


The watch had become his chief companion now. Above and about the ruins of St Gargoyle's the night was too dark for him to see the bats flitting about their food-gathering. What-ever night-creatures lodged in the burned-out shell were aware of his presence and scuttering outside the range of his vision, reminding him of their presence with the tiny sounds of claws on tiles and rubble, haunting him with imaginary images of what their true forms might actually be.

Feeling increasingly foolish, Andreas Harker took another pull from his hip-flask, replaced it in his pocket and looked at his watch again. The luminous dial showed him it was just after midnight, but he watched the sweep of the second-hand obliterate the figures briefly as it passed them on its circuit of the dial, just for the company of something moving. And sort of visible, he added mentally.

Just after midnight. Nothing at the witching hour worth reporting. But there again, that had been mechanical midnight, a man-made and therefore artificial midnight.

He performed a quick mental calculation. Sunrise would be about half four. Seven hours of darkness to this particular summer night. Three and a half into that took him to one o'clock. Under an hour away. If anything was going to happen, if anyone, any creature, was coming to model the idol upon the altar, it would be before then. Wouldn't it?

Harker stood up and stretched his cramped limbs. Despite the time of year the night was colder than he'd realized it was going to be, and his vigil was becoming increasingly uncomfortable. Time and again he fought down the temptation to look at his watch again, to say to hell with it and leave the ruins to the darkness. He even began to wonder if there was something actually there with him, whispering its temptations into his mind, then decided that such a manifestation of incipient paranoia was both illogical and potentially dangerous, and banished it with a mental effort.

The waning moon had both risen and set early. It hadn't afforded much light when it had been out, fading towards the dark point of its cycle as it was. The brightness of the stars in the clear sky served only to darken the heavens, not illuminate them, and Harker thought once again of the torch he should have brought along to lighten his darkness.

He shook his head regretfully and peered from the tower end along the length of the church towards the gloom-wrapped altar. Two specks of light appeared.

Andreas Harker closed his eyes and rubbed a hand over them. Keeping them closed he wiped at the corners with his fingers. When he looked again the specks were still there. Still glowing.

Growing.

He scowled to himself. Reflections? From what? There was nothing reflective on or near the altar. He'd checked that himself, earlier, whilst there had still been light to see by.

If not reflections, then what? Not moonbeams. Not distant car headlights. They were below the level of the shattered window behind the altar, not above it.

Harker shifted the sword-stick to his left hand and withdrew the revolver from his pocket with his right. Carefully, pointing the weapon down and away from himself, he cocked the hammer with his thumb. The sound of his heartbeat grew stronger in his ears. He felt the muscle tighten and strive to work harder beneath his ribs. The palms of his hands, dry and slightly cold before, grew sweaty.

Very slowly, placing one foot deliberately and with no mean effort in front of the other, he started along the church. Whatever he'd been expecting, whatever he'd imagined he'd find, was banished before this phenomenon. The specks persisted, strengthening in intensity as Harker's careful paces brought him closer, becoming less pinpricks than short horizontal lines in the darkness. They reminded the academic of eyes. Bright slitted eyes.

But what could they belong to? he asked himself. As he drew steadily closer, the revolver now levelled in front of him, he quickly reviewed the possibilities. If anything had entered the church he'd have heard it, or glimpsed its bulk. The dark of the night wasn't total, and the rubble on the floor made silent movement impossible, even for a cat. And those eyes, if that was what they were, were too large to belong to a cat. Too large to belong to anything he could think of. Eyes as big as . . .

Harker shivered, the pistol and the swordstick shuddering in his hands. The effort of peering lowered his eyebrows and forged a rigid band across his forehead. His mouth dried and tasted sour.

Behind the slitted eyes a heavy black bulk began to solidify. At first its outline was wavering, uncertain, but with each of the reluctant steps bringing Harker closer it deepened and strengthened, shaping itself, taking on a form both darker and more sinister than the haunted night itself.

Time began to slow for Andreas Harker. The distance between his heartbeats grew greater. His legs moved with the heavy effort of one wading in mud through a nightmare. If they're right, he thought, I'm dead already. None may look at these eyes and live, they say.

160

And they were eyes. He knew that now beyond any shade of doubt. There was nothing else, either rational or irrational, that they could be. Eyes as big as saucers. Eyes that stilled the scutterings in the ruin, that silenced all sound around him, save for the internal hammering of his heart and the scuffling of his shoes across the rubble on the tiles.

The distance between Harker and the altar slowly decreased. He drew steadily nearer, struggling to fight down his terror, to still the tide of dread rising from his bowels. He loosed and re-tightened his trembling fingers around the gun-butt, one by one, raising it in front of him, aiming uncertainly at the monstrosity which had risen up in front of the shattered sanctuary window.

*Do you think you can hurt me with that, Andreas?* a voice inside him asked, almost lazily.

'I . . .' His throat was dry with fear. He swallowed hard and worked his tongue to moisten his mouth. 'I . . . know you for what you are,' he croaked to the shape, still staring, almost as if hypnotized, at the glowing slits. 'I know you as *burghgeist* and *Chernobog*. I know you as *Madadh Dubh* . . .'

*But can you kill me, Andreas? You may know my names, but can you kill my names?*

The eyes opened fully. Their blaze hit him like twin search-lights, knocking him back. With a sharp panic cry he jerked at the trigger. He saw the flash, saw the bullet strike a mullion of the ruined window, chipping fragments of stone away, but he heard nothing. No gunshot echoed round the ruined shell of St Gargoyle's. A perplexing numbness gripped his hand, forc-ing the fingers apart, breaking his grip. The revolver clattered to the floor and lay there, useless and forgotten. The eyes burned into him, seeking out his weakness, knowing his fear, flaying his soul beneath their devilish intensity and shooting something *into* him.

*You have challenged me,* said the voice. *That was unwise. We should be god and worshipper, you and I. You should serve me, not fight me. I have need of such as you.*

A chill sweat formed on Harker's forehead and trickled down his face. He blinked hard to keep it from his eyes, realizing that he was completely powerless in the face of this creature. God, monster, werewolf, whatever it was it held his life completely in its unearthly grasp. It could maim or destroy him as it chose.

The vicious lights softened, seeming to diffuse, even to bend. Instead of being rays from those dreadful eyes they became a glow which encircled and illuminated the shape upon the altar. For the first time, through his fear, Andreas Harker gained a clear impression of the monstrosity, taking in the powerful limbs and heavy body with their deep, shaggy, tangled fur and the enormous red penis projecting beneath the belly. These details were as nothing in comparison to the head, though.

The ears stood erect, jutting outwards from the skull. The top of the head was flat, sloping down to the thick ridge above those unearthly eyes. The muzzle wasn't as long as Harker might have expected, but the bottom jaw, open, exposing the overlong discoloured canines, foam-flecked and slavering, seemed to go back all the way to Hell. Such a mouth could tear a man's head off in one bite, or shear through his backbone and rip him in half.

'You . . . *are* Black Shuck, aren't you?' Harker whispered, badly awed by the apparition.

The gape of the fearsome jaws widened, then narrowed. The academic knew that their movement had nothing to do with the answer which screamed into his brain.

*I am Shuck. Will you serve me, Andreas Harker?*

'What are you, Shuck? Are you god or devil?'

*I am neither. I merely represent. Will you do my work?*

The numbness faded from his fingers. He glanced down at the revolver, its dull metal glinting in the light from the altar. Shuck was right. He'd never kill the thing with that, assuming it could be killed at all. All that was left to him was to agree, or to stall, to play for time and hope.

'What is your work, Black Shuck?' he challenged with a strength in his voice that he was far from feeling.

*That is for you to do, not for you to know, Andreas.*

The Devil traditionally fears iron and steel, Harker told himself. It's broken the power of a manifestation before. It just might do so again. He slipped the catch on the scabbard of the swordstick, ready to sweep the blade free and hurl it into the ghastly black form in the sanctuary. He felt the tremors begin anew in his arms and legs. His heart wanted to burst, still hammering furiously in the artificial silence of the night. Waves of a disgusting foetor assailed his nostrils and he screwed up his face to tighten them against it, to keep it out of his churning stomach.

Don't think, he told himself. Just do. Catch yourself off-guard and you might catch . . .

He swept the scabbard free and hurled the blade towards Black Shuck. The monstrous animal turned its jaws, the motion almost leisurely, and caught the swordstick side-on. The huge teeth bit down and the glittering length shattered, dropping in fragments to either side of the bite.

*I cannot deny your courage,* Shuck told the gaping Harker. *Nor can I deny your folly. You need a lesson, Andreas.*

Something stung his face, tearing a tiny scratch across his right cheek. He raised his hands to slap whatever it was away. A tiny shred of darkness swooped and bit again. Then another. A fourth. A fifth. Harker glanced briefly up before he closed his eyes to protect them. Black tatters swooped and wheeled against the stars, tiny creatures with bodies less than three inches long and miniature, pin-prick teeth. He clawed one away and it flopped from his grasp, membranous wings distorted. He ground the tiny pipistrelle underfoot as its companions continued their painful, irritating assault.

Shuck was right. It was a lesson. It had taught him that the creature could control any animal life-form it chose, not just domestic pets. And whilst he knew that the attacking bats couldn't kill him, the additional strain they were placing on his overtaxed heart could leave him dead in the ruins if Shuck didn't call them off. And soon.

His breath came in laboured gasps, sometimes vocalizing into a gasp or half-scream as a new bite was inflicted. His arms and hands flailed as he stumbled back away from the sanctuary. A calm began to descend, an anaesthetic calm which resigned him to the assault. The bats didn't matter any longer. Soon be sleeping now, he told himself as he dropped to his knees and they clustered like a funeral veil over his head and shoulders. Soon be out of this. For ever.

Black Shuck felt the thought. It ordered. The bats flapped back into the night, leaving the kneeling Harker oozing rivulets of blood from tiny punctures.

*Stand up*, Shuck commanded.

He staggered uneasily to his feet, dropping a hand to the tiles for initial support. His collar was torn and stained and his face glistened as if a red dew had formed upon his features. Slowly Harker opened his eyes, their defiance now dulled with pain and a greater, more consuming fear than he had ever felt before.

*Your lesson is not over, Andreas. Stand there and wait.*

The unearthly silence resumed about him, its intensity contrasting strongly with the deafening flutter of bat-wings moments earlier. He gazed at the grim shape in the ruined sanctuary, the demonic creature squatting where the crucifix should have been. The pile of faeces didn't matter now. They had become something else, something a thousand times worse.

Gradually the silence began to break up. At first Harker couldn't identify the tiny, distant sounds which were corrupting its intensity. Scuttering sounds. Running sounds. Panting sounds. Clacking teeth sounds. He began to realize that he was no longer alone with Black Shuck, that other things were around, outside the church. They rustled in the grasses and scraped their claws against the fallen tombstones. Footsteps, fleeing footsteps, crunched on the gravel path, their panicky irregularity bringing them nearer. Gasping breaths began to sound, the breaths of a creature run to earth, only to find the earth refusing sanctuary. Now, with its flight nearly ended, with the hunters pursuing, chasing, herding it where they wanted it to go, it crashed against the barrier outside the south door, then forced itself around it and lurched into the black shell of St Gargoyle's.

Eyes wide and white in the gloom, pupils dilated with horror, Joe Pasciewicz stared wildly about himself. He glanced at Harker and briefly stretched out a hand towards the academic. The nails were torn and the wrist was bloody with teeth-marks. Harker stared back, then looked past the Pole towards the altar. Joe turned, howling inhumanly as he saw Black Shuck. He pulled his eyes away from the monstrosity and turned back towards the south door.

Teeth and claws waited at the entrance to the church, blocking his escape. He wheeled towards the Devil's Door on the north side.

More teeth. More claws. All waiting just for him.

The vodka wasn't helping now. It took him precious seconds to think about the ruined windows. By then they too were guarded by his encircling pursuers. He reached out, as if for a succour that wouldn't come, then dropped his arms to his sides in a gesture of despair and stood in the centre of the littered aisle, chest heaving, keeping his back to the altar and its nightmare occupant.

He looked at Harker, whose bloody face made him as much of an apparition as anything else in the church. His mouth formed the simple question: 'Why . . .?'

*Judas knew what he had done*, Shuck's insidious voice answered. *He punished himself. You do not know, Joseph Pasciewicz. That is why we must punish you.*

Harker ventured a brief look at the altar. The thought of the white hair forensic had found flashed into his mind, battling its way past the dull fear which threatened to consume him utterly. Shuck wasn't white. There *had* been phantom white dogs, but ghosts didn't leave impressions or hairs behind them.

Judas had delivered Christ for torture and execution. Joseph Pasciewicz had done . . . what? Remember the name, Harker told himself. Just in case I somehow get out of here. Remember the name . . .

Better still, ask him. Now.

Harker tried to speak but the words wouldn't form. He gazed at Shuck, questioning mutely, and some token in the creature's expression acknowledged responsibility. The teeth and claws still guarded the doors and windows, but now others were filing into the church, ignoring Harker, forming a dense, vicious ring about the panic-stricken Joe. The Pole turned, surveying his hunters, his captors, still seeking vainly for some means of escape and finding none.

Joe's nerves, already shredded, finally snapped. Had the creatures been wild it would have been easier to understand. That they were obviously domestic pets, many wearing collars and discs, made it much more ghastly and unnatural. 'You want me?' he screeched. 'I here. I tear you apart, fuckin' animals. I see your bones. I drink your blood. I . . .'

There was more. It spewed out as a torrent of terrified defiance. It meant nothing to anyone. Not even to Joe Pasciewicz in the last few seconds of his life. The circle about him tightened, moving slowly inwards.

'No,' Harker called. 'Shuck, no! You can't . . .'

He started forwards. A large mongrel, probably an alsatian-labrador cross, smacked into his legs and knocked him over. He tried to rise but the dog straddled his chest and snarled its rank breath down into his face. He raised his hands but wicked jaws clamped onto his wrists, restraining them, forcing them down to his sides and holding them there. Other jaws clamped his ankles, forcing his legs apart, and a pressure and sharpness around his genitals threatened worse if he dared to move again.

*I can, Andreas Harker. You will not see from where you are, but you will hear. You will hear and know that it could be you,* Black Shuck threatened.

'I tear you open, you fuckers . . .' Joe howled.

The circle closed around his ankles and feet, snapping and tearing. Joe cried and screamed as they bit and ripped at his legs. He forced his feet apart for balance and bent to thump and gouge them away. Teeth snagged and chewed his hamstrings, fastened on his buttocks and genitals, rending, destroying. His balance faltered and he crashed heavily over and down, shattering the bones of one precious, defending wrist on the tiles as he fell. They started on his arms, biting at the muscles beneath his overall, staining its shredding fabric with his blood and their streaming saliva. Claws scrabbled at his stomach, finding a way through to flesh, rending his beer-gut in their efforts to expose the intestines beneath.

Joe Pasciewicz writhed and moaned and twitched and whimpered. His liberated blood spurted and spattered against his tormentors but he still lived. He still *knew*. They were saving his consciousness as long as they could, preserving his awareness, his pain and despair, until the ultimate moment of horror. A small mongrel, Mary, hooked her canines into one of his eyes and pulled. The ball tore free of its socket, shutting out half the stars, trailing and tearing the optic nerve as the worst pain he had ever known lanced through his skull. Mary's teeth met and bit and severed. The other eye refused to come away, going out where it was as the claws probed past it into the orbit, plunging Joe into terminal darkness.

The world was completely black, completely filled with pain and torment. Yet still Joe Pasciewicz survived, lived on. He screamed until they tore open his cheeks and snapped his tongue out. He snuffled and bubbled and coughed whilst the teeth took his nose away. He heard their bloody work until the rough tongues lapped at the remains of his ears and barked in unison, shattering his eardrums.

Of his five senses only the agony which was feeling now remained, sustained by whatever life was left to leak away. Blinded, disembowelled, deafened and silenced, save for the sounds he made trying to breathe, trying to unconsciously prolong his pain a little longer, Joe felt them withdraw. They had left his heart and lungs intact, offering no *coup de grâce*. They had been ordered from him by the same creature which had commanded the attack, the same creature which squatted on the altar and commanded the release of Andreas Harker as well.

Harker felt the release and sat upright, eyes glaring, sweeping the ranks of his persecutors. Then they saw Joe.

The Pole was wriggling from side to side, struggling to use those muscles which remained intact to sit up. He was one open, gushing wound, eyeless, almost featureless, drenched in his own blood. His intestines were strung out from his belly like Christmas decorations, pulsing and quivering as the exposed nerves struggled to communicate with his dying brain. His breath hissed and squelched and became staccato as gore from his head wounds rushed into his lungs, slowly drowning him. His legs convulsed. His arms flopped in useless gestures like a broken marionette.

Black Shuck slowly closed his terrible eyes. *Your lesson, Andreas*, he hissed. *Learn it well.*

Harker struggled to his feet, then dropped on to his knees and threw up. Vomit spattered the front of his clothing and the tiles and rubbish around him. Features white, mouth open and strings of spittle trailing to his chest, he began to crawl towards the flopping, wriggling shape that had once been human. Only as he reached it, as it fell back before he could cradle its shreds in his arms and offer a final attempt at comfort, did he realize that the animals and Shuck were gone from St Gargoyle's, that he was alone with the remains of Joseph Pasciewicz.

He sat beside the mutilated corpse, crooning softly to himself. Be strong, his instincts urged. Get up. Observe. Make the effort or you'll sink into insanity. You've seen bloody death on newsreels. That was as real as this. The only difference is that this wasn't so remote. You were here, helpless, as it happened. If you'd tried to interfere they'd have done this to you as well.

But would they?

The question, a challenge called from deep inside his brain, shook him partly free of the encroaching madness. Would they have served him the same way? He was being taught, not punished. Black Shuck wanted him alive. It had to, otherwise he'd be dead right now. So his brain hadn't figured that out at the time. It was hard to figure anything when there were teeth clamped around your penis, ready to bite if you moved. Self-preservation had taken the place of logic, and even that was logical.

He forced himself upright and took off his jacket, ready to drape it over Joe's mutilated head. Only as he was about to did his eyes, accustomed to the gloom, note the way the unfortunate Pole's intestines had been laid out. It could have been random. Had it been a simple animal attack he would have assumed that it was only random. But with Shuck there, directing the torture, taking in and controlling every detail, it had to be more than that.

They say that a grown man's intestines will run the length of a soccer pitch if they're untangled and laid out. So why should it be so strange that there's enough of them to form a five-pointed star, with two points in the ascendant, to either side of the remains of Joe Pasciewicz' head?

If there'd been anything left in his stomach of the Greek meal Harker would have brought it up right then. Instead he retched dryly until his guts began to calm, then dropped his jacket and lurched away.

Harker shambled out of the church, falling over the barrier and grazing his forehead. He laughed bitterly. What did another wound matter? Dried blood from the bat attack already streaked his face. Sweat and tears had carved rivulets through the bloodstains, leaving his features with the appearance of random warpaint. His being was beginning to numb with shock as he crunched unevenly down the gravel and stumbled at the litch-gate . . .

Into the arms of P C Forrest.

'You're a bit of a mess, sir,' the policeman understated.

Harker scowled and clutched the constable for support, his legs suddenly useless. 'You should see the other fellow,' he croaked in self-parody. 'Jesus God! A bit of a mess?'

'Come along, sir. I think you'd better tell me what's happened. There were some bloody funny noises coming out of there . . .'

Andreas Harker began to shake again. 'Put me down,' he ordered. 'Get Wilson.'

'Wilson? You mean Detective Chief Inspector Wilson?'

'Harker forced a nod, then wished he hadn't as his stomach contracted again. 'That's the one. Ben Wilson, Get him here, constable.'

'Right now!'


Sally French heard the bells. They were loud and insistent and couldn't possibly belong to that boy on the push-bike. She stretched out a hand towards them and the boy and bike vanished together. Instead she felt flesh. Solid flesh.

She opened her eyes and saw the broad expanse of back above the bedclothes. It was solid, snoring, and definitely not a dream. And it wasn't Jake Lewis either. She tried to search her memory, but the bells were still getting in the way of anything approaching rational thought.

Rongg rongg. Pause. Rongg rongg. Pause. Rongg . . .

She reached over the sleeping back and picked up the telephone. She scowled at its invading presence before she said: 'Hello?'

'Hello,' a voice answered. 'Is D C I Wilson there?'

Sally looked at the back again, lowering the receiver as she did so. The name and the back seemed to go together, despite the lingering effects of getting on for three bottles of Chianti between them. She remembered something else and prodded the flesh. It grunted.

'Phone, Ben,' she urged. 'Phone. It's for you.'

He surfaced and peered at her. She handed him the receiver as he blew her a kiss. She blew one back as he began: 'Wilson. What the hell time is it, anyway?'

The question was for Sally, but another voice answered him.


Harker shuddered and pulled the blanket tighter about himself. The night was colder than it should have been, colder and grimmer than any June night he could ever remember.

St Katherine's Square was in more chaos than Wilson could

remember, except for the night of the fire. The policeman was feeling gruff and surly, displaying less sympathy than he would have done if he'd not been pulled out of a warm woman's bed. Especially for that nutter Harker, no matter what he'd found.

They'd kept the remains as Harker had left them, as PC Forrest had first seen them, as much for forensic and the photographer as for Wilson. Now the ambulance was here, blue lights flashing, together with similar lights from two patrol cars and the magnetic flasher on Wilson's own unmarked vehicle. In addition there was a plain van which belonged to the forensic team, the photographer's car and Harry Chester's as well. All lighting up the square. All parked haphazardly outside the ruined church.

Ben Wilson plodded back down the gravel path, now better used than it had been for years, towards the litch-gate. 'Stay close, Harry,' he'd instructed Chester, 'but stay out of it. I'll do this one to one.'

Harker was perched on one of the decaying seats which flanked the gateway, his teeth chattering and an unnatural shaking consuming his frame. Wilson sat down beside him, his thoughts whirling from Sally to corpses to Harker and back again.

'You want to tell me about it?' he growled.

Andreas Harker shook his head grimly. 'I don't want to tell anyone about it. There are things that nobody should have to relive. But I suppose I'll have to, sooner or later.'

'Too bloody true. Suppose you start by telling me what you're doing back here, Professor?'

The academic forced a shrug. The deliberate movement helped to calm him. Like a drunk who finds things to do to stop the world from spinning, he was glad of the opportunity to move. He'd been shot with a sedative, though he'd flatly refused to be taken to hospital as a shock patient.

'What's that supposed to mean?'

Harker sighed. 'I came back to watch, Mr Wilson. I wanted to keep a vigil and try to see what was shaping that pile of faeces on the altar.'

'And you saw?'

He shook his head. 'Not that. What I saw was worse than that.'

Wilson growled softly. 'Do I need a can-opener to get it out of you?' he demanded.

'You shouldn't. Unless you think I'm drunk and I imagined the whole thing.'

'We found a flask of brandy on you.'

'And how much of it had been drunk?' Harker challenged. 'If you'll stop behaving like some God-awful stage copper I'll tell you about it.'

Wilson thought back to Sally French. And Leader.

He'd hauled himself out of her bed and, despite her protests, forced his wearied and reluctant body into his clothes. She'd kissed him goodbye, Leader in the background, he remembered. The light had been uncertain, but he thought he remembered the Newfoundland as being more grey than the white beast he'd originally encountered that evening. Okay, the dog was his problem. So was having to leave Sally French. From the sheer look of him Harker had really been through something in St Gargoyle's, and it wasn't altogether fair to heap his own problems onto the academic.

Ben Wilson began to relax. He still had to play the copper, though.

'We found an old revolver in there as well,' he stated more gently. 'Yours, Professor?'

'Next you'll say I shot the poor devil before mutilating him with a set of false teeth,' Harker scowled.

'I'm not quite that stupid. You ready to tell me now?'

Harker sighed. 'I returned to the church before sunset,' he began. 'I wanted to watch and see if I could find your white dog for you. Sometime after midnight . . .' he paused. Sometime after midnight by the clock, he remembered. But Joe Pasciewicz must have died as close to true midnight as made no odds. 'Ask your constable what time he found me,' he instructed.

Wilson shook his head. 'Don't need to. He's told me already. One twelve is what he's logged. What makes you ask?'

'I think I'm beginning to understand this at last.'

'Good for you. Feel like sharing?'

'Not if you still have the same attitude you had last time we met.'

Wilson took a deep breath. 'Look, Professor,' he said with an effort at restraint, 'last time no-one had been killed. Now I've got something in there that looks like a trial-run by an apprentice Jack-the-Ripper. Christ, I never knew there was so much pipework in a man's stomach until I saw . . . that. Do you know who he was?'

'Shuck spoke his name . . .'

'Shuck? Black Shuck?'

'That's right!' Harker snarled, ready for the policeman's disbelief. 'Black Shuck. It was in there. It ordered that man's death. It compared him to Judas before its minions tore the poor bastard open. Do you know how long Joseph Pasciewicz took to die, Wilson? I don't. They held me down. I only managed to see towards the end and I wished I hadn't then. But I'd guess he was two or three minutes being slaughtered. Count that out, Wilson. Go on, count it out. Count to a hundred and twenty. Now think of pain going on that long. Pain and the knowledge that you're dying slowly, that there's never going to be anything better for you ever again. He was conscious, Wilson. He was conscious and struggling to the end . . .'

He buried his head in his hands and began to sob. Wilson laid an arm around his shoulders and ran his free hand over his own face. 'Joseph Pasciewicz?' he asked gently.

Harker nodded. 'That was the name. Did you know him?'

'Don't think so. We can easily find out, though.' He shot a glance to Harry Chester, who nodded and moved towards the radio in one of the patrol cars. 'So, after they'd finished with him they started on you?' Wilson resumed.

'Not at all. Shuck wanted me to know what they *could* do. He was teaching me some kind of lesson. For some reason he's let me live.'

Ben Wilson struggled to swallow his unbelief for a few minutes. 'So what happened to your face?' he asked.

'Bats.'

'Bats?'

'Bats. Tiny bats. Probably common pipistrelles. Shuck used them to break my defiance. Hundreds of them. More than you'll find in the old tower, anyway. It was his way of telling me that he doesn't just control domestic pets. He controls all animal life, any time he wants to . . .'

He broke off, his mind still struggling to comprehend, to make order out of the chaos of his thoughts. *Any* time? If that was true the monster would have made its move before this. The attack on Wilson and Chester had taken place at dusk. Joe's death had been true midnight. Both after the sun had gone down. Both with the moon waning.

He clutched Wilson's arm. 'Not any time,' he hissed. 'There are rules he has to obey. All we have to do is learn them and we have a chance.'

Harker was beginning to pull himself back together. He knew he would never be the same again, not after that glimpse of unmitigated evil he'd had in the nighted ruins of St Gargoyle's, but he was a long way from being the broken and chastened man Shuck wanted him to be. He struggled to his feet and turned back towards the church.

Wilson stood up and caught his arm. 'And where do you think you're going?' he demanded.

Harker faced him. 'Back in there, Mr Policeman. There are things I have to see for myself.'

'Oh come on, Professor. You've had enough for one night. Besides, you're due for rabies shots at the very least . . .'

Wilson wasn't prepared for the academic's next move. He'd imagined Harker would be persuaded and sit down again. Instead he shook off the policeman's restraining arm and rounded on him, his grotesquely blood-painted features set in determined lines.

'Listen to me, Wilson. You may not want my help. You may even regard me as an interfering nuisance who thinks he can get a folklore paper out of this silly jaunt. Maybe even a book. No, you probably don't want my help. But you need it for all that. And I'll tell you why.

'You're used to thinking in certain ways. You assemble data and interpret it according to set rules. So do I. In that respect we're much alike. The difference, however, is that I have the capacity to deal with the aspects you dismiss as unreal and irrelevant. If you found an ice-cube in the middle of the Sahara you'd conclude it had melted down from an iceberg deposited there some time before. You'd wonder how the iceberg got there, but that would be the logical origin. I, however, could postulate at least three other explanations. And two of them could be correct *at the same time*. The closest you ever come to parallel causality is finding two motives for one crime. Not that I'm saying such is the case here, because it isn't. You are dealing with data you can't interpret, though. It's there. It has to be there. But you won't know what to look for. I just might. And that's why I'm going back to that church, right now.'

He stalked unsteadily up the gravel path, still wrapped in the blanket like a caped Bela Lugosi. For a moment Wilson hesitated, still reeling from Harker's verbal assault, then followed him.

St Gargoyle's was ablaze with hurriedly installed lighting, most of it directed at Joe's mutilated remains and the work going on about them. A grim-faced police doctor was performing an autopsy *in situ*, his plastic-gloved hands stained with the victim's congealing blood. An assistant held a tape-recorder to catch the surgeon's monologue.

'. . . severance and almost complete removal of duodenum, jejunum and ilium, all showing lateral and transverse lacerations. Mesentery severed. Ascending colon severed at the ileum. Hepatic flexure lacerated and distended . . .'

'What did the severing?' Wilson asked.

The doctor broke off and glared at him. 'Can't you wait until I've finished?' he demanded.

'Not this time. What did it, doctor?'

The surgeon sighed and sat back on his haunches. 'I can only give you a rough guess at this time, Wilson. Without the benefit of a laboratory examination I'd say animal teeth, or claws. Or both.'

The policeman looked across at Harker, who was staring down at the grisly work with an almost feverish intensity. 'Tell me, have you moved any of the exposed intestines?' he inquired.

'Only the loop that was here. I had to displace that to get near the corpse. There will be photographs of the original placement, though.'

Harker nodded and turned to Wilson. 'Imagine that loop in place, bent into a rough point at the curve like those others are,' he instructed. 'The body lay at the centre of a pentagram composed of its own abdominal viscera. Points there, there, there and either side of the head. An inverted pentagram. The kind that's called the Devil's footprint. Now, doctor, could such an arrangement have occurred naturally?'

The surgeon shook his head. 'The components were bitten and shaped deliberately, I'd say. Look here at the way the hepatic flexure has been cut to permit manipulation.'

The professor nodded grimly. 'Thank you,' he said. 'I apologize for the interruption.' Then, to Wilson: 'This way now, my friend. I think we should take a look over here.'

His legs didn't want to respond as he forced his steps towards the sanctuary. The altar was in semi-darkness, most of the available light being concentrated around the autopsy. Wilson hung back long enough to take a torch from one of the constables, then followed the professor.

The first thing which struck them was the apparent absence of the pile of faeces from the altar. Only as they approached did they discover it was still there, though radically altered in shape and texture.

Wilson's torch wavered across the surface of the holy table, finally focusing on the flattened white mass at the centre. Harker stepped forward and raised a fragment between thumb and forefinger. As he applied gentle pressure it turned to powder and floated back down towards the stonework.

The policeman looked puzzled. 'It looks as if it's been sun-dried and flattened. I've seen old dog-shit look that white after it's been out in the sun a few days. It's like a heap of ashes.'

'That's exactly what it is. This is where I saw Black Shuck.'

'Well, so much for your idea about it being shaped into an idol. Your ghost dog's flattened that one for you.'

Harker glared at him. 'Your humour is misplaced, Mr Wilson. I may well have been wrong about that. But you tell me how faeces that were still moist this morning have been reduced to ashes in so short a time. I examined the pile this evening, before sunset. It showed no signs of drying out or sun-bleaching. Why don't you tell me how this could happen after dark. Or did I take them home, pop them in the oven, and bring them back to confuse you? After I'd bitten Joseph Pasciewicz to death, that is?'

Wilson bridled under the sarcasm. 'Suppose you tell me?' he responded. 'After all, I'm only the plodding copper in all this. You're the expert, you tell me.'

The professor nodded wearily. 'You're right. I shouldn't have snapped at you. Now, can we call a truce for our mutual benefit?'

Wilson's set features slowly relaxed into a half-smile. 'What the hell,' he muttered. 'You're my best shot so far. Not to mention being an eye-witness. Okay, Professor. Let's take it as it comes. Any ideas?'

'One. I'll need to research it, though. And if I'm right this time, friend Wilson, we'll have learned another of the rules.'

The policeman raised a quizzical eyebrow. 'I'll take your word for that. Seen all you want to?'

'No, but I think I've reached my limit for tonight.'

'Come on, then. I'll have one of my men drive you down to casualty for those rabies shots, then back to the station. I want you to wait for me there. Apart from anything else we'll need a statement from you. And for Christ's sake don't talk to the press. Not until we can figure out something that'll make sense to them.'

'Is there anyone you can let me have to help me?' the professor asked.

'Yeah. I've got a WPC called Kate Jones. She's good. But what the hell can you do at this time of night?'

'A little figuring out, perhaps.'

Wilson escorted Harker back through the church and down to the litch-gate. Despite the sirens and lights in the middle of the night not a light burned or a curtain twitched in any of the houses around St Katherine's Square.

Except one.

Salvation.


The night didn't get any shorter. Ben Wilson took Harker's statement himself, carefully saying nothing, struggling in places not to raise a disbelieving eyebrow. The remains of the swordstick had been found as well as the revolver and both men were silently aware of the number of charges that could be brought against the professor, if Wilson chose.

Despite his misgivings the policeman decided to do nothing. For all his eccentricities Harker was the only chance he had of working out what was happening in Uptown, and now that he had a full-scale murder investigation on his hands Wilson was beginning to realize just how much he needed that chance.

'I can't let you keep it, of course,' he told the academic. 'It would be in clear breach of the Firearms Act 1968.'

Harker grinned ruefully. 'For the amount of use it was I might just as well not have had it in the first place.'

'Yeah. Now that's something I don't understand at all. You say your bullet went straight through the creature, and sure enough we found it in the mullion, where you said it hit. Yet a few minutes later the thing can firm up enough to bite tempered steel in half. If that sounds okay to you I'd like to hear why.'

'It's going to depend on the results of a little research. Did you manage to find me that WPC?'

'Not yet. She's not due on 'til six and I'd rather leave her be until then. You said you had some figuring out to do?'

'If I can keep awake.'

'You might do better to get some sleep. I've arranged a cell you can borrow for the night.'

'Police hospitality? How delightful. No, I have to think this through and make my notes before I go to sleep. I can't risk losing anything if I leave it. Which reminds me. Did you find out about Pasciewicz?'

'No record. There were charges pending for cruelty to animals, though. Nothing serious.'

Harker laughed bitterly. 'Don't you find a certain irony in that?' he asked. 'The man's cruel to animals and he dies because animals are cruel to him. Can you get me details?'

'I'll get you the number for the RSPCA Inspector who brought the charges. He should be able to tell you anything you want to know. Right now, though, I'm going to grab a few hours' sleep. I'll see you in the morning. Use this interview room for as long as you want, Professor.'

'Another half an hour should see me through.'

'Okay. Good night, then.'

'Good night. And Wilson?'

'Hm?'

'Thanks. For the gun, I mean.'

Wilson winked. 'Let's say you owe me one. I'll have a word with Firearms and see if I can swing a temporary permit for you, dated today only. That should do the job.' He yawned. 'See you, Professor.'

Harker found himself alone in the yellow glare of the interview room. Its walls were plain and the only furniture consisted of a stout wooden table and three canvas-seated tubular metal chairs. He reached for a sheet of the paper Wilson had left him and began jotting random notes, setting down his impressions before they faded. Having finished with the facts that hadn't been incorporated into his statement he next listed a series of questions. Time and again he came back to the faeces on the altar. Somehow it held the key to both the secrets of Black Shuck's manifestation and purpose.

'How could I have made that mistake about the idol?' he asked himself softly but firmly. 'Point one, someone put it there. Point two, an animal, most probably a large white dog, had begun to shape it. Or at least have contact with it. Point three, Shuck manifested on it. Out of it? *Through* it?'

The Greeks used blood to give substance to phantoms in their magical rites. Blood was the staple physical symbol of the life-force. Not excrement. Excrement was spent life. Forgotten. Expelled. Useless.

Yet Shuck's presence had changed it.

Let's check the progression, he thought. Faeces placed on altar. Dog has physical contact with them. Shuck manifests on them. They change.

Andreas Harker shook his head. Whatever was there wasn't going to show up this side of sleep. He tidied his notes and, taking them with him, stood up and opened the door to the interview room. Outside a constable was waiting.

'I believe you have a cell ready for me?' the professor asked him.

# SHUCK

Granpa Hangel peered down into the square. The ambulance, which had waited there for more than an hour, had been loaded with its grisly burden and was driving away. Soon much of the police presence would follow, though one or two would remain behind at the scene of the crime.

For Pieter Hangel, though, it would not have appeared as a criminal act. It was simply obedience to the dictates of the *other*. He'd seen such blind, unfeeling obedience before, in the camp. He knew its power only too well, and had vowed all those years ago never to become a part of such a dreadful obsession. Yet the change, when it had come, had been as subtle within him as it had been within the rest of the *other*'s servants. You could only fight what you knew about, and Pieter Hangel simply didn't know.

Neither did Marge Blunson. She merely accepted that when Mary had to go out it was to do the *other*'s work. And no outsider could ever be told about that.

Pieter Hangel closed the curtains and went back to bed. It wasn't going to be long now. Nobody had told him that, but he felt it, knew it without the need for anyone to say anything. This was to be a new beginning for man and animal together, a time of newness, a second chance.

Perhaps even some kind of second coming?

He shook his head and pulled the covers close up around himself, suddenly cold. He wondered who the stranger was he'd glimpsed earlier that night, seeking the north way to the old church. Probably that was the body they'd taken away in the ambulance. Well, he'd done his work for the night. He'd been doing it when he'd seen the stranger and waved the family he was with back into their house in case they were noticed.

Their house? That was almost amusing. Nothing in Uptown seemed to belong to anyone any more. The church was dead. The houses were dying. The shops hid and waited for the demolition teams behind their shutters. Only in his great cathedral was there hope and life still to be found.

Even Salvation was doomed, he reflected as he drifted back towards sleep. His son-in-law had found another suitable property and funds were being arranged for its purchase. The work would go on. The animals would be helped and succoured. They'd have more help in the future, though. Less need of places like Salvation.

Yes, that would vanish as well. Everything would be engulfed by those enormous eyes that watched him from the foot of the bed as he plunged back into dreaming.


After Ben Wilson's precipitate departure Sally didn't sleep particularly well. The dreams she recalled in the morning had mostly been a progressive nightmare, with screeching creatures she couldn't identify chasing her along a maze of cobbled streets and alleyways.

She surfaced about half five, her body wet with a chill perspiration. Dawn had already broken outside and the birds were singing their morning chorus. Sunlight filtered readily through the curtains to touch a corner of her bedroom and all her fears were a thousand miles away, on the other side of the darkness.

Sally yawned and stretched before fumbling her way naked towards the kitchen. The first few days she'd been shy of Leader seeing her without clothes, though in this sort of weather she never normally bothered with a nightdress or gown. Now she'd become less coy, reasoning that she always saw him naked, so why did she have to preserve her modesty from her pet?

On the way she glanced into the darkened living room. Leader was curled up in his basket, a grey shape in the half-light. He opened his eyes and raised his head as she looked in, then flicked his tail and returned to sleep.

'Morning big boy,' she whispered.

Sally heaped instant coffee into a cup whilst the kettle boiled, wondering vaguely why she should be feeling rough. Only when she swallowed her first hot mouthful did she remember her visitor of the night before. She smiled to herself. He'd been okay whilst he'd been there. And she'd been damn good. Tried hard.

'You'll be back, Ben Wilson,' she whispered to herself. 'Oh yes. You'll be back.'

She carried her coffee through to the living room and drew back the curtains. She was far enough from the main road for any casual passer-by at that time not to see she wasn't dressed. Next step, once she'd begun to put her head back together, was to feed Leader.

Sally looked down at the sleeping animal, now bathed in the early daylight. And gasped.

She blinked hard enough to set spots before her eyes, just to make certain she wasn't seeing things, or was somehow still asleep and dreaming. The reality, however, persisted.

He was grey.

She bent down to look closer. He lifted his head and licked the nearest hand. Yes, it was Leader all right. His features hadn't changed. But his white coat was shot through with jet black hairs.

Sally thought for a moment. There'd been a few dark hairs the night before. But now there were masses of them. Enough to have created a positive change.

'C'mon boy,' she urged him. 'Stand up. Up, Leader. Let me have a look at you.'

He obeyed, his amber eyes glittering large.

Were those eyes a little lighter? Probably a result of his coat darkening, Sally decided. But why should that have happened?

She probed his fur to make certain. The dark hairs were everywhere, even on his feet. And his claws seemed a little longer as well.

It was Friday. She'd had Leader exactly a week. Well, the

185

shopping could go hang this afternoon. So could lunch. First thing after work she was going to Salvation to talk to Tom Greaves. Maybe he'd know why this change was taking place. He ought to. After all, he was a vet.

Sally showered and dressed and took Leader for his morning run in the park. The stick was where she'd left it the night before and she threw it harder and further than she'd thrown it before, trying to puzzle out the change in her mind. It didn't worry her that she'd taken on a white dog and now seemed .to have a grey one. He was still the same animal underneath. But the change itself was worrying. It could be something she was doing wrong. Or his health. He might be sick.

Leader chased the stick dutifully. He caught occasional glimpses of himself as he ran and knew that he was not the same as he had been. Good, he thought. It's beginning to happen. The change is coming.

Just like the *other* said it would.


Part of Andreas Harker was surprised that the humans weren't wearing ceremonial robes. Somehow he felt they should have been. That would make them more like the horror-film witches they undoubtedly were.

Black Shuck squatted, huge and demonic, on the ruined altar. His worshippers, both human and animal, had ceased their unholy capering about him and settled to a grim contemplation of their helpless captive. Harker sat on one of the fire-stained pews, ringed by slavering teeth and clacking, scraping claws, the full power of Shuck's baleful gaze turned upon him. Above and without the night was so dark it was almost luminous in its intensity.

'You have defied me once too often,' Shuck told him. 'I have been lenient with you, Andreas, and you have failed me because of my kindness to you. I sought to teach you before. This time, Andreas, I am going to punish you.'

He watched, both terrified and fascinated, as Black Shuck

excreted upon the holy table. One of the human worshippers, an old man with a tattoo on one of his bare forearms, reached for the excrement and began to fashion it into a rough human figure. A cat detached itself from the circle about the altar and advanced towards the helpless Harker. Its claws flashed out, drawing blood from his cheek. He gasped.

The cat returned to the altar and the old man bent down to permit it to dab the blood on its claw onto the image. The magical link was forged. The image of excrement had become Andreas Harker, and Harker had become the image. They were one, separated only by distance. And that distance needn't have been there at all.

The circle parted. Sufficiently for the old man to lay the image on the sanctuary steps. Harker felt the dread building inside himself, the dread of one who faces certain death and knows that there is no escape.

For a few moments silence reigned supreme. Then the howling, the barking and mewing and screeching, began. The worshippers surged towards the shaped excrement, claws and nails tearing. Harker felt his flesh begin to part as they reached the image. His liberated intestines spattered out in a star-shape about him. Sight and hearing and the rank smell of his own panic faded one by one. Teeth sank into his flesh. As talons ripped for his tongue he voiced one last desperate, pain-filled scream . . .

. . . And sat up.

Hands were on his shoulders, hands that caressed his face gently as he began to sob. 'Shhh,' an unfamilar voice soothed. 'It's all right. It's all right, Professor. You're safe.'

He struggled to peer through his tears. The face he saw was a woman's, with large blue eyes and slightly buck-teeth. It was pretty and worldly, slightly lined with the weight of knowledge beyond its years and yet desirably smooth and fleshy. The mousy hair was close-cropped, almost in a National Service short-back-and-sides, though the front was worn long in a fringe.

Harker wiped his eyes and flopped back onto the pillow,

gasping. The voice, gentle but, he felt, strong when it had to be, said: 'Drink this.'

He felt like something out of *Alice in Wonderland*. As his eyes cleared he focused on a white china mug. With an effort he raised himself obediently on his elbows and took a swig of hot sweet tea.

He grimaced. 'Couldn't you at least have managed cocoa?' he asked. 'Do you know how long it's been since I had to wake up to that stuff? Who are you, anyway?'

'My name's Kate Jones,' came the answer.

He thought for a moment, then swung his legs over the edge of the bed and nodded. It was coming back. He was in a cell at Monkhampton nick.

'Pen and paper,' he ordered.

She found his notes and offered them to him, blank side up. She took a pen from her tunic pocket and handed him that. He scribbled desperately whilst she stood watching, the mug of tea still clutched in one hand.

He finished and looked up at her. 'Good,' he smiled. 'That's going to be very useful. It's amazing how the subconscious can sort things out, don't you think?'

'I wouldn't know,' came the reply.

Harker sighed. 'No, I don't suppose you would, Constable Jones. God,' he reflected, 'that's a mouthful. Can I call you Kate?'

'Please do.'

'Right then, Kate. What time is it?'

'A little after ten. Mr Wilson sent me to wake you.'

'Did he now? Right. Give me five minutes in the loo and I'm all his. And Kate?'

'Professor?'

'Find me a cup of chocolate from one of your infernal machines, can you?'

She peered at him intently. Chocolate? At this time of day? She sighed. 'If that's what you want,' she answered.

'And find me a bloody razor as well.'

His opinion of Kate Jones began to come close to Ben

Wilson's own. She tapped at the door of the Gents about three minutes after he'd entered and handed him a disposable razor. He shaved, with ordinary soap, then completed his ablutions. As he emerged Kate handed him a cup of machine chocolate. He sipped it, sighed contentedly, then said: 'Lead on, m'dear. Let's get moving.'

She led him through the maze of corridors to Wilson's office and knocked on the glass before opening the door. Once they had settled themselves Wilson began: 'I'm getting pressure from upstairs, Professor. I need everything you can give me. Any advance on last night?'

'One, I think,' Harker beamed. 'I think I know what that pile of faeces really was.'

'Is it going to help us to know that?'

'The more we understand, the more chance we have of finding a way to stop this happening again. Yes, it is going to help us. I mentioned last night that there were rules, laws if you like, governing what could and couldn't happen. Now, with the help of this young lady,' he gestured to Kate Jones, 'who is going to make a series of phone calls for me, I can do a reasonable job of constructing those rules. Once we have them we have answers, and something else as well. We have weapons . . .'

Harry Chester rapped sharply on the door and looked in. 'Sorry guv,' he muttered. 'Chief Super's just rung down for you. Now, I'm afraid.'

Wilson nodded resignedly and stood up behind his desk. 'Go to,' he told Harker. 'The phone's right there. I'll hear the rest when I get back.'

He left them to it. Kate Jones produced a pad and pencil.

'Good,' the professor muttered. 'Now firstly I want you to call George Teacherman at Cambridge. The number's 0223 774991 and he's on extension 327. Ask him to list all dated Shuck sightings from the Willington-Cartier index. Now, when you have that list I think you ought to talk to Dr Bill Somers at the Royal Astronomical Society. I want the dates fed into his computer for a lunar phase check. He'll know what I mean. Next you're to find the nearest library with a specialist occult section . . .'

'That'll be the Fallenberg at Waventree,' Kate told him.

'Good. Get copies of Bardon's *Der Weg Zum Wahren Adepten*, Regardie's *Golden Dawn*, volume four, *The Golden Bough*, and here the abridged version will do, and anything they can recommend on the subjects of image magic and the magical link.'

Kate looked up, pencil poised. 'Sorry, what are they?'

'You don't have to know just yet. The people at the Fallenberg should understand and sort out what I want.'


Wilson's interview with Chief Superintendent Enoch was one of the most uncomfortable of his carreer to date. Enoch had a reputation for being a hard-headed stickler who played by the rules, did no favours, made no deals and expected everybody else to do the same. Even if it meant not getting the job done.

He was sitting behind his desk, the snub nose and bald pate looking out of place with his wedge-shaped face, as his secretary showed Ben Wilson in. He shuffled papers, reading a paragraph here and there, and continued to do so for nearly three minutes after he'd gestured for his subordinate to sit. Finally he tidied them into a neat pile on his blotter and sat back, hands clasped over his paunch.

'Good of you to come and see me, Weston,' he said, unsmiling.

'I'm Wilson, sir,' came the reply. You know bloody well I'm Wilson. It's just one of your tricks to fuck me up, bastard.

'Yes. Of course.' No apology. 'Now, Wilson, I've been looking over the reports of last night's business in Uptown. I see there was a firearm involved.'

'Not in the actual killing, sir.'

'That's by the way. You have this Harker fellow in custody?'

'No, sir.'

'I beg your pardon? Did you say no just then?'

'That is correct, sir. I said no, Harker is not in custody.'

Enoch's expression didn't change. 'A gun-toting mad professor, covered in blood, runs from the scene of a particularly foul and brutal murder into the arms of a policeman, and he's not in custody. Would you mind telling me why that is?'

'Because he didn't do it, Superintendent Enoch.'

'*Chief* Superintendent Enoch, Wilson.'

'Yes. Of course.' Chew on that you interfering bastard.

'How do you know he didn't do it? Were you there?'

'You know from my report I wasn't there, sir. I say he didn't do it on the basis of the forensic evidence. Point one, there was none of the victim's blood on Harker or any of his clothing, with the exception of the lining of his jacket. I doubt very much that anyone, no matter how mad we might think him, is going to try and disembowel a grown man whilst wearing their jacket inside out. Point two, the autopsy showed that the victim, Pasciewicz, was killed by animal teeth and claws. Harker had nothing about him, nor was there anything in the environs of the crime he might have attempted to dispose of, which corresponded to the murder weapon or weapons.'

'What about the swordstick? That could have done it.'

'No, sir. The nature of the wounds would have been totally different.' Why am I having to tell you all this? How the hell did you get to your present rank if you're as thick as you're making out you are?

'Even so, the man's obviously mad and dangerous. Phantom dogs that bullets from illegal weapons pass straight through? Quite preposterous. Arrest him and charge him for the revolver, Wilson.'

'I can't do that, sir.'

'Guns belong in cowboy films, not in the hands of Cambridge dons. You have a charge. I've just given it to you. I want this man in custody, if only so that the PR people can keep the press happy.'

So that's what this is about. You want a quick arrest. A man is in custody and fuck whether it's the right man or not.

'There's nothing that I could detain him on, *Chief* Superintendent.'

'Illegal possession and use of firearms is quite sufficient. Don't prevaricate with me, Wilson.'

'He had a temporary permit for use and possession,' came the reply. 'The permit's on my desk right now. As for ownership, the weapon's an antique and doesn't require an FAC under the '68 Act. So you see, sir, I can't hold him on that. And I certainly couldn't arrest him for killing Pasciewicz unless you ordered me to. And I'd require that order in writing so that I was covered when the suit for false arrest came up.'

Enoch's face was growing redder as he listened. His brows lowered. Wilson half-expected to see steam coming out of his ears at any minute. 'If he's not in custody, might I inquire what he's doing here? I believe you found him a cell to sleep in?'

'To use a good old line, sir, he's assisting with our inquiries. Will that help PR to fend off the press? They don't have to say that he's an advisor rather than a suspect, do they?'

'He's helping you? This . . . mad professor's helping you?'

'That's right. Look, sir, when I joined the strength here you told me I was a fine young officer with a reputation for getting results. I do get results, but I get them my way. Professor Harker is part of my way on this one. His theories are outlandish, I admit. But they're better than anything we've got at present. If you won't let me use him then you'll have to give the case to someone else. Jameson, maybe. Or Trench.'

Enoch was silent for a moment, his eyes narrowed across the desk. 'Wilson?' he asked at length.

'Sir?'

'Get out of my office. Do what you have to. I want a result on this one and I want it fast.'

Ben Wilson stood up. 'We all do, Mr Enoch,' he replied. Then he left the office and started walking back to his own, taking several deep breaths along the way.

*

Before Kate Jones could get started with the phone, Andreas Harker rang Terry Morris at the RSPCA. For once the inspector was actually at his desk, and he gave the professor chapter and verse on the case of Joseph Pasciewicz and a white Newfoundland dog called Leader.

While he was talking, Kate used an outside extension to get through to the Fallenberg Memorial Library and check on the availability of the books Harker had asked for. The German title seemed to perplex the librarian briefly, but he came back with an English translation. And yes, he did have Franz Bardon's *Initiation Into Hermetics*.

It was now almost eleven and Kate made arrangements to pick the books up later in the day. She didn't specify a time, realizing that the other calls she had to make would keep her tied up by the telephone for quite some time. Briefly she wondered about getting George Teacherman to phone the required data straight through to the Royal Astronomical Society, then realized that if she passed it through herself at least she'd know it had been done and be able to chase it up if necessary.

Harker finished with Morris and headed for the canteen to get something approaching breakfast. He was out of the office, and Kate Jones back in it, when Ben Wilson returned from his interview with Chief Superintendent Enoch.

Wilson sat down in one of the visitors' chairs and motioned Kate to continue her call to Cambridg . He listened as she gave the professor's instructions and watched her replace the receiver. She moved to stand up but he motioned her to stay where she was.

'Trouble, sir?' she asked him.

Wilson grinned and shook his head. 'Not now,' he told her. 'Would you believe, Enoch wanted me to arrest our loony prof for anything we could think of, just so's he could tell the press we had a man in custody in connection with last night?'

Kate's face became serious. 'He's in the canteen at present. Are you going to?'

'No way. We need that mad bugger, Kate. He's the only

193

thing that makes any kind of sense in this whole unholy mess. I know that's not saying much, but he's all I've got, and he'll be no bloody help locked up. I changed old Enoch's mind for him, somehow.' Then: 'How're the calls going?'

'I've lined up his books and spoken to this guy Teacherman. Now I have to wait for his information and phone it through to the RAS.'

'Good. When Harker gets back we'll ask him what he was trying to say earlier about that sh . . . dung-heap in the church. Not that I expect to understand his answer.'

He humped forward, leaning his elbows on his knees. 'Look here, Kate,' he ventured. 'You've read his statement and I've given you a background quickie on his theories. Is he making any sense to you at all?'

WPC Jones shrugged. 'If Pasciewicz *was* killed by animals, and the autopsy certainly confirmed that, how do we find them? We can't just walk into Uptown and confiscate every pet in the district. We'd have the press, those loonies at ALF, the RSPCA and God knows who else down on us. So *if* our Professor Harker is only half-way right we've a hell of a problem, sir. If he's all-the-way right, then at least we may find out how to stop it happening again. Maybe.'

'Strikes me *maybe* is the best we've got,' Wilson responded.

The phone rang. Kate Jones initially deferred to her guv'nor, who waved for her to answer it. She picked it up, identified herself, then listened for a moment with her pen poised before beginning to take down a list of dates.

'That was Doctor Teacherman,' she told Wilson. 'I'd better call Doctor Somers now, if that's all right.'

'Be my guest.'

He listened whilst she made the call, then stood up and leaned across his desk to pick up his diary. He flipped over the pages whilst she finished talking to the Royal Astronomical Society. As she put the phone down he snapped it shut.

'That's the biggie,' he told her. 'Depending on what this guy Somers has to say, we've got a timetable. And if Harker's right it's a bloody short one.'

'Sir?'

'Let's get the answer first. If I'm wrong I don't want to cloud your mind with my false suppositions. Did you hear what he got out of Terry Morris?'

'No, sir, I was out of the office at the time.'

They both looked up as the door opened and Andreas Harker re-entered the office. The professor sat down in the unoccupied chair and nodded, to them.

'Have a good time with your boss?' he asked Wilson.

'Nothing special. You were going to tell us about the pile on the altar, as I recall.'

Harker grinned. 'Not until I have those books,' he replied. 'I want something in print I can show you so that you don't simply think it's something I've dreamed up on my own.'

'Now would I?' Wilson smiled.

'It wouldn't be the first time. I had an interesting conversation with that R S P C A man, though.'

'Well?'

'Well, how would it be if I told you that Joseph Pasciewicz had maltreated a large white dog?'

'The next best thing to Christmas, right now. *Is* that what you're telling me?'

'That's what I'm telling you. Pasciewicz and his partner run a motor repair workshop in Uptown, though neither of them live in that district. Now, some time back Pasciewicz' wife left him. She had a dog, and it seems that the late Joseph took his spite out on the poor beast after his wife went away. Your Mr Morris responded to an anonymous tip and found the animal.'

'Was it alive or dead, Professor?' Kate Jones asked.

'Alive, my pretty Katherine. It shouldn't have been. Apparently it had been locked in a shed and starved and beaten . . .'

He broke off. *Judas knew what he had done*, Black Shuck's voice repeated.

'Professor?'

'Oh, just a thought passing through, Mr Wilson. Now, I was telling you about the dog. Yes, starved and beaten.

'Kate,' he continued, maddeningly changing the subject, 'have you made those calls yet?'

'Fuck the calls ... Sorry, Kate. Look, just stick with the dog will you, Professor Harker?'

Kate shrugged at the apology. She'd heard worse. She'd been called names that would lift paint off wood, so Wilson's lapse was neither here nor there.

'Well, Morris found it alive. He took it to Salvation and it has, apparently, survived and been rehomed.'

Ben Wilson suppressed a shudder. 'Does it have a name?' he inquired.

'Oh, yes. Yes, it does. It's a Newfoundland called Leader.'

'Jesus!' Wilson hissed. 'Look, forget the books, Harker. Get on with it. Forget about showing me things in print. Do you think that this Leader is the animal that made the print in the dog-shit and left the hair? Do you?'

His mind was racing. He'd seen that dog. He'd slept with its new owner just the night before. If Sally owned Leader, then Sally was probably in danger ...

'Yes, I believe it was.'

Kate Jones noted his agitation. 'So where does image magic and the magical link fit in?' she inquired. 'Is it connected?'

Harker snorted. 'Connected? It's the connection. Let's take this step by step. One, faeces deposited on altar, probably by one of Shuck's dispensable human servants. Two, faeces given a rough shape by something clawed that leaves a footprint and a white hair, namely this dog Leader. Three, Black Shuck manifests on those faeces. Four, the faeces are somehow dried up and turned to ashes.'

'Okay,' Wilson urged. 'So whadda we got?'

'The magical image and the magical link. I'd better explain this to you.'

'Too bloody true. Go right ahead.'

'Very well. Here goes. Have you heard of image magic?'

'I have,' Kate ventured. 'It's the old witch idea of sticking pins in dolls.'

'Good. The image became the thing it represented by magic,

and so what was done to the image was also done to the original. Now, this sympathy between image and original was created by the so-called magical link. The one not only represented the other, it *became* the other.

'Let's go a step further. Let's suppose that Leader shapes, to the best of his canine ability, an image of Black Shuck. By the principle we've just discussed that image can become Black Shuck. That's assuming a straight progression.'

'You say that as if we're not going to assume a straight progression,' Wilson remarked.

'Quite right. But we have to understand it this way round in order to understand it the other. I tried to tell you before about ways of thinking, Mr Wilson. This is going to be a prime example.'

'I sincerely hope so. And I sincerely hope it's going to get us somewhere as well.'

'It will. Bear with me. Black Shuck forms on the image. With me so far?'

'Like a leech.'

'Good. Leader is linked to the image by his pawprint, right? Don't answer that. Just remember it. There is, through that pawprint, a direct link between Leader and faeces and Shuck. The faeces are the medium. That's where I went wrong before. I assumed that they were an idol. In a way they were. They were the image forming a magical link between Leader and Black Shuck, but they were not a representation of either.'

'Sorry,' Kate said. 'I think you've just lost me.'

'The faeces were the link between shaper and manifestation. Are you with that?'

'I think so.'

'Good, sweet Kate. Now, to continue. Leader, faeces, Shuck. That's one way. Let's try it the other. Shuck, faeces, Leader. A straight reversal. We automatically assume cause and effect because that's what we're used to in the physical world. In magic, however, there is no reason why the process shouldn't be reversed. That's what we have here. It's not the end justifying the means. It's the end *creating* the means.'

Ben Wilson frowned. 'What are you trying to tell us, Professor?' he asked. 'I think you ought to cut the theory and just spell it out.'

'Then I'll do just that . . .'

The phone rang. Harker lurched for it and picked up the receiver. He listened.

'All of them?' he queried, then listened again.

'And you've double-checked, Bill? There's no possibility of error on the data you were given?'

A distant voice crackled into his ear. 'Thanks, Bill,' he said. 'We're all square now, 'till next time.'

He put the phone down and resumed his seat. Both Ben Wilson and Kate Jones had assumed that he would be smiling. He wasn't.

'You know,' Harker ventured, 'there are times when I don't like to be proved right. This is one of them. That, as you've probably gathered, was Bill Somers at the R A S. I got Kate to feed all dated sightings of Black Shuck into his computer and check them against the phases of the moon. Without exception they showed up as being during the last quarter, with the moon firmly waning to new. Like right now.'

'So this is a good time for Shuck to show up, if that's not a contradiction in terms?'

'Let's just say that supernaturally speaking, and we *are* facing the supernatural, the dark of the moon is the traditional time for acts of destruction and vengeance. Does that sound like anybody we might be getting to know?'

'I could take a pretty wild guess at it,' Wilson grunted, 'except that it wouldn't be that wild any more. Jesus, Professor. I don't believe this. If I'm honest, I don't believe any of it. My biggest problem in this whole bloody mess is that I know you're right. The new moon's in four days, according to my diary. That gives us three at the most to work this thing out. But you were saying something about the end creating the means, earlier?'

Harker nodded and stared down at his interlaced fingers. For a moment he made no reply. Then he sighed and looked up again. 'In order to understand what I am about to tell you, you will have to dispense with your established ideas about the nature of reality. You are already beginning to understand that there are realities within in real terms or adjunctival or contiguous with our own, realities that do not respond to known laws. Black Shuck is one of them. He operates in our realms, and also in others that have been forgotten or scientifically discredited through the centuries. Like magic.'

Kate Jones peered at Harker intently. 'Magic?' she queried. 'Magical link type magic?'

'Not rabbit-out-of-hat-type magic. Sorcery. The Black Arts. Whatever. This is Shuck's realm. Here cause and effect can sometimes behave in different ways. An effect can exist passively without creating means to bring it into being. To put it as simply as possible, the effect can create the means which gives it actuality.

'Now, let me relate this to Black Shuck and this dog called Leader. Shuck usually exists as a non-tangible being outside the realms of man. When he has chosen to enter them, though, he takes on a physical form. This is born out by several of the accounts, including the incident at Bungay in 1577. There he is reported to have wrung the necks of two of the congregation in the church and gripped another so hard that he shrank together and doubled up. So, this is Shuck physical, not Shuck metaphysical. He required a physical form so he manufactured one.'

'Oh come on,' Wilson groaned. 'You don't mean he built it up like some four-footed Frankenstein, surely?'

'No. Most likely he borrowed an existing body and adapted it. And that, I believe, is where Leader comes in. Leader is going to become Black Shuck. We know that Shuck can communicate with animals and humans. My guess is that he's already been in contact with Leader and at least one human. The human collected the faeces and deposited them on the altar in St Katherine's, but he or she was simply a delivery boy. Leader had to be put into contact with the mess to link him to Black Shuck through a physical medium. Forget any ideas about blasphemy or desecration. That dog-dirt was a sort of focus, rather like the wax in a wax image. Leader didn't have to shape it exactly. He only had to make contact with it. When Shuck used it to manifest, albeit temporarily, the magical link was forged and Leader and Shuck could begin to become one being.'

'Then Leader is actually turning into Shuck? That's what you're telling me?'

'I am, Mr Wilson.'

The policeman closed his eyes tightly. 'Jesus God,' he muttered. He reached across his desk and rang the switchboard. 'Get me Garmonsway and Hythe,' he ordered. 'Right now.'

Harker and Kate Jones looked at him. 'I know where Leader is,' he explained. 'I was with his new owner last night . . .'

The number rang and connected. He asked for Sally French and was told she'd gone for the day. He slammed the phone down and reached into his pocket, taking out a small notebook and looking up Sally's home number. Punching up nine for an outside line he dialled direct.

The number rang. And rang. Nobody answered.

Wilson scowled at the professor. 'You're going to cost me a bloody good relationship,' he muttered. 'We'd better find that dog and keep an eye on it. If you're right it's going to get bloody nasty before it's done.'

He lifted the phone again and asked for Tom Greaves at Salvation. 'This is our best shot,' he explained. 'If we can get Greaves to find something wrong with the dog and take it back until the moon's past new, it'll save trying to explain to anyone else.'

'Like Sally French?' Kate Jones asked him, her eyes twinkling with amusement.


He perceived the changes slowly to begin with. At first he thought the darkening of his fur was due to dirt and he attempted to clean it with his tongue, his canine contortions serving only to confirm that the alteration was taking place all over his body. When the feeling around his eyes began, though, both his vision and his perceptions began to alter.

A dull ache developed throughout his frame. It seemed to come from deep within every bone, as if their fabric was starting to stretch. It was painful, but it was also . . . expected.

The change continued throughout the morning, as it had worked slowly through the preceding night. It was a lengthening, a strengthening of his being and his purpose, an alteration which would be both permanent and consuming in its implications. Already he was aware that he was not as other dogs, that he had acquired the ability to transcend them in several ways. Those he met in Estbury Green seemed to defer to him, as if he were somehow better, more advanced than they were. Pieter Hangel's brass pentagram had been a beginning of sorts, but this continuation was more than simply a development of Leader's senses. It was a reshaping of his body as well.

And, with the restructuring of his body, aware of its discomfort as he was, his senses also expanded. He felt a power, a presence, begin to obtrude upon the very nature of his realities, expanding and developing the worlds he knew. Even his name seemed to waver in his mind, alternating between the one Ellie Pasciewicz had given him and the other name, the older name, which he realized was as much a part of him as the changes he felt, the changes he was longing to have completed.

Sally heard the phone ringing from outside. Funny how long it takes to fit a key into a lock when you're trying to hurry, she thought to herself. She fumbled in her bag and took out the office keys by mistake. By the time she'd found the flat key and unlocked the door the ringing remained only as a dying echo.

Leader looked up at her through large, bright eyes. They *were* bigger, she decided. And the darkening of his coat had continued. Now he was definitely grey. Not the same dog at all.

He barked a welcome, but even its note had changed. It was deeper, more vibrant and powerful. Not threatening. Not yet. Simply . . . different.

'Hello, boy,' she said, reaching down to scruffle his fur with a greater hesitancy than she'd previously shown. If his appearance can change this drastically, she told herself, then his nature might be changing as well. Forget lunch. Forget everything but getting him along to Salvation. Fast.

Sally found the lead and snapped it onto Leader's collar. He didn't resist or show any displeasure as she left the flat with him and, instead of heading for the pedestrian crossing, took him along to the bus stop. She'd never bothered with a car. There was a fair service into Monkhampton town centre where she worked, and anywhere she was going in the evenings was usually in her escort's vehicle. All said and done a man without a car couldn't afford to entertain her.

'Let's get you checked over,' she told him as they waited. 'You're probably as worried about this as I am.'


Tom Greaves listened to what Ben Wilson had to say. His misgivings about letting Sally French have Leader had never completely vanished and in his heart he half-welcomed the opportunity the policeman was giving him to take the animal back for a while.

'As it happens, Mr Wilson,' he said. 'I had a phone-call from Miss French this morning, from her office. She appears to be worried about Leader herself and she's bringing him in to me this afternoon. If only a fraction of what she's told me is true I won't have any difficulty in taking him back for a period of observation. How does that fit in with your thinking?'

He felt the policeman breathe a sigh of relief at the other end of the phone. 'Pretty bloody perfect,' came the answer. 'Look, can you give me a ring when she's gone and I'll come and have a look at the animal, if that's okay?'

'Fine. I'll do that.'

He put the phone down and started filling bowls for the midday feeding. He'd just finished sliding them through panels in the mesh when his wife informed him Sally and Leader had arrived. He saw them in the surgery and had to struggle not to show his alarm at the alteration in the New-foundland's outward appearance. Leader was not only darker, he was substantially larger as well.

'By his age he should have stopped growing,' he told Sally. 'And I'd have expected his coat colour to have stabilized as well. Now, you see this alteration around the eyes? There's a variety of possible causes for that, all of which don't bode particularly well for his health. As to the colour change, it's always possible that he's actually a sport reverting to type.'

Sally looked at him, perplexed. 'Could you put that in everyday terms?' she asked.

'What I mean is he could have been the only white in a black litter from black parents, carrying a changeable gene which has just stabilized and is altering his colour. It's rare, but it does happen. But even if that is the case I'd like to keep him for a few days and check these changes out. I know you'll be reluctant to part with him, but it's in the animal's interests so I feel I have to insist. Now, is there anything else I ought to know?'

Sally thought for a moment. 'Well, he's good at opening things,' she said at length. 'He managed to open my flat door a couple of nights ago. As you may remember it's a Yale, but I hadn't dropped the snub and he opened it from the inside. I found him outside the next morning with very muddy paws. I don't know where he went, but I shouldn't think that it had anything to do with this.'

'Probably not,' Tom Greaves agreed. 'It's always useful to know these things, though. You needn't worry about him getting out of here, Miss French. I've yet to meet the dog that can pick a padlock.'

The examination concluded and Sally said a temporary good-bye to Leader. As she left Salvation to go home alone, Tom Greaves rang Detective Chief Inspector Wilson and advised him that he now had Leader under lock and key. Pieter Hangel, who had just finished his lunch, overheard the call.

Wilson, together with Kate Jones and Professor Harker, drove round to Salvation. Greaves' father-in-law met them, eyed them carefully, then admitted them to the animal sanctuary. They found the vet outside Leader's pen.

'One large white Newfoundland,' Tom Greaves stated ironically.

*This* was a white dog? Wilson asked himself.

Leader's coat was now almost charcoal grey. Both his frame and his eyes had expanded abnormally, increasing his overall size by about a third. Those eyes stared out at the humans clustered beyond the wire mesh, amused and challenging. Andreas Harker stared into them and shuddered to himself. They looked all too familiar to him. He'd seen them only thirteen hours before.

'Hello, Shuck,' he said softly.

Tom Greaves heard him. 'His name's Leader,' he responded.

Harker nodded. 'Fine,' he said, grabbing hold of the mesh and shaking it. 'Just make sure he stays here.'

'He won't get out of his pen,' Greaves told him.

'I wish I could believe that.'

Leader looked at this human. He'd never seen him before but his features were familiar. Somehow he felt that this man had been taught a lesson and ought to know better. His acquiescence at Greaves' reassurance was both banal and childish in its apparent simplicity.

*Remember the bats*, he flashed into the professor's mind. *The teeth will be larger next time.*

Harker shuddered visibly and moved away from the mesh. Kate Jones gripped him firmly. 'Are you all right, Professor?' she inquired.

He forced a smile. 'Put it down to someone walking over my grave,' he ventured. Then, to Tom Greaves: 'You're *sure* he's secure?'

'My father-in-law was in a Nazi concentration camp. He's

compared these facilities to the ones he found there often enough. No, he'll not get out.'

'Then we may have found a way to stop it,' Harker said to Wilson.

The policeman scowled. I wouldn't count on it, he thought. That statement seems a bit complacent to me. Besides, there's at least one human involved as well as the animals.

'What's causing the changes, Mr Greaves?' he asked.

Greaves shrugged. 'The reason's not obvious so far. Abnormal hormone and gene properties, perhaps. I don't really know, though. It's rather beyond my experience if I'm honest. This is a remarkable animal. Its ability to open a Yale lock from inside testifies to that.'

'It can do what?'

'Oh, it's something Miss French told me. Two nights ago Leader got out of her flat. Opened the door from the inside. She found him outside the next morning, his paws all muddy.'

Harker and Wilson exchanged glances. Two days ago? The night the pile of excrement was shaped?

'Do you let him out on his own yet?' the policeman had asked Sally.

'Not yet,' came her reply. 'I have to watch him, though. He's good with doors, even bolts . . .'

Oh Jesus. The end-of-the-world-show's right here on my doorstep.

Wilson reached out and rattled the padlock. It stayed firm. 'Thank you Mr Greaves,' he said. 'I think we've learned about all we can at present. Will you keep me advised of the changes?'

'I will, Mr Wilson.'

'Thanks. Seen all you need, Professor, Kate?'

They nodded. The three of them said their goodbyes to Tom Greaves and started around the house and down the path towards the car parked in St Katherine's Square. They felt Granpa Hangel's eyes without knowing who was watching them. Harker felt he realized the implication of the hidden watcher but, still unsure as to what extent Wilson and Kate Jones believed or trusted him, said nothing.

They got in and Ben Wilson fitted the key into the ignition. 'Impressions?' he asked before he turned it.

'A larger animal than I had expected,' Harker told him. 'And the change of colour tends to confirm my theory with regard to the magical link.'

'Can it get out of there, Professor?'

'Not without human help, Mr Wilson,' Harker replied.

'Great. Tom Greaves watches Leader and our boys keep an eye on the church. Whatever goes down we've got it taped.'

In the back seat Kate Jones shuddered. 'I hope you're right, sir,' she told him.

'And so do I,' Harker echoed. 'So do I.'

In the crumbling darkness their numbers were increasing. For a few moments, as they groped their way down from the daylight, they would catch a glimpse of, perhaps even recognize, those who had arrived before them. It didn't last, though. It faded as the last trace of daylight vanished, replaced with a sudden, bewildering rush of emotions. Pride was there, briefly. Such pride as they had never thought to know. Pride at being chosen to become more than they could ever have hoped to be in some past moment. Pride in the service they would render the *other*.

And there was fear, and hope, and a desperate desire to know what would be asked of them when the moment finally arrived.

All these things passed away almost as quickly as they were experienced, replaced by a growing numbness, a lethargy of body and soul which stole over them and left them mute and passive, as the others about them were already mute and passive. Only that fragment of the *other* each harboured within continued to sustain and control them through the time of waiting, the time of lingering hidden in the darkness, living only in the power of Black Shuck.

Trish Bentham wasn't Jake Lewis's first full-time affair with a married woman, and he doubted if she'd be the last. What she was, though, he grudgingly admitted to himself, was both better looking and a better lay than Sally French.

Jake didn't spend much time in the office these days. Trish was a bloody good reason not to. Besides, the work was drying up as the last day for Monkhampton Development Corporation approached. Was it only a week or so since he'd showed that copper around and had a drink in that bloody awful pub in Uptown? Christ, time was dragging. We'll all have died of boredom by the time December gets here.

Even with Trish to take his mind off things, her husband was now off on another of his continental trips selling . . . Jake shrugged. Who cares what Tony Bentham sells, anyway. But even with him off again there was still the Friday paperwork to shuffle through. Copies of board papers. Housing and land acquisition reports (snigger). That one got shorter every time it came out. Social Development Officer's reports. Worth a look sometimes for the items on difficult tenants who might scream to the press.

He dipped and sampled at random, half an eye on his watch. Redundant personnel find it harder to muster dedication or enthusiasm. Then he spotted a couple of paras in the SDO's report and read a little harder.

Under the MDC partnership agreement with the local authority it was the borough which administered the new rented housing. That gave them some say as to rehousing their own tenants when and if they had to. A couple of the new estates were already approaching ghetto status thanks to this. But Jake wasn't interested in the nascent ghetto problem. Not this time. It did, however, affect rehousing of borough tenants on MDC estates.

He flipped open his business card folder and sorted through for that copper's number. Wilson, that was it. Ben Wilson. Interested in Uptown. Okay, Wilson, chew on this.

He dialled the number and waited for a response. Then he asked the police switchboard for Wilson by name. Time passed. It seemed to go even more slowly than ever when you were waiting on the phone.

The extension rang and was picked up. A woman's voice said; 'DCI Wilson's office.'

'Is he there?' Jake demanded.

'Who's calling, please?'

'Jake Lewis, MDC. I think I might have something interesting for him.'

Kate Jones passed the phone to Wilson, who identified himself and settled back to listen. Harker, working at a table imported specially into the office, reclaimed Kate and continued. Until Wilson hissed and waved a hand at him.

'Yeah, thanks Jake,' he said. 'Look, any chance of a copy of that item? Is there someone could drop it round here this afternoon? Great. See you.'

He put down the phone and eyed Harker and Kate across his desk. They watched him intently as he whistled the opening bars of *Riders on the Storm* and folded and unfolded his fingers.

'Well?' Andreas Harker snapped.

'I don't know if this thing gets curiouser and curiouser like Alice, or just grows and grows like Topsy,' the policeman began. 'Either way we have another ingredient to add to our Uptown brew.

'That was Jake Lewis, a guy I know at MDC . . . sorry, Professor, Monkhampton Development Corporation. The borough owned a fair proportion of its rented housing stock in Uptown and MDC's rehousing the tenants as they get moved out under the compulsory purchase orders. They're trying to preserve the old community spirit, ha ha, and settling them all together at Thorpfields. Now, MDC has some animals called Social Development Officers. In the early days they went round new arrivals brought into the town under the expansion programme and tried to help them settle in. They're trying to do that with the Uptowners as well. Except that they can't find any Uptowners on Thorpfields.'

Harker's brow furrowed. 'Would you care to take that a little further?' he asked.

'Simple enough, really. They move out of Uptown. At least, their furniture and effects do. The SDOs go round with the chat and the booklets and find . . . zilch. Nowt. *Rien*. Sod all. Oh, the furniture's there. The house is there. Everything's there except the people.

'So, our SDO calls back. Later afternoon. Tea time. Still no-one. He, she or it finishes work and tries again on the way home. Still no-one. House still deserted. Now, I take it you've moved house once or twice. The first few nights you spend settling in, right? Not our Uptowners. They fall off the bloody face of the earth. One Social Development Officer even tried a family with young children at ten-thirty at night. No hubby. No wife. No kids. No nothing, if you'll excuse the double negative for once.'

'Maybe they went back to the old house to tidy up after the move?' Kate suggested. 'I wouldn't bother, knowing it was going to be pulled down, but lots of wives would.'

Wilson shook his head. 'According to our SDO she tried that. House deserted. Borough crew had already boarded it up and made it secure. They don't want squats, so they work fast. No, that's not the answer.'

'How many people are we talking about?' Harker inquired.

'Hard to say without a copy of the report Jake Lewis was referring to. But if you reckon twenty-two families, which was the figure Jake mentioned, at two adults and two point four consenting children to a family, you get . . . something like twenty-two times four and a half, which works out at just under a hundred men, women and children.'

'You're telling me a hundred people have disappeared without you noticing?' the professor snapped. 'And this thing calls itself a police force?'

'Come on,' Wilson snarled. 'Be fair. Most MP reports are filed by relatives. And in this case the relatives have gone as well. The only consolation, if you can call it that, is that they've only been gone a few days.'

Andreas Harker stood up. 'You listen to me, Detective Chief Inspector Benjamin Wilson,' he began. 'There's something in Uptown I don't know enough about to understand, let alone fight. It's called Black Shuck and it's *nasty*. Now you tell me there's a hundred people missing? Have you any idea how much distance their intestines would cover? And before you jump down my throat think a minute. Is that or is that not a possibility?'

'You're saying the animals have had 'em?'

'Not yet. I think we'd have nosed it, as Hamlet said, going up the stairs into the lobby by now. No, I'm not saying that's what's happened. But by the same token I'm not saying it couldn't happen, Mr Wilson. And a sacrifice on that scale, and it would be a sacrifice, have no doubt about that, could unleash such power as to make us nothing more than straws before the force of a hurricane.'


Andreas Harker telephoned to Cambridge and cancelled his engagements for the next few days at Wilson's request. The relationship between policeman and professor was still uneasy, but each recognized an ability in the other which just might pull them through together, if not apart.

The books arrived from the Fallenberg and Harker checked the references he required, dictating notes to Kate Jones as he did so. By this time over fifty sheets of paper had been filled with his own jottings and his spoken thoughts.

Kate Jones found Harker possibly the strangest man she had ever encountered. He had retained the blanket from the night before in place of his jacket and, despite the obvious warmth both inside and outside the police station, adamantly refused to relinquish it. His greying brown hair with its centre parting gave him an almost venerable appearance which his features, taken singly, didn't warrant, she thought. The dark eyes were out of place with his light skin and his mouth was more often petulant than appealing. Even so, despite his outward appearance there was an inescapable inner dedication which reminded the police-woman of Ben Wilson, on the scent like a Disney bloodhound.

DCI Wilson must have seen the same thing, she reasoned.

Otherwise the professor would be looking at five years for that gun of his. Nobody got out of a firearms rap, but Andreas Harker had. Somehow.

At first she'd listened to his dictation and taken it down verbatim, not even trying to make sense of the rubbish he was spouting. It was rubbish. It had to be. Only after a while it began to make a strange sort of sense to Kate. A sense which compelled a suspension of disbelief at least.

By six that evening she'd been on for twelve hours. Harker was showing no sign of tiring, viewing and reviewing his speculative findings, seeking a way through supposition into workable fact. Okay, she decided, I'll stick with it for as long as it takes. The overtime's useful to a single girl. And besides, I'm starting to get into this.

In a pause between notes she looked across at Ben Wilson, who was snoring in his chair. He was fairly good at that, displaying an almost supernatural ability to wake and present himself as alert the second before a knock sounded on his office door. As catnaps went he was even more feline than Macavity, T. S. Eliot's *Old Possum* version of Moriarty.

Harry Chester still had some work to do on those Avenue break-ins, so Kate only saw him once or twice when he came in to explain or report to Wilson. That was just as well, she decided. There was something about the tall copper she didn't like. Too full of himself. Too much of a ladies' man, *he* thought. You could see that in the way he looked at her. There were other officers working on the Pasciewicz killing, much to Harry's disgust. Oh, the guv'nor'd put him on it, sooner or later, once they'd got enough together to go into court with on his present cases.

Around seven Professor Harker stood up and stretched. 'I need a break,' he announced. 'I'll take a walk and see if I can find my car.'

Wilson looked up and grinned. 'You needn't bother,' he said. 'It's parked outside in the car-park. We had to let forensic go over it, just to make sure you really were in the clear. You can't cut any corners in a murder inquiry. And we'd better find someone who can lend you a jacket before you start walking the streets in that blanket like a refugee. Think you can scare one up, Kate?'

'I'll see what I can do, sir.'

She left the office. When she'd gone Wilson asked: 'That comment you made earlier, about not knowing how to fight Black Shuck. Did you mean it?'

'I meant it all right. The very thought of it scares the hell out of me, for two reasons. The first is the way that Shuck let me live last night after I defied him. He didn't do that so I could find a way to beat him. The second is both more to the point and more worrying. In all the cases I've ever come across of Shuck manifesting I've only ever heard of one where he was thwarted in any way. That was in 1972.

'An Exmoor farmer was asleep beside his wife when he thought he heard a dog scratching at the bedroom door. He picked up a poker and went to see because none of his own animals were allowed in the house. On the landing was a huge black dog with fiery eyes the size of . . . yes, saucers. It moved towards him and he hit it with the poker.

'To say that this action blew the farmhouse apart would be overly dramatic, I feel. But it came close. Every window was broken. Most of the tiles came off the roof and there was no electricity for days. Now, you could put that down to a lightning strike, except that there was no storm anywhere in the area for a week either side of the incident.'

'What happened to the farmer?'

'Blown off his feet. Badly shocked and shaken but somehow the physical damage was only superficial. He never completely recovered mentally, though, and I believe he's institutionalized today.'

'I think I'm beginning to see your problem.'

'There's something else I should tell you as well,' Harker continued. 'The story I've just related is well authenticated. It also comes from a part of the country where the black dog phenomenon, though frightening, is traditionally benevolent.

It's the East Anglian Shuck that does that sort of thing, not the Devon one.

'And now, as soon as Kate's found me a coat, I'll take that walk, Mr Wilson.'

'Okay. I'd come with you, but there's no way I can get out of here just yet. Can you try not to find me any more disembowelled corpses while you're out there?'

Harker smiled gently. 'I'll work on that. Can I bring you anything back? Fish and chips or something?'

'No, I'll get something in the canteen later. You go ahead, though.'

Kate Jones came back with an old khaki combat jacket. Harker peered at it and grimaced, then tried it on and found it a remarkably good fit. He walked out of the police station feeling more like a refugee than if he'd been wearing the blanket.

He wandered down from Salmond Square towards the dual carriageway, trying to work out if he was hungry or not. Maybe he'd try something in one of the pubs a bit later.

The dual carriageway was still busy from the evening rush, though not as congested as it usually was earlier. As Andreas Harker stood at the pedestrian crossing, waiting his chance to try for the centre reservation, he looked ahead, over the traffic, towards Uptown. The Dickensian jumble of houses stretched away, a brick and slate anachronism dominated by the ruined tower of the church they called St Gargoyle's and the glass and timber dome of the old Emporium Arcade.

Somewhere out there was the solution. 'Not the same thing as an answer, my boy,' Willington-Cartier had told him decades before, 'despite any dictionary definitions you may have encountered. An answer can be right or wrong. A solution eliminates the possibility of error implicit in an answer. Remember that. It may save your sanity one day.'

Harker snorted to himself as the lights changed in his favour and he crossed to the central reservation, then darted through a gap in the traffic to the Uptown side of the dual carriageway. Sanity? Where was the sanity in any of this? More to the point, where the hell was he going to find the solution?

He passed the filter where Mike Jones and Councillor Reardon had both become statistics instead of remaining simply people. Mike would be in hospital for a couple of months yet. They'd saved one of his legs. Just. Geoff Reardon was sitting at home drinking himself slowly to a surer and more permanent death. With a bit of luck, he hoped, he'd be there before his case came up.

The professor had heard about the accident in passing when he was checking back into Joe Pasciewicz's history, but it didn't really mean anything to him. As he allowed his steps to take him into Uptown he passed Alma Terrace, where Police Constable William Forrest had spent the early years of his life. Harker's eyes, blacker than ever in their hollows, ringed around with tiredness and raw with delayed shock, probed the bricks and mortar of the crumbling houses and searched for faces at the grimy windows, several of which were now boarded up. He listened for any sounds that might be carrying on the still air of the late June evening, the sound of voices from neighbours gossiping, the shrieks of children playing or fighting, the clattering of footsteps on the cobbles as the Uptowners started out for an evening at the pub.

There had been several pubs in the area once, but they'd closed, one by one. He passed the Shakespeare, empty and deserted, main windows shuttered with flaking chipboard, door windows broken and jagged in their frames. Not even a gristly ham sandwich to be had in there, he reflected. Not even half a pint of dead spiders with the fittings ripped out by the brewery.

No sounds. Only one pub. No-one about.

Where the hell were they going to?

He stood at the junction of Inkerman Terrace and Sebastopol Street, looking along towards the Battle of Inkerman and the boarded up entrance to the Emporium Arcade. A sparrow twittered overhead, a dark tatter like a bat against the still-bright sky.

Harker shuddered.

The pub could wait, he decided, starting up Sebastopol Street. The printer's yard entrance between the houses on his left only registered as he passed it, and he retraced his steps for a closer look. It ended in a padlocked wooden door, the lock itself a bright glint in the shadows. He walked towards it, into the yard. One of his shoes kicked something away across the rough paving and he followed it with his eyes before going over and picking it up.

Just an old padlock. Probably this was another entrance to the arcade which the workmen had secured with a new lock when they boarded up the others. They'd lost the key to this one so they'd cut it off and fitted another.

A movement slightly above his normal line of vision caught his eye and Harker looked up. A cat was perched on a low, sloping roof, squinting at him with the sun on its face. A black and white cat. One of three, as the other two stalked out of the angles and lay down beside it.

Looking at him.

A tabby joined them. Then a tortoiseshell and two blacks.

All looking at him.

He looked across at the roof on the other side of the yard. Five, six . . . seven more. Humped and watching.

Harker threw the old padlock away as he felt his heart flutter and his mouth dry up. One of the black cats shifted its position, seemingly tensing for a spring. The others followed suit.

He glanced at the entrance to the yard. It was clear. Walking slowly, watching the cats, ready to dodge and run if he could, he made his way back into Sebastopol Street, where there wasn't a cat, dog or pigeon to be seen, and continued up towards St Katherine's Square, glancing warily behind as he did so.

Shuck knows I'm here, he thought. He's got them watching me. Well, I'll try not to disappoint him.

He turned into Salvation and rang the bell. Mischa Greaves answered and showed him into her husband's office. A few moments later Tom Greaves himself appeared.

'Would it be all right if I took a peep at Leader?' Harker enquired.

'Our mystery dog?'

'That's the one, Mr Greaves. Any more changes since this afternoon?'

'Well, he's getting blacker. And I'm pretty certain he's getting bigger as well. But yes, come along and see for yourself.'

They went out to the pens. Leader was back in number five and appeared to be quite docile. His coat was now a dark slate grey, and Harker no longer had any doubt that it would be completely black in a very short time. The other changes which had begun to manifest, though, were both more subtle and more alarming than his colour.

Already a large animal, Leader's size was undoubtedly still increasing. His paws and head especially appeared to be growing larger, giving him the appearance of an outsize puppy. Yet the most stunning alteration was to his features.

His muzzle had broadened, giving the Newfoundland more of the characteristics of a Mastiff. The teeth appeared bigger and sharper, and the overall expression was more fierce. The forehead was heavier, the ridge above the eyes more pronounced, and the eyes themselves seemed to have grown to at least twice their original size. And they glowed.

At first Harker wondered if it was a trick of the light, a reflection like the *red-eye* problem photographers experienced photographing faces with a flash, but even a brief look around showed nothing that could be causing the phenomenon. He was about to remark on it when Greaves said: 'I've examined him again since this afternoon, Professor. At first I wondered if the obvious growth in certain areas could be put down to canine acromegaly, which is –'

'– an excess of growth hormone from the pituitary gland in adult life. Yes, I know what acromegaly is, Mr Greaves. It isn't that. Is it?'

The question was rhetorical, but Tom Greaves answered anyway. 'No, it's not that. Frankly I'm stumped. I've spent most of the afternoon trying to get hold of expert opinion and failing miserably.'

'How does Leader feel about the changes?'

'Now that's one of the most surprising things. He seems to be accepting them as part of a natural process. There doesn't appear to be any distress or discomfort.'

'Have you given him any medication?'

'A light sedative, as a precaution. Nothing more. You see, he's still . . . Leader. He just looks different. Miss French was in to see him just before you called. She was desperately worried until he greeted her. The bark's a little deeper, but his response was the same as I've observed previously, and it reassured her somewhat. She'll be back shortly, I should think. She left her purse here.'

'Really.' The word was a flat acknowledgement, spoken with only marginal interest in what Greaves was saying. Harker's eyes had already passed from the changing Leader and were studying a detail on the entrance to the pen.

He'd seen a padlock like that one just a few minutes before, on the door at the end of the printer's yard.

Tom Greaves followed his gaze. 'He *is* secure, you know,' he asserted.

'Good.' He looked at the adjoining pens. 'You use the same locks on all the enclosures?' he inquired.

'I do. I bought a job-lot at a clearance sale. They're Havards. The firm went out of business a few weeks back and they were cheap enough for me to buy up a few dozen. They're better locks than I could have afforded normally. Havard specialized in security work and sold directly to the trade. Those new keyless electronic locks finally defeated them, I'm told. They weren't geared up to cope with the new technology so they folded.'

'Direct to the trade, eh? So you couldn't buy them in the shops?'

'No. But why the interest?'

Andreas Harker shrugged. 'Thinking out loud. I collect odd details for my rag-bag mind,' he answered. 'Well, I must be getting along. Thank you for your time, Mr Greaves.'

217

Leader watched him go, returning the obvious interest this human had shown in him. The part that was still Leader retained a natural curiosity as to the man's intentions. The other part, the part that was darkening and growing stronger with every passing minute, peered through its growing, glowing eyes at the retreating professor.

*You don't know it all yet, Andreas,* the *other* taunted.

Harker heard the taunt as a hissing in his mind. He wheeled round and stared into the pen. 'Not enough, Shuck,' he replied softly. 'Not yet. But I will, by Christ.'

'Professor Harker?' Greaves asked.

*That is why I let you live. You serve me even as you seek to defeat me. You show me my strengths and my weaknesses by what you're doing.*

*And that is why I shall win, Andreas. That is why you can never beat me.*

Harker shivered visibly. 'Are you all right?' Greaves demanded.

'A . . . slight chill, perhaps. Nothing more.'

'Would you like to come into the office and sit down for a few moments?'

'No. Thank you. I'm fine now,' Harker replied, turning away from the pen.

He was about to leave when Sally French returned for her purse. The professor had never met her before but it was obvious that her features were much prettier than the weary, haggard, tearful face he actually saw. Tom Greaves introduced them.

'Of course,' Harker responded with a forced smile. 'You're a friend of Mr Wilson's, I believe. I'm coming to know your friend quite well. Tell me, Miss French, might I buy you a drink?'

She studied him for a few moments, trying to decide whether to accept or not. Sally felt terribly vulnerable without Leader and walking through Uptown unescorted had been a worrying but necessary evil. This man, despite his rather peculiar dress of combat jacket over much better clothing, seemed concerned about her for some reason.

'What's your connection with Ben?' she asked him.

'I'm assisting him with an investigation, in a specialist capacity. But you haven't accepted my offer yet. I realize it's terribly forward of me . . .'

'Not at all,' she answered, slipping her arm through his on a sudden impulse. 'Shall we be going, Professor?'

They wished Tom Greaves good night and left Salvation together. Harker looked across the square at the ruined church. It was now after eight and the sun was dipping low on the horizon. Around the tower of St Gargoyle's the flitting black pinpricks of tiny bats were fluttering in the approaching twilight. The days were shortening visibly, he thought, in more ways than one.

'What're you a professor of?' Sally asked him as they walked down Sebastopol Street.

'Folklore.'

'You mean herbal remedies and that sort of thing?'

'Not quite. Folklore is more the study of traditional beliefs, Miss French, if I were to put it simply.'

'If you want to put it simply call me Sally.'

'Very well. Then you must call me Andreas.'

She shook her head. 'That's too heavy. Can I call you Andy?'

Harker appeared amused by this. 'That would be delightfully novel,' he told her.

They reached the corner of Inkerman Terrace without incident, the professor was relieved to note. A brief glance into the yard as they passed showed no sign of animal or human presence there.

He gestured up the terrace. 'Do you mind if we use this local hostelry? I find this area depressing, and I think a little refreshment would speed us out of here more cheerfully.'

Sally had no objections so they made their way into The Battle of Inkerman. A notice pasted over one of the door windows, pasted not taped, Harker noticed, announced a closing down party set for a couple of weeks ahead. The bar was virtually deserted and the professor speculated as to whether there would be enough people left in Uptown to make the party a viable proposition by the time it came round.

He ordered whisky for himself and a vodka and tonic for Sally. The grim-faced barman seemed to frown, as if perplexed by the novel combination. All part of the local atmosphere, Harker decided. The whole area would have been worthy of study if he'd discovered it earlier, under different circumstances.

*You serve me even as you seek to defeat me*, Shuck's voice echoed.

Hell, he was cold. He picked up his whisky and drained it whilst the landlord was touching a glass to the vodka optic. 'Another, if you please,' he said. 'A double this time, I think.'

He paid for the drinks and joined Sally at the table where he'd sat with Ben Wilson the day before. 'Do you have any cigarettes?' he asked her.

She shook her head. 'Sorry, don't smoke.'

'Do you mind if I do?'

'Go right ahead, Andy.'

He'd given up years before, but the craving still persisted at odd moments. And the moments he was living through at present were the oddest of his life so far.

Harker bought a pack of Benson and Hedges and a box of matches and took them back to his seat, unwrapping the cigarettes as he walked. He lit one and exhaled vigorously.

'So what're you helping Ben with?' she asked. 'Come to that, how come he told you about me?'

'Oh, he mentioned he was worried about Leader. As to the case I'm helping with, it's not really a pleasant topic of conversation.'

'You mean that murder last night? Ugh,' Sally shuddered. 'The news made it sound positively gruesome. I haven't seen Ben since it happened. I expect he's rushed off his feet.'

'He would be, if he knew which way to go,' Harker muttered, draining his glass. 'How's your drink?'

'It's fine. Look, Andy, don't think I'm being rude, but do you usually drink this quickly?'

'No, dear Sally, I do not. In normal circumstances I'm positively temperate.'

She caught the implication. 'And these aren't normal circumstances for you, are they? I think you'd better get yourself another and tell me about it. If it's getting to you like this it must be screwing Ben up as well.'

The whisky was warming and starting to work on his empty stomach as he ordered a second double, grinding his cigarette out disgustedly on the Senior Service ash-tray on the bar. He paid and sat down again.

'Well?'

'I don't think I ought to, Sally.'

'Come on. You know the old line about a problem shared is one that's halved. *Is* it the murder?'

'It is. And it's more. There are things going on here I don't understand. Probably I never will.' He lit another cigarette. 'If I start telling you about phantom black dogs you'll think you're drinking with a raving lunatic. I'm sorry. I didn't bring you in here to burden you with our problems.'

She studied his features intently. 'Andy,' she asked, 'will you tell me something? Is Leader mixed up in this somehow?'

'Right at the centre of it,' he replied, before he'd realized what he was saying. Oh hell, he thought. I didn't mean to say that.

'Then you'd better give me the rest of it. Right now.' She paused, waiting, but Harker made no reply. 'Look, Andy,' she continued, 'I'm the sort of person who can get involved too damn fast sometimes. I have done with Leader. I think I am doing with Ben Wilson. If there's a link I want to know it, no matter how unlikely it sounds.' She put her hand on his shoulder. 'C'mon, Mastermind. You've started so you'd better finish.'

He sighed and sipped the whisky. 'I don't know where to start,' he ventured. 'And before you tell me to begin at the beginning, there are no such things. Here's the basic premise, Sally. Believe it if you can. Remember I'm a Doctor of Literature as well as a BA, and that I hold the Antaeus Chair of

Folklore and Related Studies at the University of Cambridge. I don't tell you this to make you think I'm right. I tell you to make you believe that I think I'm right. And I think your Ben Wilson is slowly beginning to agree with me. For a policeman he's succeeded in retaining a remarkably open mind.'

Slowly, in a jumble of bits and pieces, Andreas Harker told Sally everything. The Willington-Cartier index, Black Shuck, animal murderers and his terror of the next few days all came tumbling out. So did his hypothesis for the changes taking place in Sally's dog. By the end of it his glass was empty again and his head was feeling unsteady on his shoulders.

Sally listened in silence, restraining herself from interrupting, sipping her vodka and tonic. The professor was right about his story being strange. In places it was the most ghastly thing she'd ever come across outside the pages of James Herbert and Stephen King. Occasionally she looked across at the barman, who appeared to be finding himself things to do so that he didn't look as if he was listening as well, though she knew he was. When Harker finished she stood up, picked up his glass and went to the bar for refills for them both.

The landlord didn't seem so gruff this time. Something about his expression looked worried. Perhaps even frightened.

She went back to the table and set Harker's drink down in front of him. He seemed drained, exhausted. 'So how are you going to stop whatever's happening?' she asked him.

He looked up at her standing over him. 'You believe me, Sally?'

'I'm not sure. But I believe you believe it yourself. And probably Ben does as well. It's not logical, but that doesn't make it impossible. How *can* you stop it?'

Harker sighed deeply and looked at the pack of cigarettes open on the table in front of him. 'I wish I knew,' he replied, dejectedly. 'I think it's going to take a bit more than hitting him with a poker like that Exmoor farmer did . . .'

Suddenly he stood up and drained the whisky. His hands cupped her face and he kissed her hard. 'Can you sing?' he demanded, letting her go again.

Her startled expression became a puzzled one. 'A . . . little . . .' she faltered, taken by surprise.

'Then sing. Anything you like. No, wait a minute.

> 'My old man
> Said follow the van,
> And don't dilly-dally on the way . . .

'Landlord, I bid you a good night,' he waved, grabbing Sally's hand and pulling her towards the door. 'Come along, Sally. Join in. You must know the words of this one.

> 'Off went the van with me old man in it,
> I followed on with the old cock-linnet . . .'

He staggered down the steps, still dragging Sally French. As they reached the street she asked: 'Andy, you all right? Are you drunk or what . . .?'

'Yes, I'm drunk,' he grinned. 'And I'm definitely *what* as well. But that's not why I'm singing. But don't stop. Don't stop. Not yet.

> 'I dillied and dallied, dallied and dillied,
> Until now I don't know where to roam . . .'

He's mad, she thought. Stark mad. Yet she joined in anyway, tra-la-ing where she didn't know the words.

The streets of Uptown echoed to the sound of their singing. Sally's voice was quite good but Harker would never have made a choirboy, even as a child. Quantity seemed more important than quality, though, and they belted it out together, going through *It's a long way to Tipperary* when *My old man* ran out. They were still singing when they ran into P C Forrest on the corner of Alma Terrace.

Before the policeman could begin the 'ello 'ello 'ello routine Harker took him by the arm and pulled him, startled, but, recognizing the professor, not resisting, towards the dual carriageway.

> 'Oh Constable, take out your radio,
> Aa-and contact Mr Wilson,'

the professor improvised to the tune of *Shenandoah*,

> 'Oh Constable, take out your radio,
> And then we'll keep singing here,
> Whilst he drives here to meet us.'

Forrest looked from Harker to Sally French, who was still tra-la-ing. She broke off long enough to say: 'Please. Do it. He's not mad. Get Mr Wilson here.'

PC Forrest shrugged, then radioed in on his personal transceiver. Several discordant oldies later Wilson and Kate Jones drove up and parked on the filter. Harker and Sally piled into the back.

'Drive out of town,' Harker hissed. 'Come on, man. Let's get out of here. Can you spare me sweet Kate and a car overnight? Or even Kate to drive my own?' Then he started to sing again.

'Will you stop that and tell me what the hell is going on?' Wilson demanded.

'Later. I have to get to Cambridge fast, and I'm in no shape to drive. Sally will fill you in on what she knows, but I mustn't stop singing. Not yet.'

They drove to the police station, by which time Harker was into *Whisky in the Jar* 'You'd better steal a mobile, Kate,' Wilson instructed. 'I want radio contact as soon as our tame looney starts making sense.' Then, to the professor: 'You're not just out of your tree, Harker, you're floating somewhere over the top of it. Christ knows why, but I'm giving you your head. For the last time, mind!'

The reply, not unexpectedly, came in song through *Boiled Beef and Carrots*:

> 'I've got an answer,
> I've got an answer,
> That's the stuff, lovely grub,
> And if Shuck reads my mind he'll just get this . . .'

'So that's it,' Wilson muttered. 'Okay, Kate, get him moving. And keep it legal, Harker. No more shooters and pigstickers. I won't be able to pull you out of it next time. I've enough troubles with Enoch. He wants to set up an incident room, and the only thing that'll do is get the whole bloody lot of us certified.'

Harker's voice dried to a croak, but he kept singing until Kate Jones had got him as far as Huntingdon. Only when they were passing over Godmanchester on the flyover did the professor finally relax.

'Thank God you've stopped,' Kate sighed. 'I was beginning to think you never would.'

'It could still be too soon,' Harker told her. 'I had to do it, though. I know why Shuck let me live. He didn't want me as a servant. Not in the way he wanted whoever put that excrement on the altar. He's more subtle than that.'

'So what does he want from you?'

'He wants me as his informer. He managed to get inside my mind last night. Everything I thought or did near him he knew whilst I was in Monkhampton. Then I had the beginning of an idea which might just defeat him. If I'd formulated it there he'd have discovered it and found a way to stop me. He still can, but it's the best chance we have so I have to take it. The only way to stop him finding out was to fill my mind with something else. If he picked anything out of it he just got snatches of old songs that mean nothing at all. I'm only glad you all trusted me enough to bear with me whilst I was doing it.'

'As Mr Wilson said, Professor, we don't have much choice at present. Can you tell me what we're doing next? After we get to Cambridge, I mean . . .'

Her voice trailed off as she glanced in her mirror and saw the blue light closing behind. They were doing a good eighty-five.

'This is another good reason for not taking your car,' Kate grinned. She flicked a switch on the dashboard and the rear POLICE sign lit up. The pursuing blue light dropped back and she reached for the radio handset, punching into the local frequency.

'Huntingdon Control,' she began, 'Huntingdon Control, this is Hotel Bravo One Eight Monkhampton. Do you copy?'

A voice crackled back.

'I'm in Delta One One Five November Victor Victor on A604 eastbound, urgent business for Monkhampton A Division. Please relay to local patrols. I've got one in my mirror right now. Acknowledge.'

Harker peered into the passenger mirror fitted in front of him. 'So you have,' he smiled.

'Roger, Hotel Bravo One Eight Monkhampton. Wait,' said the crackle.

After a pause Huntingdon Control resumed: 'Message received and understood. Wilco. Over.'

'Over and Out.'

Kate replaced the handset and looked at her mirror again. The patrol car following flashed its headlights twice and dropped back, turning the blue flasher off as it did so. 'Easy when you know how,' she told her passenger.

'I wish it was all that easy,' Harker croaked.

'And this from the man who's found the answer to all our problems?'

'Sarcasm won't get you any further than flattery these days,' the professor told her. 'And I didn't say I had *the* answer. I said I had *an* answer. It might not be the right one. I still have to check it out. For tonight, though, I'm going to buy you a decent meal in Michel's in Bridge Street. After that I'll put you to bed in my rooms whilst I try to scare up some help. And no argument, sweet Kate. You've been on your feet longer than I have today, and they're much prettier than mine.'

'Professor?'

'Mm?'

'Why do you keep calling me *sweet* Kate?'

'From that, dear lady, I deduce you were never fond of Shakespeare,' came the reply.

'No. Never got on with the immortal whoosit. Where do you sleep?'

'If I'm lucky I sleep on the way back tomorrow, once the facts are checked and the equipment's been scrounged and collected.'

'Equipment?'

'All totally legal. But enough. I have to do some talking to people before I'm even sure it will have a chance of working. Tell me, do you think your Mr Wilson could arrange a helicopter if we needed it? It'd be faster than driving back.'

'I don't think our force has got one. He might be able to arrange a charter, though, if it was really urgent. But won't your mind be exposed to Shuck when you go back? Or are you going to sing again?'

'If I'm right, and it's a big *if* Kate, Shuck will be too busy with his own plans to bother about me. Oh, he'll realize. But with luck it'll be too late for him to do anything.

'I hope,' he added.

Harker was as good as his word. They arrived at the college and parked the mobile, walking the short distance back to Michel's once Kate had checked in with Cambridge HU to avoid confusion and relayed her proposed locations to Wilson. The guv'nor phoned her during the meal and she told him what she could whilst the professor fretted over the quality of the food on her plate deteriorating. She resumed her seat quite quickly, though, and with an improved appetite, Harker thought.

Afterwards they returned to his rooms, where the policewoman fell asleep in Harker's bed without any argument. By now it was getting on for eleven but the professor still began to ring round, hauling colleagues out of bed or relaxation without any compunction, detailing his requirements and eliciting promises to call him back first thing in the morning. One of his contacts told him that chances were there was still a post-graduate researcher in the lab who could give him a direct answer.

He put down the phone, then dialled again. A surprised voice responded at the other end.

'Professor Harker,' he began. 'Dr Griswold said you might be able to help me. I'm interested in C–N activity around Monkhampton over the next two nights. To my untutored senses we should be about due for some, don't you think?'

He listened to the response, then held. The voice at the other end resumed and detailed what was expected. 'Estimated base?' he inquired, then listened again.

Harker jotted down the replies, nodding to himself as he did so. When he finally put the phone down he was smiling.

Good. That was everything set in motion. Now it was time to check the old man's index again, and this time he knew what he was looking for. So far it was working out quite well.

He went through the Shuck listings, studying the sighting details:

Anglo–Saxon Chronicle 1172 '. . . sounding and winding their horns . . .'

Abraham Fleming 1557: '. . . fearful flashes of fire . . . of whom divers were blasted . . .'

Norfolk 1893: '. . . a ball of fire, the air heavy laden with a sulphurous stench . . .'

Notes and Queries 1850: '. . . as if gunpowder had exploded there . . .'

Hilgey in Norfolk 1945: '. . . an ear-splitting howling . . .'

His eyelids flickered and he slumped forward as the darkness closed in around him. He walked unfamiliar corridors with an anxious heart. Shadows flickered at the edges of his vision, shadows which hardened and solidified into people as he passed. Only then did he become aware of his guide, of the old man who strode ahead of him, turning and beckoning, as the unseen carnage progressed and the horror that was Black Shuck leered and slavered in his future.

And then he was there, in the place all the corridors led to. Black Shuck, no longer Leader, stood before him at the centre of a golden pentagram. He looked down, seeing the rivulets of blood which flowed past his feet towards the witch-beast in the centre of the star. Other rivulets were running from other directions, washing over the lines of the pentagram, flowing into the growing, glowing monster in the middle.

It lapped at the blood of sacrifice, then looked up. *Too late, Andreas*, it whispered. *Too late. I have beaten you. That is why I am here, not where you thought. You see, I am too clever for you. I read your thought that night and knew what you intended. Now I have won, and I am free to run for ever.*

He shook off his fear, knowing it was too late to run, or even to submit. 'Are you, Shuck?' he demanded, extending his arms in front of himself. He watched his fingers glow as the balls of fire formed and discharged towards the creature. Shuck leaped up, his terrible jaws agape, and caught and swallowed the flaming globes as they approached it.

*And is that how you sought to destroy me, Andreas? No man has that much power. Not even one such as yourself . . .*

Self . . . elf . . . chrelf . . . chrip . . . chirrup . . . chirp . . .

His neck ached. As he lifted a hand to rub it he realized that the rest of his body ached as well. Outside him the chirping continued as the dawn chorus sang innocently out over the Cambridge morning.

He stretched, wishing he hadn't, then shook himself fully awake and stood up. Loose pages from the index lay all over the surface of his desk.

'You're wrong, Shuck,' he said to the empty study. 'I can beat you. We have the technology, as they say. You may defeat me in my nightmares, but I can defeat you in the one you're creating for yourself.'

Harker walked unsteadily into the kitchen, wondering why he felt so dreadful. Only when he was sipping his cocoa did he recall those glasses of whisky in The Battle of Inkerman the night before. He checked his watch, which had stopped because he'd forgotten to wind it for the better part of two days. The cooker clock said just after seven.

He made a pot of tea and arranged a wake-up tray for Kate Jones, knocking as he carried it into his bedroom. While she drank it and dressed he tuned in his radio from Radio Three to a local station and started listening for the news and weather.

They ate breakfast together in silence, Kate not knowing what to ask the professor, Harker still mentally running over what remained to be done. He relaxed until nine, then disappeared back into his study to make some more phone calls. Left to herself Kate found a paper in his letterbox and retired to his bedroom to read it. Less than half an hour later he came bounding in like a jubilant schoolboy.

'Time to go,' he beamed. 'We've a few things to collect. First stop is the Met lab at Pembroke College, then over to Physics at Cavendish. We'll borrow their computer to plot the necessary.'

Kate looked up from her paper. 'Isn't it about time you told me what the necessary is, Professor?'

'Not really. The fewer of us that know the better. You never know who Shuck can communicate with without them knowing. If I'm the only one who knows it all then we've a fifty per cent chance of success. If I share the information, even if only with you, that chance goes down to one in three. You've trusted me this far, and I'm afraid you'll just have to trust me for a little longer.

'Oh, and before we go, ring your Mr Wilson. I want that helicopter on stand-by here in Cambridge. I'll arrange with the Senate for it to be able to land in the court outside. You do the same at the Monkhampton end for a landing in St Katherine's Square.'

'A Chopper? He wants a chopper?'

Wilson stared incredulously across his desk at Harry Chester, who was trying hard not to giggle. Then he scowled back into the phone. 'Jesus, Kate. What the hell's he trying to do?'

'He won't tell me, sir. He says that if only he knows there's less chance of this Shuck picking it up. But he seems to have mobilized a good thirty per cent of Cambridge University behind him. We're shooting about all over the place this morning picking up equipment. I really think he knows what he's doing.'

'It's a bloody good job someone does. Okay, I'll see what I can do. One thing, though. On his own timescale we're supposed to have another two nights before Black Shuck tries whatever he's going to. You say Harker wants to keep what he's up to from the creature, yet he's coming back tonight. Won't that leave plenty of time for Shuck to pick his brains, or is he going to sing for two days? And how much gear is he going to have? That'll have a bearing on the size of chopper we need. *If* I can swing it.'

'I don't know, sir. Not yet.'

'No, I don't suppose you would. Okay, Kate. Stick with him. Meantime I'll just have to try and bypass Enoch and pray for a happy ending. Otherwise it could mean all our jobs. Keep me informed, when you can.'

He put the phone down and glared at his sergeant. 'And you can stop fucking grinning as well, Chester,' he snapped. 'Do something useful. Get onto InterForce Liaison and see if the Royal Anglians have any idea where we can borrow a five-seater military job. Civil hire will cost a bloody fortune if we have to keep it on stand-by.'

Harry Chester gulped. 'You're doing it, guv? You're going to get Harker what he wants?'

'You got any better ideas? And check the rosters as well. I want extra manpower available for tonight. I don't know why, but Harker's brought this thing forward. That's the only possible explanation for the helicopter. Oh, and one more thing. Find out where the Tactical Firearms Team's going to be. We may need them in a hurry, so I don't want them down on the Oxford range.'

'How about first tier response?'

'Locals? You know them. Two weeks learning which end of a Smith and Wesson the slug comes out of and how to put their ear-defenders on. No tactical training. Chances are they'll just stand by and wait for the civilians to identify a specific target and call it in 999. There may not be any civilians doing that. Not in Uptown.'

Harry Chester nodded. In the time they'd been together

he'd never seen Ben Wilson this wound up about anything. Part of him, the part that had seen Joe Pasciewicz' remains spread out in the church, could understand it. The other part, however, the one that regarded Harker as at least slightly mad and probably dangerous as well, couldn't work out why the guv'nor was co-operating to the point of laying his job on the line. Still, he had his instructions, and if Wilson and Harker were right then he'd be a fool to risk his own career by not carrying them out. And all in all, if it came to a choice between backing Enoch or backing Wilson, he'd go with the guv'nor every time.

He left the office for his own desk, to get on with it. Ben Wilson watched him go, then rubbed hard at the back of his neck. Despite the odd cat-nap he'd had precious little sleep since Andreas Harker came into his life, and it looked as if he wasn't going to catch up for at least another twenty-four hours. Enoch would be hammering at him soon for something else, something new, to tell the press, and apart from MAD PROFESSOR DISAPPEARS WITH POLICEWOMAN – HELICOPTER RANSOM DEMANDED there wasn't a single bloody thing to say. Not that there hadn't been developments. Naturally there had. Even supernaturally there had. The problem was what the hell to say without looking a complete idiot.

One of the few consolations he could hold on to was that the night had been a quiet one in Uptown. Bill Forrest and the others had been working double shifts since the murder, and had been briefed to be especially watchful. The question of the missing residents, though an important factor, had yet to become official. So far not a single Missing Person Report had been filed. Even so, the beat bobbies had been told to keep their eyes open.

He knew what Enoch would say to that. Wait for the proper notification, Wilson. Concentrate on the murder, Wilson. Forget all this nonsense about cats and dogs and find this pseudo-Ripper, Wilson. Go on, get on with it. Out of my office. Now.

Short-sighted bastard.

Chester checked with InterForce Liaison and, wheedling and pleading, had managed to obtain a promise of a Bell 406 Combat Scout from Lakenheath. Kate Jones had left George Teacherman's number in Cambridge as a contact point and the details were relayed there for Harker to make his own arrangements. Traffic was briefed on the Monkhampton landing sight and asked to stand by for ETA. The square would have to be cleared of traffic, but nobody expected that to present any difficulty.

One of the beat officers assigned to Uptown radioed in an odd report late in the morning. An unusual number of dead bats had been found around the west face of St Gargoyle's tower, a green froth around their mouths. There were some dead birds as well, their beaks also stained with a greenish pigment. Wilson referred the finding to Tom Greaves at Salvation, who promised to have a look later in the day. Then he began to wonder why the creatures hadn't been spotted earlier. The old church, especially since Joe Pasciewicz' death, had been scheduled for regular examination by the patrolmen. It had been light for the better part of seven hours, and bats at least were night-time creatures.

It was only a small puzzle, Wilson accepted, and human error was the most likely explanation. The small puzzles were mounting up, though, and no matter how different or diverse they might appear, the policeman instinctively felt that where Uptown was concerned there was likely to be a connection between them. He checked a list on his desk, then phoned through to Personnel.

He asked his question and listened to the answer. Putting the phone down he turned his attention to the file on the Pasciewicz killing, flipping through it and studying one of the reports in detail.

Wilson sat back and steepled his fingers. Between what he'd just read and the information he'd received from Personnel he'd created a problem for himself. It went against the grain to sit back and do nothing, yet his suspicions were such as to warrant sensitive handling. It might mean something to

233

Harker, and it should mean something to him. The problem was in deciding exactly what it meant, and in knowing how to proceed from there.

In the event he decided to do nothing for the time being. Maybe knowing, even suspecting, was enough for now.


Kate threaded the mobile skilfully through the narrow Cambridge streets, busy with Saturday shoppers and midsummer tourists, as well as the weaving cycles of the student population. Beside her Harker was still singing occasionally, but in a more relaxed fashion. Despite the weariness which gripped him, and the increasing dread of a confrontation to come, he managed to appear cheerful, almost jubilant at times.

At Pembroke College they collected two large cardboard boxes and three heavy gas cylinders, together with a nozzle adaptor, which were loaded onto the police car's rear seats. Harker also took charge of a computer print-out, which he nursed whilst they continued on to the Cavendish Physics laboratory, where data from the print-out was fed into the system and processed. Once he'd been given the results he went back to the car, where Kate Jones was waiting.

'Nearly everything,' he beamed.

'*Nearly* everything?' the policewoman challenged.

'Back to Pembroke, I think. There was something that wasn't ready for me before, but I think it will have been checked out of the stores by now. They've had quite long enough to get the signature they needed.'

'Is that all you're going to tell me?'

'For now, sweet Kate. Shall we go?'

She shrugged resignedly and started the engine. Once back at Pembroke the professor entered the lab alone and emerged some time later with a wooden case. Some of the lettering on the sides was masked out with brown adhesive tape and Harker put it straight into the boot.

'And now back to my rooms. I'll check with George Teacherman and then we can have a word with your Mr Wilson and find out how things are faring in Monkhampton. At this stage every detail is important. Come to that it always was, but never more so than now.'

'You think whatever is going to happen will happen tonight, don't you? That's why you asked for the helicopter.'

Harker nodded. 'I didn't want to say so yesterday in case it panicked anybody. But you're right. It will be tonight.'

'How can you be so sure, Professor?'

'Two reasons. One, Black Shuck won't wait for the absolute dark of the moon. With the early rising and setting we have at present the actual new moon will occur at around 2.00 pm in the afternoon. Now, desk diaries, such as Mr Wilson uses, give the middle date of three during which the moon is actually classified as new. By that time it's really beginning to wax again and pass from the dark into the light cycle. So it would have to be the night before, at the very latest.'

'That's still tomorrow.'

'Yes, Kate, it is. But he won't wait that long because of my second reason.'

'Which is?'

'That he picked enough out of my head last night to know I'm up to something. You see, this is more than just another Shuck sighting. This is something that the creature's been planning for some time. Possibly even for centuries. As I told you before, on occasions in the past he's borrowed and adapted some poor creature's body as a temporary habitation in order to enter the realms we inhabit. This time it's different. This time there's nothing temporary about it. Black Shuck intends to stay here and wreak his own particular brand of havoc. He can control both humans and animals, which makes him the better part of a god. At present his powers are limited and his habitation is temporary. Once he has Leader's body and consolidates his presence he'll be unstoppable.'

Kate shuddered. 'You still haven't told me why it's tonight.'

'It's logical progression, really. He let me live so that he could learn what I was up to. He knows I'm an authority on him and he realized that I might come up with a way of defeating him. Let me spell it out for you.

'He lets me live. Why? To learn what I'm up to, to find out how much I know, how much I'm capable of. He tries to frighten me into inactivity. Why? To stop me doing too much. There's only one conclusion I can draw from all this. Despite his arrogance towards me, despite his overt contempt, *Black Shuck is actually afraid of me.*'

'Wouldn't it have been better to kill you, rather than let you find a way to defeat him?'

Harker shook his head. 'He's not tried anything like this on such a scale before. He still doesn't know his own strengths and limitations fully. Oh, a lesson was taught in St Gargoyle's that night when I faced him, but it was Shuck who was learning from it, not me.'

Kate signalled a right turn into Trinity Street. 'Professor', she asked, 'do you know what he's going to do? I mean, how he's going to strengthen himself enough to do what he wants to?'

'Yes, Kate, I do.'

'Couldn't we forestall him?'

'We could, but he'd just try again in another place at another time. And next time he'll be the stronger for what he's learned from me. Now, here we are again. We can leave the cylinders in the car, but we'd better take the other things inside. I'll check the data on the print-out and then we've a little putting together to do. Nothing too complicated.'

As she parked he took the two cardboard boxes from the back seat and put them on the roof of the mobile. 'You take one,' he instructed. 'I'll bring the other and the case from the boot.'

He sandwiched the print-out between the two boxes and led her up the stairs to his rooms, puffing a little with the unaccustomed exertion. At the door he set them down and fumbled for his keys. As he did so Kate noticed that one of the strips of adhesive tape had peeled off the wooden surface, exposing the lettering underneath, which was printed in red.

DANGER, it said. EXPLOSIVE CONTENTS.

*

Tom Greaves studied the little bodies around the base of the tower. They lay in the broken, unnatural attitudes of the dead, stiff and already beginning to decay in the heat of Saturday noon.

He looked up. Whatever had killed these flying creatures was overhead, not on the ground, so there was little point in seeking the cause at his feet. The vet had already guessed the actual cause of death, and his visual search was purely for confirmation.

Tom shielded his eyes from the sun and studied the west wall of the tower, the only one to have remained substantially intact after the fire. Some distance from the top a thick wire projected from the stonework, curving outwards and glinting copper at the tip. The wire, stapled to the wall, ran down to ground level and disappeared. Originally it had stretched all the way to the tower roof, Tom decided.

He picked up one of the dead bats and ran a finger over the gritty foam around its mouth. No doubt about it, he decided. These creatures died of verdigris poisoning. That only answered a small part of the question, however.

Verdigris is an irritant poison, a copper carbonate which forms as a sort of rust on the surface of the metal but, unlike iron rust, serves to protect what is beneath rather than eating through it. Because it is an irritant anything touching it, even the size of a common pipistrelle, would usually be so put off by the burning sensation of the taste that it would leave it alone.

These hadn't.

They'd attacked the wire, one by dying one, replacing each other like soldier ants fighting an intruder to the colony. Not typical bat or bird behaviour at all. Then again, neither had the attack on Professor Harker been typical.

Tom Greaves frowned and turned away. The animals at Salvation had been restless again the night before, though not particularly noisy. All except Leader. The Newfoundland, and Tom realized he could no longer call it the *white* Newfoundland, had lain calmly amongst the general disquiet as if

237

detached from it, rather like a general watching his army. Now there were dead bats nearby.

Why?

Well, the answer wasn't to be found by standing here. He decided to move back and take another look at the tower from further away. As he pushed through the long grass he noticed the long metal spike, rather like a javelin, which the grass had been concealing. On impulse he grasped the end, to which a few strands of copper wire were still attached, and pulled. The spike slowly came clear of the earth and Tom held it out in front of himself, assessing its length at a little under five feet.

He studied it for a moment, then put it back where he'd found it and began to walk back to Salvation to phone Ben Wilson.


Granpa Hangel didn't respond to Tommy calling him for lunch. The boy opened the workshop door, which answered with its usual creaking, and peered inside. The old man wasn't there. Nor was he to be found anywhere else around Salvation.

The family were naturally concerned, but ate without him. Mischa recalled various other details of her father's odd behaviour recently and urged Tom to get the landrover out and drive round looking for him when they'd finished. The vet decided to wait through the afternoon and see if Granpa turned up on his own.

After lunch Tom went out to pen five and examined Leader. The dog was now completely black and looked as if he had increased his all-over size by at least a third. He didn't appear to be suffering any discomfort, and responded to Tom scruffling his shaggy coat with that smiling expression he'd been known for before.

'Is that it, Leader?' Tom asked, looking into the dog's enormous amber eyes. 'Have you stopped now? Well, we'll give it a couple more days to make sure, then you can go back to your new home. You'd like that, wouldn't you?'

Leader barked with apparent understanding. The bark was lower in pitch but otherwise ordinary enough.

Granpa Hangel didn't show up during the afternoon. Tommy Junior made a joke about him finding himself a girlfriend, which was greeted with disfavour. Mischa was seriously worried and Tom agreed to phone in details to the police.

Sally did her shopping that morning as quickly as possible and hurried back to the security of her flat. Her chance meeting with Harker and Ben the night before had left her confused and worried. There was obviously something rather horrid going on from what the professor had told her, and Ben's flat refusal to elaborate or confirm had been annoying and mystifying.

The policeman must be taking Professor Harker seriously, she reasoned, from the way in which his request to be driven to Cambridge had been complied with. And the changes in Leader, *her* Leader, must have some bearing on the situation. She'd asked Ben Wilson flat out about their meeting, realizing that it hadn't been the happy accident it appeared. 'Yeah,' he'd answered. 'But I'm glad things worked out that way all the same.'

He'd grinned at her as he'd said it, and something in that grin was infectious enough to stop her being as furious as she'd intended to be. They'd parted still friends, despite her efforts to remain chasteningly cool.

In comparison to the one before, Friday night had been doubly lonely for Sally. No Leader. No Ben Wilson. And the prospect of shopping without her canine deterrent in the morning. Well, that was behind her now. Tonight would be quiet as well, but she'd cook herself a good meal, have an extra couple of vodka and tonics and retire to bed early with the latest Dick Francis. She would go out, to see Leader at Salvation, but she'd treat herself to a taxi there and back and not risk public transport on a Monkhampton Saturday night.

Andreas Harker rang Lakenheath and identified himself. After a seemingly interminable wait he spoke directly to the Combat Scout's American pilot, Captain Nathan 'Jonah' Wayle.

'You jus' tell me what you want, Perfessor,' Jonah told him.

'We got the okay from the big boys so you jus' thinka me like some kinda air taxi.'

'That's very civil of you,' Harker responded. 'Now, Captain Wayle . . .'

'Hell, call me Jonah. You ain't gonna be formal are ya?'

'Right . . . Jonah. Now, timing is crucial. I need to be set down in Monkhampton no later than 12.48 am. It would be as well to add a ten minute margin for error and observation. Do you have any form of observation light mounted on your craft?'

'No problem. I'll get the guys ta fit a spot fer ya.'

'Good. What time do we need to leave Cambridge?'

'Lemme see. I gotta top around one-four-oh, so that makes . . . what, sixty mile? 'Bout twenny-six minutes, I reckon. You be ready ta go by 00.20 hours we're home an' dry.'

'Excellent. We'll see you then, Jonah. Two passengers and about 150 pounds weight of equipment. Is that all right?'

It was, Harker was assured, hunkey-dorey. He finished the call and looked across to where Kate Jones was kneeling on the floor of his study, matching square foil containers to what appeared to be oversize folded plastic bags. The wooden case, beside her, was now empty except for a jumble of foam sheeting on which a series of short glass phials containing a red liquid, sealed with a thin layer of wax at one end, were laid haphazardly.

'You see?' Harker smiled at her. 'I told you there was nothing to worry about. There's absolutely no danger of the fuses discharging until they're in the right place.'

Kate still looked doubtful. 'Maybe if you tell me how they work I'll feel a little happier,' she told him.

'Simple enough. The wax on those chemical fuses is designed to rupture once the container it is attached to has reached a certain height. At ground level they're completely stable unless you break them deliberately. There's a small response trigger inside the container which sets them off.'

'So what's in the foil box, Professor?'

'It can't hurt you to know that. At the lower end, where the fuse is inserted there,' he pointed, 'is a small explosive charge

240

designed to rip open the foil and deliver the payload. And before you ask it's a chemical called silver iodide. The system was first tested in what used to be called Tanganyika in 1952. Hardly the new technology, is it?'

'How about once they're in the helicopter? Won't they go off once we're off the ground?'

'No danger of that at all. Stop worrying, Kate. You just put them together and I'll scrounge some plastic rubbish sacks we can carry them in once you've finished. And check with Mr Wilson again in case he's anything new to tell us from Monk-hampton.'

He left her to it and returned some minutes later with two large black plastic sacks. 'Professor,' she began, 'I've just spoken to DCI Wilson. He's given me a couple of things to pass on to you. Well, three, actually. The first is that the old man from Salvation, Pieter Hangel, has been reported missing by Mr Greaves. The second is something else Mr Greaves reported. Apparently there were several dead bats and birds around the bottom of the tower at St Katherine's . . .'

She gave him the messages. Andreas Harker listened in silence, his features impassive. When she'd finished he demanded: 'And there's nothing else, Kate? Nothing you've left out?'

'No, Professor. Nothing. That's exactly what he told me to tell you.'

'Then things may not be quite as straightforward as I'd hoped they would be. Look, Kate, it's already late afternoon on a Saturday. Our Mr Wilson has got to get hold of somebody who can put that lightning conductor back on the tower. Understand me? It has to go back up. I don't care how he does it but it *must* be done. And if possible the old man must be found as well. But for God's sake don't stop him. Let him alone. Just find him. As for the other matter, it's best to do the same thing. Find him a mate or something, someone dependable who can keep an eye on him.

'And get him to do it straight away. This thing's just turned from a straight line into a corkscrew!'

*

Tom Greaves was permitting himself the Saturday luxury of a late film when it began to happen. Lee Marvin and Chuck Bronson were inside the château with Clint Walker, Donald Sutherland and the rest getting ready outside. *The Dirty Dozen* were preparing for the final shoot-out with the Nazis when a fair approximation of a gunshot sounded from outside.

Followed by another.

'What the devil? . . .' he muttered, turning his head to listen better.

Mischa watched him. She was mostly concerned about her missing father, but the noises were sufficiently startling to make her forget Pieter Hangel for the moment.

A third report sounded. The vet left his chair and stalked through the house towards the pens at the rear. A brown and white Springer Spaniel pushed past his legs as he stepped outside. He stared at it in blank incomprehension.

'Geordie? How did you get out? . . .'

Kerrack!

A mesh door swung open. The Collie, Rufus, sniffed at it for a moment, then left his pen.

Upstairs Tommy Junior hadn't got to sleep yet. He heard the sounds and swung himself out of bed, putting on his dressing gown. Hey, this was crazy. Sounded like a gunfight was going on outside.

For a moment Tom Greaves stood perplexed. Behind him Mischa had come out to see what was causing those peculiar noises. The vet shook his head as if to clear it of befuddlement and approached one of the now empty pens. He looked for the padlock.

It wasn't there.

Fragments of the lock littered the concrete around his feet. Other shards of the metal were buried in the brick wall of the outbuilding opposite. He started down the rest of the covered walkway to check the others. No doubt about it. Pens one to four had somehow burst their locks. Five was still secure.

Tom peered in at Leader. The dog's eyes peered back at him. Enormous. Slitted. Glowing. He reached out and took the lock in his hand, shaking it to test the strength of the shank, looking at it.

The lock exploded.

Tom screamed as his hand vanished in a spray of blood and slivered flesh. He spun, spurting blood from the tattered stump of his wrist as other fragments sliced into his abdomen and kidneys and heart. He jetted and pirouetted, already dead, as the force from the exploding padlock whirled him around, spattering mesh and brickwork and the ground beneath his failing feet.

Leader smiled. Mischa screamed. Tommy Junior scrambled down the stairs.

Mischa leaped towards Tom's collapsing body. It hit the concrete heavily and lay still. Wailing dementedly she straddled it and tried to lift her husband's remains. The padlock on pen six shattered, fragments of the metal slicing her scalp away and laying her brains bare to the night.

At the back door Tommy felt his mind reel and his heart leap into his mouth as the top of his mother's head disappeared in a bloody mist. Mischa collapsed on top of her husband like a rag doll suddenly released. For a moment her arms flapped like broken wings. The boy screamed and ran towards the broken shambles of his parents. Geordie snapped at his ankle, tripping him, bringing him down. He bounced off the bodies, howling, his dressing gown and pyjamas red with their escaping life. As the mesh door swung slowly open Leader padded out and bent over him, rank dog-breath choking his nostrils.

*Child of man, you are now the child of death*, grinned the *other*.

He tried to scrabble past the corpses and away, but his feet slipped and slithered helplessly on the puddles running from them. Leader's jaws, teeth enlarged, horribly distorted, snapped onto his genitals and tore upwards.

Tommy couldn't hear the other locks exploding through his pain. The last thing he remembered, the last thing he ever knew, was those bloodstained muzzles burrowing in his entrails, laying them out in the shape of the Devil's footprint where he'd fallen.

A beat officer called the disturbance in. 'Gunshots,' he stated, as calmly as he could. 'Sounds like dozens of 'em. From Salvation.'

They told Ben Wilson. He looked at his watch. It read just past midnight.

Why the hell hadn't Harry Chester found Bill Forrest yet?

He picked up the phone and thumped at the rest until an irritable late-night switchboard operator responded. 'Tactical Firearms Team,' he said bluntly. 'Get them into Uptown. St Katherine's Square. Right fucking now.'

It was about the same time that Marge Blunson heard the knocking at her front door. She wasn't to know who it was, or where he'd been and what he'd been looking for. Even so, Marge hadn't been to bed. She'd felt in her ancient bones that tonight was to be *the* night, so she'd stayed dressed and awake in her front room, Mary alert and watchful beside her.

She moved into the hall and opened the door. Standing outside, as if he was waiting for her, was the old man she'd seen at Salvation. For a moment she simply stared at him. Then she asked: 'Is it time?'

'It is time,' Granpa Hangel told her.

Mary snuffled at her feet. They both looked at him.

'The *other* is ready for you,' he said.

They left the house together and walked with him up Inkerman Street into the square. There Mary turned and looked at her mistress, barking once as if to say goodbye. Marge looked at her, stretched out a hand to her. Pieter Hangel took that hand.

'You have different tasks to perform for the *other*,' he told her.

She looked across the square. The shell of St Gargoyle's stared back at her, the lightning rod affixed once more upon its tower. Other pets, singly and in twos and threes, were making their way towards the ruins.

Mary barked again, then ran off to join her four-footed companions. Marge looked at Granpa Hangel. He was smiling.

'Come with me,' he instructed.

She took a last look at her retreating little love, then followed him. They passed Gertie Tomkin's boarded-up home on their way to the plywood fascia of the old Emporium Arcade. The lock on the workman's entrance seemed to have broken and the door was hanging ajar. Pieter Hangel led her inside, into the shelter and the light.

Marge looked around her. From the empty shop units, their cellar entrances open, familiar figures were emerging. ''Allo Gwen,' she called to one. 'George, Connie. Why, ain't this just like old times?'

No. It wasn't. She felt that a moment later. The automata which had been Uptown residents left the shops and stood in the aisles of the arcade, sightless, hearing nothing. Marge peered at them, suddenly wondering and nervous. Then her own senses seeped away as well.


At 12.15 Kate and Harker carried the black plastic bags down the stairs and into the court. The professor had become progressively less communicative through the evening, finally culminating in a state which Kate could only describe as sullen and broody as they removed the gas cylinders from the car and waited for Jonah to arrive with the helicopter.

The policewoman felt the butterflies in her stomach. The worst part, she decided, was not knowing what was going on. Then, wondering, she studied Andreas Harker once more.

He stood with upturned face amongst the ancient buildings of his college, watching and listening for the chopper from Lakenheath. Despite his attitude his features showed no emotion.

I don't know, Kate Jones thought to herself, and it's hard. But he does. At least, I can only assume he does. I've only got his word for what we're going to face. I don't even know what we're going to do. Hell, that scares me.

And if I'm frightened, not knowing, how much worse must it be for him?

Oh, yes, it was happening. No way could anybody call out the Tactical Firearms Team without Chief Superintendent Enoch hearing about it. Even if he was in bed at the time.

He slammed the phone down and tried not to listen to his wife's complaining as he hauled himself out of bed. That Wilson had a lot to answer for, and by God he was going to do some answering, as soon as Enoch was dressed and in Uptown.

'As far as he's concerned,' he muttered to himself as he pulled his uniform trousers on, 'the end of the world starts right here.'

He was never to know how close to the truth that statement came.

The locks were still exploding, opening the pens and liberating the animals inside them, as PC Treleaven radioed in. He was some distance from Salvation and was really guessing at the direction of the sounds. As soon as he'd finished the call he scrambled up over the north wall of St Katherine's churchyard and began to circle the ruin, moving as fast as the poor light and the long grass permitted. Only when he rounded the sanctuary end did he stop and take stock of his surroundings.

Beneath him, at road level, the animals crossing the square stopped still to watch him. Behind him, through the broken sanctuary window with its single surviving mullion, other non-human eyes stared out of humped silhouettes.

Treleaven grabbed for his radio again. 'Control,' he whispered. 'It's alive with animals. The whole bloody place is alive with animals. I'm in the churchyard. I'll try to get over to Salvation'.

He dropped down from the wall and stood on the edge of the square, opposite the animal sanctuary. Jesus, he'd never seen so many animals together at one time. They were everywhere.

The final lock exploded, freeing a cross-bred Great Dane which was now smaller than Leader. As the creatures, some with muzzles still wet with Tommy's blood, began to cross towards him, an engine roared into life. Without lights, leaving rubber squealed into the tarmac, the Landrover reversed out of Salvation and shot towards him, swinging broadside as he leaped clear, then stormed across the square and into the distance.

Shocked and shaken PC Treleaven watched it go, marvelling that not a single animal appeared to have been killed or injured. The short hairs at the back under his helmet were standing up now. In a dozen years on the force he'd never seen anything like this anywhere.

He couldn't see the number but he had a fair description of the vehicle. Summoning the little courage he had left he began to walk towards the animal sanctuary. Where the hell was his support? A gunshot message was immediately relayed to other beat officers and mobiles in the area. Okay the pubs were shut and the piss-artists all home by now, so his colleagues would have relaxed a bit, but there should be some response by now. How the hell long was it since he'd first called in? Certainly before he saw the animals . . .

Which had closed about him in a circle, sitting waiting.

He stood in the road, turning slowly, watching them. Control crackled at his lapel, requesting a progress report. His hand moved slowly, cautiously towards the transmit button.

Then he saw the blackness.

It was larger than any of the other shapes around him, and darker, much darker. The huge eyes glowed like headlamps and he was surprised not to find himself bathed in their light. He held the transceiver on and hissed into it.

'Christ, you ought to see this one! It's almost as big as a pony. And the teeth. Oh Jesus, those teeth . . .'

The witch-beast joined the circle about him. As if by some unspoken command they leaped as one, biting and clawing and slashing, bearing him down as he screamed into his radio, lacerating his tunic and trousers, puncturing and pulling at the belly flesh beneath.

Sally was wary of opening the door to begin with. At that time of night you never knew who was out there, even in Estbury Green. She slipped the safety-chain on before she undid the lock and peered out. As it happened she felt she needn't have bothered. It was the old man she'd met at Salvation, Mr Hangel.

She'd kept her promise to herself and taken a taxi to the animal sanctuary early in the evening. The visit had worried her intensely because of the severity and speed of the changes which Leader had undergone. Now, seeing Pieter Hangel, her heart leaped towards her throat.

'Is anything wrong?' Sally asked. 'Leader . . . is Leader? . . .'

'I think you should come with me, Miss French,' Granpa Hangel replied. 'There has been some alteration in Leader.'

'Oh Christ! Look,' slipping the chain off, 'come in, won't you? I'll get dressed and be right back.'

'That is kind. Thank you.' The old man stepped inside, smiling sympathetically. 'I have a Landrover waiting outside, when you are ready.'

Jonah checked the section of the enlarged city plan on his clipboard. He had the map reference right, so that should be the court. He reached down and flicked on the spotlight, the rotors throbbing overhead.

There they were, waving up at him. Man and a woman. Two black sacks. Three colour-coded gas cylinders. Hey, that stuff was helium, wasn't it?

The Combat Scout settled down into the courtyard and landed gently on its skids. Jonah knew these mixers backwards. They'd stand on their tail rotors if he asked them nicely enough.

The world around Harker's feet began to rush away in the draught from the helicopter. He left Kate Jones determinedly holding on to the bags and struggled forward with a gas cylinder tucked under each arm. The pilot slowed the engine and opened his cockpit door.

'You Perfessor Harker?' he yelled above the engine noise.

'That's me. You're Jonah? We'll just get this stuff inside and we'll be right with you.'

Jonah motioned for him to go round to the other side. Bent low, his hair streaming and whipping around his features, Harker complied. The pilot leaned over and opened the other door.

Harker slid the cylinders on to the floor and ran back for the third, sending Kate on ahead of him with the sacks. They tugged back behind her like water-wings as she crouched and moved forward. With them loaded she climbed into the remaining space on the rear seat and waited for the professor. He joined her quickly and rattled the third cylinder down on top of the other two before climbing in and shutting the door behind him.

The noise inside the helicopter was only marginally less than it had been outside. All over the court lights were flashing on and faces had appeared at the windows of the ancient buildings. The sound of the rotors echoed back from the stonework, magnified, and every scrap of litter was dancing and racing in the miniature whirlwind created by the blades. Jonah twisted in his seat and clicked Kate into a restraint belt, then he did the same for Harker. Next he plugged radio headsets into the centre panel and handed them to his passengers.

'They're not much,' he said loudly, 'but they're better than trying to shout. All set, folks?'

Harker gave him a thumbs-up, then wished he hadn't. The ground rushed sharply away beneath and his perspective on the world tilted violently as Jonah banked into a climbing turn. They were above the college and following Bridge Street's light westwards before his stomach even began to catch up.

'Keep yer feet on those cylinders, lady,' Jonah instructed. He checked his instruments, then his watch. 'Twelve twenny-one, Perfessor,' he beamed. 'That ain't bad, huh?'

'Not bad at all. What's our E T A?'

'What you asked fer. I gotta clear flight path. Y'all hang on there an' I'll show ya what this here mixer can do.'

He was as good as his word. The city lights beneath them had vanished almost before he'd finished speaking. Behind him Kate kept her feet pressed down on the helium cylinders to prevent them moving around too much. In the seat beside him Andreas Harker, fighting a rising surge of panic, began to sing.

> 'They're shifting father's bones to lay a sewer,
> They're digging father up for ten-inch drains . . .'

'What the hell kinda crap is that?' Jonah demanded.

'Very droll,' Harker forced a smile. 'Explain to our driver, Kate.'

'He has to sing, Jonah,' Kate called into her headset. 'He has to keep what we're doing out of his mind. It's crazy, I know, but it's vital.'

> 'Because some high-born twit
> Wants a pipeline for his excrement . . .'

'Christ, I'd a charged ya double if I'd known about this.'

> 'They're digging up the poor old boy's remains . . .'

'Look, I gotta turn my ears off. Y'all wanna say anythin' jus' gimme a tap, huh?'


Hotel Bravo One Three screamed up Sebastopol Street, light flashing and siren wailing. Its headlights caught the sight ahead as it entered St Katherine's Square. The animals moved aside to give its occupants a better view.

The driver managed to stand on his brakes and stall the mobile before he threw up all over the inside of the windscreen.

Beside him his ghost-white partner stared, wide-eyed, mouth working.

'That . . . that's Mick Treleaven . . .' he whispered, raising quaking hands to wipe the sprayed vomit from his face. 'Oh fuck! What do we do, Jim? What the fuck are we going to do?'

His voice was rising as he spoke, rapidly approaching a hysterical level. The driver wiped a patch on the glass with his uniform sleeve and fumbled at the ignition.

Hotel Bravo One Three refused to start.

'Look what they've done to Mick,' his partner continued. 'Look at the poor bastard. He's spread out like that poor guy the other night . . .'

'Shut up!' Jim snapped. 'Shut the fuck up. If you want to talk then radio in. Christ, this bugger won't get moving.'

'They're all round us. Everywhere!'

'Call in you stupid bastard! Call in!'

He kept twisting the key uselessly. In the headlights several bloody-muzzled creatures were approaching, circling the police car.

'They'll get in . . . They'll get in and do . . . that! To us!'

'Jesus, Archie. For Christ's sake try to stay calm. Call it in. We might have a chance that way. But don't fucking panic or we *are* dead.'

With trembling fingers his partner reached for the handset. Behind them another siren wailed gradually closer. Then another behind that.

'Thank God,' Jim muttered.

Wilson's car, with Harry Chester driving, was third into the square. Harry swept round in a wide circle, his full beam picking up as much of the scene as possible. The animals around Hotel Bravo One Three broke their circle and began a leisurely withdrawal towards the ruins of St Gargoyle's, their feet depositing glistening wet prints from Mick Treleaven's blood behind them.

Ben Wilson didn't permit himself more than a brief glance at the constable's remains. Even that was enough to tell him that he'd died the same way as Joe Pasciewicz. And this time

251

there had been police witnesses. That dozy bastard Enoch could chew on that for a while.

He looked at his watch. 12.41 am. Harker should be well on his way by now. Whatever the mad professor was up to had better work first time. It was unlikely that any of them would get a second chance, assuming they lived that long. And where the hell was the Firearms Team?

'Quick chorus of *Land of Hope and Glory*, guv?' Harry asked, straight-faced.

Nobody wanted to get out. They sat there, watching, as the creatures made their way into the churchyard and from there into the ruined church. An ambulance, called by the second mobile, hee-hawed into the square. As it stopped Wilson opened his door and leaped out, running across to it, warrant card held out, eyes darting into the shadows for signs of murderous life concealed in the darkness. Behind him Harry Chester edged the car forward to offer his guv'nor a chance of shelter if the worst came to the worst.

He reached the ambulance and banged on the nearside cab door. It opened and he pulled himself in, shutting it after him.

'There's sod all you can do for that poor bastard,' he grunted, slightly out of breath. Just stay here. Keep the doors and windows shut. If you want to know how dangerous it could be out there just turn your lights on that body.' He turned to get out, then added: 'And tell your control. Any other calls into Uptown must be treated with extreme caution until we give you an all-clear.'

He stepped down from the ambulance into the square, still glancing warily around. As he walked over to his car he cupped his hands and called to the other two police vehicles: 'Okay. Get out. But stay by your cars.'

'I thought you'd had it that time,' Harry Chester told him, unfolding his long body from behind the wheel.

'You and me both, sunshine. Look, get on the horn and find out what's happened to Traffic. This area should have been sealed off for Harker's landing by now. I know it's late on a Saturday night but I'd expected better of them than this. Hello . . .'

His voice tailed off as two more vehicles swept into the square. One was the large police van housing the blue-over-alled Tactical Firearms Team. The other was a private car which Ben Wilson knew only too well. It belonged to Chief Superintendent Enoch.

Chester saw them too. 'I reckon the shit's a half-inch from the fan,' he muttered.

'Forget Traffic,' Wilson ordered. 'You get the team out facing the church. I'll handle Enoch. Or die trying.'

A figure climbed down from the van and approached Wilson's car. 'Who's in charge?' it demanded.

'My show,' Wilson said. 'Look, Sergeant Chester's got the details. Can you liaise with him while I talk to the Chief Super?'

He continued past the TFT Inspector towards Enoch's car. As he reached it he began: 'Sorry, Mr Enoch. Could you move your vehicle over there? We need this space for a helicopter landing.'

Enoch looked about ready to explode. 'Helicopter?' he demanded. 'You've called out the TFT and organized a helicopter? You've some explaining to do, Wilson.'

At least the bastard's got my name right, Ben Wilson thought to himself. That's a sure sign he's bloody furious. Heigh ho.

'Fine. Just move your car, will you?'

As if to emphasize his words the distant sound of rotors chopping the night began to sound over Uptown, gradually growing louder.


Harker stopped singing. He tapped Jonah on the shoulder and pointed. 'Fly over that ruin,' he ordered. 'I want to see what's going on inside it.'

'How low d'ya wanna go?' the pilot asked him.

'Low as you can. Shine your light on the altar.'

253

Jonah hardly seemed to touch the controls of the Combat Scout, but it fell like a stone, hovering less than thirty feet above the reinstated lightning rod. He stabilized, then turned his 'mixer' until the spotlight hit the empty altar.

'Jeez,' he whispered. 'That place is fulla cats 'n' dogs. I never seen anythin' like it, Perfessor.'

'Just pray you never do again, my American friend. I was afraid of this. Now, one last little job and then you can set us down.'


Enoch grudgingly moved his car. Traffic arrived and sealed off the square, then found themselves suddenly co-opted into a baffling and apparently dangerous operation which centred on the old church.

Harry Chester did as he'd been instructed and liaised with Inspector McGovern of the TFT. 'Anything animal comes out of there, shoot the bugger,' Harry said, gesturing towards St Gargoyle's.

Ben Wilson began the hassle with Chief Superintendent Enoch. Trying to explain a chopper and the TFT on the say-so of a mad professor wasn't easy. Enoch didn't believe a word of it.

'You're saying that church is full of domestic pets that kill people?' he yelled above the noise of the hovering helicopter. 'You must be as mad as your friend Harker. Well, I'll see this farce through, Wilson. Then I'll have you. By God I'll have you.'

He began to stalk towards the church. Chester realized what the Chief Super was up to and moved to stop him.

'Take your hand off me, Sergeant,' Enoch ordered. 'I'm going to see for myself if you're all mad or what.'

He continued towards the litch-gate and passed beneath it. Wilson rushed towards him but Harry caught him by the shoulders. 'Let him go, guv. If he sees he'll have to believe you.'

'Yeah, but it could be the last fucking thing he does see.'

Chester's grip tightened. 'If you go after him that could be true for you as well. For Christ's sake stay here!'

Wilson tried to push past him. One of the sergeant's hands left his shoulder, balled and punched into his stomach, winding him.

'Sorry guv,' Chester said, unsmiling. 'Bust me later.'

Enoch strode up the gravel path towards the barrier, wearing what he considered to be his best important-policeman look. It fell away as he stepped into the church. The eyes turned towards him.

He stared. His mouth dropped open. 'Oh no,' he pleaded. 'Nooo!'


Granpa Hangel realized what the lights ahead had to mean and parked the Landrover beside the entrance to the printer's yard. Sally, in the passenger seat, looked at him suspiciously.

'This isn't Salvation,' she said questioningly. 'Why have we stopped here, Mr Hangel?'

'Leader is not at Salvation,' he told her. 'We have had to move him to another place. The changes have made him . . . contagious.'

He was pleased with the word. It said everything so simply. Yes, it was good to know a second language as well as his own.

They heard the noise of the helicopter overhead. Sally stared up into the night. It wasn't as clear as it had been. Some of the stars were now obscured by cloud.

Pieter Hangel started into the yard and, somewhat hesitantly, she followed him. The changes in Leader must be serious if Tom Greaves felt she ought to see her pet at this time of night. Really he was a more considerate man than she had ever suspected.

She wasn't to know that his ruined body had yet to be discovered outside Leader's pen.

The Sebastopol Street entrance to the Emporium Arcade stood open, shards of the lock littering the yard. Granpa Hangel stepped into the darkened doorway and beckoned to her. 'This

255

way, Miss French,' he instructed. 'Be so kind as to follow me.'

She followed, entering the black corridor which led out into the eastern arm of the arcade. As she reached the broader area with its broken and empty shop-fronts she became aware of the motionless figures which stood silently to either side, like zombie sentinels in Pieter Hangel's cathedral of the damned.

Sally gasped and raised a hand to her mouth. These weren't dummies. Yes, they were people. Living, breathing, motionless people. What was Leader doing in a place like this?

She turned. In the tunnel of darkness behind her the open entrance called out like the voice of sanity striving to break through madness. She was moving towards it when the old man's hand caught her wrist and spun her back. She raised her free hand to strike at him, but he caught that as well.

'You . . . you're not taking me to Leader . . .' she began.

'But I am, Miss French. I am,' came the reply. 'Or rather I am taking you to the *other* which your Leader has become.'

Despite her futile resistance he dragged her towards the great glass and timber dome at the meeting of the arcade's arms. The shape was waiting for her, dense and black. Only the glinting of its slitted eyes distinguished it from the shadows nestling around it.

Hangel threw her to her knees before the *other*. She reached out and her fingers touched the outline of the brass pentagram in which it sat. They recoiled as if burned by the metal. She gasped with pain.

*That's good*, Black Shuck told her. *That's very good, my one-time mistress.*


The unholy paean began. Nearly a thousand animal voices began to howl their triumph to the clouded sky above. It echoed, it reverberated off the walls of the burned-out shell of St Gargoyle's with sufficient force to drown Enoch's screams, almost with force enough to blot out the sound of the helicopter landing in the square outside.

As the first skid touched solid ground again Harker had the door open and began hauling the equipment clear of the fuselage. Ben Wilson glared at Harry Chester and struggled upright, lurching towards the professor.

'There are gas cylinders here,' Harker yelled over the noise of the rotors. 'In those bags are balloons with foil canisters attached. Get the balloons filled and launched as quickly as you can, Mr Wilson. Meanwhile we need metal wire, preferably copper, and the aerials off at least three of your vehicles.'

'Isn't it time you told me what you're up to, Professor?' Wilson called back.

'Listen to me,' came the reply. 'You should be able to guess by now. No, I still can't tell you. Shuck must know what I'm doing, but what he picks up he'll only pick up from *my* mind. That still leaves us a chance.'

'What was all that business with the lightning rod?'

'Simply a diversion. It kept Black Shuck believing he'd fooled me for a while longer. He's not in the church, Wilson. He's not there.'

'You mean the animals there are just a diversion?'

'Not at all. They're waiting to do him homage, once the final metamorphosis has taken place. He's not at the height of his power yet. He still has the sacrifice to perform.'

'Then if he's not in the church, where the fuck is he?'

'There.' Harker pointed towards the Emporium Arcade. 'But keep your men out here. Don't tip him off. There's nothing you can do to stop him anyway.'

Whilst they were talking Kate, previously briefed, was organizing men to help her fill the balloons from the helium cannisters. They began to float up into the night, one by one, launched well away from the Combat Scout's flailing rotors. Once the equipment was clear and Kate had stepped down onto the ground Jonah pulled back on the stick and took off back into the night.

'Now,' Harker demanded. 'The wire and the aerials. Come on, man, we're only about ten minutes from true midnight. We need every second.'

257

'And where am I supposed to find wire at this time of night?'

'Try the workshops at Salvation. There must be something for temporary mesh repairs. Don't worry, there's no animals there. I checked that when we flew over. Just a heap of bodies out by the pens. Probably Greaves and his wife, and their son.'

'Jesus. Not his father-in-law?'

Harker shook his head. 'If I'm right the old man's in there with Black Shuck, and everyone else who's disappeared in Uptown. Including your PC Forrest.'

'Okay. I'll do what I can. That'll have to be good enough.'

'You're too right, Mr Wilson. When I step inside that arcade in five minutes time I'll be counting on you to bring me out alive.'

'You mean it's up to me? I thought you were the one who knew what he was doing.'

'I do, but I need outside help. Now get the wire and the aerials!'

Supported by one of the TFT men Harry Chester made a wary approach to Salvation. It wasn't as wary as he would have liked, considering it was the scene of a reported shooting, though it was only when they reached the workshops behind that they discovered the true horror of the scene. Tom Greaves and his family lay beneath the covered walkway, their entrails spread out like human pentagrams.

'Oh fuck,' Harry whispered. 'That makes four with Mick Treleaven, so far.'

They rapidly searched the workshops, finally discovering some suitable wire coiled on a roll. The aerials had been taken along and whilst the armed policeman stood guard, Chester set to work with pliers to construct the device Andreas Harker had demanded.

'Now for that side entrance,' he grunted, two of the aerials tied together at one end of the reel and the third attached to the other end. 'How long have we got?'

The man looked at his watch. It read two minutes past one.

Retracing their steps to the square they were awed by the full nightmare of the scene. The helicopter with its noise and draught had long vanished back into the sky. TFT men stood ready, facing the south side of St Gargoyle's, from which an unholy and terrifying cacophony of animal sounds was rising. The ambulance team were removing PC Treleaven's body. They looked white and one was distinctly unsteady on his legs. Wilson and Harker stood together with the remaining policemen, staring towards Salvation. Chester flashed his torch at them, then started towards Sebastopol Street, through the barrier Traffic had set up and past the local radio cars which had collected there, despite the lateness of the hour. A reporter tried to stop them but Chester brushed the man roughly aside.

In his haste he went past the printer's yard at first, then realized and doubled back. Once inside he stared up at the low roofs to either side.

'What's your name?' he asked his companion.

'Connors, Sarge.'

'Okay, Connors. Gimme a leg up. I got to get to that dome up there. How's the time?'

'Four minutes past.'

'Jesus. We're cutting it fine.'

Connors helped him onto one of the slate roofs and handed up the wire and aerials. At the end of the yard the door into the arcade stood ajar. In the darkness of the corridor a deeper darkness began to approach. As it reached the doorway it screeched and launched itself at the TFT man. Connors raised his pistol, then hesitated. The screaming shape was wearing a police uniform.

Chester looked down. 'Forrest!' he yelled. 'Forrest, snap out of it . . .'

He was too late. Bill Forrest was on top of Connors, tearing at the TFT man's throat with his fingers. The hesitation had cost Connors dear and he'd been born over backwards, hitting the yard heavily, his weapon spinning away out of reach. He writhed and twisted beneath his assailant, feeling the almost supernatural strength of the grip trying to crush his trachea.

With a last desperate glance back at the fight beneath him Harry Chester began his climb.

'Time for me to get on with it,' Harker stated flatly.

The last of the balloons began its ascent into the clouded night. On the other side of the square the howling from the ruins had become rhythmic, as if some kind of inhuman ritual, orchestrated like a proper church service, was now in progress. Calls had gone out for the first tier response officers to cover the other side of the ruin in an attempt to contain its savage occupants. They would also bring extra weapons to arm the patrolmen at the scene. Two fire engines with water-cannon had also been drafted in and the spotlights and headlights of the attendant vehicles were trained on the broken church.

'You sure you don't want a gun?' Wilson asked the professor.

Harker shook his head. 'Useless last time,' he replied. 'This time Shuck will be even stronger. He may be in a body, but don't make the mistake of thinking it responds to the same physical laws as our own.'

'Professor, let me come with you,' Kate Jones pleaded, grabbing his hand as he turned towards the boarded entrance to the Emporium Arcade.

He prised her fingers away, making an effort to stop himself from shaking. He'd told Wilson he could get out of there alive, but in his heart he didn't really believe that. Black Shuck no longer had any use for him, especially as he'd been able to thwart the use Shuck had intended. All that remained was to stall, to try to stay alive until Harry Chester and the balloons did their work. That way there was a tiny chance of destroying their demonic adversary.

'Sorry Kate,' he told her. Then, to Wilson: 'Keep her there.'

'At least take a torch,' Wilson offered. 'There's no light in here.'

Harker took the torch as it was held out to him. 'Except Shuck's eyes,' he whispered. 'Now, it's five past one and I'm late for a meeting. You know, I don't normally like to be late for meetings.'

He stepped through the workman's door and entered the arcade.


At just under 5000 feet the first of the balloons entered the base of the layer of cumulo-nimbus clouds drifting over Monkhampton. It continued to rise unchecked, born aloft by the helium, through the tendrils of water-vapour which bristled and brushed around it with unsubstantial fingers.

Not yet. Still some way to go yet.

The balloon continued to rise. Beneath it the trigger device at the bottom of the foil container moved microscopically, preparing to activate. At 12,000 feet it began to touch the wax on the chemical fuse. At 15,000 feet the wax ruptured, releasing the chemical.

With a small explosion the foil container burst open, scattering its silver iodide contents into the cloud and bursting the balloon above it. Their work now done, they began a more rapid descent back to earth.


It was Gillimore, the young reporter from the weekly free paper, the *Post Advertiser*, who followed Chester and Connors towards the yard. Something usually happened on a Saturday night and you could often get a good story out of it, especially if you'd got the gear to monitor the police wavelength, like Gillimore had. He wasn't going to stay with that crappy little rag any longer than he had to, and that meant making a name for himself, bloody fast.

He watched the two policemen disappear inside and counted ten before he went after them. As he turned into it his eyes widened as he witnessed the end of Connors' struggle against Bill Forrest. Knowing he was onto something good (it *had* to be good if you had two of the filth knocking shit out of each other), he moved as close as he dared.

His foot struck metal. Keeping his back to the wall, his eyes firmly fixed on the combatants, he reached down and touched Connors' revolver. His grasp closed about the butt.

Overhead, Harry Chester hauled himself onto the next roof. This one covered the shop and office units and ran parallel to the glass and timber structure over the arcade's walkways. It led directly to the central dome. Another two minutes, maybe, and he'd have the aerials in place.

Gillimore picked up the gun as Forrest's fingers dug like daggers into Connors' throat and ripped upwards, tearing through windpipe and arteries alike. The reporter cried out as the fountain of death erupted, drenching the demented survivor of the struggle, and raised the gun to defend himself. Forrest saw him and nodded, eyes aflame, rising to his feet and lurching forward.

The first shot went wide and chipped a large hole in the brickwork on the other side of the yard. The second scythed Forrest's ear off. The third and fourth blew away half of his left shoulder and carved a tunnel through his lungs. But none of them stopped him picking Gillimore off his feet and slamming him against the wall with skull-cracking force. Released, the reporter dropped like a broken shop-dummy.

Forrest ignored him. His tunic smoking from the proximity of the last two shots, his own blood merging with that of the murdered Connors, he began to climb up after Harry Chester. The pain didn't matter. The fact that he was almost certainly dying didn't matter. The *other* had told him to stop Chester, and that was exactly what Bill Forrest was going to do.


Wilson and the others heard the shots. 'You two,' he ordered the nearest T F T members, 'with me. The rest of you stay here. In exactly two and a half minutes get in there and bring Harker out!'

They raced along the square and past the barrier, down into

Sebastopol Street. The shots had also attracted the pressmen and flashes were spattering the two bodies in the yard whilst voices gabbled into mikes and recorders. Wilson and his men forced their way through and ordered the media savagely away, the sight of armed policemen reinforcing the command.

He checked the bodies briefly. Neither of them was Harry. He looked up towards the dome. Two dark shapes, close together, were silhouetted against the skyline.

One of the policemen raised a rifle but Wilson slapped it away. 'You might hit Chester,' he scowled. 'And there isn't time to get another man up there.'

Thirty seconds had passed. Andreas Harker had been inside the arcade for a whole minute. For all Wilson knew he was probably dead already.

Harker stepped through the entrance and stood perfectly still, eyes tightly closed. Then he opened them and was surprised at how much light there was inside the Emporium Arcade.

'I'm here, Shuck,' he began, trying to keep the choking constraint of fear out of his voice.

*So you are, Andreas. I'm pleased to see you, even if you have tried to fool me. Come closer. Pieter, escort Professor Harker a little closer.*

Granpa Hangel shuffled down the aisle of the arcade towards him. To either side, lined up like sentinels outside the shop units, stood the missing residents of Uptown, silent and motionless. Behind the old man, beneath the dome, Harker saw two as yet indistinct shapes. One black, one white.

'Will you come with me,' Hangel said flatly, his voice as lifeless as his expression. 'I am to take you to the *other*.'

Harker began to follow, to approach the waiting creature beneath the dome. Outside came the rattle of gunfire. Three ... four shots, the professor counted. Oh God, they couldn't have killed Harry Chester, could they?

He passed the first of the motionless residents, half expecting them to fall into step behind him. They didn't. In many ways they were dead already.

*You wonder why these people are here,* Shuck continued, *why*

263

*I need them. Over the years, Andreas, I have lent each of them a little of myself. Now, through them, I am greater than the sum of my parts. They are here to repay the debt. Let me show you.*

It sounded like wet cement slopping out of a bucket, only faster. Harker turned at the sound and gaped in horror as the two figures nearest the entrance suddenly flew open, spraying out their entrails in an unmistakable star shape before they collapsed into ragged heaps of torn flesh. As each body exploded a flash of yellow the colour of Shuck's eyes hurtled up the arcade towards the monstrosity in the pentagram, momentarily lighting the dull, uncaring features of the surviving residents. And Shuck himself. And the white shape on all fours which waited motionless before him.

The naked white shape of Sally French.

Harker's stomach heaved. Shuck had made him sick before, he remembered. But not this time. No matter what evil, what torment the creature revealed to him he had to keep himself together. Another couple of minutes. Just another couple of minutes.

The professor straightened up and continued to follow Granpa Hangel towards the pentagram. 'I can beat you, Shuck,' he called. 'I can beat you. You shouldn't have let me live.'

Taunt him. Distract him. Keep hoping.

Blood from the bodies began to trickle past his feet.

Shuck's features became clearer, stronger. The eyes were now fully open. *Too late, Andreas,* the monster whispered, the whisper echoing through the renewed stillness of the glass-roofed structure. *Too late. I have beaten you. That is why I am here, not where you thought . . .*

Those words were familiar. He'd heard them spoken before . . .

*You see, I am too clever for you. I read your thought that night and knew what you intended. Now I have won, and I am free to run for ever.*

The dream.

His arms were half extended before he remembered the

264

rest. No that wouldn't work. Only the original plan now stood a chance of working. Too late to run. Too late to submit, no matter how much his terror might want to send him grovelling to Shuck's feet. He'd just die like the others, feeding the creature with his life.

The sounds and flashes came again, in sequence. Marge Blunson was amongst the ones who blew apart this time, sending globes of fire hurtling down each of the arms of the arcade towards the dense, waiting black malignity that was Shuck.

'Let . . . the girl go,' he pleaded. 'She's done nothing to you. She tried to help you, to love you, when you were Leader . . .'

*I was never Leader, Andreas, though Leader is now me. The girl is mine, as she was Leader's. She is waiting for me to be ready, Andreas. Then we will mate and she will bear the first litter of my true servants. And I shall be ready very soon, Andreas.*

It was true. The last of the changes was taking place. Black Shuck was beginning to pulse with strength, with an inner darkness blacker and more terrible than even his outside form could ever have suggested.

Harker reached the edge of the area beneath the dome. Granpa Hangel stood before his master and announced. 'I have brought the one you wanted to you.'

Then sprayed out his life in the star sign.

The professor averted his eyes, glancing up towards the dome. There should have been a shape there by now. There should have been sounds as well, apart from the cacophony from the animals across the square.

Shuck was right. It was over.


Harry reached the point where the roofs intersected and the dome began. A wooden catwalk, curved flush with the surface but slightly proud of it, extended to the apex. He tested it gingerly and decided it would bear his weight, just.

265

Jesus, he thought, this must be about like what the shit Bobby Ferrow had to put up with. Oh what the hell . . .

He still had a minute. That should be long enough to get the aerials in place, break the glass and scramble clear like he'd been told to. Then the hand gripped at his ankle. He twisted, falling full-length onto the catwalk, feeling it begin to give as its weathered, decaying timbers took the strain, and glimpsed the bloodstained, demented features of Billy Forrest beneath him.

Connors must be dead, he thought. I'm on my own with this madman.

His free foot stamped down onto Forrest's face, crushing his nose. As the constable fell away, sliding down the tiles, desperate fingers clutching for the guttering at the edge, Harry Chester felt the first few spots of rain begin to fall. He turned back and continued towards the apex.

The guttering buckled, then held. Forrest hauled himself back onto the roof and moved towards Chester once again. Harry reached the wooden centre of the dome and jammed the sharpened end of the lower of two aerials lashed together into the woodwork. Now all that remained was to check his watch, wait for true midnight as 1.08 crept round on the second hand, punch that hole in the glass and drop the third aerial, attached to the other end of the wire, down into the centre of the arcade.

He exerted as much pressure as he dared to onto the aerials projecting from the dome. They had to take the weight of the wire and the other one as it fell. He was still pressing down when Bill Forrest renewed his attack, hurling himself onto Chester's stretched-out body.

The catwalk groaned. Wood cracked and popped, dull and rotten, beneath them. Rain started to fall in shafts, lashing the two men as they fought, the seconds of their conflict ticking away towards true midnight. In the yard beneath, Ben Wilson looked on helplessly, then started towards the open entrance to the arcade. He was almost through it when he noticed that Kate Jones was with the other two men behind him.

He grabbed her by the shoulders and stared grimly into her eyes. Whatever was happening inside the old Emporium Arcade wasn't for her to get mixed up in. He had enough doubts and fears about how he was going to cope with it himself.

'Go back to the square, Kate,' he ordered. 'This isn't for you. I don't want to have to worry about you in there as well as Harker.'

He was almost too stunned to stop her as she brushed his hands away and pushed past him towards the entrance. 'Have me about it later,' she said firmly. 'I'm going in.'

Harry Chester kept punching at his attacker. He should have knocked the breath out of Forrest by this time, but the horrifying thought was beginning to dawn that there wasn't any breath left in the ruined, animated corpse. Even so, he felt Forrest's assault begin to weaken. If only the rotten, splintering catwalk would hold he had a chance. With a desperate effort he hurled Forrest away from him and punched a hole through the glass of the dome, lacerating his right hand on the jagged edges.

Now get the other aerial and the wire in place, he told himself.

With a surge of panic he realized that the wire had broken. He grabbed at the nearest end and swept about for the other to tie them together. With inhuman determination the battered, blood-soaked remains of Bill Forrest renewed the attack. The tortured catwalk began to buckle ominously.

Rain hit the dome, echoing in the arcade like muted gunshots. Andreas Harker shuddered, almost hurled backwards as he felt the full force of Shuck's eyes. This time they were more than just glowing pits of evil, the professor noted grimly. This time there was something in them he hadn't seen before.

For a fleeting instant Black Shuck had shown him uncertainty.

Sounds from the struggle on the catwalk overhead filtered down through the dome. Fragments of glass and splashes of blood from Harry Chester's injured hand hit the reddened floor about the pentagram.

'No, Shuck,' Harker announced defiantly. 'It isn't over yet.'

The eyes threatened to incinerate him where he stood. The cold chills sweeping his backbone were now so familiar as to have become a fact of his life, however much or little there was left of it.

*'You think not, Andreas? Even if the time has now come for me to summon my worshippers?'*

Black Shuck threw back his monstrous head. For a moment the slavering lips drew back, exposing the massive, discoloured fangs they had concealed in a grim and unconscious parody of Leader's smile. Then the creature began to howl.

In the yard outside, Ben Wilson heard it and shuddered. So did Harry Chester, fighting for his life against a dead man on the catwalk overhead. Both of them had heard that sound before, on the night they'd been attacked outside St Gargoyle's.

The howl reached out through the darkness and crossed St Katherine's Square. The paean of animal voices in the ruined church began to falter, then slowly died away. The animals surged forward, out of the broken, fire-stained shell, hurtling towards the churchyard wall and the litch-gate. The men in the square opened fire and large calibre bullets and shotgun pellets combined to cut swathes through the four-footed ranks, shattering heads and limbs, gutting bodies, blowing patches of fur and flesh from the advancing creatures.

But failing to stop them.

They swept across the square, pulling down and tearing, ripping, slashing and clawing everything in their path. Their master had called. Shuck needed them and they would not fail to answer his summons. The plywood fascia across the entrance to the Emporium Arcade began to splinter and bow inwards before their assault.

Black Shuck gathered his power more quickly. Along the arms of the arcade standing bodies flew apart, sending their globes of yellow fire and their liberated blood towards the monstrosity in the pentagram. He sat, howling and feeding, as the Uptowners collapsed like exploding dolls into the star-shaped offal of their own bodies. Harker tried not to watch, knowing that at any moment the same thing could happen to him. There had been a moment, a forgotten moment, when he had faced the *other* in the ruins of St Gargoyle's, when Shuck had planted one of those monstrous seeds in his own body.

That was how Shuck had been able to reach him. That was why he'd needed to shield his thoughts from his adversary. Hold on, he told himself. Defy him. Give the others the time they need.

'I told you it wasn't over yet,' Harker taunted.

No police were going to rush in from the square and pull him out of there. They either lay dead amongst their own spilling entrails of were too busy fighting for their lives. But even reeking with power as he was, enthroned amongst the litter of the dead, Harker sensed Shuck's fear. The creature must be at the height of its power now. He was only seconds from true midnight, when he would come into his undreamed-of kingdom, yet he was afraid.


Wilson heard the rush as some of the animals swept towards the printer's yard. Following Kate and the others into the arcade he turned and slammed the door shut behind him, his eyes darting about for something to jam it in place with. If the creatures got through they were all dead, and there'd be nothing he or anyone else could do about it.

The first bolt of lightning struck close to the police station in Salmond Square, disappointingly outside Uptown. The second hit the reinstated rod atop St Gargoyle's ruined tower, flashing to earth and charring the few tardy creatures which had yet to leave the ruin.

Count the thunder, Wilson remembered his mother telling him. One elephant, two elephant, three elephant ... That's how you tell how close the storm is. An elephant a mile, Benjamin.

Flash and thunder were less than an elephant apart.

Harry Chester managed to throw P C Forrest off him as the catwalk began its final ominous creaking, the ancient woodwork punished beyond endurance. In a lazy, time-suspended moment he watched the policeman's body arc out over the suddenly busy rooftops, past the surge of sharp teeth and claws and night-bright eyes that were heading for his life. Their coats were drenched and spiky with the lancing rain, but that didn't make them any the less deadly.

The final second ticked away unnoticed. True midnight came.

'*I've been so lonely through the centuries, Andreas*', Shuck told him. '*Watch me now, before I destroy you. Watch me father young in my own image that will go out into the world to do my will.*'

Sally French, her clothes gone, crouched on all fours before the creature, her hands and knees stained red with the blood that had flowed towards the pentagram. Her eyes were wide with shock and horror. Hardly a muscle twitched in her rigid frame as Shuck reared up and prepared to cover her. Harker's eyes goggled with horror as he saw the true size of the creature for the first time.

The animals burst through the arcade's square entrance and hurtled towards Harker, claws scraping on the bloody tiles and concrete as they passed the gaping bodies of the Uptowners. One cat, out ahead of the rest, an ear torn away by shotgun pellets, reached his feet and he kicked it away with rib-shattering force.

At the end of a lesser arm Kate Jones glimpsed the evil blackness of Shuck rearing above Sally French and saw Andreas Harker kick the cat away. Unthinking, she started towards him.

Harry Chester felt the teeth go for his feet. Buckling and splitting the catwalk crunched through the dome. Broken glass sliced down towards black Shuck, fading into nothing before it reached the rearing terror. Sally French, as docile as any of the dead, waited for his assault in mute incomprehension.

Harker saw Kate and Wilson. 'Get out of here!' he yelled, gesturing wildly.

The animals were all over Harry Chester now, their weight forcing the tortured catwalk further through the dome. Shards of glass slashed at him, increasing his pain as the fingers of his good left hand groped urgently for the other end of the broken wire.

And found it.

With a bellow that was part pain and part triumph he forced himself upright, forcing his tormentors to fall or hook their claws into his flesh to save themselves. As he twisted the two ends of the wire together the last braces on the catwalk gave way. Still upright, the third aerial clasped in his bleeding right hand, the repaired wire uncoiling behind him, he plummeted down towards the pentagram and its ghastly occupant beneath him, a rain of animals and glass and timber about him as he fell.

The lightning struck a third time.

A jagged flash shot from the seeded clouds and struck the upper of the two aerials embedded in the apex of the dome. Its charge travelled on down the copper wire.

Harry Chester erupted into flame as he thrust the aerial he was holding between Shuck's upturned jaws.

Harker grabbed Sally French and tore her clear of the pentagram, swinging her towards Kate and Ben Wilson, then threw himself after her.

In an eruption of smoking flesh Harry Chester and Shuck showed briefly blue. The brass pentagram buckled and shattered. For a moment Wilson and Kate Jones glimpsed man and monster writhing together, then the force of the electrical discharge tore a crater in the bloodstained floor of the arcade. The world slowed and stopped as the dome above them cracked and shattered, then started again with the lethal, slashing rain of its collapse.

Sally, bruised and grazed, landed at Ben Wilson's feet. Kate removed her tunic jacket to try to cover her nakedness. The surge of animals faltered. Its purpose changed. A mongrel terrier called Mary came forward and barked, forefeet raised in a begging position, before Professor Harker. The terrier was very old and very tame.

Harker bent over to stroke her. He was laughing and crying at the same time. Around him the Emporium Arcade was settling into a stunned silence spiced with smoke from the hole beneath the remains of the dome.

'Good dog,' Harker whispered, reaching to pat her head. 'Good, normal dog.'

Andreas Harker never actually touched Mary. His hand missed her altogether as his tortured muscles, numbed with terror and relief, gave way and he pitched over onto his side.

Kate rushed forward and shook him. 'Professor,' she urged. 'Professor!'

He managed to open his eyes and force a wink at her.

'Go 'way,' he muttered. 'I want to go to sleep.'

The final discussion at Monkhampton took place in Ben Wilson's office, though it was the Assistant Chief Constable who actually sat behind the desk. Wild stories had already reached the national media, but they were so disjointed as to make those who printed or published them appear rather ridiculous. After all, that sort of thing doesn't happen, does it? Killer pets foiled by lightning strikes? Quite ridiculous.

Despite his position, the ACC was more of an observer than a participant in what followed. Harker and Wilson told their stories as best they could, though it was the professor who found himself answering most of the questions.

'I knew it had to be the arcade,' he ventured, 'when we flew over the church and found the altar empty. That wasn't the only thing, though. You see, I'd spotted the lock on the Sebastopol Street entrance. It could only have come from Salvation because it wasn't the same as the ones on the other arcade approaches. If the workmen who sealed the place had had Havard locks they'd have used them all the way round. And there was something else as well.'

'Which was?' the ACC asked.

'Black Shuck became over-confident. He taunted me through my dreams and gave too much away. I knew he wasn't going to be in the church because I'd dreamed he wasn't. He gave me the solution to the excrement through dreams, and he gave me the new location the same way. That's why I had Jonah Wayle fly over it before we landed.'

'You still haven't explained the lightning,' Ben Wilson told him.

Andreas Harker nodded. 'You can blame the Exmoor farmer for that. The only way anyone could make sense of his story was that when he struck Black Shuck with the poker it had attracted lightning, which ruined his home and, as you might say, Mr Wilson, fucked up his electricity. That Shuck and electrical activity went together I had deduced from the reports in the Willington-Cartier index. It was a gamble that a discharge when he had already absorbed more power than he had ever done before would tip him over, but it seems to have worked. The rest of it, seeding the clouds to produce the storm and so on, was pure mechanics. Nothing more.'

'So why didn't we find Shuck's body?' Wilson demanded.

'You yourself have already said that forensic are still trying to sort out which body is which. You've even drafted in specialist teams from outside the area to help. But you're quite right. I don't expect you to find either Shuck's body or Leader's. You can only stop something like that by the means I employed. You can't destroy it.'

'You mean Shuck is still around somewhere?' asked the ACC.

'I would say so. The essential Shuck, anyway.'

The two policemen offered no response. Each individually was reviewing the death-toll from the Uptown incident, as it was becoming inadequately known. Eleven members of a TFT unit, eight traffic policemen, six mobile patrolmen and two beat officers were dead, let alone five members of other civil forces and a reporter. Thirty-five with Enoch and Harry Chester, and as for the many Uptowners . . . It was too many. Certainly it was too many to explain easily, especially if some of them had been your friends.

'So he'll be back?' Wilson asked at length.

'I've no doubt of it. Though probably not in this area. Shuck will assume we've learned our lesson and try somewhere else. And he *will* try. He's probably prepared the attempt already. I'm sorry to appear to be depressing about this, but I think I know my adversary now, gentlemen. And now, if you'll excuse me, term isn't quite over yet and I still have the odd tutorial to take, though none of them will be as odd as what's happened here.'

He stood up and shook hands with his two companions.

Wilson held on to his grasp. 'Let me know what happens, Professor,' he said. 'I want to know. Even if I don't understand I want to know.'

'I'll do that. Now it's time you let me go.'

Wilson released his hand and watched as he left the office. Harker had scarcely closed the door before Kate Jones was standing in front of him.

'I'm resigning from the police,' she told him.

He looked at her carefully. Still pretty, though a little more lined since that night in Uptown. She'd come through, though. All the survivors had somehow come through. Even Sally French.

'That's your decision, sweet Kate,' he answered. He moved past her.

Kate's eyes followed him. 'You'll need help,' she called. 'You didn't face Black Shuck alone this time. Next time it's going to be even harder. You'll need me, Professor.'

He turned and looked back at her, smiling gently. He thought for a moment.

'That's the best offer I've had so far this year,' Harker replied.


He watched them as they searched the cellars and the shop units. He watched them as they carted the dead away and zipped plastic body-bags. He watched them, and reflected.

Defeat was bad enough, especially defeat as he'd approached the zenith of his powers. Now, he realized, he would know what it was like to be hunted. They wouldn't find his body, so they'd be looking for him.

It didn't matter. By the time they were organized enough to think about that hunt he'd be long gone.

There were others, in other places, who had learned to serve him. He could be served again, grow strong again. After all, when you were the next best thing to immortal time was on your side. You could even wait for the future, for Professor Andreas Harker to die, before you tried again.

Black Shuck melted with the shadows, the taste of defeat bitter in his mouth. No, he wouldn't be waiting that long. He had a score to settle with Ben Wilson's mad professor. Death was too small a price to exact from Andreas Harker. It had to be more.

Black Shuck hugged the shadows and began to move away. Yes. Other times. Other places. Uptown would be torn down, but it could just as easily have been a shopping mall or a new residential estate. It could be anywhere. Anytime.

And then he'd have his revenge. And come into his glory. For ever.